UNEXPECTEDLY MINE

A Birch Crossing Novel

STEPHANIE ROWE

Authenticity Playground, LLC

CHAPTER ONE

CLARE GRAY KNEW it wasn't the same as that night fifteen years ago.

It wouldn't happen again.

It *couldn't* happen again.

But as she inched her car along the twisting mountain road, staying as far as she could from the washed-out edge, she couldn't help but remember the night she'd become an eighteen-year-old widow. The awful night she'd lost a husband, and her tiny daughter had lost a father.

It had been a night, a storm, and a road just like this one.

Her tires slipped on rain-slicked pebbles, and the car slid several feet down toward the edge. "Oh, God, no—"

The rubber caught, and the car stopped. She clenched the steering wheel, her hands shaking as she tried to calm herself. Her heart was hammering frantically, her chest so tight she felt like a vise was crushing her ribs. She couldn't catch her breath, her mouth so dry she couldn't swallow.

The wipers hammered as they fought the onslaught of rain. The thundering of the rain on the roof was nearly deafening, and all Clare could see in her headlights were sheets of water cascading across the dirt and gravel road.

Her phone rang, the shrill sound making her jump. Her daughter's ringtone. Clare set the emergency brake, then grabbed the phone. "Katie? Are you all right?" All she could hear was crackling. "If you can hear me, I'm on my way. Just stay where you are, okay?"

The connection went dead.

Damn it! Clare checked the phone. No reception. Her body shaking with frustration and anxiety, she jammed the phone into the console so she could reach it if Katie called back.

She'd had it with the untainted quality of life that was so important to her town. She was bringing up the cell phone reception issue at the next town meeting, and she wasn't going to let it die this time. This was why they needed a cell phone tower in Birch Crossing. Even charming Maine towns had teenage children who went camping and got stranded in storms.

Dear God. It had been almost two hours since Katie had called, asking for help. Two hours in that freezing rain, stranded in the woods—

The phone rang again, and Clare lunged for it. "Katie?"

"Mom?" Her daughter's voice was barely audible over the interference. "Where are you? We're so cold!"

"I'm on my way, sweetheart." Clare desperately eyed the muddy water streaming over the road, like an insidious threat trying to keep her from her daughter. "Another twenty minutes." God, she hoped she could get there that soon, that the road wouldn't betray her.

"What?" The phone crackled again. "Mom? Can you hear me?"

"Katie!" Clare shouted, frantic to be heard over the static.

"Stay where you are. Don't try to find a dry place. Just wait for me. I'm coming! Don't go anywhere!"

"If you can hear me, bring blankets." Katie's voice was thin and fragile, and Clare gripped the phone tighter, clutching it so tightly she felt like her hand was going to snap. "And food. Our stuff went over a cliff into a river after Jeremy fell in."

After Jeremy fell in? Clare's stomach dropped. "Is everyone okay? Did he get out?"

"Mom? I can't hear you!"

"Katie! Is everyone all right?"

The phone disconnected again. "No!" Screaming with frustration, Clare bowed her head and pressed her hands to her forehead, fighting desperately to maintain her composure, to stay focused enough to navigate the mountain road and make it to her daughter. *Please, God, take care of them until I can get there.*

She took a deep breath, then raised her head, staring grimly through the windshield at the sheets of rain that had turned the mountain road into a muddy river.

If she screwed up and crashed tonight, what would happen to Katie? Who would take care of her? Her daughter had already lost a father. What if she lost a mother too? Katie would be all alone. Terrified. Clare's heart started to hammer, and panic hit—

"No!" Clare spoke the denial out loud. "Tonight is not the night for any of us to die. Everything is going to be fine." She had all-wheel drive. New tires. And a very smart fifteen-year old-daughter who would stay put until Clare got there.

It was going to be okay. It had to be okay. She was going to make it okay.

Clare set the phone in her lap in case Katie got through again. Then she shook out her shoulders, released the emergency brake and carefully, precisely, eased her foot onto the gas and the car began to creep forward again.

~

GRIFFIN FRIESÉ LIKED THE RAIN.

He liked the way his tires spun out as he shot up the dirt road. He liked to feel his truck strain beneath him as it fought the earth for survival. Truck versus nature. Someday, maybe, nature might win, but she'd have to put forth a hell of a show, because his truck had a winning streak that had never been seriously challenged.

He hadn't thought about nature since he'd left home at age seventeen to head to the city and make a life for himself that didn't involve the carpentry, deep woods and logging that had consumed his existence as a kid and driven his parents into an early grave from hard work and financial stress. But being back in the Maine woods was making him remember how much fun it could be to challenge nature head-on and come out the victor. He'd always had an infallible instinct about how far he could push it and still come out on top, and it felt good to know he hadn't lost his touch.

The trees were bowing and lashing in the wind, dodging in and out of his headlights. Pine branches still loaded with needles littered the sodden road in front of him. The truck bounced and jagged across the debris, as if it were waltzing with the great Mother Earth herself.

Griffin hit the off button on his radio, silencing the satellite broadcast of Beethoven's Fifth. The truck immediately filled with the howl of the wind, the drumroll of rain, the splash of puddles, and the roar of his engine.

He rolled down his window and breathed in the freshness of the air. The rain pelted his face and dripped down his neck, bringing life and vitality into the vehicle that had spent too many hours in his condo's parking garage and on paved streets. Mail he'd collected just before driving out of Boston flew around the interior of the truck, sticking to the damp windows.

Instinctively, he swore and grabbed for the papers...then he saw what was in his hand. An ad for a Neiman Marcus sale addressed to his ex-wife.

Griffin usually dealt with more critical documents than two top level executive assistants could handle, but there was nothing important in the mail for him right now. Next week, life would resume. But today, not a damned thing.

It had been a week since he'd sold his company. Seven days to wrap up the business that had been his life for the last fifteen years, pack his truck with critical necessities, and haul ass up to the mountains to reclaim what was his.

He let the flyer drop and watched the white scrap flutter around the cab of his truck like a dove in its final stages of death.

Maybe it was time he let certain things die.

But as he punched the accelerator and made the truck leap forward, he knew he wouldn't.

GRIFFIN ROUNDED the bend in the road and saw the red tail-lights of a car stopped directly in front of him. He instantly realized he had no time to stop on the wet dirt, so he jerked the wheel and swerved to the left. His front bumper barely missed the rear of the stopped vehicle as he bounced up the side of the embankment. His tires skidded across the muddy hillside, and the truck fish-tailed several times before finally coming to a stop at an angle that would have been fun as hell in his younger days.

Today, it was just an impediment to his forward progress.

A massive tree was down across the road. The roots were still wedged high up on the hillside, and the branches were hanging down over a ravine on the other side of the road. Headlights from the stopped car were illuminating the obstacle, and a small figure was attempting to shimmy precariously over the trunk. A woman? Or a teenager?

What did she think she was doing? She was going to get herself killed.

Griffin backed his truck off the ridge and turned his floodlights onto the tree. The climber raised an arm to block the light, and the hood fell back.

A soggy reddish-brown ponytail and fine cheekbones made it clear that it was woman, definitely not a teenager. Sudden, shocking awareness hit Griffin, a rush of heat so intense he forgot to breathe. Her face was pale, stripped by the rainy cold, but there was a fierce set to her delicate jaw that burned with a courage he rarely saw. Her shoulders were narrow, her legs slim in those dark jeans, but he could practically feel the determination coursing through her body.

A need to protect surged over him, a nearly insurmountable instinct to haul his ass across the wet road and hurl himself between her and that damned tree, shielding her from the lethal risk he knew it presented.

Griffin threw open the door of his truck and stepped out into the downpour. His high-tech jacket and boots kept him dry, but his jeans were soaked through within a few seconds. "Hey!" he shouted into the roar of the wind. "Get off the tree!"

She waved at him and yelled something back, but he couldn't hear her. But when she grabbed a branch and braced her foot, he realized she was still going to climb over it. Screw that. No one got to die when he was around.

Griffin sprinted across the rain-soaked road, latched his arm around the woman's waist and hauled her off. "That thing could come loose any moment," he shouted over the storm. "Get off it!"

"Hey!" She twisted around in his arms, shoving hard at him to let her go.

Heat leapt through Griffin as his hands slid over her curves when she turned in his grasp. She was all woman, this petite firestorm in his arms, and that realization was like a spark, igniting a fire that had been dead inside him for so long. He was shocked by the bolt of desire rushing through him, jolting him with an awareness long forgotten.

Apparently oblivious to the lust she'd ignited in him, the woman glared at him, her blue eyes vibrant in the glare of his floodlights as she struggled to get free of his grip. "Why did you do that?" she demanded. She was furious, but there was a vulnerability in her voice that got his attention in a hurry. "I was almost over!"

"Those roots are loose in the soft ground." Still holding her securely, he jerked his chin toward the almost fully exposed tree base. "The tree could slide over the cliff at any time, and if you're on it, you'll be going for a ride."

Her eyes widened, and she looked quickly at the tree. He saw her rapidly assess the situation, and she pounded his arm in frustration as she realized he was right. The fight faded from her body, and she sagged in his arms as he set her down, holding her to make sure she wasn't going to fall. He could feel her trembling, and the protective instinct he hadn't felt in so long surged even more powerfully through him.

"Tonight isn't the night to be driving around in the mountains," he said, his grip tightening on her small waist, fighting his ridiculous caveman urge to sweep her up in his arms, toss her over his shoulder and whisk her away from this dangerous situation. "Turn your car around and come back after the storm when it's safe."

She shook her head, and he saw anguish on her face that

turned his very soul. "My daughter's up there. I have to get her."

"Your daughter?" Instinctively, Griffin glanced up the road, into the pitch darkness of the storm and woods. Adrenaline shot through him, and every muscle in his body tensed. Shit. Daughters shouldn't be in those woods during this kind of weather. "Up where? In a car?"

The woman whirled away from him, her boots splashing in the puddles as she paced frantically alongside the tree, searching for a way over. "She went camping with friends."

"Camping?" The woman looked far too young to have a daughter old enough to go camping by herself. There was an innocent beauty to her, despite her tormented eyes and her storm-ravaged appearance. She was courageous, no doubt about that, but there was such desperation in those sapphire-colored eyes, such utter vulnerability that it touched his core.

She needed him. This sodden, frantic, sensual woman needed him. Griffin knew it, and he damn well liked how it felt. It had been a long time since a female had needed anything but cash from him. "Where is she? Is she with adults?"

"No, just friends. They got dropped off." Her expression tightened with frustration, and for a split second, he thought she was going to cry. She wiped the back of her hand across her cheek, her hand shaking and pale. "I didn't know she was going." She took a deep breath, as if willing herself to find the courage to cope, and then pointed to the road on the other side of the tree. "They're at Pike's Notch. It's about eight miles up the road."

"Eight miles." Griffin swore under his breath. He felt her pain in every move of that small, determined frame, and he practically vibrated with the need to ease her anguish and relieve that soul-deep torment. "And were you planning on hiking up there after you got over the tree?"

The woman raised her chin, her eyes flashing with anger, which was what he'd hoped would happen with his quip. Anger could be channeled into productivity. Fear and panic couldn't.

"I can't get my car up there," she said. "So what am I going to do? Leave them?"

That was a question that didn't need an answer. Those kids had to be retrieved. End of story. Griffin rubbed his jaw as he surveyed the washed-out road leading into the darkness, his mind working at rapid speed to figure out how he could fix the situation. "It's too far to hike up there in this weather."

"So? I'll do it anyway." The wind caught her jacket and blew it open, and he caught a glimpse of a light blue sweater that managed to make a modest cut incredibly sexy as it hugged her curves. Again, wholly inappropriate desire surged through him, a heat that he hadn't felt in years. Not that he'd do anything about it, but damn, it felt good to be reminded that he was a man.

She quickly pulled her rain jacket tighter around her and zipped it up, but he noticed that her jeans were drenched, and her boots were old and frayed. He was sure her feet were already soaked. Her skin was almost translucent in the glare of the lights. Water streamed down her cheeks and dripped off her makeup-free eyelashes. She looked young, vulnerable, and terrified. "I have to get her," she said. "I—"

The tree shifted suddenly, and she leapt away from it with a startled yelp. Griffin caught her, yanking her away from the branches as the tree slid several feet toward the gully. He had a sudden vision of it dragging her down into the ravine, and he tucked her against him, using his body to shield her from a branch as it almost clipped her.

But this was one damsel not in the mood to be rescued, apparently.

"Maybe we can pull it out of the way!" She twisted out of his grip and ran over to the tree. She grabbed one of the branches and threw all her weight into it, trying frantically to continue its descent into the gully.

"Whoa!" Griffin leapt after her, ready to yank her back if the tree shifted again.

To his relief, the beast hadn't moved by the time he reached her, but the idea had potential, depending on how loose the tree really was.

Griffin grabbed the branch just behind hers, putting himself between her and the cliff's edge. If the tree started to go, she'd have to go through him to fall in. "On three," he shouted.

"Okay." Her shoulders were narrow in her oversized jacket, but her feet were braced as if she knew how to leverage the most out of her small frame.

"One!" Griffin gripped the tree, but the bark was slippery and hard to hold. "Two!"

She dug her boots into the gravel.

"Three!"

He threw all his weight against it, straining his muscles to their limit, but it didn't budge. He swore and released the branch. So much for that few inches of movement. Nothing but the illusion of opportunity. "This tree's not going anywhere until Mother Nature decides she is."

"Oh, come on!" She pounded her fist on the trunk. "Don't do this to me! I can't leave her there!" The despair in her voice tore at his gut.

Suddenly, with the rivulets rushing past his boots, the howl of the wind, the sound of water crashing down the side of the mountain, Griffin was reminded of the nightmare that haunted him so ruthlessly. His daughter. Caught in the undertow. He couldn't get to her—

Shit! Not this time. This time he wasn't trapped in the

helplessness of a nightmare. This time he could get it right. This time, he was owning the result, and there was going to be a happy freaking ending.

There was only one option.

He grabbed the woman's shoulders just as she turned back to attempt another fruitless assault on the tree. He forced her to look at him, his grip tightening as she tried to bat his hands away. Thick drops were rolling down those pale cheeks. Rain or tears? Now, he wasn't so sure. "Listen. I'm going to drive my truck around the tree. Stay back by your car. If I dislodge the tree, I don't want you anywhere near it when it goes. I'm going to help you."

"Help me? What are you talking about?" A little furrow creased above her delicate eyebrows, but he could tell he'd caught her attention. There was such disbelieving hope in those blue eyes, as if she couldn't comprehend that someone would come to her aid. He swore under his breath, wondering what kind of life she'd endured that had taught her that she had to fight every battle by herself.

"Just stay by your car." He pulled her away from the tree, deposited her by her Subaru, then sloshed through the rushing water to his truck. He swung into the driver's seat, then backed up so his lights were on the hillside that was gripping the tree so precariously.

The grade was steeper than he would have preferred. His truck was heavy, but was it heavy enough to keep from flipping over?

Hell, yeah. He'd never crashed his truck before, and he wasn't going to start tonight.

He gunned the engine and headed straight toward the side of the mountain.

DUCKING her head against the raging storm, Clare hugged herself while she watched the huge black pickup truck turn its headlights onto the steep hillside. She was freezing, and her muscles wouldn't stop shaking. She was so worried about Katie, she could barely think, and she had no idea what this stranger was going to do. Something. Anything. *Please.*

The truck lurched toward the hill, and she realized suddenly that he was going to drive straight up the embankment in an attempt to go above the roots and around the fallen tree that was blocking the road. But that was crazy! The mountain was way too steep. He was going to flip his truck!

Memories assaulted her, visions of when her husband had died, and she screamed, racing toward him and waving her arms. "No, don't! Stop!"

But the truck plowed up the side of the hill, its wheels spewing mud as it fought for traction in the rain-soaked earth. She stopped, horror knifing through her as the truck turned and skidded parallel across the hill, the left side of his truck reaching far too high up the slippery slope. Her stomach turned as she saw the truck tip further and further, until she could see the roof.

A feathered angel was painted beneath the floodlights. An angel? What was a man like him doing with an angel on his truck?

The truck was almost vertical now. There was no way it could stay upright. It was going to flip. Crash into the tree. Careen across the road. Catapult off the cliff. He would die right in front of her. Oh, God, *he would die.*

But somehow, by a miracle that she couldn't comprehend, the truck kept struggling forward, all four wheels still gripping the earth.

The truck was above the roots now. Was he going to make it? *Please let him make it—*

The wheels slipped, and the truck dropped several yards down toward the roots. "No!" She took a useless, powerless step as the tires caught on the roots. The tires spun out in the mud, and the roots ripped across the side of the vehicle with a furious scream.

"Go," she shouted, clenching her fists. "Go!"

He gunned the engine, and suddenly the tires caught. The truck leapt forward, careening sideways across the hill, skidding back and forth as the mud spewed. He made it past the tree, and then the truck plowed back down toward the road, sliding and twisting as he fought for control.

Clare held her hand over her mouth, terrified that at any moment one of his tires would catch on a root and he'd flip. "Please make it, please make it, please make it," she whispered over and over again.

The truck bounced high over a gully, and she gasped when it flew up so high she could see the undercarriage. Then somehow, someway, he wrested the truck back to four wheels, spun out into the road and stopped, its wipers pounding furiously against the rain as the floodlights poured hope into the night.

Oh, dear God. He'd made it. He hadn't died.

Clare gripped her chest against the tightness in her lungs. Her hands were shaking, her legs were weak. She needed to sit down. To recover.

But there was no time. The driver's door opened and out he stepped. Standing behind the range of his floodlights, he was silhouetted against the darkness, his shoulders so wide and dominating he looked like the dark earth itself had brought him to life.

CHAPTER TWO

SOMETHING inside her leapt with hope at the sight of him, at the sheer, raw strength of his body as he came toward her. This man, this stranger, he was enough. He could help her. Sudden tears burned in her eyes as she finally realized she didn't have to fight this battle by herself.

He held up his hand to tell her to stay, then he slogged over to the front of his truck. He hooked something to the winch, then headed over to the tree. The trunk came almost to his chest, but he locked his grip around a wet branch for leverage, and then vaulted over with effortless grace, landing in the mud with a splash. "Come here," he shouted over the wind.

Clare ran across the muck toward him, stumbling in the slippery footing. "You're crazy!" she shouted, shielding her eyes against the bright floodlights from his truck. But God, she'd never been so happy to see crazy in her life.

"Probably," he yelled back, flashing her a cheeky grin. His perfect white teeth seemed to light up his face, a cheerful confident smile that felt so incongruous in the raging storm and daunting circumstances.

But his cockiness eased her panic, and that was such a relief. It made her able to at least think rationally. She would take all the positive vibes she could get right now.

He held up a nylon harness that was hooked to the steel cord attached to his truck. "If the tree goes over, this will keep you from going with it."

She wiped the rain out of her eyes. "What are you talking about?"

"We still have to get you over the tree, and I don't want you climbing it unprotected. Never thought I'd actually be using this stuff. I had it just out of habit." He dropped the harness over her head and began strapping her in with efficient, confident movements. His hands brushed her breasts as he buckled her in, but he didn't seem to notice.

She sure did.

It was the first time a man's hands had touched her breasts in about fifteen years, and it was an unexpected jolt. Something tightened in her belly. Desire? Attraction? An awareness of the fact she was a woman? Dear God, what was wrong with her? She didn't have time for that. Not tonight, and not in her life. But she couldn't take her gaze off his strong jaw and dark eyes as he focused intently on the harness he was strapping around her.

"I'm taking you across to my truck," he said, "and then we're going to get your daughter and the others."

"We are?" She couldn't stop the sudden flood of tears. "You're going to help me get them?"

He nodded as he snapped the final buckle. "Yeah. I gotta get into heaven somehow, and this might do it."

"Thank you!" She threw herself at him and wrapped her arms around him, clinging to her savior. She had no idea who he was, but he'd just successfully navigated a sheer mud cliff for her and her daughter.

For an instant, he froze, and she felt his hard body start to pull away. Then suddenly, in a shift so subtle she didn't even sense it coming, his body relaxed and his arms went around her, locking her down in an embrace so powerful she felt like the world had just stopped. It felt like the rain had ceased and the wind had quieted, buffeted aside by the strength and power of his body.

"It's going to be okay." His voice was low and reassuring in her ear, his lips brushing against her as he spoke. "She's going to be fine."

Crushed against this stranger's body, protected by his arms, soothed by the utter confidence in his voice, the terror that had been stalking Clare finally eased away. "Thank you," she whispered.

"You're welcome."

There was a hint of emotion in his voice, and she pulled back far enough to look at him. His eyes were dark, so dark she couldn't tell if they were brown or black, but she could see the torment in his expression. His jaw was angular, and his face was shadowed by the floodlights. He was a man with weight in his heart. She felt it right away. Instinctively, she laid a hand on his cheek. "You're a gift."

He flashed another smile, and for a split second, he put his hand over hers, holding it to his whiskered cheek as if she were some angel of mercy come to give him relief. Her throat thickened, and for a moment, everything else vanished. It was just them, drenched and cold on a windy mountain road, the only warmth was their hands, clasped together against his cheek.

His eyes darkened, then he cleared his throat suddenly and released her hand, jerking her back to the present. "Wait until you see whether I can pull it off," he said, his voice low and rough, sending chills of awareness rippling down her spine. "Then you can re-evaluate that compliment." He tugged on the harness. "Ready?"

She gripped the cold nylon, suddenly nervous. Was she edgy because she was about to climb over a tree that could careen into the gully while she was on it, or was it due to the intensity of the sudden heat between them? God, she hoped it was the first one. Being a wimp was so much less dangerous than noticing a man like him. "Aren't you wearing one?"

He quirked a smile at her, a jaunty grin that melted one more piece of her thundering heart. "I only have one, and ladies always get first dibs. Besides, I'm a good climber. If the tree takes me over, I'll find my way back up. Always do." He set his foot on a lower branch and patted his knee. "A one-of-a-kind step ladder. Hop up, Ms.—?" He paused, leaving the question hovering in the storm.

"Clare." She set her muddy boot on his knee, and she grimaced apologetically when the mud glopped all over his jeans. "Clare Gray." She grabbed a branch and looked at him. "And you are?"

"Griffin Friesé." He set his hand on her hip to steady her, his grip strong and solid. "Let's go save some kids, shall we?"

As CLARE SHUT herself into the huge, black truck and Griffin began to drive them into the dark, isolated mountains above Birch Crossing, she realized just how much she'd entrusted to a complete stranger. Her life. Her daughter's life, potentially. The children of her friends.

But it was a little too late to back out now.

Except for the summer tourist crowd, which was still two months away, there were no strangers in Birch Crossing, and any unknowns who came to town were regarded with distrust until they'd proven their worth for at least a decade.

She'd lived here her whole life, and she'd never heard of the man sitting inches away from her.

"How old is your daughter?" he asked as the truck roared up the road, bouncing over rocks with a little too much fervor.

She grabbed the overhead grip and braced her left hand on the console. "Can you slow down a little?"

He shot a surprised look at her. "Aren't you worried about your daughter?"

"It won't do her much good if I die before I get there."

Griffin stared at her for what felt like a full minute before he seemed to grasp her point. "You think I'm going to crash?" He asked the question as if he couldn't quite comprehend that fear.

"Well, maybe slide over the edge or something." Clare peeked out her window, but it was too dark to see the steep drop off she knew was just below her side of the truck. She also couldn't see clearly enough to determine whether there was a safe expanse of road between them and the sheer cliff. Oh, God. She tightened her grip on the overhead handle and ordered herself not to dissolve into a sniveling lump of terror. "Stuff like that happens."

"Clare."

She turned her head toward Griffin at the low urgency in his voice. "What?"

His face was blue-lit by the dash, showcasing a hard set to his jaw and tendons flexed in his neck. "I'm not going to crash." His voice was calm and non-judgmental. Just a simple stating of fact.

His hands were relaxed on the steering wheel. No tension. No fear. Yet, the energy rolling off him was a hyper-vigilance, as if he knew the exact location of every stone his tires sprayed up.

He exuded confidence. Not crazy, blind brashness. He had the unconcerned demeanor of a man who was fully aware of what fate could do to him and was absolutely certain he had the tools to triumph. His faith was reassuring, and she felt her grip on the handle loosen slightly, and the pressure in her chest eased off.

He smiled. "There you go. Relax. Enjoy the scenery. Soon enough, the truck will be full of kids and our intimate moment will be over."

She almost choked at his words. "We're not having an intimate moment!" But even as she made the protest, she became aware of the closed quarters of the truck. The damp heat of the air, warmed by their bodies, moistened by the rain. Of Griffin's scent, a mixture of wet leather, Old Spice, and something more refined. His shampoo, maybe? And a deeper, lower fragrance, the aura of pure man, an intimate scent that usually only lovers would get close enough to experience.

Suddenly, the cab felt very small, Griffin seemed extremely male, and the distance between them was temptingly close. Clare watched the strength of his hands on the wheel, and a long-forgotten warmth curled through her belly, a sensation that absolutely terrified her... and filled her with the most delicious fascination, which she couldn't afford. Not now. Not ever. She cleared her throat and dragged her gaze off him. "Really. We're not."

Griffin grinned, his low chuckle wrapping around her like a warm seduction. "What? You don't have intimate moments with complete strangers you meet in the middle of storms on mountain ridges? What kind of woman are you?"

She bristled at his accusation, at the words she'd heard so many times questioning her choices, her competence, her life. "There's nothing wrong with me—"

"Whoa!" He held up his hand, his voice gentling. "I was just teasing. Trying to lighten the moment." He raised his brows as the truck bumped over another ridge. "How would I have any idea if there's anything wrong with you? I don't even know you."

Yeah, okay. He had a point. Clare rubbed her hands over her arms, embarrassed by her outburst at the man who had galloped into her life on his white horse and played the gallant knight for her, a heroic rescue so foreign to her she still had trouble believing it. "I'm sorry. Habit. I'm a little stressed right now."

He shrugged and shot her a mischievous wink that told her all was forgiven. "No apologies necessary. Takes a lot more than that to offend me." His smile faded, and his voice became serious. "But you should know, I don't judge people. People are who they are, and it's cool."

She was surprised by his words, and by the truth she sensed in him as he spoke. It felt good. It felt safe. "I like that."

"Good." He swerved the truck sharply, and she braced her hands on the dashboard as he appeared to head straight into the woods.

"Where are we going?"

"The sign said Pike's Notch. Isn't that where we're headed?"

"Yes, but there's a bigger road further up."

"Why do we need a bigger road? Plenty of room for a truck here."

Clare grimaced as the trees appeared in front of the headlights, flashing by so close she half-expected one of them to clip off a mirror. Dear God. What kind of person was he? She learned her lesson fifteen years ago about men who didn't like to play by the rules. "Who are you, exactly?"

He frowned. "I told you. My name's Griffin Friesé—"

"No, I mean, who *are* you? Do you live around here? If so, for how long? How come I don't know you? What do you do? Why—"

"There they are," he said, interrupting her string of desperate questions.

"Where——" Then she saw them. Up ahead, barely visible through the trees, she could see the pale blue of her daughter's wind-breaker, along with the huddled bodies of three other teenagers, including Jeremy, in his familiar neon-green jacket. She clutched the dash, her throat tightening at the sight of her daughter, standing up, still alive, still safe. "Honk the horn, Griffin," she said, tears so thick in her throat she could barely whisper them. "Tell them we're coming."

He hit the horn, and the quartet spun around. For a moment they froze, and then they started shouting and waving and jumping up and down. Clare laughed through her tears, her heart aching with relief. "Look at them trying to get our attention. Do they really think we might drive by without stopping?"

Griffin pulled up and slowed the truck. "No parent would, despite what some people might think."

"Who on earth would ever think a parent would drive past?" The comment seemed strange, but she sensed heavy tension in his words... as if someone had accused him of doing that? "You mean, someone thinks you would?" That was insane. The man had driven his truck up the side of a mountain for kids that weren't even his, for heaven's sake.

Instead of answering, Griffin stopped the truck and jerked his chin at the windshield.

She turned and saw her daughter's face. Worried, scared and pinched with cold. Tears sprang in Clare's eyes, and her composure fragmented with the relief of seeing her daughter. "Katie!" She shoved open the door and nearly fell out of the truck as Katie ran up.

"Mom!" Her darling daughter, who suddenly seemed so much younger than fifteen, threw herself into Clare's arms. As Clare wrapped herself around the trembling body of the most precious thing in the world to her, she looked over her daughter's shoulder and saw Griffin watching them with a wistful expression, longing etched so deeply in his face that she wanted to reach out and sweep him into their hug.

Her heart ached for him, for this powerful, strong man who had taken on the storm and commanded a happy ending. His eyes were dark, his damp hair tousled, his broad shoulders nearly taking up the whole front seat. He was so masculine, a man who wanted no comfort, and yet that's all she wanted to give him. There was a small smile playing at the corners of his mouth, but she sensed a deep sadness from him as well.

Clare wanted to hold out her hand to him, to offer him the kind touch she sensed he craved, but then his gaze met hers, and the vulnerability vanished from his eyes. He nodded, a satisfied gleam in his eyes of a job well done.

And it was. She smiled at him and mouthed her thank you. He flashed a real smile and winked, a special look only for her that made her belly tighten.

Then he turned away and stepped out of the truck to help the other teenagers, who were scrambling for their gear.

As she hugged her daughter and watched Griffin make his way toward the kids, getting them organized with a few commands of encouragement and reassurance, she knew she owed him a debt she would never, ever be able to repay.

No matter who he turned out to be.

WRIGHT & Son was as busy as always on a Sunday morning.

Normally, Clare loved walking into the local general store and seeing half the town streaming through its doors to get a morning coffee, or gathering around the wooden tables for a gossip session over breakfast and fishing poles. She loved the scent of coffee, freshly-baked muffins and hot chocolate, and she usually enjoyed the rowdy discussions that almost overwhelmed the store. But on this particular morning, after last night's stressful escapade in the mountains, she suspected her head was going to explode from the noise the moment she stepped inside.

All she wanted was to sit on her own back porch with coffee and silence, so she could figure out how to deal with the terror of last night, the unexpectedness of Griffin, and her daughter's illicit camping adventure. But people were expecting her, so there would be no quiet Sunday morning for her.

Balancing her stack of pastry boxes, Clare pushed open the door with her shoulder, and a five-year-old boy with a shock of red hair ducked under her arm and sprinted out onto the porch. "Sampson!" The top box on her stack started to slide, and she yelped, trying to catch it.

"Got it, sweetie!" Ophelia Wright, the wife of the current proprietor, swept up the wayward box. Her short gray hair was tucked neatly behind her ears, and the necklace of the day was blue and yellow sea glass with driftwood bits mixed in. "We've been getting requests for your cupcakes all morning. Glad you finally got here."

"Morning, Ophelia," Clare said to Ophelia's retreating back as the old but very solid woman carted the box of Clare's homemade cupcakes back toward the deli. The cupcakes were supposed to be located in the bakery section, but Ophelia always took some for her deli and forced them upon whoever she thought needed one, free of charge, of course.

The fact that Clare got no money for those cupcakes? Not a concern. Ophelia figured that the town's estate planning attorney could afford a few freebie cupcakes to those in need.

Sadly, Ophelia was not quite as right as Clare wished.

"Clare!" Beckoning from one of the tables by the front window was Clare's best friend and office mate, Astrid Monroe. Astrid had moved to Birch Crossing only three years ago, but their connection had been instant, filling both their lives with a beautiful friendship so strong that Clare felt like she'd know Astrid forever. Her brown hair was cascading in all directions, held at bay only by a colorful scarf twisted artistically through her curls.

Ah...relief was on its way. Clare grinned, her whole body relaxing at the sight of her friend. There was nothing like coffee with the girls to keep her head from actually spinning off. "I'll be over in a sec." Nodding greetings at assorted patrons, Clare worked her way through the crowd to the front register.

Sitting on his high stool, his ancient black ball cap on his head, was Norm Wright, the second generation of Wright men to anchor Wright & Son. Norm was leaning back against the wall, arms folded across his chest as he observed the chaos. A few strands of gray hair peeked out from beneath his cap, and his two-day beard was as white as the snow-tipped mountains in January. Despite being in his early seventies, Norm was still as sturdy and low key as she remembered from her childhood.

"Good morning, Norm." Clare set the boxes on the counter, happy to see the man who had been an icon in the town her whole life. Even though he plunked himself in the middle of chaos by running Wright & Son, Norm had a relaxed, unhurried way about him that always eased her stresses and made her smile. "How are you doing?"

"Always good." He gave his standard answer, his pale gray eyes focusing on hers with alert interest. "Katie okay after last night?"

Clare stifled a sigh. Of course Norm had already heard about the crisis in the mountains. Knowing Norm, he probably also knew she hadn't sat down with Katie to talk about it yet. Last night had been about comforting each other, and Katie had still been sleeping this morning when Clare had left the house. Dinner would be interesting tonight. "Yes, she's fine."

Norm nodded once. "Listen to what she has to say."

Clare smiled. "You mean, after I ground her for the rest of her life?"

"No. Before." Norm's gaze was unwavering. "She's a good kid."

"I know." Clare warmed as she thought of Katie. She never would have made it through the last fifteen years without her daughter, even if Katie did make her crazy sometimes. "I brought an assortment of cupcakes today. A few extra, since you keep selling out, but remember—"

"If they don't sell out, I have to toss 'em at the end of the day," Norm finished with a wink. "Clare, the world won't end if someone eats a day-old dessert."

"I won't have anyone thinking that I make dried-out cupcakes." Clare's stomach rumbled. Coffee and food could be delayed no longer. She leaned over the counter and kissed his cheek, laughing at the way he still turned red when she did it. "I'll see you later, Norm."

He winked at her, and she waved her farewell as she headed over to the deli. The refrigerated glass cases looked like they were the same ones that had housed salads, sandwiches and deli meats for the last fifty years, and the pine counters were dented and worn, but as always, completely immaculate. Above the grill was a painting of Wright's the first year it opened, and the old white building looked exactly as it had ninety-two years ago.

Her plaid sleeves rolled up to the elbow and flour covering her faded pink apron, Ophelia already had coffee, scrambled eggs and a blueberry muffin on the counter for Clare. "Here you go, Clare."

"Blueberry today?" Ophelia's muffins were the best in the state. She claimed her special ingredients were the milk from the Daniels' farm and the local berries she froze for use all year long. Whatever it was, they were legendary and Clare was delighted to see that Ophelia had saved one for her. "Thanks, O!"

Ophelia blew her a kiss. "Anytime, sweetie— Wait a sec." Ophelia plucked a cupcake from Clare's box and set it on the plate. "Here."

Clare laughed. "I have a dozen at home. I'm all set." She tried to hand it back.

"Doesn't change the fact you need one today. I can see it in your eyes." Ophelia waved her off and turned away to deal with a local carpenter who was attempting to order an omelet without ham, much to Ophelia's disgust. According to Ophelia, the man was too peaked to forego some good, solid protein, and she was going to make sure he got it. Clare had been dismissed.

Resigning herself to the pink and white dessert on her antiqued wooden tray, Clare hurried across the deli, avoiding friendly chit-chatters and diving into the seat across from Astrid. "The store is bedlam today."

"I know." Astrid's dark brown eyes were gleaming. "The energy of this place always fires me up. I'm ready to go to work!"

Clare laughed, already buoyed by Astrid's energetic presence. "It's Sunday, Astrid. Take the day off." Astrid designed and created nature-inspired jewelry, and she sold it both locally and on the Internet. Her friend was truly gifted and adored what she did. Her signature was an "A," beautifully designed in the shape of an orchid blossom, though she had never explained the significance of the orchid to Clare. The peacefulness on Astrid's face while she worked always made Clare a little envious. There was nothing like looking up from an hour of bleary-eyed document-reading to see Astrid's eyes gleaming with delight as she wove another magical pattern out of her jewels and wire.

"Never! If I don't spin a few pairs of earrings, I'll lose my mind." Astrid lowered her voice and leaned forward, her eyes dancing. "So, tell me about the guy. Is he as hot as I've heard, and more importantly, is sex finally going to become a part of your life again?"

CHAPTER THREE

FOR A SPLIT SECOND, the only word Clare could think of in response to Astrid's question was a resounding *yes,* the kind of yes that started deep down in her soul and reverberated through every inch of her body, a yearning so powerful it tore at her heart and made her belly pulse with need.

Her mind flashed back to the previous night. The torrential rain, the anguish and helplessness she'd felt when she'd encountered the tree blocking her path, and the relief that had poured into her when Griffin had climbed out of his enormous black truck and strode across the drenched road.

The moment she'd seen him, she'd known everything was going to be okay. She wasn't one for fantasies and knight-in-shining-armor yearnings, but last night, she'd been desperately out of answers, and he had carried himself with the aura of a man who always got it right.

And he had. This total stranger, this man from nowhere, had delivered everything she'd needed. For the first time in fifteen years, she hadn't needed to figure out the solutions on her own and make it happen. It had been the most incredible relief to surrender everything to him.

"Clare!" Astrid waved her sparkly pink manicure in front of Clare's face. "You here? Tell me about the guy."

Yanked back to the present, Clare ducked her head and peeled the top off her coffee cup. "What guy?" she managed to ask, struggling to regain her composure.

"The one who helped you rescue Katie and her friends." Astrid gave her an impatient look. "I heard about it from Richie, who heard it from Jenn, when he called her this morning to talk about the fundraiser for the new rec center, who'd heard it from her nephew who was with Katie last night."

Clare inhaled the rich aroma of her coffee. The Columbian brew was mixed with vanilla today, always her favorite. Ophelia knew she loved her coffee that way, but that didn't mean the woman was always willing to make it for her. Clare was glad today had been one of the days Ophelia had taken pity on her. "His name's Griffin Friesé."

"A very manly name." Astrid's eyes gleamed. "And who is he? What's his scoop?"

Clare shrugged and broke off a piece of muffin. "I have no idea." Excitement was strumming through her. "He has strong hands, though." She could still remember when he'd grasped her to help her over the tree, the way his hands had supported her, reaching nearly all the way around her waist. He'd lifted her as if she'd weighed nothing, and tossing her over the massive tree had been no strain at all.

He'd been all man, and it had been a very long time since there had been a man in her life, even for a fleeting moment.

"You should see your face!" Astrid grinned. "Girl, you look dreamy. I've never seen you look dreamy in your whole life, except the day you came running into my house and told me you'd met this cute boy named Ed Gray."

Clare's excitement faded. "Yeah, well, look how well that turned out—"

"It did turn out! Ed was your moment of true romance and love. He opened your heart, he gave you a daughter, and he made you smile." Astrid shrugged. "Sure, he died, but that doesn't change that you were so happy when you came home and said that your heart had taken flight."

Yes, well, maybe not quite all happy in the end. Clare sighed and spun the coffee cup in her hands. Ed was a good reminder not to get involved...but she still couldn't stop thinking about Griffin. The moment in the truck, when she'd been consumed by the scent of leather, man and—

"Wow." Astrid leaned back in her chair, a thoughtful look on her face. "You've got that expression again. You look a thousand years younger than you have in ages."

"A thousand years, huh? That's quite a statement." But Clare did feel a little perkier than usual, she had to admit. She'd been a little bit giddy dreaming of heroic rescuers in muddy boots last night.

Fanciful moments while sleeping were one thing, but real life was another matter entirely. Clare picked up her fork and took a bite of her eggs, trying not to get caught up in Astrid's excitement. She had things to do. A daughter to raise. A business to run. Bills to pay. "I don't have time for dreamy. I have no idea who Griffin is, and I'm sure I'll never see him again—"

"Oh, I know who he is." Eppie Orlowe, the oldest and dearest friend of Clare's mom, pulled up a chair beside them. Like everyone else in the store, she was wearing jeans and hiking boots, but her head was adorned with a hot pink straw hat with artificial sunflowers and a tiny stuffed turtle. "Griffin Friesé is the Slipper King."

Clare flicked one of the sunflowers out of Eppie's wrinkled face, trying to muster up a smile at Eppie's intrusion. She loved the interfering old lady, but right now, she wanted to be all giddy about Griffin for a few more minutes before being subjected to another lecture on how she was letting her daughter down by her parenting skills. "What's a Slipper King?"

"You haven't heard?" Clare's best friend from elementary school, Emma Larson, pulled up a chair and sat down, her blond hair up in a ponytail and already speckled with enough paint to suggest she'd been in her studio for hours already. Clare was a little worried about how much Emma was painting these days, but she was afraid to bring it up. If painting was all that was keeping Emma from crumbling, maybe it was okay that it was consuming her friend. Or maybe not. She didn't know.

"Griffin Friesé is the owner of Free Love Slippers," Emma said.

"Free Love?" Clare remembered the rainbow colored slippers that Katie had *begged* to have for her eleventh birthday. Every girl in Daniel Webster Middle School had owned at least one pair, and the flashing lights on the toes had become a common sight on every street once the company had started putting real outsoles on them. Free Love had gone platinum nearly overnight, and Clare and her friends had often lamented that they hadn't been the ones to think of the silly things.

"Griffin *was* the owner," Eppie clarified. "Before he went insane."

Clare's attention jerked back to Eppie. "Griffin went insane?" Her Griffin? That made no sense.

"He doesn't sound insane," Astrid said with a smug look at Clare as she leaned back with her latte. "He sounds quite fine indeed."

"Really?" A wary look came over Emma's paint-speckled cheeks. "Is he handsome?"

"Apparently, quite deliciously so," Astrid said. "Strong hands."

31

"Strong hands!" Emma smacked Clare's shoulder with genuine concern. "How do you know how strong his hands are? Seriously, Clare. What were you doing up there on the mountain?"

Clare picked up her coffee, feeling her cheeks burn. "He helped me over a tree."

"Is that the *au courant* euphemism?" Astrid asked. "Because I could use a man to help me over some trees—"

"He abandoned his wife and daughter," interrupted Eppie's best friend, Judith Bittner, as she dropped another chair beside the table. Unlike Eppie, Judith was wearing her Sunday best, and was no doubt heading to church in her flowered skirt, lavender blouse and silver-tinted hair. Her gold framed eye glasses were perched on the end of her nose, and the sparkly chains hanging from the ear pieces were her only jewelry.

Clare was startled by Judith's claim. Griffin had abandoned his family? The man who'd risked death to help a stranger? That didn't make any sense. "Are you sure about that?"

"Damn straight I'm sure," Judith harrumphed as she set her plate of bacon and hash browns on the table. "Walked out on them, just like Ed abandoned you and Katie by dying. Don't be getting yourself tangled up with another outsider, Clare."

Clare held up her hands to try to stave off the lecture. "Calm down, Judith. I'm not getting involved with anyone! He actually helped me over a tree—"

"You should get involved," Astrid said, her eyes twinkling over the rim of her coffee cup. "Especially with handsome men who rescue you in the middle of the night."

"I don't know about that," Emma said. "I need to hear the story first. What's he like?"

"I'll tell you what he's like. Griffin Friesé is bad news."

Eppie leaned forward, her hat sliding to the side, weighted by the flowers. "He lost his business, abandoned his wife and daughter, and then completely snapped." She nodded sagely and lowered her voice. "That man is on the fast track toward a complete breakdown, and you would do best not to have anything to do with him, Clare."

"Men on the verge of a complete breakdown are sometimes the most interesting," Astrid said. "Clare, you need some excitement in your life. I vote you go for it."

"I'm too busy to go on dates," Clare protested. But the thought of a date was interesting for the first time since she could remember. Despite Eppie and Judith's attempts to malign Griffin, Clare didn't buy it at all. In fact, she was kind of drawn to the idea of getting dressed up and showing Griffin what she looked like when she wasn't drenched, terrified and muddy. It wasn't just any man who would suffice. It was Griffin Friesé. His power. His strength. His—

"He showed up in town last night," Judith said, peering at Clare through her glasses. "Got a room at the Dark Pines Motel. What kind of millionaire takes a room at that place? He's already snapped, I'm telling you."

Clare stiffened. "He's in town? Now?" Her entire body leapt into awareness, and she bolted upright, belatedly searching the store for him. What if she saw him again? What if he wasn't a mere shadow that had flitted through her life for only the briefest moment? Her heart started to pound, followed by swift disappointment when she saw he wasn't there. Oh, God. What was she doing? She couldn't obsess about him. She sat back and raised her chin, fighting for composure.

"Oh..." Astrid said, her eyes gleaming. "I think maybe you should go thank him personally for his help. A one-night stand might be just the thing you need."

"I'm not having a one-night stand with him," Clare said,

glaring at Astrid. Hello? Did her friend *really* have to bring up sex in front of Eppie and Judith? But the thought of Griffin and sex sent a sudden pulse of desire rippling through her, just like last night when she'd been in Griffin's arms. Twice in twenty-four hours? There was no way for her to stop her small smile. It felt amazing to remember what it felt like to be attracted to a man.

"His ex-wife and daughter escaped him by moving to River Junction." Eppie plucked a sunflower off her hat and twirled it oh-so-casually in her fingers. "They live less than twenty miles from here."

"The Slipper King has come to stalk his family, kill them and then go back to Boston," Judith said, folding her arms over her bosomy chest. "It's a sad state of affairs, it is. From a happy marriage to this. Money ruins everything, I'll tell you that right now."

Emma looked down at her coffee, and Clare put her arm around her friend and hugged her gently, knowing Judith was making Emma think about her own recent escape from a hellish marriage. "Oh for heaven's sake," Clare said, interrupting Judith before she could gain momentum. "I'm sure Griffin's not here to kill anyone. He was a hero last night, for heaven's sake—"

"A hero?" Eppie pointed a sunflower right at her. "Listen here, young lady. I swore on your mother's deathbed that I'd look after you and Katie, and I'll honor that promise until the day I die. If you so much as utter one complimentary word about that dangerous man, I will lock you down until we run him out of town."

"May God rest your mother's spirit," Judith added emphatically. "That man's no good, and if you start dallying with him, it'll endanger everything you've worked so hard to provide for Katie."

"Katie and I are doing just fine," Clare bristled, clenching her fists under the table. "So just stop—" She paused and forced herself to take a breath. These women had been her mother's dearest friends. She had to honor her mother's love for them. She managed a smile. "I appreciate your concern very much," she said evenly. "But you don't need to worry because I'm not going to date him, talk to him or get involved with him in any way."

"Too bad," Emma said. "I think he sounds just wrong enough to be worth getting involved with."

Clare looked at her usually cautious friend, unable to suppress the swirl of nervous anticipation at Emma's comment. "What? Aren't you all about staying away from him?" She really didn't need her friends encouraging her to get all dreamy-eyed about Griffin. She was having enough trouble not remembering how her entire being had trembled when he'd enfolded her in his arms with such strength.

"He sounds like a good choice for you." Emma shrugged, stealing a corner of Clare's muffin and popping it into her mouth. "He apparently has a decent streak to him or he wouldn't have helped you, but you won't be fooled into thinking he's Mr. Right. He's safe to date because it would get you back into the game, but he's got so many issues that he wouldn't tempt you long term. You need to get back out there before you get so desperate that you make a huge mistake like I did." She smiled thoughtfully. "I think he actually sounds interesting."

"Much more interesting than any of the men we get around here," Astrid agreed. "I've never had the opportunity to date a handsome knight who's on a mission to kill his family. Maybe I'll date him if you're not?"

"What? You? I don't think he's your type." Clare sat up quickly before she saw her friend's teasing expression.

"Ah, she does care," Astrid said quietly. "Methinks he did make an impression."

A warm feeling eased through Clare. He *had* made an impression. A big one. And it felt good. Maybe it felt so good because she knew he didn't live in town, so she never had to actually consider acting on it. She could fantasize, but she'd never have to risk anything that mattered to her.

"It's about time a man made an impression on Clare," Emma said. "It's been too long. Dry spells of that length can lead to dangerous decisions."

"Fifteen years too long," Eppie said. "Katie needs a father. A responsible one," she added. "One that will be there for her. You need a solid, responsible man, Clare, and it's time you stopped being selfish about your freedom and found one."

"Clare needs passion, not a husband," Astrid announced. "A few orgasms and some nights with the massage oil."

Clare's cheeks heated up, Emma clapped her hand over her mouth to stifle a giggle, and Judith looked horrified.

But not Eppie. Oh, no, of course not Eppie. "Sex?" Eppie said brightly. "You're talking about sex, aren't you? Well, you may think that old Eppie doesn't know about sex, but we all have our need for passion—"

"Okay." Clare stood up. Hearing Eppie talk about sex was too much for a Sunday morning, and that would be the fast track toward deflating any residual fantasies about Griffin. "I need to work. I'll see you all later."

"I'm going to work, too." Astrid leapt up, and grabbed her coffee. "Emma?"

"Me, too. I need to paint." Emma hurried to her feet. "Today's a painting day, for sure."

"I'll see you later, Eppie. Judith." Clare nodded at the gray-haired duo, but before she could follow Astrid out the door, Eppie took her hand and patted it tenderly.

"Clare, darling, I know sometimes I drive you mad, but

we're just looking out for you because we love you and Katie," Eppie said.

Clare's irritation with the older women faded, and she smoothed Eppie's wrinkled collar. "I know, and I appreciate it. It's reassuring to have someone looking out for me."

Judith patted her arm. "We're always here for you, Clare, and when you're ready to date, you just let us know, and we'll find a good one for you."

Clare smiled fondly. "Thanks, but I'm all set." She kissed each one on the forehead. "I have to run and get some work done before Katie gets up. See you later."

They waved her on, and they were already spreading more gossip about the Slipper King before Clare made it to the front door. By the time Griffin woke up, he was going to discover he'd already murdered ten people, six dogs and a hamster. He wouldn't last in this town past noon. Being a hero only went so far if you were an outsider.

As she stepped outside, the thought of Griffin leaving town cast a pall over Clare. She instinctively glanced in the direction of the Dark Pines Motel, but no big black truck was driving toward them. He was either already on his way out of town, or the roof had collapsed on him and pinned him to his bed.

As it should be—well not the roof collapsing, but it really was best not to run into him again. She couldn't afford him. He belonged in her heart and her memories as a romantic amazing moment that would always be perfect because real life could never taint it by turning their brief connection into a real relationship. Griffin was her mythical savior, and now it was time to get practical.

Clare lifted her chin resolutely. Emma and Astrid fell in beside her as she headed down the steps of the store toward the street.

"I'm sure he's not a killer," Emma said as the trio crossed

Main Street toward Clare's office, which was just down the block.

"I agree that he's probably not here to go on a killing spree." Clare sighed, feeling oddly deflated. Whether it was the thought of Griffin leaving, or the reminders of her mistake with Ed, she didn't know. She just felt tired. Not sleepy tired. Soul-tired. "But Eppie's right. I don't need another outsider."

"Screw Eppie," Astrid said as they stepped up onto the sidewalk.

"No!" Clare set her hands on her hips and glared at her friend, knowing she needed to quell any romantic longings before they could take hold and render her incapable of accepting the life she had. "I would never have survived those early days without Eppie taking care of Katie while I went back to school."

"But that doesn't mean she's right about this guy." Astrid sighed. "Clare, you're only thirty-three, and you haven't dated in fifteen years. Even for a nun, that's kind of a bit anti-social."

"I don't have time." Clare pulled open the door to the quaint little building that housed their offices. Clare's was full of legal documents, and Astrid's was full of jewels, precious metals and all sorts of design sketches.

"You don't *make* time," Astrid said. "There's a difference."

Clare gestured at her desk. "I have clients to deal with, a daughter to raise, bills to pay, and my house needs a new roof. When does that leave time for dating? And why would I want to? I have everything I need."

"Do you really?" Astrid picked up a double-heart necklace that was her biggest seller, and she dangled it. "Are you so sure about that?"

"Well, no." Clare looked at the list of names on her desk. "I need a new roof for free. Other than that, I'm good."

"Speaking of good, I really want to hear the whole story about the Slipper King, especially the strong hands part." Emma leaned against the door frame as Clare crossed the room and sat down at her desk. "All I know is that some guy who drives a big black truck did the hero thing last night, and he might be an insane murderer. Who is he? What happened?" Her dark brown eyes met Clare's, and they were full of an understanding and empathy that had deepened since Emma had returned to town last fall. "And are you okay, Clare? Really okay?"

Emma's gentle inquisition made Clare's defenses fall, and she sagged down in her chair, unable to stop the aching loneliness from cascading through her. "I'm a wreck."

Emma laughed softly. "A wreck because you met an appealing guy? I'd probably be the same way."

"Or are you a wreck because you finally want to break out of that shell of yours, and you're scared?" Astrid asked. "It's okay to be terrified about men. Why do you think I never get serious with one? It's all a facade for the fact that being in another serious relationship terrifies me beyond words."

Clare smiled at her friend's confession. "We've been telling you that for years, Astrid. You need therapy."

"To talk me into a husband? Never. My jewelry is all I need." Astrid smiled gently. "But you, my dear, don't even date. That's not normal. Raw, debilitating terror is not a reason to skip out on a chance to get in touch with your womanly side."

"I'm not terrified." Clare thought back again to last night, but this time, the memory of Griffin's lean and well-muscled body striding across the sodden earth toward her didn't flood her with warmth and peace. Instead, tension tweaked her chest, her belly churned and fear rippled through her body. Well, okay, maybe a little terrified. She'd lost so much already, and she couldn't afford to lose anymore. She knew it would break her beyond what she could take.

Eppie might be an overly protective gossip, but the older woman was right. Clare *had* made a grievous mistake fifteen years ago, far more than anyone, even Astrid and Emma, knew. And Griffin was that same kind of mistake.

She'd come too far, and she was clinging to a thread that was too perilously thin to be able to afford another mistake, or take a risk, any kind of risk. Astrid was right. She *was* terrified. But for all the right reasons.

"Clare?" Emma prompted. "I want to hear the details."

Clare turned on her computer, the bleak void in her heart so powerful that her chest actually hurt. "It was nothing," she said quietly. It had to be nothing. She couldn't handle it being anything more.

Her friend gave her a skeptical look, and Clare knew she didn't believe it.

Unfortunately, Clare didn't either.

CHAPTER FOUR

THE SITUATION WAS INTOLERABLE.

Griffin could still feel the skittle of little claws across his forehead as he drove down what was apparently Main Street. Not that he had a problem with rodents per se, but waking up to find one trying to pluck out a few hairs for its nest had not been exactly what he'd had in mind when he'd asked a local for a place to crash last night.

He did not sleep with rodents. Period.

He should have known better than to take directions from a man wearing ear flaps in the middle of April, especially one who had taken such a long and skeptical look at Griffin's truck and asked him point blank whether it had cost more than his house. But the man who'd been standing roadside at ten o'clock when Griffin had driven into town had been the only resource in sight, and Griffin had been wet, muddy and yeah, a little distracted by the prior two hours.

Hence a night with the rats.

Griffin slowed his truck as he saw a crowd of cars ahead. He'd expected the town of Birch Crossing to still be asleep at seven thirty on a Sunday morning, but the number of cars and people crowding in front of Wright & Son told him that he might find a reference to better lodging.

He parked his truck and reached in back for his leather jacket, but his fingers hit something softer, wetter, and fluffier than should ever have been in his vehicle. Instinctively, he jerked his hand back, but nothing squeaked in outrage.

Cautiously, he peered over into the rear of the truck and saw a hot pink scarf sitting on his back seat. His mind flashed back to last night, and he remembered that Clare's daughter had been wearing that scarf when she'd gotten into his truck.

He picked it up, turning it over in his hand as he recalled the previous evening. He thought of Clare. Of Katie. Of all the kids that had been piled in his vehicle. Fighting over his blankets. Teeth chattering. All of them talking over each other, trying to tell Clare what had happened and how they'd ended up stranded in the woods. A feeling of rightness settled over him as he recalled the chaos that had reigned in his truck last night.

For those twenty minutes it had taken to get them back to Clare's car, his truck had been overrun with people, with teenagers. He'd forgotten what that felt like to have the windows steam up because there were so many people in his space. He hadn't remembered what it felt like to have someone's foot accidentally knock his arm off the arm rest. He'd lost the memory of what it sounded like to hear teenage laughter. Their screeches of protest ringing in his ears.

He laughed softly, remembering the teens competing to tell the story of Jeremy falling into the river, trying to talk over each other to be the one to deliver the final blow to the poor kid's dignity, explaining how he'd been peeing into the river at the time he'd fallen in, and he'd had an all-too-revealing zipper in his jeans when the girls had pulled him out.

Griffin's smile faded as he looked around his truck,

suddenly aware of its emptiness in a way he hadn't felt when he'd bought it. It had been perfect. Pristine. Flawless. Exactly as he liked it. Now, there was dirt on the seats and floor and smudges on the windows. He nodded. Yeah, that was how a truck should be. Lived in.

On the floor of the passenger seat were thick chunks of dirt on the mat. From Clare's boots. His adrenaline spiked as he recalled her sitting in that seat, gripping the dashboard like it was all she had to keep from falling apart. He'd felt like a fucking hero when he'd seen her stumble out of the car and hug her daughter. He'd fixed something and made it right, something he felt like he hadn't done in a long time.

The high he'd gotten was addictive as hell. What if his own daughter could have seen him in that moment? Maybe she would look at him the way Clare's daughter and her friends had, like he had delivered them from the very bowels of hell into salvation, instead of being that hell himself. But she didn't. She hadn't looked at him like that in a long, damn time.

Scowling, he clenched the scarf in his fist, and a few drops spilled out and dripped on the leather console.

Like the drops that had been dripping down Clare's cheeks when she'd climbed into his truck and pushed back her hood.

For a moment, he hadn't been sure whether they were tears or raindrops. Still wasn't, in fact. But he could still recall with vivid clarity those huge blue eyes staring at him in desperation, in a silent plea for help.

He laughed softly, remembering his asinine inspiration to drive his truck up the side of a damn cliff. Anything to take the strain off the face of that petite female who'd been ready to climb over a monstrous tree and hike eight miles in a storm to find her daughter.

In that moment, when Clare Gray had climbed into his

truck, drenched his new seat, and turned toward him...he would have driven off a damn cliff for her.

Getting caught up in playing the hero for a woman was something he didn't need. Not now. Not ever. He'd learned his lesson, and he'd learned it well. It was a role he didn't fit.

The only female in his life from now on would be his daughter.

As soon as he got her back.

Until Brooke was home, there was no time for thinking about a woman like Clare. Even if she did have the most expressive blue eyes he'd ever seen.

"Hey!" A man about Griffin's age wearing a faded army jacket and an old flannel shirt smacked the hood of Griffin's truck. "You like her?"

"Her?" Griffin shot out of the truck as the man flattened his palm on the gleaming paint. Was the man talking about Clare? Did he know where she was? "Who?"

"This truck." The man stroked his hand over the hood again. "I'm saving up for one of these babies. Ralph is going to let me know if someone turns one in at his lot. If it's got less than seventy thousand, I'm getting it."

The truck? Griffin scowled, trying to pull his thoughts back from the woman who'd been on his mind all night. It was guy time. Truck talk. A much safer topic. "Less than seventy thousand? Miles?" Griffin hadn't kept a truck past thirty thousand in twenty years.

"Yeah, man, that's when she gets into her prime." The man stuck his hand out. "Jackson Reed. Welcome to Birch Crossing, my man."

Griffin hesitated, then clasped Jackson's callused hand. "Griffin Friesé."

"I know. Nice job last night, my man. Nice job." Jackson clapped his palm on Griffin's shoulder. "You going in for a cup of coffee before you kill them off?"

"Kill them off?" Griffin was too surprised to come up with a more coherent response. He'd heard a lot of comments in his day, but this was a first for him. "What are you talking about?"

"The rumors are going, man. The rumors are going." Jackson nodded at the market. "I'd stay and introduce you, but I've got to get to work on the new rec center. Grand opening in a couple days, and it's not ready." He slapped Griffin's back. "But if you need anything, you give me a holler. I know what it's like to be the new kid."

Griffin raised his brows at the offer, surprised that anyone would think he needed someone to pave his way. "Thanks, but I'm sure I'll be fine."

Jackson laughed. "Yeah, I'll remind you later that you said that." Still chuckling, Jackson strode past Griffin, his heavy work boots thudding on the sidewalk as he headed toward an ancient red pickup that was loaded with fresh lumber, covered in rust, and armed with enormous, brand new tires.

Griffin studied the tires, impressed by the size and quality of them, especially in comparison to the old vehicle riding on them. Jackson Reed knew where to put his money at least. A foundation was the core to anything, and the man had four good tires holding up his payload.

Griffin shook his head in amusement as he turned toward the market. Damn if he didn't like the guy already, just for his tires.

Still chuckling, Griffin vaulted up the stairs and threw open the door to Wright & Son. He stepped inside and stopped abruptly at the chaos that assaulted him.

People were everywhere, voices raised, pipe smoke drifting out the door, a damn dog barking by a tank of lobsters, and a well-oiled chain saw sitting on one of the tables, being ardently discussed by a trio of men with more gray hair than Santa Claus.

And then, like a whisper on the wind, one by one, heads turned toward him, conversations ceased and the world became focused on him. And none of the faces were friendly. He stopped just inside the doorway, adrenaline spiking at the obvious hostility. Exactly who had Jackson said was going to be killing off whom?

The door suddenly slammed into his back, and the doorknob jammed into his kidney.

"Norm!" A woman called out from behind him.

Griffin's whole body tensed, and something sprang to life inside him at the sound of that voice. That lilting sound that struck a chord all the way down in his chest. A melody that made the chaos fall away, replaced by nothing but the sound of her voice.

He turned slowly as Clare Gray peered past him, looking across the store, and his breath literally stuttered in his chest as he saw the woman who'd invaded his dreams all night.

Clare was real. He hadn't imagined her. He hadn't exaggerated his response to her. Her energy, her fire, and her allure were every bit as powerful as they had been last night when he'd been unable to walk away from the hero role for the first time in his life.

"I accidentally left the cupcakes for Emma's niece here." She pushed past him, apparently too preoccupied by the cupcakes to glance his way and realize he was beside her. "You didn't sell them yet, did you?"

Griffin caught a scent of lilac, fresh soap and subtle natural springtime as she walked by, and every cell in his body ignited. No heavy perfume for Clare, just purity and lightness, and it was perfect.

She looked so different than she had last night. Her face was vibrant and alive, instead of drawn and terrified. No longer pinned to her head in sodden clumps, her dark hair tumbled down around her shoulders, messy and free, as if she hadn't bothered to tame it this morning. Her jeans curved over her backside in an altogether tempting way, and there was a spring to her step he hadn't seen last night. She'd been compelling then, but now, she was vibrating with life, and she was utterly riveting, awakening in him a raw desire that had been dormant for so long.

She strode past him, her steps confident and sure. Her shoulders were pulled back, and it dawned on him that Clare looked like a woman to be reckoned with, not a woman to be rescued.

His adrenaline faded as he suddenly realized the truth. Despite last night, Clare was a strong, independent woman who didn't need help or support. Not from any man. Not from him. Ever.

Just like his ex-wife.

Well, hell. Griffin shoved his hands in his pockets and narrowed his eyes, his good mood gone. Not that it mattered. He was there to get his daughter back, not to get caught up in a woman like Clare.

But as he watched her hips sway as she walked across the store, he couldn't stop the rise of anticipation at the thought of her finally turning those decadent blue eyes his way and realizing he was standing behind her.

CLARE WAS JUST LIFTING the box of cupcakes off the front counter when she became aware of the utter silence of the store. Even at the funerals of her parents, she hadn't heard this kind of silence in Birch Crossing.

Awareness prickled down her arms, and she looked at Norm. She could have sworn that there was amusement crinkling his gray eyes when he nodded toward something behind her.

"Oh..." Astrid's squeak of surprise told her that her friends had followed her into the store.

Clare spun around, and there he was.

Griffin Friesé.

Her mystical knight in shining armor.

Her heart began to race as she met his gaze. His stare was intense, penetrating all the way to her core. She was yanked back to that moment of his hands on her hips, his strength as he'd lifted her. The power in his body as he'd emerged from his truck during the thundering rain and raging wind. Her body began to thrum, and his expression grew hooded, his eyes never leaving hers, as if he were trying to memorize every feature on her face.

He was wearing a heavy leather jacket that flanked strong thighs and broad shoulders. His eyes were dark, as dark as they'd been last night in the storm. Whiskers shadowed his jaw, giving him a hard look. His boots were still caked with mud, but his jeans were pressed and clean. His light blue dress shirt was open at the collar, revealing a hint of skin and the flash of a thin gold chain at his throat. His hair was short and perfectly gelled, not messy and untamed like it had been last night. A heavy gold watch sat captive on the strong wrist that had supported her so easily.

Today, he wasn't the dark and rugged hero of the night.

Well, okay, he was. His power transcended mud, storms, nice watches and dress shirts.

But he was also, quite clearly and quite ominously, an outsider, a man who did not fit into the town of Birch Crossing.

Then he smiled, a beautiful, tremendous smile with a dimple in his right cheek. "How's Katie?"

A dimple? He had a dimple? Clare hadn't noticed the dimple last night. He looked so human, and so endearing with a dimple. Suddenly all her trepidation vanished, replaced by a feeling of giddiness and delight to see him. She smiled back, unable to keep herself from responding in kind. "She's still asleep, but she's okay. Thanks for your help last night rescuing her."

"My pleasure." His smile faded, and a speculative gleam came into his dark eyes. "And how are you?"

No longer feeling like a total wreck, that was for sure. Not with Griffin Friesé studying her as if she were the only thing he ever wanted to look at again. Dear God, the way he was looking at her made her want to drop the cupcakes and her clothes, and saunter with decadent sensuality across the floor toward him, his stare igniting every cell in her body. "I'm fine." She swallowed, horrified by how throaty her voice sounded. "Thank you," she said. "I owe you."

"No, you owe me nothing." He shook his head, and an odd expression came over his face, as if the words he was thinking didn't quite make sense to him even as he said it. "Seeing you hug Katie was plenty."

"Oh, dear Lord," Eppie muttered behind her. "Now he's going to kill Katie, too."

Clare stiffened and jerked her gaze from Griffin. The entire store was watching them in rapt silence, listening to every word. Oh, God. How had she forgotten where they were? Wrights General Store was the epicenter of gossip in Birch Crossing, and everyone had just witnessed her gaping at this handsome stranger.

Assuming her decades-old role as Clare's self-appointed protector, Eppie had folded her arms and was trying to crush Griffin with her glare, for daring to tempt Clare.

Astrid and Emma were leaning against the doorjamb, huge grins on their faces, clearly supportive of any opportunity to pry Clare out of her dateless life of isolation. But Norm's eyes were narrowed, and Ophelia was letting some scrambled eggs burn while she gawked at them. Everyone was waiting to see how Clare was going to respond to him.

Oh, man. What was she doing nearly throwing herself at him? She quickly took a step back and cleared her throat.

Griffin's eyebrows shot up at her retreat, then his eyes narrowed. "Kill off Katie, *too*? " He looked right at Eppie. "Who else am I going to kill?""

Eppie lifted her chin and turned her head, giving him a view of the back of her hot pink hat.

"The rumors claim that you're in town to murder your ex-wife and daughter," Astrid volunteered cheerfully. "But don't worry. Not all of us believe them."

"My daughter?" Pain flashed across Griffin's face, a stark anguish so real that Clare felt her out heart tighten. Just as quickly, the vulnerability disappeared from his face, replaced by a hard, cool expression.

But she'd seen it. She'd seen his pain, pain he clearly kept hidden, just as she suppressed her own. Suddenly, she felt terrible about the rumors. How could she have listened to rumors about him when he was clearly struggling with pain, some kind of trauma with regard to his daughter?

She realized he was watching her, as if he were waiting for something. For what? To see if she believed the rumors?

She glanced around and saw the entire store was waiting for her response. Eppie gave her a solemn nod, and Judith did the same, encouraging her to stand up and condemn this handsome stranger. Sudden anger surged inside her. "Oh, come on," she snapped. "You can't think he's really here to kill his family?"

Astrid grinned, Eppie shook her head in dismay, and the rest of the room was silent.

No one else jumped in to help her defend Griffin, and suddenly Clare felt very exposed, as if everyone in the room could see exactly how deeply she'd been affected by him last night. How she'd lain awake all night, thinking of his hands on her hips, of the way his deep voice had wrapped around her, of how he'd made her yearn for the touch of a man for the first time in a very long time.

Heat burned her cheeks, and she glanced uncomfortably at Griffin, wondering if he was aware of her reaction to him. To her surprise, his face had cooled, devoid of that warmth that they'd initially shared, clearly interpreting her silence as a capitulation to the rumors.

He narrowed his eyes, then turned away, ending their conversation.

Regret rushed through Clare as she glanced at Astrid, torn between wanting to call him back, and gratefully grasping the freedom his rejection had given her, freedom from feelings and desires that she didn't have time to deal with.

She felt so frazzled right now. "I'm going to work." She grabbed the cupcakes and headed for the door. "Emma, here you go—"

"I need a place to stay," Griffin said. "A place without rats, preferably."

Griffin's low request echoed through the room, and Clare spun around in shock. Then she saw he was directing his question to Norm, not to her. Relief rushed through her, along with a stab of disappointment.

No, it was good he wasn't asking to stay at her place. Yes, she owed him, on a level beyond words, but she couldn't afford to get involved with him, for too many reasons. Staying at her house would be putting temptation where she couldn't afford it. There was *no way* she was going to offer up her place, even though her renter had just vacated, leaving her with an unpleasant gap in her income stream.

"He stayed at the Dark Pines Motel last night," Judith whispered, just loudly enough for the whole store to hear.

"Really?" Guilt washed through Clare. The Dark Pines Motel was quite possibly the most unkempt and disgusting motel in the entire state of Maine. How had he ended up there?

"Fitting, I should think," Eppie said, "for a man like that."

A man like what? A man who would risk flipping his truck so he could help a woman he didn't even know? Anger began to simmer inside Clare at the way Griffin was being maligned. Didn't anyone care that he'd come to the rescue of four teenagers?

Clare paused, warring with the urge to go back and defend him. It was one thing for Eppie and Judith to orchestrate her well-being, but doing it at Griffin's expense was wrong.

But as he leaned his hands on the counter, his broad shoulders flexed, Griffin didn't look like a man who needed defending. He looked strong, powerful and utterly unconcerned about what anyone thought about him. Clare's heart sank a little bit. There was nothing she could do for him. He didn't need her, and he never would. He wasn't the kind of man who needed anything. What could she possibly offer a man who had everything he needed?

"Well, now, Griffin," Norm said, as he tipped his chair back and let it tap against the unfinished wall. "Most places won't open for another month when the summer folk start to arrive. And the Black Loon Inn is booked for the Smith-Pineal wedding for the next week. It's Dark Pines or nothing."

Clare turned toward her friends. "Let's go."

Astrid raised her brows. "Strong hands, indeed."

Emma lowered her voice. "He might be a killer, but if I could have a man look at me that way for one minute of my life, it might almost be worth it."

Clare felt her cheeks heat up, and she glanced back at Griffin. He wasn't even looking her way. So, yeah, that heated look between them had meant nothing. Resolutely, Clare pulled open the door. "Just stop already."

"Looks like you'll have to pick another town, Mr. Friesé," Eppie said cheerfully. "There's no place for you to stay here."

"Yes, perhaps you should go back to Boston," Judith added, peering at him through her glasses. "Maine isn't the right place for a man like you."

Clare bit her lip against the urge to jump in. What purpose would it serve? Griffin could defend himself just fine, and she didn't need the grief she would get if she interfered. She had to live in this town, and she already had enough people chastising her for how she wasn't doing enough for her daughter or herself. She knew Eppie and Judith's hostility came from their need to protect her, and she would stir it up even further if she started defending him.

Both she and Griffin would be better off if she didn't defend him, and it was pretty clear from his body language that he didn't want her interfering anyway. The magical moment in the storm had not translated to real life, even though for a split second, when he'd looked at her so intensely, she'd thought maybe it had.

It hadn't, and she had to move on. Life was not a fairy tale.

Clare wished she hadn't let her mouth drop open in an awed gape when she'd seen him. The only reason the town was giving him such a hard time was because they thought there was a personal relationship between her and Griffin, thanks to her dramatic reaction to seeing him. Yes, if he was a total stranger, they'd still think (or hope) he was a soon-to-be murderer, but they'd be more curious than hostile. The hostility was her fault, and she regretted that. She glanced at him, wishing there was a way she could make things right with the man she owed such a debt to.

Griffin was frowning as he spoke to Norm. "There has to be something. A bed and breakfast?"

Norm shook his head. "Not this time of year, but I probably have some rat traps in the back I could loan you for your stay.'

"Rat traps?" Griffin echoed. "That's my best option?"

Astrid grinned at Clare, a sparkle in her eyes that made Clare's stomach leap with alarm. She grabbed Astrid's arm. "Don't you dare—"

"Clare's renter just moved out," Astrid said, her voice ringing out in the store. "Griffin can stay in her spare room. No rats, and it comes with free Wi-Fi. Best deal in town."

Oh, dear *God.* Clare's whole body flamed hot, and she whipped around. *Please tell me he didn't hear that.*

But Griffin was staring right at her.

Of course he'd heard. And so had everyone else.

CHAPTER FIVE

GRIFFIN'S INSTINCT had been to turn down the suggestion of staying at Clare's house, but his refusal died in his throat the moment he saw her stricken face.

Her eyes were wide with horror, and she was clutching her precious cupcakes so tightly he was certain she'd crushed them. In that moment, he saw the woman he'd met last night. The one whose passion, courage and vulnerability had made him want to whip out a sword and slay all her dragons.

Yes, there was still confidence and strength emanating from her, but there was also a frailty that touched something inside him. Clare might put on the persona of being tough and independent, and she might even live that life, but inside that courageous exterior was a softness that touched the very depths of his being.

When Clare had strode in there to retrieve her cupcakes, Griffin had been compelled by her energy and dynamism. But when she'd looked around and realized that people were watching, she'd shut him out faster than his ex used to do on a regular basis.

He knew what it was like to have a woman retreat on him,

and he'd known instantly when Clare had shut him down. He didn't waste time with that crap anymore, and as soon as she'd done it, he'd checked out. Done.

But as he saw her gaze flicking nervously around the room, he saw fear in her expression that belied the apparent aloofness and independence. Clare was vibrantly alive, unabashedly emotional. She was thrumming with fire and passion, and something inside him flared back to life at the realization.

Her gaze snapped back to him. "I don't think you'd like my place," she said, her voice strident across the store, but now that he was listening for it, he could hear a tremulous waver in her voice. "There's no privacy. Shared bathroom and kitchen. It's just a room. I'm sure you're used to your own space."

"I am." And he damn well liked his space, too. He basked in his gleaming penthouse condo, he appreciated his massive office with floor to ceiling windows, and he liked to order in whatever he wanted for dinner.

Relief flickered across her face, her emotions on such display that his heart softened even more. "Well, so, then great. I mean, yes, I'm sure you'll find something else—"

"There's nothing else," the old man behind the counter said. "Not until next week."

"Oh, well..." Clare swallowed, her nervousness apparent. "Well, if your wife and daughter are in River Junction, there are some nice places near there—"

"Ex-wife," he interrupted. How in God's name did she know about Hillary and Brooke?

"She's his 'ex' because of his rages," the old lady with the lavender hair whispered loudly enough to be heard all the way back to Boston. And from the way the energy in the room shifted, it was clear that everyone there was right on board with her sentiments.

"Ex-wife," Clare repeated, and there was something softer in her voice, something he couldn't decipher. But that gentleness drew his attention back to her, and suddenly, the world was gone again. Just them.

His life was a crazy whirlwind of action, negotiation, movement, and people. Never had it closed down into a single moment, a single person, a single thought.

But in this moment, with Clare, he was consumed by her. By nothing but her. He felt his entire body thrum with focus and energy, and he knew he wasn't finished. Not with this moment. Not with this woman. Not with this feeling. "I'm not going to stay in River Junction," he said to her, only to her. "I'm going to stay here."

Her forehead furrowed anxiously, and tiny tension lines creased around her eyes. "Why?" Her question was almost desperate, as if she could will him to go somewhere else.

Because you're here. The thought sprang unbidden into his mind, and he dismissed it as quickly as it had come. He was here because he'd plotted his strategy, and this was the best place to launch his assault. Like Jackson and his tires, Griffin knew that every successful invasion began with a solid foundation, and Birch Crossing was his launching point. "Because this is where I need to be."

Clare pressed her lips together, and he smiled. No, she was definitely not the cold, ruthless female his ex-wife was. Clare was different. She couldn't conceal all the emotions rolling so turbulently through her, and he relished that expressiveness. Her passion was such a tremendous relief after spending so many years fighting to get past the hard shell with his ex-wife, to have some glimpse of the humanity beneath. Clare poured everything she was out into the world, and it ignited a response in him that made him want to stride across the room and bury himself in everything she was.

"You don't want to stay at my place," she said. "The roof is leaking and I'm always up late working..."

"You have Wi-Fi?" he asked, already knowing the answer.

"Well, yes, but—"

"Rats?"

"No, but sometimes a squirrel will get in the kitchen—"

"I'm in."

The room came alive as people began to whisper. He didn't even bother to look at the two older women behind him, but he could feel their stares. He simply kept his gaze on Clare, waiting for the play of emotions he knew he'd see on her face, waiting for her answer.

The tension was thick, the silence intense, but Griffin didn't move, his body taught with the need for her to say yes.

Clare's friends broke into wide grins, but Clare simply stared at him. She looked shocked and utterly uncertain how to answer. But he was pretty sure he saw a flash of interest in those crystal-blue eyes of hers, even as her small hands tightened around the smashed box of cupcakes.

"Okay, that's it, young man." The woman with the garish pink hat walked up to him. "You do not get to prey on the women in our town. Leave now, or we'll have you escorted out—"

"He can stay," Clare interrupted, her voice rising defiantly over the crowd. Her gaze met his, and her face softened. "You can stay," she said more quietly, and he knew she was talking only to him.

Hot damn. Intense satisfaction pulsed through Griffin, along with hot anticipation. Clare had stood up for herself, for him. She had courage, and he liked that. Damn, did he like that.

Her cheeks were red with emotion. But her shoulders were back, and she was holding her chin aloft. She was a woman with substance, standing firm despite the pressure in that room to walk away from him. Her fear was evident in the way she glanced nervously at the pink hat lady, but her conviction was clear. She was going to protect him, and the only way she knew how was to invite him into her home.

His determination to stay with her softened at her show of courage, and he strode across the room toward her.

The tension in the room began to rise as he got closer to her, and Clare lifted her chin even higher, but she didn't step back as he came to a stop directly in front of her. As he got closer, he could see the gold highlights in her auburn hair, pure natural beauty that made him want to sift the strands through his fingers.

Quietly, without a word, he took her arm. Her muscles were rigid beneath his grasp, and her arm was so tiny. But it was strong beneath that denim jacket.

She watched him warily as he bent his head so his lips were next to her ear. Her hair brushed his cheek, and he caught the faint floral scent of her soap. Natural, but so appealing in its femininity. "Clare," he said in a low voice, for her ears only.

She caught her breath and stiffened, and her hand went to his forearm. Her grip was tight, almost desperate, and electricity leapt through him at her touch. She turned her head so her cheek was next to his, her breath brushing his ear, as she mimicked his pose. Almost touching, but not quite. "What?" Her voice was soft and feminine as she responded, her quiet question for him and no one else.

Total privacy, shutting out the crowds even while in the midst of them. Intimate.

"You don't have to let me stay," he said quietly. As much as he burned to accept her offer, to move into the home of this woman who awakened a fire inside him he hadn't felt in years, there was no way he would compromise her integrity or take advantage of her. The same need to protect her that he'd felt last night was hammering at him, even if it meant protecting her from himself. "I don't want to make things uncomfortable for you."

She didn't respond for a moment, and regret weighed in his chest. She was going to accept the escape he'd offered her.

But then she pulled back, just enough so she could look at him, but she didn't let go of his arm, and she kept the intimate, private distance between them. She searched his face, as if she were looking for answers that only she could see. "I owe you," she said, so softly that even her friends standing next to them wouldn't have heard.

"No." Griffin was so tempted to lift one of those wayward tendrils away from her face, but he didn't. "You don't owe me." He could not allow her to make a choice out of guilt.

Defiance flashed in Clare's eyes, as if she was going to argue with him, but then she seemed to change her mind. She simply shrugged. "You can stay with me. The reason doesn't matter."

Relief cascaded through him at her certainty. He wanted to stay with her. And he wanted it with a fierceness he didn't even understand. "You sure?"

"Yes." Then a twinkle danced in her eyes. "But you have to pay me up front. Once you get arrested for murder, I don't want to have to track you down for the rent payment."

He laughed, his voice echoing out over the silent room that he knew had been trying so desperately to hear what they were saying. "I agree."

She smiled then, a real smile full of vibrancy and life. "My office is across the street. Come by in an hour, and I'll have the rental agreement ready for you to sign." She spoke in normal tones, and the occupants of the store began to whisper excitedly. He was pretty sure he heard someone mention aiding and abetting a murderer.

"A rental agreement?" He was surprised by the formality.

It seemed out of place for this small town, for the passionate woman whose grip on his arm had softened to a temptingly intimate touch. "For a stay that's going to last only a few days?"

She released his arm and patted his cheek. His adrenaline spiked at the warmth of her touch, the intimacy of skin-to-skin, and sudden heat rushed through him. "I'm a lawyer, Mr. Friesé. Of course I have paperwork for you to sign." She waved at the room. "See you all later. Have a fantastic day."

Then cupcakes in hand, she spun around and strode out the door, leaving with just enough extra haste that he knew she was thoroughly rattled by her decision, which made him smile.

Her friend with the headband grinned at him as she followed Clare. "Welcome to Birch Crossing, Griffin Friesé. You're going to love it here, as I'm sure you can tell."

The gal with blond hair gave him a more thoughtful look. "Be nice to her," was all she said, but he felt the sincerity and love behind that comment. Clare had friends who cared deeply for her.

The door slammed shut behind them, and he moved to the window to watch the women hurry across the street into a small, white building down the block.

His vulnerable, delicate Clare Gray was a lawyer.

Damn. He hadn't seen that one coming.

Was she the tough lawyer who'd strode into the store this morning? Or the vulnerable, passionate woman who'd caught his attention so thoroughly?

He grinned. He didn't know, but he was looking forward to finding out.

SEVERAL HOURS LATER, Clare ran up the steps to the side

door of her house as Griffin's enormous truck pulled in behind her Subaru. As she reached for the doorknob of her rambling farmhouse, she suddenly noticed that the dark red paint was chipping, and that her home looked older and more worn down than she'd ever noticed. She'd been so proud the day she'd bought it five years ago, finally being able to give a real home to Katie, but suddenly, it looked rundown instead of charming. What would Griffin think, with his new truck and sparkling gold watch?

He stepped out of the truck, pausing to study the house. She became uncomfortably aware of the missing shingles on the roof and the overstuffed gutters. Her yard looked so drab compared to Griffin's shiny truck and his pressed shirt. How would he react to it?

Then she scowled and fisted her hands. Hadn't she learned her lesson about trying to change who she was to impress an outsider? She loved this drafty old farmhouse with its huge yard and the beautiful oak tree by the street, and she was so proud that she owned it. This was her triumph, and she wasn't going to feel embarrassed just because it wasn't pristine, modern and fancy like she was sure Griffin's home was.

If Griffin deemed it unworthy, he was more than welcome to go back to the Dark Pines Motel. "Come inside when you're ready," she called to him, not bothering to wait for him.

"I'm ready." He immediately turned and began heading toward the door, his stride lithe and almost predatory as he headed toward her, closing the distance between them with alarming speed.

Ack! He really was coming in! Clare pulled open the screen door and hurried inside, casting nervous glances at the misplaced shoes, jackets and school books on the floor. "Katie?"

"In here." Her daughter's voice drifted from the family room, and Clare was thankful her daughter was out of bed at least.

Clare set her purse and backpack in the small foyer and walked to the door of the family room. Katie was curled on the faded navy couch watching television and eating cereal. She was still wearing her pink pajamas and her brown hair was in disarray from going to bed with it wet. The poor thing had been so cold that she'd stayed in the shower until all the hot water was used up, and then had wanted even more.

"How are you feeling?" Clare asked, her heart softening at the sight of her daughter all curled up on the couch.

Katie shrugged, not bothering to look away from the television. "Fine."

"Really?" Maybe her daughter *was* fine, but to Clare, Katie looked so small and vulnerable under the big, fluffy blanket she'd apparently dragged down from her bed. She looked like a fifteen year old girl, not the woman she wanted to be.

Not the grownup Clare was about to ask her to be. "I rented out the room."

"Mom!" Katie groaned and rolled her eyes, tossing the remote control on the couch with visible annoyance. "Again? I hate having people in our space."

"The money helps—"

"If you need money, then don't send me to MIT this summer." Katie gave her a long-suffering look that was artfully accentuated by an expression of heart-melting pleading.

As if they hadn't had this discussion a thousand times already. "That summer program will help you get into college—"

"I want to stay here."

Clare gritted her teeth. "I know you think you do, but

63

trust me. You'll love being away from here and it will help give you options—"

"Trust you?" Katie set the bowl down with a thump that sloshed cereal all over the coffee table and the magazines strewn across it. "How do you know what's right for me?" She folded her arms across her chest and slouched back against the pillows, clearly preparing to battle it out.

Clare heard the thud of heavy, booted feet on her steps, and she hurriedly picked up several of the couch pillows and set them back on the sofa. "Katie, this isn't the time to discuss this—"

"It's never the right time." Katie lurched to her feet and faced Clare, hands on her hips. Her cotton pants were too low across her belly, and her zippered hoodie was getting a little snug across her chest. How much longer was Clare going to have any influence over her at all? Katie was quickly leaving behind girl and heading towards woman. "That's why I went camping last night. I knew you wouldn't let me go, but I wanted to be with my friends and do something for *me* instead of always having to work and study."

"Studying *is* for you! If I hadn't had good grades, I would have had no options after Dad died." Clare picked up the remote control and set it on the end table. Why was there so much stuff on the floor? She realized with dismay that the room looked cluttered and messy. How had she let it get this bad? "The fact I had great grades in high school enabled me to get into college and get my degree—"

"So you could do what? Work on Sunday mornings at a job you hate, but still not have enough money to fix a leaky roof?" Katie flung up her arms in exasperation and rolled her eyes with a snort of disdain. "Wow, Mom, I can't wait until I'm old enough for that—" She stopped abruptly and her mouth dropped open.

Clare felt the unmistakable heat of a powerful presence behind her.

"Am I interrupting?" Griffin's deep baritone filled the room with a masculine warmth and a presence that had never graced these walls.

Clare glanced back at him, embarrassed to be caught in a poor parenting moment. Griffin was leaning casually against the door, his jeans slung loosely across his hips, an amused smile making his dimple appear. His shoulders were so wide, he took up nearly the entire doorway, and his head almost reached the top of the frame. He radiated such presence, a man who owned his space and dominated the room. What had Clare been thinking, bringing him into her house? Into her private sanctuary where she didn't have to worry about men or judgment? "No, it's fine. We were just—"

"Oh my God!" Katie's face lit up, and she beamed at Griffin. "You're here!" She raced across the room and threw herself at Griffin, giving him a huge hug. "Thank you for last night!"

Griffin caught her, but the look of surprise on his face was so stark that Clare almost started laughing. If, of course, she wasn't feeling a little disgruntled that her daughter would shift from turning on her own mom to embracing a potential murderer in less than a second. But at the same time, Katie's exuberant reaction gave her reassurance that it was okay to have Griffin there.

Kids were perceptive, often more so than adults, and if Katie was comfortable with Griffin, then Clare would relax and trust that her own instincts about him were on target.

"Um, yeah, no problem," Griffin muttered. His hands were sort of stuck out at a strange angle, as if he had no idea how to hug Katie back and hadn't the slightest clue where to put his hands.

Suddenly, Griffin didn't seem so intimidating. He seemed

endearingly human and vulnerable, a man who was just a man, despite his money and his presence. Clare couldn't help but smile, relaxing at the sight of her daughter making this successful businessman look so adorably awkward.

Katie pulled back, clinging to Griffin's arms as she grinned at him. "So, wow, that was the coolest thing ever the way you hooked us up to that harness to get us over the tree. I mean, seriously! And when the tree started to slide— My God! You got over that huge trunk to unhook me so fast! How did you learn to do that?"

Griffin grinned at Katie, and Clare could practically see his chest puffing out with pride at her daughter's adoration. "I did that kind of stuff as a kid. My dad knew that kind of shi— I mean, stuff."

"Okay, Katie." Clare took her daughter's hand to pry her off Griffin and give him some space. "Give Griffin a chance to get acclimated."

"Acclimated?" Katie's eyes widened. "Are you our new boarder? Seriously?"

Griffin glanced at Clare, and his eyebrows went up. Giving her one last chance to back out? Her heart softened toward him. Would she really relegate her daughter's savior to living with rats? No chance. "Yes, Katie, Griffin's our new renter. Just for a few days—"

"That's awesome!" Katie beamed at them both. "Mom, you are the coolest ever! He's so much better than that old lady who smelled like mothballs and spent hours in the bathroom."

Clare laughed, relieved by her daughter's enthusiastic response, glad to know this wasn't going to wind up being yet another battle between them. "Yes, well, Patty was very nice and once I started washing her clothes, she smelled better."

Griffin gave her a speculative look. "Does that mean you'll be washing mine?"

Clare had a sudden vision of his undergarments in her wash. Men's underwear mixed in with hers? "Um, that's a little personal, I think."

He grinned, mischief sparking in his eyes. "You washed Patty's."

"She was a woman," Clare said, mortified by the sensation of her cheeks heating up. Was she actually blushing at the idea of washing Griffin's underwear? "It's different with a man."

"Oh, get over it, Mom," Katie snorted. "He's just a guy. Jeremy leaves his underwear in my laundry all the time. I don't have a problem washing his shorts."

Clare looked sharply at her daughter, sudden chills running down her spine. "Why on earth is Jeremy's underwear in your laundry hamper? How come his clothes come off at our house?" Dear Lord, she was going to pass out. "You're fifteen!" Only three years younger than Clare had been when she became a widowed mom. It couldn't happen to Katie, not her daughter, not becoming a mother at age eighteen.

"Jeremy runs over here sometimes before we go out. He changes out of his running clothes after he gets here." Katie shrugged. "Not a big deal mom. We're just friends."

"Naked friends are not allowed! There will be no more naked men in this house," Clare said, her palms breaking out into a sweat. "None!"

Her daughter and Griffin looked at each other, and then back at her. Griffin was grinning and so was her deviant daughter, already co-conspirators against her. "And what?" Katie asked. "Griffin and Jeremy are just supposed to shower with their bathing suits on?"

"Well, not Griffin," Clare stuttered, then her face heated up *again* at Griffin's wicked smile, and her daughter's burst of laughter. "I mean, because he's going to live here! But no boys, and not in your room—"

Griffin set his hand on her shoulder. "It's okay, Clare. I won't get naked if you don't want me to."

"Jeremy will," Katie said. "I can't stop him. Boys just like to be naked and—"

"Enough!" Clare glared at them both. "You both are going to eat lentil soup and liver tonight." She pointed at her daughter, her hand trembling, but she had to know. She had to understand the truth and face it. "Have you ever kissed Jeremy?" She'd given that boy full reign of her house and her daughter for years, assuming that they were just friends. But nakedness? "Have you?"

Katie giggled. "You're so uptight, Mom. If you let someone kiss you, maybe you'd realize it isn't such a big deal."

Clare couldn't bring herself to look at Griffin's response to that remark, and a cold dread beat at her as she faced her daughter, preparing to ask the question she'd been fearing since Katie was born. "Katie, are you having sex with Jeremy?" Her heart stuttered and a sharp pain ricocheted through her chest. *Please God, let the answer be no.* "I won't judge you, but I need to know—"

"Mom!" Katie looked appalled at the question, sending a stricken glance over to Griffin to see if he was listening. "I'm not having sex with him, or any other guy! Jeremy is always in the bathroom, alone, when he's changing. I haven't seen him naked since we were about five! Okay?"

Clare let out her breath. She knew her daughter well enough to know she was telling the truth. Her body began to shake with relief, and her legs suddenly felt weak. "Okay." It was okay. Her daughter wasn't about to get pregnant. It was still okay.

Griffin raised his brows at her. "Are you all right?"

"Yes, fine, just an overactive imagination." Clare shook out her hands and took a deep breath.

Katie grinned, her eyes radiating with excitement. "But

Jeremy did kiss me last night when we thought we were going to die," she sang. "It was pretty cute."

"He did?" Clare couldn't help but smile at the twinkle on her daughter's face, remembering that excitement of a first kiss, but at the same time, she felt her heart sinking. Her little girl was too young to be heading down this path. Yes, it was just a kiss, thank heavens, but still. "Do you like him?"

Katie shrugged. "I don't know. We'll see." She glanced over at Griffin, who had been watching the whole exchange with an increasingly furrowed brow. "Can I have Jeremy and Sara over for dinner? Jeremy is dying to see Griffin again, and Sara wants to meet him."

Oh, right. The last thing Clare needed was for Eppie to hear that she was getting Katie and her friends emotionally invested in a serial killing outsider. "No, I don't think so. Not tonight."

Katie ignored her and turned to Griffin, directing her question at him. "Is it okay with you? They'd go crazy if they got to have dinner with you."

Clare blinked at her daughter's dismissal of her. "Hello? Who's the mom here?"

Griffin glanced at Clare, then back at Katie. There was an expression on his face that she couldn't decipher. There was uncertainty, discomfort, but also a sense of surprised delight. Of what? Her daughter's adulation? He turned to Katie. "I'd like to get to know Jeremy a little better," he said. "Bring him over."

"No!" Clare stepped between them, needing to reclaim her space. Yes, she was pretty sure Griffin wanted to terrify Jeremy into keeping his underwear on anytime he was in her house and she appreciated it, but she could handle it. She *had* to handle it, because where would she be if she let Griffin fight her battles, and then he left? "Griffin has work to do, and he won't be sharing dinners with us the way other renters have."

"Are you serious?" Katie gaped at her. "Why not? What's wrong with Griffin?"

Other than the fact he made Clare's entire body melt with desire and all sorts of womanly feelings that she barely even recognized, let alone knew how to deal with? "Nothing, but—"

"You just don't want a man at our table, do you?" Katie grabbed her cereal bowl in a dramatic display of disgust. "Jeremy thinks you're frigid, you know. That's why you never date anyone."

"What?" Clare gaped at her daughter as Griffin started coughing, doing a pathetic job at hiding his amusement.

"If you are frigid, that's cool with me, but don't make Griffin starve because of it." Katie sighed as she walked past them. "I'm going out."

Clare didn't dare even look at Griffin. *Frigid?* Really? "No, you're staying here today."

Katie shot Clare a look of bored condescension, as if it was so beneath her to have to educate her mother as to the basics of life. "I'm going to the library to study with Sara. Physics test tomorrow. I can't pass it without her help."

"Physics test? And you were going camping?" Clare felt like banging her head against the wall. "What kind of responsible decision is that?"

Katie met her gaze, her eyes steely and rebellious. "I hate physics, and I'd rather fail it and have a fun weekend, than stay in all weekend and pass the test. I don't want to go to MIT this summer, Mom. I really don't. I don't want to spend my summer with a bunch of geeks creating some robot that can sift through sand on Mars. Seriously. "

Clare sighed. "I know you don't, sweetheart." She was

beginning to suspect she was never going to convince her daughter it was a good idea.

Katie met her gaze, waiting. "So?"

"So, you still have to go."

"You're impossible!" Katie groaned with aggravation and stomped out of the room. There was the clank of her bowl being dropped on the counter, and then the quick tempo of her feet as she raced up the creaky old stairs.

Clare sighed, and then she saw Griffin watching her. Assessing her parenting capacities? She didn't need that. She got enough grief from Eppie. "Not a word," she said to him, holding up her hand to stave off any comments. "I don't want to hear it."

He held up his hands in surrender, his face so innocent she almost laughed. "Since I can't eat dinner here, I was just wondering where I'm going to get takeout in this town. Got any suggestions?"

"Takeout?" Was she really going to make him order takeout? Clare capitulated at his innocent expression. No, of course she wasn't. And not just because the rental agreement he'd signed specified that food was included. She didn't want people messing in her kitchen, and she'd learned long ago that the best way to keep them out was to feed them until they couldn't bear the thought of even going near her kitchen except at mealtimes.

The truth was that she actually did kind of want a man at her dinner table. Not just a man. This one. This stranger from the outside, with obligations and baggage, a man who didn't know how to hug a teenage girl, yet somehow managed to cull utter adoration from the same. He got Katie to smile. And that was something she would treasure.

But as Clare heard Katie's door slam, she grimaced. What was she doing, bringing Griffin into their home? Into their lives? He'd be gone the minute they got used to him. She couldn't afford to rely on him—

Then she felt his hand on her shoulder. Her body tightened, and she looked up into his intense dark eyes. "What?"

His thumb rubbed softly over her shoulder. "The summer study at MIT is a great program. I went to it when I was fifteen. We worked on computer chips for NASA. Coolest experience I've ever had."

Oh, God, it felt unbelievable to be touched like that. "Are you serious?" She could barely concentrate on his words, she was so startled by the sensation of his hand rubbing her muscles. "You went there?"

He nodded. "Sure did." He glanced at the stairs, moving his hand slightly so he could rub the base of her neck. "Katie must be very smart to get into that program."

Clare smiled, unable to hide her pride, even as a part of her began the slow process of melting at the decadently sensual sensation of his fingers against her bare skin. "She is. She works really hard." Then she sighed, closing her eyes to focus on Griffin's touch. It had been so long since anyone had touched her like that, and she didn't want to miss a second of it. "But she's a little resistant, as you can see." She tilted her head, giving him more room to work on her neck. The slide of his fingers across her skin was delicious, the kneading of his knuckles was a luxurious sensation that made her want to surrender to his touch and turn herself over to him on every level.

Maybe Astrid was right about the benefits of occasionally letting a man into her life. Because this felt amazing, unreal, magical...words she couldn't even think of, creating sensations within her that she could barely even fathom. "Would you maybe talk to Katie about MIT? Tell her how much you enjoyed it? I mean, she thinks you're so cool that maybe she'll listen and—"

"Sure."

Relief rushed through her, and she opened her eyes, startled to see Griffin watching her intently, as if he were trying to see right into her soul. "Really?"

He nodded as he continued to dig his fingers into the knot in her neck. His offer to help and the soothing allure of his massage eased the tension that had kept her captive for so long. "Of course I will," he said. "Consider it done."

A weight began to lift from Clare and she smiled at him, hopelessly lost in the intensity of his gaze. What if he could help Katie see the benefit of MIT and good grades when Clare had been unable to do so? It was worth the risk. "You can eat at my table."

His hand stilled, and his eyes darkened. "I would like that."

She swallowed at the sudden heat that flared in her belly. "It's not personal," she clarified. "It's only to help Katie." And then, she blurted out, "And to prove to my daughter that I don't have a thing against men." Oh, no. Had she really said that?

His eyebrows went up, and a wickedly sexy smile curved his mouth. "Clare, there's no chance in hell I would ever believe you're frigid."

Her heart began to race. "No?"

His gaze went to her mouth, and then back to her eyes. "Not with the way you look at me."

She swallowed, her body vibrating at the intensity of his gaze, and the weight of his hand as he caressed her neck. "How do I look at you?" she whispered, her voice too breathy.

"Exactly how I want you to." His voice was low, and his hand paused as his gaze dropped to her mouth again, and this time, there was no mistaking the desire that flared in his eyes.

Oh, God. Her stomach jumped, and she felt light-headed. "What does that mean?"

He winked. "Figure it out. I'm going to get my bags." He squeezed her shoulder and then, without another word, he turned and walked back out the door, leaving her to wish desperately that the extra bedroom was not right next to hers.

And, at the same time, unable to stop thinking about the fact it was.

CHAPTER SIX

IT WAS ALREADY six o'clock by the time Griffin finally got his gear settled in Clare's spare room, the afternoon somehow consumed by bringing in firewood, cleaning the mud off his truck, helping Clare unload mulch for her yard, and getting the Wi-Fi going. She hadn't asked for his help with the chores, and he hadn't thought to offer, but somehow, he'd ended up doing it.

And he hadn't really minded. He'd actually enjoyed the day.

He was grinning as he finally strode into his room to get his own things taken care of. The room was old and worn, and there were water marks on the wall that gave credence to Clare's claim about the deteriorating roof.

But the blue and red plaid quilt appeared to be hand-made, and the birch log lamp beside the bed was topped with a soft, white lampshade that cast a warm light over the room. There was a lake scene hanging over the bed, which he was guessing was the Black Bear Lake that edged up against the south side of town. Faded green curtains treated the windows, and the old dresser had a few dents, but everything was clean, neat and smelled fresh.

Griffin was accustomed to stainless steel fixtures, off-white walls with carefully selected artwork of the highest caliber, and glossy wood floors. But as he surveyed the room, something about it felt comfortable. It actually kind of reminded him of the way his mother had kept house. Old but with a charm and an elegance that couldn't be found in a new high rise like the one he lived in.

He ran his hand over the door frame, noting that the joints were smooth and perfect, and the wood was beautifully grained beneath the stain. It was a house that had been made with skill and care, a personalization he hadn't thought about in a long time, not since the days he and his dad had spent at their mountain cabin, building furniture and getting simpatico with the life of a woodsman.

Clare's house fit her perfectly. Warm, natural, with an elemental beauty that could never be artificially created.

He smiled to himself as he walked across the room and retrieved his phone from the pocket of his jacket, which he then tossed on the bed. What was he doing staying in this place? He was a hotel guy, not a bed and breakfast guy. He liked his space. He liked his privacy. He liked people to leave him alone.

But this morning, in that store, with all the rumors of his murderous tendencies flying around, Clare had seemed like an oasis amidst the hell. Now that he was here, it still felt like the right call.

Griffin's warmth faded as he contemplated the rumors that had been circulating at the store this morning. He was here to murder his ex-wife and daughter? What was that about? He was used to people not being fond of him, but a murder rap was new, and he wasn't really liking it.

Had his ex-wife started it? Tension roiled through Griffin

at the thought. That wouldn't be unlike her. Doing anything she could to get his daughter to hate him. But a murderer? During their brutal divorce, she'd worked so hard to turn Brooke against him, and his battle to keep a connection with his daughter had been even more draining than the divorce itself. Once Hillary had met her new husband and taken off to Maine, his daughter had finally slipped out of his fingers completely, no matter how many times he'd called and emailed, trying to reach her.

It had been a year since he'd seen Brooke, but he was done being shut out. He was going to get his daughter back, and he wasn't going to give up until he'd succeeded.

Swearing under his breath, Griffin picked up his phone and speed-dialed the number that hadn't successfully connected with a live person in far too long. It rang. Not going directly into voicemail this time. Hope flared—

"Hi, this is Brooke. You missed me. Leave me a message, and maybe I'll call you back."

Griffin sighed at the familiar sound of his daughter's recorded voice. "Hey, Brookie. It's Dad. I'm up in Maine now. I'd like to swing by and take you to dinner tomorrow. How about I pick you up around six? If I don't hear from you, I'll assume that works and I'll see you at your place."

He paused as he pulled a small, white jewelry box out of his pocket. He flipped the lid and studied the delicate gold chain with a single pink pearl. "Got a birthday present for you that I know you'll love. I'm... yeah... I'm sorry I missed your birthday. I'll make it up." The image of Clare and her daughter hugging each other in the pouring rain flashed in his mind, and his throat suddenly thickened. He closed his eyes and pressed the phone to his forehead, blowing out a breath before continuing. "Anyway, yeah, hope everything's going well. Talk to you tomorrow."

He disconnected the call, suddenly feeling the emptiness

of the room. Of the house. Yeah, he could hear Clare and Katie talking in the kitchen, and the clank of pots echoed through the house, but it wasn't *his* daughter who was down the hall. Why hadn't Brooke answered his call? He'd left at least six messages telling her that he was coming to town.

Scowling, Griffin strode across the room and raised the window sash. Warm, moist wind blew in, as if the lake was waking up from its winter nap and filling the air with its energy. He propped his boot up on the wooden sill and let the breeze rush into the room, filling it with life.

Keeping it fresh.

A hollowness settled upon Griffin as he watched the pine trees waving in the gentle wind, the leaves skittering across the lawn that spring had just barely touched with green. He shouldn't have decided to stay here. In this home. With a mother and daughter bonding. It made him remember what it felt like to be alone in his own home. In his office, while he heard Hillary and Brooke giggling in the other room.

He'd been an outsider in his own home, and now he was there again.

Shit.

His phone rang and he jumped to answer it before the caller could change her mind. "Brooke?"

"No, sorry, it's Phillip. Have you spoken to Brooke yet?"

Griffin swore under his breath at the sound of his business partner's voice. Phillip Schnur had been his number two guy at Free Love Slippers, and they'd broken away from the slipper biz together, ready to pursue new ventures, several of which Phillip was currently investigating while Griffin was tracking down his daughter.

"I haven't reached her." Griffin turned away from the window and grabbed his briefcase off the floor. "I'm going to see her tomorrow." He unzipped it and removed his laptop.

"Well, you better step it up. Things are moving faster here than we anticipated."

Griffin set his laptop on the card table that Clare had set up as his desk. "What's going on?" The sale of Free Love had been completed only last week, and it had taken Griffin too long to get everything organized for his trip up here. He'd left Phillip in charge of due diligence for several businesses that they'd been tracking for a while, but he hadn't expected anything to happen so soon.

"In Your Face, that family business with the designer jeans for the teen market, is more viable than we'd even hoped," Phillip said, his voice fired up with excitement. "It's a strong product, and they have great designs for some future expansion."

Griffin nodded. "I expected that." He'd been watching In Your Face for several years, and that company was part of the reason he'd decided to divest himself of Free Love, so he could be in a position to acquire it.

"Here's the deal," Phillip said. "They want to sell, and they've already got a lot of interest. We'll have to move fast. I sent you an extensive report on their financials. Can you look at it tonight?"

"Yeah, I'm on it." Griffin booted up his computer, and the electronic beeps felt discordant with this woodsy setting. He should be back in his office, dealing with work, not languishing in Maine. "But I'm not rushing just because there's someone else interested."

"Agreed, but this is a good one. It's hot, and we need to move now."

Griffin swore. He couldn't return to Boston until he'd retrieved Brooke. "I can't go back yet." He opened his email program and saw the messages from Phillip.

"Then get your daughter and get down here. We don't want to miss this." Another line buzzed, and Phillip said, "I need to take that call. Call me back after you've looked at the file."

Griffin disconnected without replying as he opened the first email from Phillip. He wanted that company. He needed to step it up, but he was not leaving town until he had his daughter—

A loud shriek of laughter from Katie jerked his attention back to the present, and he felt a stab of frustration. No doubt Hillary and Brooke were having that same kind of bonding moment that Katie and Clare were having, and that was why Brooke hadn't answered the phone. Hell, for all he knew, Hillary had taken Brooke's phone so he couldn't reach her. Dammit. He needed to at least talk to his daughter—

He suddenly noticed the landline sitting beside the bed. He contemplated it for a moment, then he looked down at his own phone. Would it be that simple?

He tossed his phone on the bed, picked up the landline, and dialed Brooke's phone. She answered on the first ring. "Hi, Katie."

The sound of his daughter's voice was like a sling straight to the gut. For a moment, Griffin couldn't even speak, so overwhelmed by the realization that his daughter was there, talking to him, connecting with him. Then he realized the implications of her answering the phone when he'd called on Clare's land line. Son of a bitch. She'd been screening his calls. That familiar ache jabbed his chest, but he shoved it aside and kept it light. "Hi, Brookie. It's Dad."

There was silence.

"Brooke?"

"Why are you at Katie's house?" she asked without preamble. No greeting. No reaction at all to hearing his voice for the first time in months. She actually sounded a lot like Hillary. Cold, unemotional, distant.

He gripped the phone tighter, frustration mounting. "I'm

in Maine, Brookie," he said, keeping his voice casual, not wanting to give her an excuse to shut him out. "How about dinner tomorrow night? I'll be by around six—"

"I can't," Brooke interrupted. "I'm busy."

Griffin set his hand on the bedpost and dug his fingers into the wood. "Then what time? I can come earlier. Later. What works?"

"Nothing works! I'm busy!"

"Brooke—"

"Hello, Griffin."

He stiffened at the sound of his ex-wife's cool, emotionless voice. He'd forgotten how low and hard her voice was, or maybe it was just in comparison to Clare's light, warm tones. "Hillary."

"Brooke has a life now," Hillary said. "She has a family now. Let her go."

Griffin's hand slipped off the bedpost, and he swore as the tightness crushed harder in his chest. "She's my daughter, Hillary. You can't take her away from me."

"You haven't seen her in a year," Hillary said. "I'm not taking her away from you. She doesn't want you. She wants this life, and this family."

Griffin ground his jaw and paced over to the window, but the breeze was no comfort now. "I haven't seen her because you took her away from me, carting her off to Maine—"

"It's okay, Griffin. You don't need to feel obligated." Hillary's voice became softer, almost gentle. Not like Clare's, of course, but there was an element of acceptance he hadn't heard from her before. He barely recognized it. She'd never spoken that way to him before, as if she actually recognized that he was a human being.

"I'm not obligated," he said. "I *want* to be with her—"

"You're free now," Hillary said, her words devoid of acrimony, judgment or recrimination for the first time in years.

"Brooke has a father. I have a husband. We are loved, and we are taken care of. Your daughter is good, Griffin. She's found her peace. Go live your life. You don't have to play the role anymore. We grant you your freedom."

"I don't want my freedom," he snapped. "I want my daughter—"

"Do you?" A familiar challenge returned to Hillary's voice, the edge that had grated on him for so long. "Do you want that beautiful spirit that belongs to Brooke, or do you simply want to be able to claim success at fatherhood?"

"I—"

"Griffin," Hillary said firmly. "You aren't meant to be a husband, and you aren't meant to be a father." She sighed. "I've finally accepted that, and it's okay. It really is. You're great at business, but you've got nothing when it comes to family." Those were the words she'd thrown at him for years, but this time, there was no hate or anger behind them. Just acceptance, like she'd given up on him.

Screw that. She wasn't going to manipulate him into walking away from his daughter. "I'm a good dad—"

"You're not, and it's time for you to accept it. I have. You won't be happy as long as you're trying to force yourself to be the man you aren't. Let yourself go back to Boston. You deserve to find peace, and so do we. Good-bye, Griffin.

And then she hung up on him.

The phone buzzed in his ear. What the hell had just happened? In their sixteen-year marriage, all he'd gotten from Hillary was grief about his work schedule, and *now* she was saying it was okay? She was telling him he had no chance to be a decent dad? Screw that. He was Brooke's father, and he wasn't some washed up bastard who didn't deserve her. Griffin scowled and began to dial Hillary back—

A light knock sounded at the door, and he looked over to see Katie standing in the doorway. She grinned at him, her eyes gleaming with delight. "Dinner's ready," she said. "Jeremy and Sara are here. Mom made lasagna and garlic bread."

The teen was wearing a faded gray sweatshirt, and her hair was pulled up in a ponytail, just like Brooke used to do. Sudden sadness bit at him, a sense of loss so deep it almost staggered him. He remembered how Brooke had answered the phone, asking him why he was at Katie's house. If they were friends, maybe Katie could give him some insight on how to reach her. "Do you know Brooke Friesé?"

"Of course, I do—" Katie paused, and her eyes got wide. "*Brooke* is your daughter? You're the dad who took off on her?"

"I didn't take off on her," he snapped. What the hell? Was there no such thing as privacy in this damned town? "How do you know her? Are you good friends with her?"

Katie's eyes narrowed, and there was no mistaking the sudden coolness of her tone. "She lifeguarded at the Wenopequat Beach last summer, and I hung with her at some of the lifeguard parties." She gave him an accusing look. "She said you abandoned her."

Griffin swore. "I was working—"

"You left." Katie lifted her chin, an old, deep-seeded loneliness flaring in her eyes. "You had a daughter who wanted you, and you walked away. Maybe you should have traded spots with my dad, who actually loved me but didn't get to hang around." The accusation in her voice was bitter, too damned similar to what Hillary had flung at him for so long. "If you were dead, at least you would have an excuse for ditching your own daughter. My dad at least had a reason for leaving me." Then she spun around and flounced off, her pony tail bouncing as she strode down the hall.

Son of a bitch. What was it with all these people? He hadn't left. They'd walked out on him.

Griffin scowled as he heard Katie stomp back to the kitchen. Her laughter with her friends and Clare drifted down the hall, a world he didn't fit into. He'd walked into a thousand boardrooms in his life, but he had no idea how to walk into that kitchen with all those people.

And he didn't need to. Not anymore.

He wasn't in Maine to play family time with people who judged him. He was there to get his daughter back. Hillary didn't know what she was talking about. Katie didn't know him. He would be there tomorrow at six to reclaim his daughter. Period.

And in the meantime, he was getting his business back on track. When Brooke came home with him, he was going to show her that he could give her anything she wanted. Anything. He looked at the necklace again, and set it on the bed. Tomorrow she would see. Tomorrow she would realize that she was wrong about him.

Of course he wanted to be her father.

Of course he saw the beauty of her soul.

He always had, dammit. Just because he worked long hours didn't mean he didn't get it.

As more laughter drifted down the hall, Griffin grabbed his laptop, his briefcase and his phone, then walked out his door. He paused in the hallway just outside the kitchen. Three teenagers were sitting around the table, munching on French bread, but he barely noticed them.

All he could focus on was Clare. Her hair tucked in an adorable, messy bun, she was unwrapping foil from what smelled like hot garlic bread. She looked domestic and happy, her eyes dancing as she chatted with the kids. He almost smiled, drawn in by her obvious peace with the moment. He didn't remember Hillary ever looking that soft or appealing. He felt like he could stand there all night and watch her.

"When's Griffin coming?" Jeremy asked. The kid was

wearing jeans and a red tee shirt, and he was watching Katie with an interest that made Griffin want to go in there and toss the kid out on his underwear-clad ass.

Katie looked up and saw Griffin. Her face hardened. "Griffin isn't coming to dinner," she announced.

Clare turned quickly to her daughter. "He's not coming to dinner? Why not?"

Griffin's sense of peace retreated swiftly. It was the same thing all over again. Why wasn't Griffin coming to dinner? Why wasn't he participating in the family event?

Dammit. Hillary was wrong. She was *wrong*. He deserved his daughter, and he was going to get her back.

"Is Griffin sick?" Clare wiped her hands on her jeans. "I'll go check on him—" She turned toward the door, and Griffin ducked out of sight.

He booked it out the side door and was already at his truck by the time Clare pushed open the screen door and came out on the back stoop. He met her gaze, and for a moment he hesitated. There was no recrimination on her face, just concern.

But that was how it started.

The hostility and accusations always came eventually. He didn't have time to be reminded of his failings. He had a daughter to rescue, a business to buy, and a life to reclaim.

He did not need to invest himself in some small town in Maine, or in a woman whose blue eyes could suck the life out of a man...or give him enough fuel to survive anything. A woman who could make him feel like he owned the world, and then rip it out from under him the moment she deemed him unworthy. No, he didn't need that again.

He yanked open the truck door and set his gear inside.

"Griffin?" Clare walked down the stairs. "Is everything all right?" Her voice was gentle and worried, and her eyes were filled with warmth. She barely knew him, and already she was opening herself to him, bringing him into her circle. She'd done it when she'd announced to the entire store that he could stay at her house, and she was doing it again.

For a split second, Griffin was tempted to let himself accept her concern, to yank her into his arms and breathe in the purity of her essence. But for what? So she could take it all back the moment he spent too long at the computer? Screw that. No more loss for him. He wouldn't start down this path again, not when he knew where it would go. Clare was all about home and family, and she would eventually hate him just like Hillary had. "I have to go."

Her forehead furrowed with concern, with worry, utterly without judgment. "Where?"

But he wasn't going to fall for it. "I just need to go." He started the truck, shifted into reverse, and peeled out of her driveway without looking back.

He would not go back to a world of accusation and blame.

There was only forward.

Only forward.

Only forward.

CHAPTER SEVEN

THE OX HILL PUB loomed dark and moody as Griffin sped down one of the side roads that had led off Main Street in town. Neon beer signs flashed in the window, and there were a scattering of pickups in the dirt parking lot.

Not the same as the bar at the Four Seasons, but he'd take it for now.

Briefcase in hand, Griffin yanked open the door of the bar and headed inside. Dark wood beams bisected the white ceiling, and the walls were bare wood, decorated with black and white pictures that seemed to document a hundred years of history. Farmers with their pitch forks. Old tractors. A couple of guys in hip waders holding some bass.

The low-lit bar smelled like a wood stove and fresh bread, and he was surprised by the hum of energized conversation. There were dining tables to the right filled with families who'd taken their kids out for an early Sunday dinner. But to the left was a bar. Quiet at this hour on a Sunday, and exactly what he wanted.

No one seemed to be attending the door, so Griffin

headed inside, grabbed a table in the corner and set up his office.

Two beers and a burger later, he was immersed in Phillip's file and the world of teen fashion. The creators of In Your Face jeans had expanded into jackets, and he was damned impressed. The two Berkeley grads had taken their start-up into impressive places, and were selling their product to some powerful outlets. They were onto something, and it smelled the same as Free Love Slippers had when he'd first scented that gem.

He clicked on a pair of jeans with the IYF logo on the hip—

"You're a fashion guy?" Jackson Reed, the guy with the good tires, leaned over Griffin's shoulder, peering at the computer screen. Jackson had spiffed up with a pair of dark jeans and a collared shirt. His hair was slicked back and the man was freshly-shaven.

"It's a business I'm thinking about buying," Griffin explained. This was his comfort zone. Business talk with a guy who invested in good tires. No one ever accused him of failing to deliver when it came to work.

"Yeah?" Jackson pulled out a chair and sat down. "I'm thinking about buying out my boss. Risky shit, going into business on your own, isn't it?"

Griffin couldn't help but grin with satisfaction. "It's the best deal on earth." He hadn't been accountable to anyone in years, and he would never go back.

"Yeah?" Jackson cocked an eyebrow, folding his massive arms over his chest, the body of a man who lived by hard labor, much like Griffin's dad had. "What if it goes belly up? You lose everything?"

Griffin shrugged. "It's a risk, yeah, but not likely if you know what you're doing."

Jackson barked with laughter. "Yeah, if it was that easy,

everyone would be doing it. Hell, I'd have started my own company years ago."

Griffin leaned back in his chair as the waitress set another beer in front of him. It felt good to have a little man time. "What's your business? Construction?"

"Yep." Jackson tipped his chair back and propped his booted foot on an empty seat. "Been with the same company since I was eighteen. Jeff Green took me on when I showed up here on my way to nowhere, and I've never left. This town was the best thing that ever happened to me."

Griffin didn't bother to comment on that. "Why don't you buy it?"

"Well, yeah." Jackson let the foot fall back to the floor. "Jeff's retiring, and he wants to hand it off to me." He shrugged as he helped himself to one of Griffin's fries. "Can't do it now, though. Things being what they are and all."

As if he had any clue what Jackson was talking about. "Why can't you do it? It's always the right time to go out on your own."

"Why can't I?" Jackson grinned suddenly, his face lighting up. "Shit, man, how do you not know? You've been in town for twenty-four hours. Everyone knows."

Griffin ground his jaw. "Yeah, well I'm not tapped into the gossip chain yet." At least when it came to others. Apparently, his personal life was a well-covered topic.

"Just giving you grief, my friend." Jackson slapped him on the shoulder, then grinned. "Trish's having a baby, big guy. A baby!"

Griffin blinked. "Trish?"

"My wife!" Jackson looked so proud Griffin half expected him to leap on the table and start beating his chest. "I'm going to be a damned father. Can you believe that shit?"

Griffin couldn't help but grin at Jackson's enthusiasm, and he raised his beer. "To the new dad."

Jackson slammed his drink against Griffin's so hard that the amber liquid sloshed over the table. "Hell, yeah, man. Hell, *yeah.*"

Griffin eyed the other man as Jackson took an enthusiastic slug of his beer. He couldn't quite remember what his reaction had been when he'd found out Hillary was pregnant. In fact, he couldn't even remember finding out. Just one day, his daughter was there. But he was pretty sure he'd never been as fired up as Jackson.

"So, now you see why I can't buy out Jeff," Jackson said.

Griffin tried to figure out the connection between the baby and Jackson's inability to buy the business. "I'd think that now would be the time to make the move. Get the security of being your own boss—"

Jackson shook his head instantly. "And risk Trish and the baby? No chance."

Griffin frowned. "How does buying out your boss risk them?"

"Don't you get it, Griff?" Jackson leaned forward, his face serious. "They're counting on me now. I have to provide for them. A house, food, clothing, all that shit. If I sink all my savings into a business, then I've got no security for them to count on. And what if the business tanks? We've got nothing." Jackson shook his head. "Different story if I was single, but when you're single, what the hell does it matter anyway? Who are you doing it for? The dog?" He grinned and his face was at peace. "I've got a new job now, and it's not the one that pays the bills." He slammed his fist on the table. "I'm on it, Griff. I'm going to be the best damn father any kid has ever had and—"

"Jackson? Sorry I'm late." A woman with long blond hair streaming down around her shoulders waved from the entrance to the bar. She was wearing a thick sweater, but there was no obscuring the swell of her belly. She smiled at Jackson, her face beaming at the sight of him.

Shit and damn. Griffin had never had a woman look at him like that. Jackson was a lucky bastard.

"Trish!" Jackson bounded out of his chair, his face glowing. He was by her side in an instant, his arm around her shoulders and his hand resting protectively on her stomach. "How are you?" His question was earnest, and he said no more as he waited for her answer.

She smiled and touched his cheek. "I'm great."

"Good." Jackson tucked her against him and turned toward Griffin. "Trish, this is Griffin Friesé. Griff, this is my wife Trish."

"Nice to meet you." Griffin nodded at her. "You've got a good man."

"Oh, I know." Trish smiled warmly at Jackson before turning back to Griffin. "It's great to meet you. We're so glad to have you here." Trish beamed at him, and Griffin was surprised to see sincere welcome on her face. No judgment like there'd been from the others in the store. No fear that he would murder her unborn child or her grandma. "I've heard so much about you," she said cheerfully.

Griffin laughed softly, spinning his beer between his palms. "If you've heard that much about me, you shouldn't be talking with me."

"Griffin." Trish walked over and took his hand, holding it between hers. He was so startled by the contact he almost jerked his hand away before she squeezed it with genuine affection.

"Thank you for taking care of Clare and the kids last night," she said earnestly. "They were so lucky you were there for them.

Griffin stared at her for a second before he could muster up an answer, momentarily undone by the strength of her welcome. "It's no problem," he finally muttered, embarrassed but pleased.

She smiled cheerfully, a twinkle of mischief in her blue eyes. "Jackson and I are so glad that you're in town and staying with Clare. She needs you."

Griffin's warmth at her welcome faded as he registered her comment. What did she mean that Clare needed him? Was Clare in trouble? No, no, no. He couldn't go there. "I'm just renting a room at Clare's. Nothing else."

Trish's smile widened. "No one just rents a room in Birch Crossing."

"I'm only going to be here a couple days." Maybe less. "I'm just passing through."

"So was I," Jackson said. "Twelve years later, I'm still here." He slung his arm around Trish's shoulders, and kissed her temple. "Gotta get my girl some dinner before she gets cranky. Talk to you later."

"Yeah, sure." Griffin leaned back and clasped his hands behind his head as he watched Jackson and Trish head off toward the restaurant section. Their heads were bent toward each other, and they were talking quietly. Intimately.

He pulled his gaze away, feeling like he was intruding, and he focused his attention back on the computer. Jackson might think the key to being a good dad was to be someone else's workhorse, but Griffin knew better.

And as soon as he bought In Your Face and launched his new business, Brooke would see that he was the only father she needed.

But as Griffin scrolled through the next product line, he couldn't quite keep his gaze from drifting across the restaurant to the couple who'd just left.

But Jackson and Trish were out of sight.

With a resigned sigh, Griffin went back to work.

～

ALMOST SIX HOURS LATER, Griffin paused on the steps outside the back door of Clare's home, listening for the sounds of activity inside the farmhouse. All was quiet, as he'd hoped. He'd worked until closing, and then he'd done another hour in his truck before driving back to Clare's.

It was almost midnight now, and even Wright & Son had been closed and quiet when he'd driven by. Surely, Clare and Katie would be in bed by now.

He frowned at the thought. Yeah, his goal had been to walk into the house and be left alone to do his thing, but now that he'd managed to make it work...he almost regretted it. Was walking into silence better than getting grief from Clare for bailing on dinner? He thought of those intense blue eyes and wasn't sure anymore.

Not that it mattered. He'd set it up the way it needed to be. He had one job to accomplish up here, and he was going to get it done, without distraction. Plus, as soon as he got inside, he was going to hook up to the Wi-Fi and send the emails he'd written to Phillip while at the bar, and get that moving as well.

He tested the door knob, wondering if would be open. Clare hadn't given him a key, claiming that she never locked the door, and she'd ignored him when he'd questioned the wisdom of that (murderers abounded in this small town, yes?). Would she really leave it unbolted? Or was she going to punish him for bailing on dinner and lock him out?

But the chipped white knob opened easily, and Griffin stepped inside.

He was immediately assaulted with the scent of baking cake. The air was filled with chocolaty sweetness, swirling so thickly he could almost taste it. It reminded him of walking into his house as a kid, and having his mom in the kitchen. It had been years since he'd smelled cake baking in his own house. Domestic as hell. And it smelled damned good. He smiled. More cupcakes from the lawyer, apparently.

The house was dark, except for a faint glow coming from beneath the kitchen door. There were no lights from upstairs where Katie's room was, or from Clare's bedroom at the end of the hall. Just the kitchen.

Griffin shut the back door and headed down the corridor toward his room. But he paused outside the kitchen when he heard someone typing on a computer. Clare?

He reached for the kitchen door to push it open, then dropped his hand. For what purpose? So she could berate him about how he'd ditched everyone? How the kids had waited for him and he hadn't been there? Screw that. He was going to bed—

"There are leftovers in the fridge if you're hungry," Clare said, her voice just barely audible through the closed door.

Griffin froze, waiting for more, for the recrimination, for the blame. But she didn't say anything else. And she hadn't sounded mad.

He'd walked out without an explanation or an apology. Was he really such an ass that he'd ignore this offer as well, and head to his room without acknowledging her?

Hillary would say he was.

Eppie would hope he was.

Katie would predict he would be.

And Brooke... would she even care anymore, or was she too busy with her new father? Dammit. He wasn't the ass they all thought he was. But would Clare think he was if he ignored her this time?

He thought of her concern when he'd skipped out on dinner, the way she'd stood up for him in Wright's, and suddenly he wanted there to be one person in the world tonight who didn't think he was pond scum. And he wanted that person to be Clare.

So, he shouldered his brief case, shoved open the kitchen door and walked inside.

～

GRIFFIN WAS WELL aware of how much he liked Clare's captivating blue eyes. He was on board with his physical reaction to her in the store. He knew that she'd brought out the hero-wannabe side of him.

But he was still unprepared for the potency of his physical reaction to her when he walked into the kitchen and saw his disheveled and utterly unpretentious landlord hunkered down for a night at home. Her hair was up in a messy bun on top of her head. She was wearing faded jeans and a light pink tank top without a bra, revealing the soft curve of her shoulders and the decadently temping swell of her breasts. No makeup, just her natural features. A silver chain with a heart pendant hung from her throat, nestled against her chest. There was white flour dusted across her shoulder, and pink frosting in her hair.

She was leaning back in her chair, knees propped against the table, her feet dangling to reveal rose-pink toenails. A folder was on her lap, a pen in her hand, and her laptop was open on the kitchen table.

She looked studious, intelligent and innocently sexy, all at the same time. He had a sudden, driving need to walk across that floor, ease his hand through those dangerous locks of hers, and allow his primitive side to take over.

She looked up at his entrance and gave him a weary but welcoming smile. "Hey," she said.

"Hey." He leaned against the door jamb, content to just watch her. The aggravation of the evening, the frustration of trying to arrange dinner with Brooke, the judgment by Hillary, the pressure to get a bid in place for the company he wanted to buy... it all seemed to melt away as he stood there, breathing in the fullness of Clare and her kitchen.

The cabinets were painted a shade of green that reminded him of the pine trees in her yard, and their carvings told him they'd been made back in the day when people took the time to create beauty and personalization in their work. The counters were old wood, polished and gleaming.

There was nothing new. Nothing pristine. No glitz. No glam. As far from his condo as it was possible to get. He'd spent a lot of money creating his haven, but this place...something about it eased him. Something about Clare eased him.

"Everything okay?" The buzzer from the stove rang out, and Clare hopped up, padding across the wood floor in her bare feet. Her voice was calm, her body relaxed as her hips swung gently as she walked. She was so natural, so comfortable in her own skin, so completely at ease that his entire body sizzled with the desire to claim her and lose himself in the magic that seemed to emanate from her.

"Yeah." He realized that she really wasn't mad at him. She wasn't going to give him grief for bailing on dinner, which immediately made him want to apologize. "Sorry about taking off like that."

Clare picked up a pink potholder with hearts on it and slipped it over her hand, looking at him carefully, as if debating whether to believe his sincerity. "You're a boarder here, Griffin. Your life is your own."

Griffin frowned as she pulled a tray of cupcakes out of the oven. They were a decadent chocolate brown and smelled amazing. "Yeah, well, I just wanted to apologize because I said I'd be there for dinner, and I wasn't." He did mean it, and for some reason, he wanted her to believe him. It mattered to him.

Clare set the tray on the counter and turned to face him. She gave him an understanding yet quiet smile. "Griffin. You rent a room here. You come and go as you please. I'll always make enough food for you, and you can grab leftovers whenever it works for you." She met his gaze, and her eyes were full of emotion he couldn't decipher. "You will be leaving soon," she said carefully. "And that's good."

He scowled, sudden resistance roaring through him at the idea of leaving, at the notion of her wanting him to leave. "Why is it good?"

Wariness flickered through her eyes. "Never mind." She turned away and began removing the cupcakes from the tray. He noticed there were already several dozen spread out over the counters. "Have some lasagna and don't worry about missing dinner. It's totally fine."

"I already ate." Why was it good he was leaving soon? Was she mad at him? He studied the relaxed curve of her shoulders and knew she wasn't. So why did she want him to leave?

"Then go to bed," she said, not looking up from her dessert-fest, setting a visible distance between them. "Or go work. Or whatever it is you wish to do."

Griffin ground his jaw at the wall she'd thrown up between them, cutting him off from her warmth and inner circle. She was giving him exactly what he wanted. Space to do his thing. But for some damn reason, he didn't want to go back to his room.

He wanted to stay right where he was.

No, not where he was.

He wanted to walk into that room, sit down at that table and insert himself right into the moment. He wanted to rip down that wall she'd erected and shove himself back into her sphere. He wanted her to look at him as if he ignited fire in every damn corner of her being, like she'd done at the store and earlier in her living room. And then, he wanted to wrap his hand around the back of her neck, lower his head, and kiss her until there was nothing between them but raw, raging heat, and desire so intense that it consumed them both, sucking them into a kiss so fierce that they were both lost in it forever.

Yeah. *That* was what he wanted to do.

CHAPTER EIGHT

Clare wasn't looking at Griffin, and she wasn't even facing his direction, but she knew the moment he decided to stay. Maybe it was a current in the air that suddenly came alive. Maybe it was a shift in his breathing from relaxed to something more intense. Maybe it was simply her own desire for him to stake a claim in her world. Whatever it was, her belly clenched in anticipation even before he took that first step into her kitchen.

His feet were heavy as he walked across the floor, and the sound of his briefcase landing on the table made her jump. "Mind if I work in here for a bit?"

She stole a peek at him. His hair was messier than it had been when he'd walked out hours ago, and his dress shirt was crinkled. He looked more reachable, less perfect, and utterly appealing, and he was watching her intently. Why did he look at her like that? Why? "Yes, sure, that's fine," she managed. "I'll be up for a while."

He said nothing as he opened his briefcase and booted up his computer, but she was so conscious of his presence. When he'd left tonight without a word, it had been good.

Really good. It had served as a much needed and very powerful reminder of exactly who he was.

After Katie's embrace of him, his support of the MIT program, and his humorous wit as he'd helped her bring in logs, Clare had started to relax. She'd begun to enjoy him. She'd forgotten about all the warnings, rules and plans she'd lived with for so long.

Tonight when he'd walked out on her like that, it had been all too reminiscent of the day Ed had left her. Ed hadn't been able to stay in Birch Crossing, and neither would Griffin.

If she got involved with Griffin, it would end badly, and the repercussions for Katie and herself would be significant if they became accustomed to having him around. Eppie and Judith were right. She had to stay focused. Be safe. Protect her space—

"What's with the cupcakes?"

Heat washed over Clare at the sound of his deep voice. Dammit! What was wrong with her? Why was she reacting like this? There was a man in her kitchen. So what? She was smarter than this. She really was. "These are for Wright's. Norm sells them for me." She pointed to a batch at the far end of the counter that was already frosted. "Those are for a boy in Katie's class. It's his birthday tomorrow, and I made the cupcakes for him to take to his classroom."

Griffin walked over to the counter and inspected them. "Red Sox cupcakes? You have every player on there."

"I repeated a few." Clare sighed as she looked at the vast quantity still left to be frosted. "We had too many kids in the class, so I doubled up some of the stars."

"These are incredible."

Warmth flooded Clare at the genuine admiration in his voice. "Thanks."

"Seriously." He ambled down the counter, looking at some

of the others that she'd already finished. He picked up one of the loon ones, and then the pink rose. "These are works of art, not cupcakes."

She smiled at his enthusiasm. "Well, I don't know about that—"

He looked at her then, and there was something burning in his eyes. A fire. An intensity. Her body responded instantly, thrumming with energy and heat. "What?" she asked.

He held up one of the cupcakes. "It takes passion to make these."

"Passion?" Interesting word choice. She swallowed, unable to stop the heat building low in her belly, the awareness rippling through her of his broad shoulders, the strong angle of his jaw, the way his lips curved in a half-smile. What if he kissed her? What if he put that cupcake on the counter, closed that distance between them and locked her down against him for a kiss that shook her to her very core?

"Yeah." He set it down and studied her, his eyes dark with heat as his gaze flicked briefly to her mouth, as if he were imagining that same kiss. "I specialize in buying and rebuilding companies in the fashion industry. I have no design skills myself, but I have a visionary ability to identify creative brilliance. And you've got it."

"Really?" She grinned at his genuine admiration. "No one's ever called me brilliant before. I like that."

"You must love making cupcakes." He folded his arms over his chest, his face thoughtful. "You can't create that kind of magic unless you love it."

"Well, yes, of course I do." Clare was unsettled by his intensity, so she tossed the potholder back on the counter and retreated to her computer. "I don't have time to do it as much as I would like, though." She held up the folder, trying to remind herself of what she needed to focus on. "I need to pay the bills, you know?"

Griffin sat down next to her, too close. He braced his arm on the back of her chair and leaned forward, into her space. "Why don't you pay the bills with the cupcakes?"

Clare burst out in nervous laughter. "Pay a mortgage, student loans, rent for my office and my daughter's summer program on cupcake proceeds?"

"Yeah, sure." His gaze went to her mouth again, and heat crashed through her. "I made millions on slippers. It happens. No reason why cupcakes can't turn a good profit."

She stared at him. "Make money from my cupcakes?" For a split second, something flared inside her. Hope? Desire? Interest? What if— Then she laughed, knowing it could never happen. What if indeed? "The fastest way for me to lose the joy I get from baking is to try to earn money from it. It's my respite, and if I taint it by trying to profit from it, then it won't be fun anymore."

He frowned, as if he couldn't understand. "Why not?"

Clare held up her folder. "I'm good at being a lawyer, but it drains me. I need to refresh. There's no way I could work late at night if I wasn't getting up every twenty minutes to work on the cupcakes. It energizes me. But if I *had* to bake and *had* to make them beautiful, then they become another source of stress and pressure, and another opportunity to screw up. I get enough of that with the day job already."

Griffin folded his arms as he leaned back in his chair, giving her space she didn't want now that she'd gotten used to him being so close to her. "If your work doesn't energize you, then you've got the wrong job."

"The wrong job?" She smacked him on the head with the folder. "I better not have the wrong job. I owe too much money in student loans and too many hours of free babysitting to Eppie to have made a mistake." She leveled the folder at him. "Don't even suggest it, Griffin. Those kinds of words will get you sent to bed without dinner."

He laughed and caught her wrist, deflecting the folder. "A man can't risk not having food. I'll never broach the topic again."

"Good." He was still holding her wrist. Lightly. But with a hint of possession. She stared at him, and the laughter faded until the only sound was the click of her oven working.

This time, when his gaze went to her mouth, she didn't have to wonder what he was thinking. Hot, raw desire burned in his eyes, and her entire body leapt in response. Her pulse began to hammer in her throat, and she couldn't bring herself to pull away.

She knew it was a bad idea, oh, she did. But it didn't matter. All she could think about was what it would be like to have Griffin lean forward, slide his hand through her hair and stake his claim on her. She wanted to be claimed by him. She wanted him to rip through her shields and make her unable to deny the hot desire racing through her, desire she'd thought was so long dead.

Griffin was making fire burn through her veins and pulse deep in her core. It was terrifying, but at the same time, her very soul cried out with the need for him to stoke that heat, to show her what it could be like, to make her burn from his kisses. What would it feel like to have his mouth on hers? To feel his palm slide over her belly? To cup her breast? To feel his hard, muscular body sinking down onto hers, making her his in every way?

His eyes darkened, and he slid his hand along her jaw, his touch a sinfully erotic sensation as it eased along her skin. "Clare," he whispered, his voice raw with such need that she ached for him.

Yes.

He leaned forward, closing the distance between them, and she knew he was going to kiss her—

A loud thump from upstairs made them both jump.

Griffin went still as they heard the sound of Katie's footsteps padding across the floor and the rush of water from the sink in the upstairs bathroom.

Oh, God. What was she doing? Reality rushed over Clare with the cold ache of loneliness and responsibility. She couldn't do this, not to Katie, and not to herself. Griffin was leaving. *He was leaving.*

Slowly, her heart screaming at her not to retreat, Clare forced herself to pull back from Griffin. Regret flickered in his eyes, and he released her, but he didn't take his gaze off her, raw lust still burning in those eyes. He was a man who had conceded the moment, but he hadn't acknowledged defeat.

She felt her cheeks heat up. "I need to work."

He nodded. "I do, too."

For a long moment, neither of them moved, the possibility still hovering between them. Was he going to kiss her anyway? Would she stop him this time, or would she tumble into his spell again?

The bathroom door slammed upstairs, and Griffin grimaced and finally turned away, breaking the connection and severing her last bit of hope.

Intense relief and agonizing disappointment filled Clare as she quickly picked up her folders and tried to regroup. While she shuffled papers, Griffin woke his computer from standby and began to read.

For a few minutes, she couldn't concentrate. She was too aware of his breathing. Of the creak of his chair as he shifted position. The faint scent of his aftershave mingling with the cupcakes. The slide of his boots across the floor as he concentrated.

His presence was enormous, even though he was saying nothing.

Griffin looked up, caught her watching him, and he

smiled, flashing her that dimple. He tapped her keyboard with one finger. "You'll be mad at yourself if you don't work. Step it up, Ms. Gray, or you won't have time to frost."

She laughed, and her tension dissolved. "Keep being pushy like that, and you won't get any cupcakes."

"I like mine frosted, so work."

She grinned at his serious tone, amused by the twinkle in his eyes. She was still smiling as she began to study the document again. This time, the feel of his presence wasn't distracting. It was nice to have company, even if he was a potential murderer who would be leaving town shortly. After all, it wasn't as if she had to *date* him. She'd managed to resist kissing him, right? Appreciating his presence was perfectly safe, and even Eppie wouldn't be able to object.

So, she breathed him in, and carefully, slowly and with decreasing trepidation, she allowed his presence to wrap around her as they sat side by side, each in their own work, sharing space, sharing air, and sharing the moment.

～

"TALK, GIRL! TALK!"

Clare grinned as she walked into her office Monday morning and found Astrid and Emma waiting for her. Astrid's thick hair was accented with delicate pieces of pink lace woven into a few of the strands, and Emma was wearing a tight, black long-sleeved shirt that revealed just how much weight she'd lost since she'd been back in town.

A cup of Ophelia's finest was already on Clare's desk, waiting for her as steam spiraled out of the lid. "Aren't you supposed to be at work today, Emma?"

Emma was at Astrid's work table with a paint brush, and the sun was streaming in the windows, making all the half-finished projects glitter. "I took the morning off. Astrid needed some artwork for a custom project." She pointed the brush at Clare. "What's going on, girlfriend?"

"Did you sleep with Griffin yet?" Astrid was at her computer, no doubt downloading another dozen lucrative orders. "Because he's hot."

"No, I did not sleep with him." But she'd certainly dreamed about it. All. Night. Long.

Trying not to think about the sensual images still dancing around in her head, Clare set her computer on her desk, noticing, for the first time, the contrast between her office and Astrid's. Astrid's walls were covered with cheerful paintings, bright curtains and assorted scarves and silk hanging from lights and dangling from the ceiling.

Clare had three bookshelves crammed with law books. Two locked filing cabinets. One sickly looking ivy dangling from the top of one of the bookshelves. The office felt so empty and stark, compared to the living intensity of her kitchen last night. It had been so amazing with the cupcakes, the laughter, the coziness of her beloved kitchen, and, of course, Griffin. Her office was devoid of life. Why hadn't she ever noticed that? Or bothered to decorate it the way she'd done with her kitchen? And why was she noticing it now?

But she knew why. It was because of Griffin's comment about her day job. About how it was wrong for her. It couldn't be wrong. She couldn't afford for it to be wrong for her. He didn't know what he was talking about. "Griffin's just a boarder. Not a potential date."

But even as she spoke, she felt the lie. The connection between them was so intense and so powerful that it was undeniable. She and Griffin had worked last night until almost two in the morning. She usually hated working late at night, with the silence of the house pressing down on her, as it always did when Katie was asleep or out. But last night, it hadn't felt lonely, and she hadn't minded working, even when they'd been sitting in silence, each immersed in their own work.

And when she'd taken breaks to decorate the cupcakes, Griffin had chatted lightly with her. Nothing intense. Just company. And it had been nice. Really, really nice. Having him in her kitchen had been like lighting a fire in the hearth and letting the heat and warmth of the flames penetrate the darkest corners of the room.

"There's nothing 'just' about Griffin Friesé," Astrid said. "Take advantage. He's exactly the man to get you out of your dry spell."

Clare opened her computer and saw a pink frosting thumb-print on it. She smiled, remembering how Griffin had filched some frosting right before helping her pack up her computer. She touched the dried icing that had permanently preserved Griffin's fingerprint. "It's not like that with him. He's just renting a room. He's—"

"Not like that?" Astrid snorted. "I was there in the store, Clare. I saw the way you guys looked at each other. I *felt* the way you two looked at each other. Things were so intense between you that Eppie actually came by here this morning to ask me point blank if you were already having sex."

Clare gaped at her friend. "Are you serious?" The thought of Eppie's interference made her stomach clench. Even though she and Griffin had never even kissed, the current between them was intense and amazing, and she didn't want it tainted by Eppie's judgment or disdain.

"Dead serious." Astrid twirled her dangling earrings, making the turquoise stones flash in the sunlight. "Honestly, it sort of freaked me out to have to discuss sex with Eppie, but she was surprisingly knowledgeable about it. I'm thinking that girl gets out more than we know. We think she and Judith go to bingo on Friday nights, but I'm starting to wonder."

Clare grimaced, her heart sinking at the idea that the town had been dissecting her relationship with Griffin. What they had was private, something special, not something to be flaunted and evaluated by people who didn't understand what it was: just a basic, human connection, not some rampant sex-fling. "Does everyone else think we're sleeping together?"

Astrid shrugged. "Who cares? It's not their life."

"I don't want them to think—"

"Clare." Astrid leaned forward, her tousled hair dangling precariously close to her cup of coffee. "You're the one who has to live your life. Eppie doesn't lie in your bed at night all alone. Eppie doesn't watch late night movies and have to wonder if any man will ever touch her body again. Eppie doesn't see a thirty-three-year-old face in the mirror and see the hardness that has formed in an attempt to go it alone."

Clare's throat thickened at the comments that were far too accurate. "I'm fine by myself."

Astrid's face softened. "I know you're fine, but we all deserve to be a lot more than fine."

She lifted her chin. "And sleeping with Griffin would change that?"

"It would shock a little life into you," Astrid said. "And that's what you need. He might not be the right guy. I'm not arguing that. But if you can just let yourself go and feel a little bit of life in your heart, it'll do you a world of good." She pulled open a drawer and tossed something at Clare. "Here. I bought these at the store. I told Norm they were for me because I've decided to become a prostitute, so your reputation is intact for the moment."

Clare caught the box and nearly dropped it when she saw what it was. "Condoms?"

"Have sex, Clare," Astrid said, her face completely serious. "Just try it."

"No," Emma interrupted, finally jumping into the conversation. "Don't you dare sleep with him."

Clare tossed the condoms onto her desk, her heart thumping. Condoms. Seriously? "I'm not going to—"

"Why shouldn't she?" Astrid asked Emma. "You want her to die a shriveled old lady who has forgotten how to be a woman? Just because she's a mom doesn't mean she's not a passionate, sensual being with needs."

Clare thought about how Griffin had made her body come alive simply by the way he'd looked at her. She hadn't felt that kind of energy rippling through her in ages.

Astrid's words made her realize that her friend was right in some ways. She hadn't felt like a woman in so long. She hadn't even thought about it. But it had felt so amazing last night in the kitchen with Griffin. He hadn't even kissed her, and it had still been the most intense sexual moment of her life. With the box of condoms on her desk and memories of last night with Griffin in her mind, it was a little difficult not to think about making love with him. What if she did have sex with him? What if she tossed aside all the rules and restrictions in her life and let herself go for a night, or two, or for however long he was in town?

"Clare." Emma laid her paintbrush carefully on a white cloth and turned her chair toward Clare. Her friend's face was intense, worried. "You're this amazingly tough single mom, but we all know that your heart is just a giant mushball."

Clare fiddled with the coffee as her throat clogged up. "I'm fine."

"I know you are," Emma said. "But you're not hard-wired to sleep with a man and not have it matter, and not have it affect you. You're too soft. We all know that. Griffin's going to leave, and you deserve more than to let your world be upended just for a week of nookie."

Deflation settled down on Clare, and she flicked the condom box, inching it away from her. "I know, but—"

"Don't do it." Emma shook her head. "You'll get crushed, and you can't afford that." She smiled softly. "Trust me, it can derail you in a way you can't afford."

Clare saw the pain Emma had been trying so hard to set aside. "You'll be okay again, Emma."

"Yes, you will, sweetie." Astrid put her arm around Emma's shoulders and squeezed. "You, on the other hand, aren't allowed to sleep with anyone yet, Emma. I'll use my pitchfork on any man who tries to get into your pants, I promise."

Emma laughed. "Well, thank God for that at least. I was afraid I was next on your list to get laid."

"You need to be celibate for at least fifteen years to get on my 'You Need Sex' list."

"I thought you were exaggerating yesterday." Emma looked at Clare curiously as she leaned her blond head against Astrid's dark one. "Has it really been fifteen years? You weren't with anyone while I was living in New York?"

"Fifteen years isn't so long. It's not like you forget how to do it—"

"That's almost half your life!" Astrid said.

"Fifteen years is a long time," Emma said thoughtfully. "It's too long."

"See?" Astrid exclaimed. "Even Emma agrees."

"I agree that Clare needs to have sex," Emma said. "But I'm not sure Griffin is the right choice. I mean, he's incredibly compelling. He could suck the willpower right out of a woman with one kiss, I would imagine."

"I can't imagine any man better equipped to bring Clare's sex life into the present," Astrid said, her eyes gleaming with anticipation. "He's so hot, but he's also so obviously wrong for her that she won't fall for him. She's way too smart."

Emma grimaced. "But he's so compelling. Jake was like that and I had no chance against him, even though I knew he was wrong for me."

"You were twenty-three," Astrid said. "How would you have known? But Clare's in a totally different situation. She can trust herself."

"That's true." Emma chewed her lower lip. "Clare's way more stable than I ever was. If anyone could sleep with Griffin and not fall for him, it would be Clare—"

"Oh, for heaven's sake." Clare gave her friends an exasperated look, the conversation bringing her back to reality, to the truth that she absolutely couldn't invest herself in him. "I'm not sleeping with him. He's a murderer, remember?" And he was leaving. Emma was so right, there was no way for Clare to have sex with Griffin and not let it touch her heart. She simply wasn't wired that way.

Astrid and Emma simply looked at her. The faces of the two people she trusted most in the entire world. People who loved her. Clearly both thinking that she needed to get laid if she had any chance at a decent life. "At least put the condoms in your purse," Astrid said. "Just in case."

"She has a point," Emma said, clearly resigning herself to the power of Clare's libido. "I mean, he is living at your house. A late night food fight with chocolate frosting could get a little out of control. Take the condoms, but remember that he's going to leave you."

"I know he's going to leave. I would never fall for him." Clare looked at the blue box sitting on her desk.

"Then you should do it," Emma said. "Otherwise, you're going to be too vulnerable to the wrong guy."

"Agreed. Have sex, and then tell us all about it," Astrid said.

"No, I—" Clare's computer beeped and she glanced over at the screen. At the top was an email from Griffin. The subject was blank, and there was a one line note. *A good night. Thanks.*

A good night.

A good night.

She looked at the email, and then she looked at the box of condoms sitting so innocently on her desk.

She wasn't going to sleep with him.

Really. She wasn't.

She wasn't that kind of girl.

But what if...

"Oh, fine." She picked up the box and shoved it into her purse.

And when her friends started applauding, she couldn't quite keep the smile off her face.

CHAPTER NINE

AT EXACTLY SIX o'clock the next evening, Griffin drove up to his daughter's new home. He parked in front of it, a strange sensation unsettling him as he studied the house. Brooke was right there. Behind those walls. Yards away from him. He was going to see her for the first time in a year. Finally.

Yes.

Griffin shoved his hand through his hair and fiddled with the collar of his dress shirt as he peered at the house. It was smaller than Griffin had expected. Plainer. Not nearly as warm and inviting as Clare's red, rambling farm house, or as luxurious as the home he'd once provided for his family.

It was a simple gray house of a modest size. Black shutters. A small yard. A swing set sat beside a side deck that was furnished with a picnic table with a bright red umbrella. The lawn was mowed, the grass lush and verdant. Flower pots flanked the front door. A white cat was snoozing underneath a bush, the tip of its tail flicking periodically. It was domestic, more so than he would have imagined Hillary living in. But he noticed that the paint on the clapboard was pristine, the yard neat, a picture-perfect existence that Hillary craved, just like she'd forced him to live with for so long. At the thought of his ex-wife and the life he used to live, tension rippled through Griffin and he flexed his fingers, trying to loosen his muscles.

He draped his arms on his steering wheel restlessly, forcing himself to pause and take stock of his competition. It was nothing more than a small, ordinary home, one that was the exact opposite of Clare's house with its well-worn look. He liked Clare's better.

Griffin let out his breath, his restlessness easing as he thought of the previous evening. He'd enjoyed working with Claire in the kitchen. There had been no pressure from her to be a certain way, a certain type of man. He'd liked working with cupcake paraphernalia strewn all over the place in casual domesticity. The lasagna had been damn good. Best he'd ever tasted.

Sitting next to Clare, breathing in that delicate fragrance he was coming to associate with her, had been an intimate, easy comfort. He'd been distracted from his own work too many times, watching her forehead pucker as she worked through a difficult document, listening to her laughter when he made a joke...yeah. It had been a good night. He'd woken up energized and ready to attack his work.

Griffin had been so involved in going through the documents for In Your Face this morning that he'd missed breakfast, and the house had been empty when he'd walked into the kitchen. But there'd been a note from Clare on the table, telling him that there were fresh muffins on the counter and coffee was loaded into the coffee maker, ready for him to start it. Again, no judgment for the fact he'd missed breakfast, just an acceptance for who he was.

She'd written the note in green pen, and her handwriting had been flowing and womanly, as if she'd enjoyed the mere act of creating the words.

Yeah, a great night. Unexpectedly so, and he smiled.

A gray squirrel raced across the driveway, drawing Griffin's attention to his ex-wife's Mercedes. The flashy coupe was a stark contrast to the neighbors' driveways, which had practical well-worn cars that were a quarter the price and half as shiny. Hillary might claim to have it all with her little Maine existence, but the fact she was still driving her Mercedes said she hadn't totally abandoned all affection for the finer things in life, which meant Brooke was probably feeling the same way. Those were the things Griffin could provide, and the new man in their lives couldn't.

Calm determination settled inside him at the reminder of what he had to offer. See? This was going to work just fine. He had the goods, and he knew damn well he wasn't as bad of a guy as everyone said he was. If he were, he was pretty sure he wouldn't have gotten the lasagna offer last night from Clare when he'd tried to sneak past the kitchen. Clare wouldn't put up with shit, and she had invited him right into her space. So, yeah. It was good.

Griffin flipped his door open, swung out and headed up the brick steps. He knocked on the door, and stepped back. Six o'clock. Right on time, just like he'd said. Let them try to give him grief for always being late. Not anymore.

He heard rustling inside and sudden relief rippled through him, nearly staggering him with its intensity. Brooke was really home. She hadn't skipped out. *He was going to see her.*

Suddenly on edge, Griffin shoved his hand into his pocket and wrapped his fingers around the jewelry box holding the necklace he'd bought for Brooke. Should he give it to her right away, or wait? Should he hug her or shake her hand? Should he tell her that he'd missed her, or play it cool?

The doorknob turned, and Griffin cleared his throat—

A man pulled the door open. Not Griffin's ex-wife. Not his daughter. A man.

Son of a bitch.

The guy was tall with shoulders like a freaking mountain and a beard like a grizzly bear on growth hormones. His jeans were baggy, and his hands and arms were splattered with lavender paint, as if he'd been painting the bedroom of a certain teenage girl. He had an attitude of ownership about him that suggested he wasn't a hired contractor, but the man who'd replaced Griffin.

"I'm here to see Brooke." Griffin pulled his shoulders back, raising himself almost to the man's height. "I'm her father."

The behemoth stuck out his hand. "Dan Burwell. Brooke's stepfather."

Stepfather? Something dark rippled through Griffin, but he managed a grim smile as he grabbed the beefy fist, keeping his own grip just as strong as the mountain man's. "Griffin Friesé."

"Figured." Burwell scrutinized him intently.

Griffin shoved his sleeves a little higher up his forearms. "I'm here to see Brooke."

Burwell shook his head once. "She's not here."

Fierce disappointment jabbed Griffin in his ribs, but he kept his voice even, even as his daughter's present burned in his pocket, taunting him. "Well, where is she?"

Dan narrowed his eyes. "Listen, Friesé. You walked away from this family. I didn't."

Griffin ground his jaw to keep from growling. He was getting really tired of that rumor. "Hillary took Brooke away from me," he snapped. "I didn't leave them." He still remembered that day he walked in after work and found the condo empty. The furniture had still been there, but the soul was gone. He'd known instantly that they'd left, and he hadn't had to look in the closets for missing clothes to know the truth. It had taken him almost a week to track them down, and he'd nearly gone mad with worry during that time. "I don't know what Hillary has told you—"

"I'm taking care of them, and it's my job to protect them. That includes Brooke."

Griffin's hands curled into fists. "My daughter doesn't need to be protected from me."

"No?" Dan set his arms over his chest, his huge forearms straining against the folded cuffs of his plaid shirt. "You make her cry. That's not okay with me."

Griffin's aggression faded at the idea of his daughter crying. Brookie? Crying? Because of him? "I don't make her cry—"

"You do." Dan jerked his chin at the road, silently telling Griffin where to go. "Hillary and Brooke aren't here, and they won't be here no matter how many times you come by, so take a hike."

Griffin gave the man a steady, hard stare. "You can't keep my daughter from me." It was true, and they both knew it. "I will not hesitate to enforce my rights."

"Yeah, you can call in the law," Dan said, his voice dark with challenge. "But are you willing to destroy Brooke by forcing her?"

Griffin faltered. Destroy his own daughter by enforcing his right to be her dad? He would never do that to her. Ever. Suddenly, all his plans, his well-laid, infallible plans began to unravel around him, and he had no idea how to stop it.

Dan closed in on Griffin's hesitation. "Listen, Friesé. I've got nothing personally against you, but we both know that the only reason you're here is because another man took your place, and that pisses you off." He slapped Griffin's shoulder. "It's a guy thing. I get it. But get over it. Your job with them is done. It's mine now, and unlike you, I love every damn minute of it."

Griffin stared into the ruddy face of the lumberjack who'd

taken over his family's life. There was pride gleaming in the man's eyes. And ownership. Unyielding, fierce, protective ownership.

Shit.

This was a complication he hadn't anticipated.

～

CLARE BOLTED UPRIGHT IN BED, her heart racing.

Wind was howling. Rain was pounding at the shutters. Was that what had woken her up? Bad weather? It was just another spring storm in Maine, and this time her daughter was safe at home, not stranded in the mountains. A little inclement weather wasn't worth vaulting out of bed in a panic.

Chill out, Clare.

She flopped back on the blankets, staring at the ceiling as she listened to the sound of water pouring off the roof, like a waterfall right outside her room. Branches were scraping against the side of the house, and the wind was whistling through the gaps in the window frames. Was Griffin still out in this weather?

He still hadn't come back by the time she'd gone to bed, and after the last evening's late night, she'd been too tired to work past ten. Katie had needed help with her math homework, and a new client had needed a will before surgery in the morning, so cupcakes (and the rest of her work) had been abandoned for the night.

Clare sighed. No delivery for Wright's tomorrow. No assortment of sweets on her counters. No wonder she'd been woken up by a little feisty weather. She always felt a little off if she didn't get a chance to bake. She hadn't even had time to go through her emails, let alone frost a single dessert.

She knew the lack of baking wasn't the only thing bothering her though. The house felt empty without Griffin, and she didn't like that. This was her home. She loved it. She treasured every moment in it, and she was so proud that she'd managed to buy it. Katie had a home. She had a home. And it was perfect.

So, why did it feel so empty without Griffin? How could she have let that happen in a single night with him? One night of camaraderie, and he was already destroying the sanctity of her dear home.

Clare rolled over onto her side, facing the windows, so she could watch the water hammer against the glass, trickling in little rivulets down the panes. She needed to forget about the condoms. Emma was right. She couldn't get involved with Griffin in that way. He was already invading her oasis too much, and her world was too fragile and too precious to risk it for a week of nookie, as Emma had put it, though she had to admit the idea was tempting in an unnerving way—

A loud shout from Griffin's room caught her attention. Relief flooded her at the realization he was home, but it was quickly chased away by concern. It was nearly two in the morning. What was getting him worked up at this hour?

Another shout, mumbled words, and foreboding rippled over Clare's arms.

He was in trouble. Something was wrong.

Clare leapt out of bed and hurried out the door. There were more shouts, and undecipherable words. He sounded like he was in pain. He sounded the same way her dad had those last nights before he'd died.

Sudden panic hit her, and she raced down the hall to his room. She flung the door open without knocking and ran inside. The room was dark, and all she could see was Griffin's shadowed outline in the bed. He was thrashing and groaning. "Griffin!" She ran over to the bed and touched his face. He was drenched in sweat, and he sounded like he was in horrible agony. "It's okay," she said urgently. "Calm down."

He rolled over, still tossing and moaning. Cold fear gripped her, and her hands started to tremble. Was Griffin sick? Like really sick? Like her father had been before he'd died? "Griffin!" She grabbed his shoulders and shook him. "Wake up!" She had never been able to get her father to wake up, because it hadn't been a dream that had been consuming him. It had become his reality, a horrible illness taking his mind and his body away from him.

Not again. *Please, God, not again.* "Griffin!" He fought her, shoving her hands away. His skin was hot, and his hair was plastered to his head. She shook him again, desperate, frantic. "You have to wake up!"

"Clare?" His voice was thick and confused, but his eyes opened. He was awake.

"Griffin." Relief surged through Clare, and she sank onto the bed beside him, suddenly too weak to stand. "Are you okay?"

"Clare," he mumbled. Still sounding dazed and mostly asleep, Griffin rolled onto his side, facing her, and she set her hand on his shoulder. He was trembling, his powerful body shocked into submission by whatever he'd been dreaming about. His skin was slick with perspiration.

"Let me get you a towel." She started to slide off the bed.

"No." His arm clamped around her waist and yanked her back beside him. "Stay." He shifted so his head was on her leg, using her thigh for a pillow. He kept her anchored against him, like a terrified child in desperate need of comfort to ward off the monster under the bed.

"Okay." She settled back against the headboard and began to stroke his head. "It's okay, Griffin. It was just a nightmare."

He said nothing, and she let her hand still, suddenly

feeling a little silly about comforting a grown man as if he were a child.

"Don't stop," he said quietly, his voice harsh with anguish. "Please."

She realized that he needed her: her touch, her comfort, and her help. Tears filled her eyes, and a powerful feeling surged through her. She immediately began to stroke his head again. "I won't stop," she said. She weaved her fingers through his hair, the damp strands slippery and soft beneath her touch. "I'm here, Griffin. You're safe."

He reached for her free hand and entwined his fingers through hers, holding onto her with a weariness that spoke of a soul that couldn't survive by itself for one more minute.

She snuggled deeper against the pillows, moving so her body was against his. Letting him feel the reassuring strength of human contact. Of being held. Of not being alone.

He draped his leg over hers, his body heavy as he pinned her to his mattress, still holding tight to her hand.

Clare smiled gently and continued to stroke his hair. "Whatever is chasing you," she whispered. "It can't get you right now. I have you. It's okay."

Griffin said nothing, but as she held him, the tremors began to ease from his body, and his muscles began to relax. But his breathing didn't change, and she knew he was still awake.

He shifted, nestling his head more snugly against her hip, and he wrapped his arm around her leg, as if to ensure she didn't sneak away. His hand was gripping her inner thigh, and suddenly she became aware of exactly how little she was wearing.

A pair of silky shorts and a camisole top. Griffin was wearing only boxers, and his legs were bare against hers. Skin to skin, over the lengths of their bodies, wrapped so intimately around each other.

His breathing shifted, and she knew that he had just noticed the same thing. His arm tightened around her thigh, ever so slightly, but even that small movement was enough to send ripples of awareness over her body.

She didn't need this. She really didn't. He needed comfort right now. Not sex. She needed space. Not sex. She shifted, trying to extricate herself. "Griffin—"

"I dreamed she was drowning," he said, his voice muffled and hoarse.

Clare stopped, frowning at the shadowy figure tangled around her. "Who?"

"Brooke. My daughter."

"Oh." Clare's heart tightened, and she scooted down on the bed so she could look at him. Her eyes were adjusting to the darkness, and she could make out the features of his face. Enough to see the tendons rigid in his neck and the agony in his eyes. "I'm so sorry," she whispered. "It's terrifying to imagine harm coming to our children."

His head was resting on the pillow now, facing her as he anchored his leg over hers again. "I dreamed that I was standing on the shore of the ocean, and there were huge waves," he said, his voice raw. "Brooke was in the water, being tossed around. She was screaming for me, waving her arms. 'Daddy! Daddy! Daddy!' Just screaming my name over and over and over again. She kept getting sucked under, and I thought she was gone, and then she would come up again, screaming for me."

"Oh, Griffin." Clare laid her hand on his cheek, trying to ease his torment. "That's a horrible dream." For years after Ed's death, she had been haunted by the nightmare that she was dying, and her little girl was crying for her, left behind without anyone to take care of her. A shudder went through Clare as she remembered the depths of the terror that would grip her for days afterwards, not fear of her own death, but fear of the devastation it would do to Katie if she died. No wonder Griffin was still shaking. She rubbed his shoulders the way she'd wished for someone to rub hers all those times. "But it's just a dream—"

"I was shouting for Brooke," he continued, his tension rising as he relived it, working himself up again. "I kept trying to get through the waves to her, but they kept throwing me back to shore." He was starting to tremble again, and she knew he was getting sucked back into the terror of the nightmare. "The waves were crashing all around me, and I couldn't see her and I couldn't get to her, but I could hear her screaming. I was shouting her name, reaching for her, but I couldn't get to her." His voice broke. "My baby was drowning, and I couldn't save her. I was too late. Too fucking late." He stopped suddenly and rolled onto his back, throwing his arm over his face. "Fuck!"

Clare stroked his arm, trying to soothe him. "It was just a dream, Griffin. She's not drowning. She's okay."

"No, she's not! She's not okay." He swore and punched the pillow.

"Yes, she is!" She grabbed his arm, her heart breaking for his anguish. "Listen to me, Griffin! It was a dream!"

"She's not okay, and I can't get to her. I can't reach her. I can't fucking help her!" He punched the pillow again.

"Hey!" Clare climbed on top of him, grabbed his forearms and shoved them back against the bed. "Stop it! Your daughter is okay, and you haven't done anything wrong!"

Griffin grabbed her arms and in a move quicker than she could prevent, he rolled over, pinning her beneath him. He pinned her hands against the pillow above her head, his hips weighing her down. He glared at her, anger rolling off him. "You have no idea what is going on with my daughter!"

His body was rigid with fury and the residual trauma of his dream, and his face was angry. But Clare could feel his pain and fear, and she wasn't afraid. Despite what anyone else might say, there was no danger in this man. When Ed had died, she'd struck out in rage like Griffin was doing now, and she knew it was just the residual effects of the terrifying dream, the body's defense to a terror so deep it could break a person completely. "Griffin," she said quietly, trying to coax him back into sanity. "I'm not the enemy. It's just me."

He stared at her, as if he couldn't understand her words, as if he couldn't grasp what was happening. Her heart bled for him, for this strong, powerful man who had been brought to the very depths of fear and panic because he was worried about his child.

This was the man who Eppie had accused of being a murderer?

This was the lunatic who had supposedly driven his family off with rages or abandoned them, depending on which rumor you listened to?

No. This was the beauty of a father who loved his daughter, of a man with more passion in his heart than he knew how to handle. "You're a good man," she said quietly.

He searched her face, and she saw the desperation in his dark eyes. She felt the intensity of his need to believe her words. "You don't know me," he said.

"No, I don't."

"Then you don't know if I'm a good man." His grip was still secure on her wrists, and his body was heavy on hers, but she sensed that he would release her if she asked. He was holding her down because of his own need to be connected, a need she suspected he didn't even comprehend.

"I do know," she said. "You lost your connection to your daughter in the divorce, and you don't know how to get it back. That doesn't make you a bad person. It simply means you have a heart that actually works." She smiled. "That's a good thing, Griffin."

"What?" Confusion laced his voice, and his forehead was furrowed.

"Katie filled me in on what Brooke had told her about you. There's a disconnect between the two of you, isn't there?" Her legs were starting to ache from his weight on them, but she didn't want to dislodge him.

His grip tightened on her wrists, his gaze desperately searching hers for understanding. "I went there tonight to take her to dinner."

Clare shifted her legs, sliding them outside his. The moment she did that, he sank deeper against her. Okay, maybe not quite the right solution. She focused on Griffin, trying to ignore the pressure of his body between her thighs. His slowly growing hardness between her legs. "And she wouldn't go with you?"

"She wasn't there, but Hillary's new husband was. It didn't go well." Griffin's eyes began to darken, and his gaze drifted to her mouth. "She's trapped in that house, and I can't reach her. It's like my dream, only this time it's real, and I still can't reach her."

Clare swallowed, her body beginning to respond to the heated way he was studying her lips. This wasn't good. She couldn't do this. "Have you spoken to Brooke?" she asked, trying to keep the conversation directed to a safe topic.

"Yeah. She told me to leave her alone."

Clare's heart tightened for the pain beneath his words. "Don't give up on her. She needs you."

Griffin stared at her, and then a faint smile softened his hard features. "Thank you for saying that."

She smiled back, happy to see the hint of peace in his eyes. "I believe it."

"I know you do." He began to rub his thumb over the inside of her wrist. "And that's why it was so beautiful."

Tremors rippled down her arm from his touch, and a pulse began to beat low in her belly. "Griffin—"

"No," he said. "No more words. Not right now."

Then slowly, ever so slowly, he bent his head.

He was going to kiss her. She knew he was. She should push him away. Get out of bed. Run screaming. *Go, Clare, go!* "Griffin—"

"Tonight, you are my savior," he whispered. "That dream tortures me constantly, but tonight you took it away. You gave me room to breathe again."

Tears filled her eyes at the earnestness of his words, and then he kissed her.

CHAPTER TEN

GRIFFIN'S KISS was everything Clare had dreamed of for years.

Feather-light and tender, his lips brushed over hers, a fleeting connection of desire and endearment that was over before she had a chance to take a breath.

He pulled back and studied her, as if trying to gauge her reaction.

She couldn't tear her gaze away from him, couldn't keep herself from being mesmerized by the depths of his dark eyes. She wanted him to kiss her again. And again. And—

"You're trembling," he said.

She blinked. "I am?"

"Are you cold?"

"No." She couldn't seem to find words.

He raised one eyebrow, and then a slow, seductive smile spread across his features. No dimple this time, just the awareness of a man and his power over a woman. "Hmm..." He released her wrist and laid his hand against her head, his fingers tangling in her hair in a sensual caress that sent spirals of pleasure cascading through her.

Still smiling, he kissed one corner of her mouth. And then the other. And then her nose.

Clare closed her eyes, afraid to breathe, terrified of shattering the moment. This precious, amazing moment. She drank in every touch, the warmth of his lips as they touched her skin, the gentleness of his hand in her hair, the heat of his breath against her cheek.

There were no words between them. No words to describe the wonder of what it felt like to have Griffin touching her. She reveled in the sensation of his skin against hers, the weight of his body pressing her to the mattress, the exploration of his lips over the curves of her face, the heat from her skin mingling with the damp fire rising from his.

Then he kissed her mouth again, and this time, the kiss was deeper. More insistent. More intimate. Seeking her response.

Desire blazed through Clare, answering his summons, and she began to kiss him back, tentatively at first, not sure what he wanted, or how to respond. But when Griffin made a soft growl of pleasure and deepened the kiss, sweeping his tongue across hers, she forgot to be worried. She forgot to fear. She just kissed him back, following his pace, setting her own. She became lost in the kiss, in his hands in her hair, in his body moving against hers, his hips nestling more deeply between her thighs.

His skin felt so magnificent as she moved her leg, sliding her bare foot along his calf. She basked in the hardness of his muscles as he supported his upper body, the sheer raw man that he was. She'd forgotten, oh, how she'd forgotten, what it felt like to be in a man's arms, to be kissed as though she were the most precious being in existence.

No, not *a* man. Griffin. It was only Griffin. His legs tangled around hers, his woodsy scent filling the air, his mouth nibbling so seductively along her collar bone.

Griffin lightly bit her lip, then the kiss changed. It deepened, it pulsated with power, and with urgency. With need.

Answering need rushed through Clare, and she shifted her legs apart a little further as he moved his hips against her, pressing into her. She tentatively set her hands on his shoulders, needing to feel his skin, wanting to pull him closer, not sure how to do it, not sure if she should.

"I like that," he whispered. "Hold me."

Excitement poured through Clare, and she wrapped her arms around his neck, kissing him back, feverish desire racing through her. It was beautiful and amazing and—

"Mom?"

Clare froze at the distant call, her heart hammering with desperate need as Griffin pulled back. For a moment, they simply stared at each other, as if they could will away the interruption and fall back into the magic that had begun to build between them. But as they lay there in frozen stillness, Clare felt the cocoon that they'd built around themselves beginning to unravel. The intimacy being torn apart. This special moment, this incredible feeling of being in Griffin's arms was crumbling through her fingers. Her hands dug into his shoulders, as if she could hold onto it, keep it from slipping away from her—

Then she heard footsteps descending the stairs. Coming toward them. "Mom."

This time, Clare heard the stress in her daughter's voice, and she knew she had to go. "I'm sorry, I—"

Griffin caught her face and kissed her once, hard. "Go," he said.

He smiled, and she smiled back, and something flashed between them. An understanding as parents? As lovers? She didn't know, but it felt beautiful, as if she wasn't alone.

"Go!" Griffin lightly smacked her bottom, and she scrambled off the bed and raced for the door as she heard Katie's feet at the bottom of the stairs.

Safely out of Griffin's room before Katie could see where she'd been, Clare hurried out into the hallway and intercepted her daughter as Katie reached the bottom step. "What's wrong, sweetheart?"

"Bad dreams." Katie was hugging Harvey, her ancient pink bunny who found his way into her bed only on really tough nights. Her hair was hanging across her face, and her shoulders were bunched. "Can I sleep with you?"

"Of course." Clare put her arm around Katie, guiding her back toward her bedroom. Katie closed her eyes and rested her head on Clare's shoulder, barely awake even as she walked.

As they reached the back hallway, Griffin leaned out his door. He nodded at Katie and raised his brows in question.

Clare smiled at his concern. "She's okay," she mouthed, as she smoothed her daughter's hair back from her face.

Griffin nodded and slipped back inside. She heard the soft click of his door shutting as they walked past.

Their moment was over.

~

"You had sex!" Astrid declared as Clare walked over to the corner table of Wright's with her cup of coffee the next morning.

Astrid's hair was pulled back in a thick ponytail, but she'd woven delicate red and blue beads into a few of her strands. The beads were today's daily reminder to herself that she really was the artist she wanted to be.

"Astrid! Shut up!" Clare glanced around her at the bustling crowds, but on this Tuesday morning, everyone seemed to be too busy to notice to Astrid's attempt to embarrass her. Clare did a careful check of the table by the door, but Eppie wasn't at her customary spot, thankfully. Eppie would not have missed that comment, for sure.

Clare made a face at Astrid as she slid into the chair beside Emma. "Seriously. I really don't need anyone in this town talking about my sex life."

Astrid wrinkled her nose and glanced around. "Sorry," she said. "I was just so excited when I saw your expression when you walked in." She raised her brows and lowered her voice expectantly. "You slept with him, didn't you? Your eyes are totally sparkling."

Clare felt her cheeks heat up. "I—"

"No, you didn't. I can tell." Emma gave Clare a thoughtful look as she picked at a cupcake. Emma was paint-free this morning, which hopefully was a good sign. Since she'd been back in town, Emma had been up before dawn painting, no matter what time she'd gone to bed, and Clare was starting to worry about her need to bury herself in her studio. There was, however, a cupcake on Emma's tray, which suggested that Ophelia, at least, thought Emma was having a tough day. "You're not glowing or traumatized enough to have done the tango with him." Emma patted Clare's shoulder. "Good girl."

"I didn't have sex with him." Clare wrapped her hands around the coffee cup and let the heat penetrate her palms. Katie had had an early study session at school, and Clare had bailed before Griffin had emerged from his room, not quite sure what to say to him after last night. She peeked behind her to make sure no gray-haired ladies had zoomed in, but the backfield was clear. So, she leaned forward and lowered her voice, unable to keep the grin off her face. "But he kissed me."

"Really?" Astrid clapped her hands, a delighted smile on her face. "How was it?"

Clare replayed that moment when Griffin's lips had

touched hers. The strength and heat of his body on hers. "Amazing. It was just incredible."

"Oh," Astrid said. "You look so happy right now. I'm so glad."

Even Emma smiled. "Really?" She sighed and put her hand over her heart. "That's so beautiful. You deserve a good kisser. They're really wonderful."

"And?" Astrid prompted. "What else?"

"Katie came downstairs and interrupted." Clare had gone over that incident a thousand times in her head since last night. What would have happened if Katie hadn't woken up? Or if she'd come down five minutes later? Clare still couldn't decide whether she was glad Katie had come down, or not.

"Well, that's okay. It builds anticipation." Astrid sat back in her chair, her eyes dancing. "This sounds promising. Are you excited?"

Clare spun the cup around in her hands, trying to find the words. She'd sat there staring at that box of condoms this morning for at least ten minutes before getting into the shower. If anything happened with Griffin, it would be only a night, or two, and then real life would be back, facing her every morning. Could she really gallivant to the heavens with Griffin and be able to return peacefully to her world?

Emma leaned forward. "What's wrong, sweetie?"

Clare eyed the cupcake that suddenly looked very tempting. "I don't know what to do."

"About sleeping with him?" Astrid asked.

Clare shrugged. "About everything. I mean, it's been so long. I'm totally not rational about it. When he was kissing me, I thought I'd died and gone to heaven. I have no frame of reference or foundation or anything." She picked up the dessert and realized that it was an old one. From yesterday? It was totally against her morals to eat it, but she broke off a piece of the hardened frosting anyway, craving the chocolate.

"I mean, it was the most amazing sensation ever, to feel his body against me like that. I wasn't even thinking logically. I just wanted more. I would have hung from the rafters with him, and that was just from a kiss! What will happen if there's more? I'll be insane. I won't even know how to think or act or respond."

"Of course you will," Emma said. "It's natural—"

"And that's not all!" Clare popped another bite of the day old dessert in her mouth and made a face even as she chewed. It was dried out and crumbly, but the sugar hit her system in a well-needed boost. "Do I even like him? Or was it just the feeling of a man giving me attention? And what happens if I do like him? And then he leaves?" She shoved the rest of the cupcake into her mouth. "It was so much better before he reminded me of what I'd been missing from my life." She groaned and put her forehead down on the table. "I'm such a wreck."

Astrid laughed and put her arm around her. "Oh, babe, it's okay. You'll be fine."

"No, I won't," Clare moaned, not lifting her head. "I don't know how to have sex anymore. I don't know how to kiss. I was so in awe of his hands in my hair that I think I would have fallen down if I hadn't already been in his bed."

Emma whistled softly. "You were in his bed? How did that happen?"

"Because I'm so ignorant when it comes to dating and men that I got myself into his bed half-naked without even *thinking* about the fact it could turn sexual. What else am I going to do? Hop into the shower with him by accident?"

Astrid was laughing openly now. "If you get in the shower with him, there's no way I'm going to believe it's by accident."

"It's not funny!" Clare sat back and folded her arms against her chest. Her breasts felt heavy against her arms, and she could almost feel Griffin's chest against them. "Emma was right. I'm in no shape for intimacy with a man. Some women are supposed to be celibate, and apparently, I'm one of them."

"If you were," Astrid said cheerfully. "It wouldn't have felt so incredible, now would it?"

"It felt too incredible. I can't be trusted." Clare groaned. "I don't even know what I'm doing." She searched the faces of her friends for answers she didn't have. "Would I really have had sex with him? I mean, I don't even know him. He's an outsider. He'll be leaving soon. He's everything that's wrong."

"And yet he's completely tempting." Emma drummed her fingers on the table, chewing her lower lip as she always did when she was in the middle of thought. Her white cotton blouse was soft, making her look even more fragile than she already did. "Maybe he should move out. I'm not sure that his staying there is a smart idea. Things could happen because of the proximity, not necessarily because you've thought it out and decided you were willing to take the risk of the fallout."

Astrid raised her brows at Emma. "You think she should kick him out?"

"No!" Clare's panicked response came out before she could stop it, and she saw the knowing looks from her friends at her intense reaction. "Oh, God. I'm already too dependent on him. I do have to make him move out, don't I? Or I'm going to jump him while he's sleeping."

"Oh, no." Astrid gave her a contemplative look, absently fingering the double heart necklace she was wearing. "You aren't just attracted to him. You actually like him."

"Yes, you do," Emma agreed with a grimace. "I thought sex would put you over the edge and make you get emotionally involved. But all it took was one kiss, and you already like him?"

"Well, yes, but it was a really good kiss." Oh, Clare didn't like how that made her sound a little too harlot-like. "Plus, he's a good man," she added hastily, as she brushed the cupcake crumbs off the table. Had she really scarfed an entire day old cupcake in two bites? Yes, she had. It was official. She'd lost her capacity to cope.

"He might be a good man, but he has major baggage with an ex-wife, and he lives in Boston," Emma said gently.

"I know, but—"

"It nearly wrecked you when Ed died," Emma said. "Don't get emotionally invested in a man who's guaranteed to leave you. If you're going to like a guy, at least pick one that has a chance of working out."

"You know, Clare," Astrid said. "I still believe you need to start dating again, and get some action, but I agree with Emma." She looked at Clare with concern. "Your heart is too big, and you've already opened it to Griffin. You can't sleep with him. You have to let him go."

"You're right." Clare bit her lip, trying not to think about that amazing kiss. "I know. You're right." She made a face. "But I really, really liked kissing him."

"Liked kissing who?" Ophelia asked as she walked up, carrying several plates of food from the deli. A personal delivery from the store owner meant one thing: that Ophelia was about to get personally involved, unless Clare could deflect her.

"Ed," Clare said quickly as Ophelia gave Astrid a warmed croissant and an orange. "My late husband. We were reminiscing about how he won me over."

Ophelia waggled a finger at her. "Now, now, missy, don't try to lie to me."

"I'm not. I—"

"I may have been married for fifty-three years, but I know a good looking and good-hearted man when I see one, and that Griffin Friesé is all that." Ophelia set another cupcake down in front of Clare, giving her a knowing nod that made Clare realize Ophelia had seen her scarf the cupcake and concluded she needed another one. "It's natural and right that Griffin would look at you the way he does, and what girl with a beating heart would be able to resist those smoldering looks he dishes your way?"

"He 'smolders' at me?" Clare grinned. Okay, if she wasn't going to convince Ophelia that she'd been talking about Ed, she might as well abandon the pretense and enjoy dishing about Griffin. Seriously. It wasn't every day someone told her a man like Griffin Friesé was giving her dark, lusty looks. "Really?"

"Oh, yes," Astrid said.

"'Fraid so," Emma added. "Are you going to eat that?" She pointed at the cupcake on Clare's plate. "Because if you're not, I'm going to, seeing as how you ate mine."

Clare looked at the cupcake and saw that the frosting definitely looked a little bit crustier than it should. "These are all from yesterday." She frowned at Ophelia. "You're supposed to throw away the old ones. You know it's against my rules to serve old ones."

"Well, we didn't get any new ones today because our cupcake baker didn't come through. Live with it."

Guilt twinged through Clare. She hated letting people down, and she was religious about delivering to Wright's. There were people in town who'd had one of her cupcakes every day for the last five years for their afternoon sugar high. "I had work."

"Oh, I'm teasing, girl." Ophelia waved her off. "Day-old cupcakes don't bother me, and they can still help the spirit revive." Ophelia rested her palm on the table, balancing the pot of coffee on her hip, her hazel eyes focusing on Clare. "Now, listen to me, Clare. Norm and I have been watching you for the last fifteen years...well, we've been watching you for the last thirty-three, but it's those later ones that matter right now."

Clare glanced across the room and saw the ancient owner of Wright's studying them beneath the rim of his red hat. Always watching. Always vigilant. She smiled at him, and he gave her a nod.

"We've been waiting for the light to return to your eyes," Ophelia said, drawing Clare's attention back to her, "and we're tickled pink to see that it's come back."

Clare was surprised. Had her light been out for so long? Twelve hours ago, she would have denied it, but after her response to Griffin last night, she had no defense. Last night he'd brought her to life in a way she hadn't felt in a very, very long time. Maybe even fifteen years? Maybe longer? Oh, God, she hoped not.

"But a spark like that is fragile," Ophelia continued. "It can be snuffed out in a heartbeat when it's still so new. Griffin could be the one to either bring it to full flame, or knock it right out for good."

Clare stiffened. "He's a good man—"

"So he is. But sometimes, that's just not enough." Ophelia pushed the cupcake toward Clare just as Emma reached for it. "Be careful, Clare. If not for yourself, for your daughter. That girl of yours can go on only so long watching her mama's spirit fading away. You need to live, my dear. Don't go back to where you were, not ever again. Nurture that spark, and coax it back to life. Got it?"

"Yes, I got it." Clare's response got a skeptical sniff from Ophelia, but Norm called her away before Ophelia could press harder.

Clare stared after Ophelia as she shimmied up to Norm and nuzzled the old man endearingly, her heart sinking. "Was I that bad? I mean, I'm pretty happy, right?"

Emma put her arm around Clare's shoulder and squeezed.

"Don't listen to her, Clare Bear. You're doing a great job with Katie."

"Am I?" She sighed, thinking about the night before. "Katie's fifteen, and she still sleeps in my bed several nights a week. She's started having nightmares about me dying and leaving her all alone."

Astrid looked surprised. "You never told us that before."

Emma nodded. "It makes sense. She lost her dad, and now she's hit puberty. Teens become aware of things they didn't notice before. You're her world, Clare."

"I know." Which was why she had to do right by her. Ophelia was totally correct. Clare had to make her daughter's world safe. But what was the answer? To retreat back to where she'd been in her safe, protected world? Or to start exploring the feelings that Griffin had stirred in her? To stoke the fire, as Ophelia might say.

Clare watched Ophelia sneak behind the counter and talk to Norm. He bent his head toward hers, and his wrinkled old hand held onto Ophelia's as they spoke. There was such beauty between them, a connection as old as the earth. A partnership where they talked about things together, shared their worries, helped each other with solutions.

Clare had watched them huddle up hundreds of times, and she had always thought it was sweet. But for the first time, watching them made her feel empty inside, because she realized now what she didn't have in her life. Last night, helping Griffin with his crisis about his daughter had felt good. She'd never had that kind of bond with a man, sharing burdens, understanding each other, connecting. Not even with Ed.

She'd never even thought about the lack of it in her life before. But now she was so achingly aware of it, of the hollowness in her chest. Clare realized then that the appeal of last night hadn't just been about the kissing.

It had been about the man himself. His mind. His heart. His fears. And, of course, the way he'd held her and kissed her and—

"Look who just walked in the door," Astrid whispered. "And he is looking mighty fine."

Clare turned sharply, and there he was.

The man himself.

GRIFFIN GAVE Norm a cheerful salute as he stepped into Wright & Son. The old country store was bustling, and there were people everywhere. But this time, Griffin didn't feel overwhelmed. He was just in a damned good mood, and he grinned at a couple of locals discussing the best fishing spots on the lake as he headed toward the owner. "Good morning, Norm."

The grizzled old man tipped his hat back. "Things going well, I see."

"Oh, yeah." Griffin swept a New York Times off the counter and tucked it under his arm. "I had a great sleep last night. The best I've had in years."

Norm gave him a speculative look. "The Maine air will do that for a man. Nothing like the fresh scent of Mother Nature."

And the scent of a certain woman that had lingered on Griffin's pillows all night long. Last night was the most vivid that nightmare had ever been. Sleep was always a lost cause after that dream. But last night, Clare had soothed him. By the time she'd left, Griffin had been at peace and had decided to try sleeping again. He'd crashed hard and woken up feeling completely rejuvenated. Somehow, with her soft voice, earnest concern, and sensual kisses, Clare had chased away

139

the demons brought on by his failed trip to River Junction to see his daughter.

Speaking of River Junction... Griffin contemplated the older man for a moment. A potential resource? "Hey, do you know anything about Dan Burwell?"

Norm nodded. "Sure do."

Griffin grinned at the news. It had been hard as hell to walk away from Dan last night without engaging, but he'd made the call that he needed to reassess his strategy. Now that he knew Norm had information about the man who'd supplanted him, Griffin was glad he'd followed his instincts to step back and regroup. The key to a successful war was good information, and now he was going to get it. "Well, what's he like? Tell me about him."

Norm tipped his head, studying him. "Known the guy for forty years."

Anticipation rushed through Griffin. This was what he needed. He leaned on the counter. "Talk to me."

Norm's gaze drifted over the busy store, and Griffin noticed that a line had formed behind him. There were already eight people in it. "Come back tonight after closing," Norm said. "We'll talk."

Griffin ground his jaw, frustrated by the delay, but he knew it would be worth the wait. One thing he'd learned in business was not to move too soon. He'd run into complications with Dan Burwell, and he would take the time to figure out the best approach. "What time do you close?"

Norm shrugged. "Whenever the last person leaves." He nodded past Griffin, dismissing him. "Morning, Patsy. You want to put that on your account?"

Griffin moved aside as a young woman with a baby on her hip stepped up to the counter. He glanced around the store, inspecting the crowds, and then he saw Clare, her blue eyes focused on him. She froze when he caught her gaze, and the rest of the store vanished instantly, and all that was left was the two of them.

There she was, the woman he'd dreamed about last night, sitting with two of her friends. Her hair was pulled back in a loose bun, a few strands hanging loosely around her face, tempting him to wrap those locks around his fingers and tug her over to him. She was wearing a loose peasant blouse and a long skirt that flowed decadently around her legs. He knew how soft her skin was below that casual top, and he knew what it felt like to have her legs wrapped around him. And he knew, with vivid clarity, exactly what it felt like to kiss her.

Griffin grinned, tossed money for the paper onto the counter, and headed right toward Clare.

CHAPTER ELEVEN

"OH, HE'S COMING OVER HERE," Clare whispered as Griffin began to work his way through the crowd toward them. She instinctively touched her hair to make sure it looked all right, then jerked her hand down. Hadn't she already decided she wasn't going to get involved?

"Of course he is." Astrid watched him approach, her eyes gleaming in anticipation. "You teased him and left him hanging last night. No man can resist that kind of temptation."

Clare grabbed Emma's chair. "Move closer so he can't sit next to me—"

"What are you, thirteen years old?" Emma pushed her hand away. "That's way too obvious. Deal with it."

"Good morning, ladies," Griffin arrived at the table, a wide grin on his handsome face. The dimple was in full bloom today, and his eyes were bright and cheerful. He was wearing jeans and his hiking boots again, a white button down shirt, and a hip-length leather jacket that gave him just the right edge of sophistication and ruggedness. He was clean-shaven and looked ready to dominate the day.

He looked way fresher than Clare felt. She was guessing he hadn't spent the night in anguished debate over what direction their relationship should take. So unfair.

"Good morning." Astrid held out her hand, showcasing three inspirational bracelets that she'd finished only last week. "I'm Astrid Monroe. I share office space with Clare. Sorry I missed you the other day when you came by to sign the lease."

He gave her a firm handshake. "Griffin Friesé. Potential murderer, at your service."

Astrid grinned. "Always good to advertise. Word of mouth is the most powerful marketing tool."

"Yep, it sure is." He turned to Emma with a questioning look.

"Emma Larson." Emma gave him a thoroughly contemplative inspection. It wasn't quite as friendly as Astrid's had been, but she wasn't taking aim with a deadly weapon either, which was about all that would keep Clare safe from him right now, given the hum strumming through her body at his nearness. "It's nice to meet you, potentially," Emma said.

He flashed Emma a wicked grin. "I'm not as dangerous as my reputation, I promise."

A small smile quirked the corner of her mouth. "Danger is subjective."

"Excellent point." And then Griffin did what Clare had been both dreading and eagerly anticipating. He turned his full attention onto her. "Good morning, Clare."

She clutched her coffee cup. "Hi." There he was. Inches away. The man who had kissed her last night so thoroughly and so decadently that he'd awoken the woman she'd forgotten she was.

"Come sit." Astrid pulled a chair up between her and Emma. "It's girl time, but as long as you promise to put on lipstick, you can join us."

Clare waved her hands in protest. "No, I'm sure he has to go—"

"Thanks for the invite. I look great in lipstick." Ignoring Astrid's strategically placed chair, Griffin grabbed a seat from a nearby table, set it next to Clare and sat down. His shoulder brushed against hers, and he leaned his knee against hers beneath the table. "What's the topic today?" he asked.

Clare shifted casually in her seat to put some space between Griffin and herself. How could he have sat next to her like that, when there was an empty chair on the other side of the table? She didn't have to look around to know that people were watching.

But she looked around anyway.

Yes, people were watching. Surprise, that.

"Men. Sex. Dating. That kind of thing," Astrid said. "Typical girl talk."

Hello? Bring up men, sex and dating in front of Griffin? Clare kicked Astrid under the table, while Griffin burst out in a deep chuckle. "At eight on a Tuesday morning?" he asked. "What about work?"

"Not nearly as interesting," Astrid said. "Clare's an estate attorney. What's interesting about that?"

"She's also a cupcake phenom," Griffin said as Ophelia set a cup of coffee down in front of him with a wink. He nodded his appreciation at Ophelia as he continued to declare Clare's talents. "Her desserts are works of art." He set a proprietary arm across the back of her chair. "And incredibly delicious, as well."

"That's not work," Clare protested, but she could tell she was beaming from his remarks. She knew she had a special talent for cupcakes, but not everyone really understood how she poured her emotions into them. But Griffin seemed to, and that was a beautiful rarity. "Making cupcakes is pleasure, not work."

"It could be both," Griffin said. "Follow your passion, Clare."

Clare rolled her eyes at him. "We already went over this—"

"Oh!" Astrid smacked the table with a yelp. "I totally forgot to tell you. Harlan told me that The Bean Pot is for sale. You should buy it and turn it into a cupcake shop."

"What?" Clare burst out laughing. "You're kidding. A cupcake store in Birch Crossing? That's crazy."

"Oh...I love that idea," Emma said. "That would be amazing."

"What's the Bean Pot?" Griffin asked. "And who's Harlan?"

"Harlan's my brother, and he does some real estate work on the side. The Bean Pot used to be a coffee shop just down the street," Astrid said excitedly. "The owners retired to Florida about ten years ago, but they always come back up in the summer when the lake is packed with visitors. They called Harlan and said they didn't want to do it anymore, so they asked him to put it on the market."

"That would be so perfect," Emma chimed in. "That location is great. And there's a kitchen in back, because they used to make those really good coffee cakes there, remember?"

Clare did remember. "Didn't one of those end up in my hair when we were sixteen, because Pete Harmon asked me to the junior prom instead of Emma?"

"It wouldn't surprise me." Astrid leveled a finger at her. "You're a no-good, man-stealing 'ho, you know."

Clare burst out laughing at Griffin's shocked expression. "She only talks like that to those she loves. When she calls you a bastard, you know you belong."

Griffin grinned. "Well, damn, and to think I was angling for a more standard signal like, 'great guy,' or 'brilliant addition to our town,' or something that is clearly too mundane."

"I abhor the mundane," Astrid said cheerfully.

Griffin raised his coffee cup. "Amen to that, sister."

Astrid clicked her cup, and Emma added the same. "To abhorring the mundane," Emma said.

Griffin looked over at Clare. "You joining us?"

"I'm a trusts and estates attorney," she explained. "I can't afford to abhor the mundane."

Griffin locked his fingers around her wrist, placed her coffee cup in her hand and raised it up. "My darling, you could be a tax attorney in a black suit and glasses and you would be as far from the mundane as it is possible to get."

Clare couldn't stop the huge smile that spread over her face, or the warm gooey feeling that filled her belly. She wasn't sure if it was the endearment or the compliment, and she wasn't sure it mattered. The whole statement was simply melt-worthy.

"Oh, now, that's just really sweet," Astrid said.

"And correct," Emma said. "Clare Bear is not mundane."

"No," Griffin said. "She's not."

"You guys are crazy." Clare surveyed the three grinning faces, all of them holding up coffee cups. Even Emma was relaxed, and Clare realized that Griffin had won over both her friends. The man was a heroic rescuer of stranded teenagers, he was an amazing kisser, he was fire-starter to her hormones, and he could charm the girls over coffee and muffins.

"To cupcakes," Griffin said.

"To cupcakes," Emma and Astrid echoed. All three of them were beaming at her as if they knew some secret worth gloating over.

"They're just dessert," Clare protested.

"No," said Griffin. "They're passion."

"Oh..." Emma nodded. "He's right you know. Just like my art and Astrid's jewelry."

Astrid grinned and slid a key across the table toward her.

"Harlan slipped me the key to the Bean Pot when I told him that you might be interested."

"I'm not interested." But Clare couldn't help but stare at the shiny silver key that looked like it had just been cut. It was sitting on the table so close, just waiting for her to pick it up. A sudden yearning pulsed through her. What if there was a way to make a living by doing what she loved? What if—

An envelope dropped on the table in front of her, and she looked up to see Jackson Reed standing behind Emma. "Morning, Clare. Here's Jeff's estimate for your roof." He gave her an apologetic shrug. "It's not as low as you were hoping for, but it's the best he'll offer. Let me know if you want to do it."

"Okay, thanks." Clare picked up the envelope with a resigned sigh. This was her life, this was her reality. Would a few cupcakes pay for her new roof? No chance. Was she going to force her daughter to sleep in the car so she could play in the kitchen? No, she wasn't. She was going to do her job and take care of her daughter. The Bean Pot would just have to go to someone else. "I'll look at the bid and get back to you."

"Sounds good." To her surprise, Jackson didn't leave. Instead, he nodded at Griffin, as if they knew each other. "Hey, Griff."

Griff? Griffin Friesé was so not a "Griff."

But Griffin shook Jackson's hand in one of those rough and tough handshakes between men who understood each other. "Morning, Jackson. Give my best to Trish."

Jackson's smile lit up his face. "Will do, my man. Will do." He nodded at the rest of them. "Take care, ladies. Be nice to Griffin. It's one against three at this table."

Astrid laughed. "I think he can take care of himself."

"Agreed." Jackson grinned at them all, then headed out the door toward his truck.

"How do you know Jackson and Trish?" Clare asked.

Griffin shrugged. "Small town. He's a good guy."

Clare smiled at his perceptiveness. "He is. Trish is wonderful, and he's so good to her."

Griffin got a thoughtful expression on his face as he watched Jackson get into his truck. "Yeah, I noticed that."

Emma pushed the key closer. "Take it, Clare. Just go take a peek at the store. That doesn't mean you have to do it."

"Trust me," Astrid said. "Turning your passion into your work is amazing. I'll even help you with the internet stuff. I bet you can get a serious online client base—"

"No." Clare folded the roof estimate in half and put it in her purse. Yes, for a moment, she had been almost tempted. But she was too sane to get caught up in irresponsible fantasies. "Now isn't the right time. Maybe when Katie is done with college and—"

"You'll be fifty by then," Astrid said.

Clare snorted. "I'll barely be coming into my prime." She stood up. Nothing like a bill for necessary house repairs to motivate a woman to hustle off to the day job. "I have to go to work. I'll see you guys later." She turned to Griffin. "I'll see you later—"

He stood up. "I'll walk you."

Excitement rippled through her. "It's okay. I can manage."

"Doesn't matter if you can manage or not." He set his hand on the back of her chair and moved it out of her way. "I'm still walking you."

"I'm not ready to leave yet," Astrid said as she picked her coffee back up. "You kids go on ahead."

"Yes." Even Emma leaned back in her seat, apparently giving Griffin the green light as well. "I'm not done either. See you later. So nice to meet you, Griffin."

"My pleasure." Griffin smiled at them both, and then set

his hand on Clare's back as she began to weave her way through the crowded store.

His action announced to the world that she was his.

She wasn't. She absolutely wasn't.

But she couldn't quite get herself to move away from him. It just felt too lovely to have his strong hand supporting her.

Griffin reached past her to open the door for her, and as he pulled it open, Eppie walked in, wearing her rainbow straw hat with artificial tulips. Her sharp eyes took in Griffin's possessive stance, and she gave Clare a long, hard look.

Clare stiffened and tried to duck away from her escort, but Griffin swept her past Eppie before she could extricate herself from his grasp.

"Good morning, Eppie," he said as he passed her. "You look lovely today. Where did you get such a fashionable outfit? You look like an apple blossom on a sunny day."

Eppie's brow furrowed in confusion at the enemy's politeness, and then they were out the door.

～

CLARE BURST out laughing as soon as she and Griffin were outside Wright's. "An apple blossom on a sunny day? Seriously? Eppie had no idea how to respond to that. How on earth did you come up with that?"

Griffin grinned. "I'm an expert at getting people to part with things that matter to them. Money, their business, whatever it takes. Apple blossoms seemed like it might work for her."

Clare waggled her finger at him as he guided her across the street. "You are a dangerous man, Griffin Friesé."

He cocked an eyebrow. "That I am." He kept his touch light, but there was no mistaking the possessiveness of his hand still strategically placed on her lower back.

She giggled again, feeling so liberated by the interaction with Eppie. Somehow, with one well-placed comment, he'd managed to spare Clare any judgmental comments by the older woman. "Well, I appreciate it. Thanks."

"My pleasure." Griffin followed her up the steps of the charming white building that housed her office, and for a moment, she contemplated inviting him in. She had no clients for an hour—

Seriously, Clare?

Instead of grabbing him by his sexy leather jacket and dragging him inside, she stopped on the porch. It was time to tell him he had to move out. The fact she was even contemplating an on-the-desk-ravishment meant that she was losing her mind. She set her hands on her hips. "Griffin—"

"Thanks for coming to my rescue last night." His eyes were dark and penetrating again.

"Oh, well, sure. I mean, you sounded like you were in trouble." She cleared her throat, trying to steer the conversation and her thoughts away from his soul-melting kisses. "But—"

He slipped his hand behind the back of her head, his fingers massaging her neck. "I really enjoyed kissing you."

She swallowed, her heart starting to race. Why did his hand have to feel so unbelievably amazing against her skin? Between the shivers racing down her spine and the desire spiraling through her belly, she could barely even remember how to talk, let alone resist him. "Um, thanks, but—"

"And I look forward to tonight." Then the rapscallion kissed her.

In broad daylight.

In the center of town.

At rush hour.

With half the town passing by, or across the street at Wright's.

And dammit, if she didn't kiss him right back. With great enthusiasm, unabashed passion and altogether too much tongue tango.

She melted right into the kiss with a delighted sigh, and her entire body spiked with desire when he locked his arm around her lower back and hauled her against him. The kiss turned hot and fierce almost instantly, their bodies pressed against each other with a desperate wanting far too intense for eight o'clock in the morning on a public street. Within moments, she was out of breath, her body was trembling and she was utterly lost in the demands of his mouth and his body—

"We can't do this here." Griffin swore and pulled back, raw lust burning in his eyes.

Clare clung to his arms, fighting desperately to catch her breath, to gather herself, to keep herself from screaming, "Yes, we can!" and dragging him right off the porch into her office.

He tunneled his fingers through her hair, his eyes gleaming with anticipatory delight. "I'll see you tonight." Meaning was heavy in his words, and her whole body shouted with eagerness.

Clare shook her head. "No, we can't. It was a mistake—"

"Not by me." Then he kissed her again, a dominating kiss of promise and intention that swept away her resistance and replaced it with a quivering ball of burning need.

He pulled back, a satisfied grin on his face at her utter capitulation to his kisses. "Until tonight, my darling." Then he turned and took the stairs two at a time, hitting the sidewalk before she had time to protest.

Oh, no. This was so not happening. "Griffin—"

He turned toward her, walking backward as he headed down the street. "Live a little, Clare. Life is too short."

Then he was gone, loping across the street toward his truck.

Damn the man. But Clare couldn't keep the smile off her face as she touched her lips. What had she gotten herself into?

Nothing. She wasn't getting into anything. She was going to work late tonight.

Really she was.

She was entirely unprepared to handle this kind of thing with this kind of man in this kind of town.

And she never, ever went into anything unprepared.

At least not anymore.

She'd learned her lesson.

Really. She had. *Really*.

CHAPTER TWELVE

GRIFFIN WAS NOT GENERALLY a patient man.

He made things happen.

But apparently, in the town of Birch Crossing, it was Norm Wright who had the power. And Norm was apparently a man with more patience than a turtle.

Griffin braced his arms on his thighs as he restlessly swayed the bench swing that Ophelia had directed him to when he'd shown up at nine, which was the time that Wright's officially closed.

It was now nine forty-five, and he could still hear Norm inside discussing the loon nesting situation with a man that seemed to be about his same age. Twelve nesting pairs last year, five babies, but only eleven had been sighted this spring so far. Where was the missing pair?

Griffin groaned and dropped his face to his hands.

"Here now, Griffin," Ophelia came out the door, wiping her hands on her white apron and holding a beer. "Have a cold one while you wait."

"Thanks." Griffin accepted the beer and read the label. "Birch's Best?"

"Local beer, made by some fellows down the street." Ophelia winked at him. "Much better than some German import, but it'll give you a kick in the pants that might keep you up all night. You sure you're up for it?"

Griffin grinned. "Sounds like just the thing I'd be looking for tonight."

Ophelia set another one down on a small pine table beside his swing. "For later."

"Thanks." Griffin took a swig, and his head nearly blew off. "Damn."

Ophelia raised her brow. "Too much for you, Boston Boy?"

"No." But hell, he'd never look at beer the same way again. "What's in this stuff? Dynamite and Tabasco sauce?"

"No one knows. It's a well-kept secret." Ophelia peeked at Norm, then walked over and sat beside Griffin. "Hand me that beer, young fellow." As soon as Griffin handed it to her, the gray-haired deli-owner took a swig twice the length of his. "Brilliant stuff. They really need to go regional with this." Ophelia held up the beer. "Hear you're looking for a new venture. Go with these guys. They're going to change the world."

Griffin didn't even bother to ask how she knew he was looking for a new business. He was beginning to suspect that even his thoughts weren't safe from the town's gossip channels. "I'll think about it."

Ophelia leaned back and studied the sky. "She's a good girl, our Clare Bear."

Griffin smiled. "She is."

"But she's been dead for a long time."

Griffin glanced over at her. "What do you mean?"

"Like you."

He shot her a quizzical look. "Me? I'm not dead."

"You've woken her up." Ophelia took another long drink.

"But if this venture with you goes south, we'll lose her forever. She'll never come back."

Griffin ground his jaw. "Clare's not that fragile. She has amazing strength and courage. No one can stop her if she doesn't want to be stopped."

"This is true." Ophelia set the beer on her knee and swung her feet gently. She'd changed out of her day shoes, and was wearing a pair of faded, white house slippers that softened the edges of the tough old gal. "That's the thing, Griffin. Clare has to want to come alive. If she wants to retreat, she'll do that better than anyone has ever done in the history of this town."

Griffin spun the bottle in his hand. "What's your point?" Was she about to give him grief that he was too much of an ass to be worthy of Clare's time? He wouldn't have thought it from Ophelia, but he supposed he should have. Women seemed to be of a mutually-shared opinion about him.

"My point, young man," Ophelia said, "is to stop thinking and start feeling."

Griffin turned his head to look at her, not quite able to decipher her unexpected comment. "What does that mean?"

She tapped his forehead. "It means to shut this off." She then banged her fist against the left side of his chest. "And turn this on. Then you'll be just fine."

"Turn off my mind? No chance." Griffin rubbed his chest where Ophelia had thumped him with surprising vigor. "That's my greatest asset."

"Are you so sure about that?" Ophelia asked.

"Of course I am."

"Well, then, there's nothing more to say," Ophelia sighed as Norm opened the door and stepped out onto the porch.

A beautiful smile lit up Ophelia's face as she rose to her feet, making her look a dozen years younger. "He's all yours, Norman."

Norm's face creased into a soft expression Griffin had never seen on the older man's face. "I'll be up soon. Wait for me." He held out his hand as Ophelia passed by, and the couple clasped hands gently.

Their fingers drifted off each other, but their gazes stayed on each other's faces until the door shut behind Ophelia.

And even then, Norm stood and watched his wife as she walked through the store, shutting the lights off as she went. "Have you ever seen a sexier female than that?" He set his hand over his heart. "Every man should be so lucky."

Griffin grinned as Norm turned toward him. "How many years have you been married?"

"Fifty-three." Norm eased down into an Adirondack chair, a Birch's Best beer in his hand. "Met her when we were thirteen, but her father made me wait until she was eighteen before I married her. Longest five years of my life."

Griffin raised his bottle. "Here's to another fifty-three."

Norm chuckled as he tapped his beer against Griffin's. "Oh, it'll be more than that."

Griffin raised his brows at the sincerity of the older man's comment. "Will it?"

"Yes." Norm leaned back in the chair and rested his head against the wooden slats. "Ophelia and I are connected in our souls by an invisible thread that can never be broken. We'll be together forever."

Griffin felt the contentment in the older man's words, and it was a peaceful sensation. "That's beautiful." He used his foot to slide a stool over toward Norm.

"Ah, it is." Norm set his booted feet up on it, resting his beer on the flat arm of the chair. "The fact you realize it makes me think there's hope for you, young man."

Griffin grinned. "I'm not so young, and I don't believe in hope."

Norm closed his eyes. "And what do you believe in?"

"Making sure I get what I want. Hope has nothing to do it with."

Norm smiled. "Hope is what gives us life."

"No, it's not."

"Then what is it that gives us life?"

Griffin's mind immediately went to Clare. The way she laughed at him. The way she'd held him last night when he'd been freaked out. The way she glowed when she was baking cupcakes. Instinctively, he touched his front pocket, where he'd stashed the key to the Bean Pot that she'd left behind at the store. Astrid had seen him take it, and she hadn't stopped him. "Women, maybe." The answer surprised him. Wasn't it work that gave him life? Wasn't that the answer he'd intended to give?

But Norm laughed, accepting his response. "Now, that is true. A wise man you are, Griffin Friesé."

"Yeah, well, I try." Griffin glanced at his watch. It was already almost ten, and he was eager to get home before Clare went to bed. The kiss outside her office this morning had been on his mind all day while he'd been working with Phil on the In Your Face project. "I know it's late, and I don't want to keep you. What can you tell me about Dan Burwell?"

"He's a good man." Norm pointed at the sky. "Have you ever noticed how many more stars there are in the Maine sky than in Boston?"

Griffin didn't look up. Now that he had his audience, he wanted to get the information about his daughter's guardian, and then get back to Clare. "What are his weaknesses? How far will he go to keep my daughter from me?"

"Look at the stars, my boy."

He realized Norm wasn't going to answer until Griffin did what he wanted. Flexing his jaw impatiently, Griffin glanced up, then paused at the vast expanse of twinkling darkness. "Holy shit." Norm was right. He'd never seen so many stars in his life. The sky was endless with more stars than he could even have conceived of.

"We're small in this earth, Griffin," Norm said. "There's so much beyond us. So much power that we don't have to generate. It's not our responsibility to make the earth turn, or to light up the night with the stars."

"Yeah, true." He'd grant him that fact, but Griffin's brain clearly wasn't operating on the same wavelength as Norm and his wife tonight, because he felt just as confused with Norm as he had with Ophelia and her talk about being dead and turning off his brain. "But how does that help me with Dan?"

Norm finally looked at him. His eyes crinkled around the corner, almost as if he found Griffin's confusion amusing. "This is about human nature, Griffin."

"I'm in trouble then." Griffin laughed softly. "People say I'm not very good with human nature."

"No, I can't imagine you are, yet," Norm agreed. "So, I'll give you some advice. You've made your move with Brooke. She knows you're back, and you aren't going away this time. Let her digest that. Hillary and Dan aren't her voice, but as long as all three of you are yelling, no one will ever hear Brooke. Even she won't hear herself."

Griffin mulled over that bit of advice. "It's like when I make an offer on a company, and then stand back and let them come to me."

Norm smiled with a wisdom that befit his age. "Something like that, yes."

"Makes sense." Griffin dangled his beer bottle between his fingers and watched it sway as he swung it from side to side. Norm was right. He'd made his move, and now he needed to give Brooke time to adjust. "I'll give her a couple days, and then call her again."

Norm took a swallow of his beer. "Good choice."

"But you still haven't told me about Burwell."

"Why? You want to bring him home, too?"

Griffin snorted. "He's in my way."

"Only if you notice him."

Griffin frowned, contemplating Norm's words. "You mean, it's about me and Brooke. That Burwell doesn't matter?"

"Not to you, no."

"I still want to know about him."

Norm looked at him. "Dan is a good man. He'll take good care of Hillary and Brooke. If you go back to Boston, Brooke will grow up fully loved and taken care of."

A dark mood rolled over Griffin. "That's not what I wanted to know."

"But it's what you need to know." Norm leaned forward, his gray eyes fixed intently on Griffin. "You have no responsibility anymore, Griffin. They're okay without you."

"I don't give a shit if they're okay or not! I'm not here because of obligation! I'm here because she's my daughter, and I miss the hell out of her, dammit!" He slammed his beer down on the table so hard it sloshed all over his hand.

Norm said nothing, and the night echoed with Griffin's shout as it faded into the darkness.

"Shit." Griffin laced his hands behind his head and took a deep breath against the sudden tightness in his chest. "I really do miss her."

Norm grinned. "And so we finally see the heart of the man begin to emerge." He raised his beer. "It's about damned time, Griffin. It's about damned time."

$\sim$

IT WAS ALMOST midnight by the time Griffin vaulted up the stairs of Clare's house. After the conversation with Norm he was feeling restless and unsettled. He wasn't sure why, exactly, but he just felt off.

He knew he had to give Brooke space, but he wasn't used to cooling his heels when he was in pursuit of something. And he was rattled by the realization that he missed her. Really missed her.

He was too busy to miss anyone, and he wanted to re-ground himself with Clare. He needed to cleanse the conversation with Norm from his mind and get himself back on track. He had to be a ruthless man on a mission, not some sap who saw beauty in fifty-three-year old relationships and gawked at the stars when he had things he needed to do. He was uncentered and he needed Clare to find his balance again.

Yeah, usually it was his work and his computer that got him back on line, but right now, it was Clare that he craved, and he was too restless to try to figure out why that was the case.

Griffin eased open the side door and stepped inside. The house was silent. There wasn't even a light on under the kitchen door. Damn. He knew he'd spent too long at the store. Norm had started telling stories about the town, and Griffin was pretty sure he'd still have been there if Ophelia hadn't come downstairs in a cotton nightgown and given Norm a come-hither look that had gotten the old man off his chair in a hurry.

He grinned, recalling the look on Norm's face when his seventy-one-year-old bride had walked out on the porch in her sleeveless nightgown. Oh, yes, there wasn't going to be any sleeping in the living quarters above Wright's tonight.

Or at Clare's house, hopefully.

Griffin strode down the hallway, not bothering to turn on the lights. The moon was casting white beams through the windows, breaking up the darkness of the house. And Griffin knew exactly where to step, as if he'd already claimed the place as his own.

He reached the end of the hall and instead of turning toward his room, he headed toward the white door that protected Clare from the world. He strode up to the door and reached for the doorknob.

And then, with the knob half-turned, he stopped, Ophelia's words echoing through his head. Her warning about Clare's vulnerability to him.

He would be leaving as soon as he got his daughter back. Did he really have a right to turn Clare's life upside down?

He didn't.

He should leave her alone.

But his whole body recoiled at the idea of walking away from that door. He wanted to see her. He wanted to connect with her. He wanted Clare.

But he owed her the chance to say no.

Griffin released the doorknob, and instead he lightly rapped his knuckles against the door. One signal was all he needed. One tiny sign that she was on board. That last night hadn't been the mistake she'd claimed it was this morning.

But there was no sound from the room.

Griffin tilted his head toward the door, listening intently as he knocked again.

No sound. Not a creak of a floorboard. Not a squeak of a mattress spring.

Shit. Was she asleep? Or lying there awake, waiting for him to take the initiative? "Clare," he called out quietly. "You up?"

No reply.

Griffin swore and leaned his forehead against the door, his hand resting loosely against the knob as he warred with the urge to throw that door open, invade her space and lose himself in the respite she gave him. "I'll give you tonight, Clare," he finally said. "But I'll be back."

He blew a kiss at the door, and then gave her space.

For now.

~

BY TWO O'CLOCK the next afternoon, Griffin was pretty sure he was going to lose his mind. He had three goals: Brooke, Clare and his new business, and he couldn't do a damn thing about any of them.

Phillip was doing follow-up on In Your Face, and further action had to wait until they had the additional information.

Brooke: waiting mode.

And Clare? She'd been out of the house before he'd gotten up, and he'd intentionally been up and in the kitchen by six. A trip to Wright's hadn't revealed her, and she hadn't been in her office. It had been more than twenty-four hours since the kiss, and he hadn't been able to follow up. Seal the deal. Assess her state of mind. He was hamstrung, hog-tied and restless as hell.

Inaction was not his forte.

Three things. All of them on hold. And without another business to run, he didn't have a single thing to do with his day. Was this what retirement would be like? Nothing to do? Why in God's name would any man want to retire?

He'd split and stacked all the firewood he'd found in Clare's backyard.

He'd been up on the roof to inspect the damage, and found it was as extensive as she'd claimed.

And he'd even folded his clothes and put them in the dresser in his room.

What the hell did people do who didn't work all day?

Griffin braced his palms on the window frame and peered

out his bedroom window. Woods. Grass. Flowers. A trickle of vehicles heading past the house. His truck was sitting in the driveway, the only brand new vehicle he'd seen. But it didn't look new anymore. It fit right in, thoroughly covered in mud and dirt.

He could wash it, he supposed. He hadn't washed his own car in twenty years, but he hadn't seen any sign of a car wash in town. He laughed softly to himself as he headed toward the back door. Norm would probably think it was great he was washing his own truck—

"Mom!" The side door swung open and Katie raced past him into the house, throwing her backpack to the floor with a crash. She was wearing jeans and a shirt that was tighter than Griffin thought a fifteen-year-old should be wearing, just like Brookie liked to wear.

"Mom!" She sounded frantic as she raced down the hall, running into Clare's room.

Upon finding it empty, she screeched in frustration, and then came running back down the hall toward Griffin. Tears were streaming down her face, and he realized she was crying. Shit.

"Hey." Griffin caught her as she tried to run past him to the stairs. "She's not here, Katie."

Katie stared at him, as if she hadn't even noticed him standing there. "Where is she? I have to talk to her." Her lower lip was trembling, and she looked devastated.

Protectiveness surged through Griffin as he gripped her shoulders. "What's wrong? Who hurt you?" Son of a bitch. He'd go bust ass—

"No one! Let me go! I need my mom!" Katie tried to pull free as a fresh sob spilled from her.

"She's not here." Something snapped inside Griffin at the sight of those tears, and he softened his grip and rubbed her shoulders. "Tell me what's wrong, Katie. Maybe I can help."

She gazed at him through teary blue eyes that were so much like her mother's. "Jeremy just wants to be friends," she sobbed.

"The naked guy?" Oh, shit. This was about dating stuff? He'd been ready to go out and take down someone who'd tossed her against the side of a bus or stolen her favorite bracelet. Kissing and boys was not what he was equipped to handle.

"Yes!" Katie began to cry again. "He kissed me on the mountain, you know?"

"Yeah, okay." Griffin looked around, trying to find something to give to her. A box of tissue was sitting on the front hall table, so he grabbed it and held it out to her. "Here."

"So, Jeremy's been avoiding me all week, you know?" Katie took a tissue and plunked herself down on the bottom stair, clearly deciding that he was going to have to suffice to help her through this crisis.

Now that he knew it was about boys, however, Griffin wasn't so sure he wanted the green light. "I didn't know, but now I do." Griffin hesitated, then he eased himself down beside her. Where the hell was Clare? This was mom territory. "Boys can be bastards. I mean..." Hell. "Boys can be jerks."

Katie blew her nose, making a noise that sounded like a goose on a bender. Shit. Since when could someone that small make a noise that big? "So, today, after school, on the bus ride home," she sniffled, "he didn't even sit with me. We always sit together, ever since second grade." She held out the dirty tissue to Griffin. "Here. Can I have another one?"

Griffin stared at the snot-laden tissue as she set it in his hand, but he said nothing and simply held up the tissue box. "Just because he didn't sit with you doesn't mean anything. Boys do weird things when they like a girl."

"That's what Sara said." Katie blew her nose again. Again

with the noise. "So, I went and sat with him, and I asked him why he was avoiding me."

Griffin grimaced. "Didn't go well?"

She looked at him, great big tears sliding down her cheeks. "He said the only reason he kissed me was because he thought we were going to die, and he didn't want to die without having kissed a girl. So, he kissed me because I was the girl standing closest to him."

"Oh, hell." Son of a bitch. He wanted to take that kid and... He took a deep breath and put his arm around Katie. "He's a scum-sucking pig, then."

Katie stared at him in disgust. "A scum-sucking pig? That's so old school."

Griffin raised his brows. "Then what is he?"

"An asshole."

Griffin burst out laughing. "Well, I agree, but I was trying not to taint your innocent ears."

Katie gave him a tentative smile. "I'm not that innocent."

"Innocent enough." Griffin paused, trying to think of what to say. "Sometimes, men, and boys, aren't that good at expressing their feelings. Or even understanding them. We're kind of impaired that way."

Katie leaned against him, resting her head on his shoulder. Protectiveness surged through him, and he kissed the top of her head.

"Jeremy was pretty clear about his feelings." She blew her nose again and sniffled.

"Well, yeah, but what he said might not have been how he really feels. Even if he thinks he's going to die, a guy isn't going to kiss a girl unless he's attracted to her. We're shallow that way."

Katie lifted her head to look at him. Her eyelashes were clumped together from the tears, and her face looked so vulnerable and fragile. "So, you think he likes me?"

Oh, shit. He didn't want to give her false hope. "I'm pretty certain he thinks you're beautiful, or he would never have kissed you."

A smile worked its way onto Katie's tear-stained cheeks. "Really?"

"Yes." He thumbed the tears off her cheeks. "But that doesn't mean that he's ready to date you."

Her face crumpled. "Oh."

"No, it's a good thing." Griffin's chest tightened at Katie's anguish. Damn. He had no skills at this. Hillary had always taken the crises with Brooke. But he couldn't walk away from Katie. The kid had no one else. He had to figure it out. "You can continue to be his friend," he said slowly, stalling for time while he tried to think of what might make Katie feel better. "But as his friend, you can sit there smugly, knowing that he's thinking about how beautiful you are, and remembering that kiss. He's longing for you, Katie, and you have all the power."

Katie stared at him, and he saw a thoughtful look dawning. "I'm not sure that makes sense, but I like the idea of me having the power."

"Power is good," he agreed.

"Huh." Katie looked down at the shredded tissue in her hands. "I still feel stupid for liking him."

"Yeah, well, we all feel that way sometimes."

She gave him a skeptical look that only a teenager would be able to muster with such effectiveness and disdain. "When have you ever felt stupid about something you did? Or for liking someone who didn't like you back?"

Oh, shit. He was supposed to come up with an answer for that?

"See? You didn't." She stood up and started to walk up the stairs. "Nice try, Griffin, but—"

"I felt stupid when I walked in my condo after work and discovered my wife and daughter had left me, and I'd had no idea it was coming." Yeah, he'd felt stupid right about then. How in God's name had he not seen it coming? How had he lost control of his family? The list of ways he'd felt stupid that night was pretty damn long.

Katie paused, studying him intently. "That's really what happened?"

"Hell, yeah."

She gave him a contemplative look. "That's even worse than having Jeremy tell me he just wants to be friends."

"This is true." He realized that she believed him, and something tightened in his chest at the fact that there was a person in this world, a girl the same age as his daughter, who believed him.

She leaned on the banister. "Then why did Brooke tell me you left them?"

Griffin sighed and leaned back, resting his elbows on the next stair. "I don't know."

"Maybe you should ask her."

Griffin laughed softly. "I'll consider that, next time we chat."

Katie nodded, her face serious. "My mom says that it's always best to talk instead of being mad in silence. We always talk it out."

"You're mom's a smart lady."

Katie smiled, a real smile. "She's cool, isn't she?"

"Yeah." Griffin hesitated, thinking of all the weight on Clare's shoulders as she tried to manage things. She'd taken care of him when he'd had his nightmare, and he owed her a little relief. Now that Katie wasn't treating him like a pariah, maybe he had a shot. "You know, I attended that MIT summer program when I was a sophomore."

Katie's smile faded, and she folded her arms over her chest. "Now, you're on my case, too?"

"I'm not on anyone's case. It's your life. But I just wanted you to know that I went, and it was the best summer I'd ever had. I loved being away from home, the kids were cool, and I enjoyed the work." He shrugged. "Might not be that bad."

"Yeah, I guess it might not." She sighed and sat down on the step below him. Her shoulder was leaning against his knee, and he realized he'd passed her test, whatever that was. He was no longer hated, and he realized that felt good. It was a relief, quite honestly. "But I want to stay here."

He sensed that was more than a casual desire. "And do what?"

Katie's eyes shifted away from him. "You won't tell my mom?"

Shit. How could he make that promise when he didn't know her answer? He was getting way over his head here. How did parents respond to that kind of question? "What do you want to do?" He settled for not giving her an answer, and hoping she didn't notice.

It worked.

Katie's eyes gleamed as she turned to face him. "I want to stay here and do the Shakespeare Festival." A huge smile broke across her face. "It comes every year, and all these actors and actresses come from all over the North East. They do performances all summer, and it's one of the biggest tourist attractions in the region."

Well, damn. He hadn't seen that coming. That seemed pretty innocent to him. "You want to be an actress?"

"I don't know. I just want to do the festival. You have to be sixteen to work in it, and I'll be sixteen in May." She grinned. "That's how my dad met my mom, you know. He was in town for the festival, and they met and fell in love right away."

Griffin nodded, understanding now what she was doing. Trying to resurrect her father. "I think you should tell your mom about this." Having Katie trying to connect with her dead father by re-living the summer her parents had met was definitely something Clare needed to get involved in.

"No," Katie sighed. "She would make me go to MIT if she knew that's why I want to stay. I have to find a way to avoid MIT and not tell her I'm going to do the festival." She leveled a finger at him. "Don't you dare tell her!"

"I won't." He held up his hands in defense. He was honored Katie had confided in him, and he didn't want to break her trust. "I wouldn't recommend you lie to your mom, though. That won't go well. She seems like she's a pretty straight shooter." Which was one of the things he liked about Clare. She wouldn't fester in silence if she was upset with him, which meant that if she was kind to him, he could trust it. After Hillary's out-of-the-blue defection, Clare's honesty was like a bright ray of sunshine and relief. He knew Clare wouldn't disappear without warning. If she wasn't happy with him, she would let him know immediately, which meant he could trust her warmth when she gave it to him.

"I know." Katie sighed, her face sad again. "I'm sure I'll end up at MIT, so it won't even matter if I tell her or not."

A heavy silence fell between them, and Griffin shifted uncomfortably. How did one cheer up a fifteen-year-old girl? "I'm going to wash my truck now. Want to help?"

Katie gave him a disbelieving look. "Because that sounds like fun."

He shrugged, even as an idea came to him. It had been decades since he'd done it, but he knew one surefire way to make anyone smile, even a teenager sporting a broken heart. "Will you at least show me where the hose is?"

"Fine." Katie hauled herself to her feet and headed toward the door. "Come on, then."

Griffin stood up, grinning to himself. Did the girl have no understanding of what a car wash meant to teenagers?

Water fight on the way.

CHAPTER THIRTEEN

IT WAS SUPPOSED to be a casual drive-by to see if Griffin's truck was still at her house. A quick check to see whether it was safe to duck into her place for a snack and some yoga before heading back to the office after her trip into Portland.

The phone call Clare had gotten last night had made her nervous, and by the time she'd finished with her meetings in Portland today, she'd been on edge like she hadn't been in a long time. She'd hoped it was going to go away. She'd prayed it wasn't going to transpire. But after today, it was clear. She was being sued for malpractice, and there was nothing she could do to stop it.

She felt like she was going to snap.

There was simply no more room for her to stretch, and she didn't know how she was going to make it. Right now, she needed to be away from everyone. She wanted to pull out the yoga mat she hadn't used in months, ground herself, and try to figure out what she was doing so wrong.

The last thing she had time for was dealing with Griffin. *Please let his truck not be there.*

But as she rounded the corner, she was dismayed to see

the big, black truck parked in her driveway, covered in suds. Griffin was leaning over the hood, his muscles flexing as he rubbed it down. Didn't the man have a daughter to retrieve? But no, he wasn't off trying to track her down. He was at her house, in her driveway...washing his truck? Seriously? In a tee shirt? What was a man like that doing owning a tee shirt, let alone wearing one that revealed a bicep that was so sinfully tempting? Didn't he have a hundred businesses to buy? But there he was, soaping up the hood of his truck with one of her giant sponges, claiming her sanctuary as his own.

She ground her jaw as she hit the gas to drive past, but then she saw Katie sneaking around the side of the truck holding their garden hose. Clare frowned, easing up on the accelerator as Katie peered around the tailgate.

Griffin didn't look up, his muscles flexing as he worked on his truck.

Katie crept closer, and then she held up the hose and sprayed Griffin.

Clare slammed on the brakes, expecting Griffin to whirl around in outrage and shout at her daughter.

But he simply hurled the soapy sponge as Katie shrieked with delight and tried to retreat behind the truck. The sudsy sponge hit Katie in the back, and she screamed with laughter as she grabbed it and lobbed it back at Griffin. When Griffin looked up to snatch it out of the air, Katie sprayed him right in the face with the hose.

"Hey!" His shout was filled with amusement and cheerful threats as he sprinted after Katie, chasing her with the soapy sponge.

Clare smiled, her heart warming at the happiness in her daughter's voice. She realized it had been too long since she'd heard her daughter laugh like that.

A car honked behind Clare, and she realized she was blocking traffic. She started to drive on, but at the last second, she pulled into her driveway and put herself right in the middle of the chaos, energy and social interactions she'd been so determined to avoid one minute ago.

She parked a safe distance away from the battle, and then got out of her car. "Hello?" But Griffin and Katie had disappeared. Chasing each other into the backyard?

She smiled at the thought of Katie having so much fun and headed up the driveway, peeling off her suit jacket as she went. She so rarely put on a suit for work, but as soon as she'd gotten that call last night that the heirs who were suing her had agreed to meet with her to negotiate a settlement, she'd known she needed to portray the image that a suit would give her. But now that she was home, all she wanted to do was get it off. "I'm home," she called out.

But again, there was no response.

Some of her anticipation flagged, and she felt the weight of her day descend upon her shoulders again. How was she going to manage this? It was too much—

Cold water crashed over her head, knocking the wind out of her. She whirled around to see Katie grinning at her, a red wash bucket in her hand. "Hi, Mom." Her daughter's eyes were dancing, and she had a look of complete and utter delight on her face. "Welcome home."

Clare smiled at her daughter's ebullience, at the radiance illuminating her face. "You look beautiful."

Katie's smile widened. "I know. I'm completely gorgeous." Her gaze flicked behind Clare. "Uh, oh—"

Clare turned sharply and promptly got a face full of water. "Griffin!"

He eased off the spray, and he looked as amused as her daughter did. His dimple was in full force, and water pinned his tee shirt to his body, revealing muscles that she'd only been able to suspect until now. But as he stood there dripping and grinning like some mischievous little boy, his dark hair spiked and wet, and a day's worth of whiskers along his jaw, she felt a little bit like melting right there into the wet ground.

Then Katie set a bucket of water at her feet, and it sloshed over Clare's pumps. "Here you go, Mom. He's tough to get, but between the two of us, I think we can take him." She backed up, leaving Clare alone to face him. "I'm going to cut off his supply. Be back in a sec."

"I'm in my suit," Clare protested, even as she peeked at the bucket. It looked so tempting and soapy. It had been years and years since she'd had a water fight.

"Your suit's already wet," Katie called out as she headed toward the house. "It's already ruined."

"Ruined?" Clare looked down at her skirt, and she sighed when she saw the water stains oozing along the fabric. Now wasn't the time to have to buy a new one. Then she realized that her white blouse was also wet. And somewhat transparent. And plastered to her. Yes, she was wearing a bra, but even that had been rendered a little too friendly by the water. Oh, dear Lord. She was way too old for a wet tee shirt contest—

"Clare." Griffin's eyes gleamed with wickedness that made her belly alight. "I'll buy you a new suit. No excuses. Step up and defend the honor of the Gray women." He waggled the hose. "Or are you afraid?"

Clare's fingers twitched, and she couldn't help mimicking Griffin's wicked expression. "I have to work." She did. She really did. But the challenge in Griffin's eyes was tempting. "I'm not afraid."

"No?" His gaze went to her mouth, and then slid down her body, in a slow, heated perusal. "You, of the closed doors, not afraid?"

She felt her cheeks heat up as she thought of last night when Griffin had knocked at her door. "Um—"

His smile widened, knowledge flashing in his wicked eyes. "You were awake last night, weren't you? You heard me knock."

"I had to get up early," she protested. But oh, how she'd lain there, listening to his deep voice calling her name. The knowledge that he was so close. Right outside her door. She'd stayed so still, terrified he would decide to walk in...and praying he would. And then she'd been so furious with herself when she'd heard the floor creak as he'd walked away.

He raised the hose, challenging her. "I dare you to live, Clare."

Katie was in the flower beds by the faucet that the hose was attached to. "Come on, Mom! Don't fear him. We can defeat him."

Griffin's brows went up in challenge. "No chance. You both will go down." He brandished the hose. "I'm the one who's armed—"

The water suddenly stopped coming out of the hose. Griffin looked over his shoulder at Katie, who waved at him from the spigot, where she'd just cut off his water supply. "Go, Mom!"

Clare grabbed the bucket and hurled the contents at Griffin while his head was turned, catching him full on the side of the head. He bellowed in protest and whirled around as she dropped the bucket and began to scramble backward, laughing at his outraged expression. Water and soap were dripping off him. He was totally drenched.

Clare shrieked as Griffin charged her, laughing as he grabbed her around the waist and tossed her over his shoulder, holding her tightly. "You girls are going down now!" He sprinted up toward the faucet, and Katie shrieked and dove out of the way as he turned it on again. Clare braced herself against his back, laughing as she bounced. "Put me down! I'm going to throw up."

"I've got you covered, Mom! Stall him!" It was a race back toward the hose, but Katie beat Griffin to it, grabbed the hose first, and sprayed it.

Griffin immediately turned so the spray caught Clare full in the face. "Hey," she sputtered, laughing. "Katie!"

"Sorry!" Katie laughed. "It's sort of hard to get a clear shot at him with you hanging all over him."

"I'm not hanging all over him," Clare protested. "I'm being held captive."

"Well, move!"

Oh, right, because it would be easy to pry herself out of the steel pistons masquerading as arms that had her locked down. Clare looked down at the broad back that she was clinging to, surveyed the rigid muscles, and had a flash of brilliance. "Are you ticklish?" She poked her fingers into his sides and wiggled them.

"Hey!" Griffin twisted around with a yelp of protest, and she kept tickling as he spun around, trying to get her off. "Stop!"

"No way!" Totally amused that the big, tough man was ticklish, she attacked him relentlessly, laughing at his howls of agony. Katie was laughing so hard she had to sit down, and Griffin was spinning around, trying to protect himself without dropping Clare.

"Enough!" He flipped Clare off his shoulder, and Katie immediately sprayed him with the hose.

"Victory!" Katie shouted.

But as Griffin faced them, dripping like a waterfall, the tempestuous fire of a warrior burning in his eyes, Clare knew the battle had just begun.

And she was so looking forward to every minute of it.

∼

"I HAVEN'T HAD that much fun in years," Clare said as she walked around the front of the house to where Griffin was sitting on the front step, enjoying the early afternoon sun.

Griffin watched her approach, and he felt something primal stir inside him as she neared. She had put on a sweat-shirt and a pair of jeans, and her damp hair was curling around her shoulders. She wasn't wearing any makeup and her only jewelry was a pair of silver hoops dangling from her ears. She looked unsophisticated, natural and infinitely alluring.

He held up his hand to her, inviting her to join him. "You look beautiful."

"Thank you." She smiled and allowed him to take her hand just long enough for her to sit down beside him. Not quite touching him, but close, so very close.

"You're welcome." Griffin rested his arms on his knees. He hadn't bothered to change after the water fight and had finished waxing his truck while the women had gone inside to warm up and dry off. He had to admit, there'd been some-thing elemental and satisfying about polishing his truck, and he'd enjoyed it far more than he would have expected. "I haven't had a water fight since I was a kid."

"Me either." She lightly brushed her finger over his hair. Her cheeks immediately turned pink when he looked at her. "There was soap in your hair," she explained, jerking her hand back.

"You don't need a reason to touch me," he said quietly, something pulsing deep inside him in satisfaction at her inti-mate gesture.

"I know. I mean, I guess. Thanks." She rolled her eyes at herself, as she folded her hands in her lap, a response that wasn't quite what he'd been hoping for. "I was awake last night when you came by."

Her confession made him smile. "I figured you heard me."

Clare pursed her lips, as she fidgeted. "I haven't dated anyone since Ed died."

He set his hand over hers, stilling their restless movement, wanting to ease her sudden tension. "That's a long time," he said gently, letting her know that he understood what she was trying to say.

"I know." She studied their entwined hands, but didn't try to pull away. "I find the entire prospect of you daunting."

Griffin chuckled as he picked up one of her hands and set it on his knee. "I find the prospect of you intriguing beyond words."

Clare made a noise of protest. "I don't think I'm capable of handling you when you say things like that." But she didn't remove her hand from his knee.

"Nothing to handle." Griffin tucked a stray curl of hair behind her ear, then took her other hand in his. "Just accept the words and enjoy them."

She bit her lower lip and lightly scraped her fingernail across his knee. "How long are you staying?"

Griffin rubbed his thumb over her palm, relishing the softness of her skin. "I don't know. A few days. A week. Two at the most."

Her eyes darted nervously to his face. "You wouldn't consider moving up here with Brooke?"

"No," he said automatically. "My life is in Boston."

"Okay." Clare took a breath and flattened her hand on his knee. "I needed to hear that."

He could feel her tension, and he saw the uncertainty flicker across her face. Shit. "Deal breaker?"

But she surprised him by shaking her head and tapping her fingers against his knee. "I don't know yet, but I needed to know the truth so I don't delude myself about the reality of the situation."

He smiled at her serious expression, so different from the

carefree woman who had let herself get caught up in the water fight. "Do you ever let yourself just go and not analyze every decision to death?"

She raised her eyebrows at him skeptically. "Do you?"

Ah...she had him there. "Touché," he acknowledged.

They said nothing for a few moments, nothing between them but the small circles he was drawing on her hand, and the weight of her hand still on his leg. Her fingers were still again, no longer caressing, but she was still touching him, maintaining their connection. It was a perfect moment of connection, one that made him want more, one that made him take a risk and try for more.

"What are your plans tonight?" he asked, surprised that his heart was racing a bit. "Can I take you to dinner?"

Clare's gaze shot to his, her eyes wide with sudden panic, but her fingers dug into his knee, as if she were trying to hold onto him to keep herself from retreating. "You're asking me on a date?"

"Yeah, I guess." He held her gaze, willing her not to run away. Now that he'd put it out there, he realized that was exactly what he was doing: asking the woman he was craving out on date. He felt as nervous as a fifteen-year-old hoping she would agree to go out with him.

A smile flirted across her face, and relief rushed through him. She was going to say yes.

But then she sighed and shook her head. "I can't," she said. "I have plans. Softball game against the Grizzlies. I'm selling cupcakes as a fundraiser for the new rec center."

Ditched for a softball game? Adrenaline charged through Griffin, a need not to give in, to pursue what he wanted. Hmm...could he change her mind? Griffin pressed his lips to her palm. "Who are the Grizzlies?"

"Men's softball. Our town's team is the Pirates." Watching him nervously, Clare toed her sneaker through the dirt, leaving behind a circular pattern that reminded him of a design she'd put on her cupcakes the other night. Always the artist. "The whole town shows up for their games," she told him. "This is the first of the season. There will be a barbecue and games and stuff. It's really fun."

A small town softball game? Griffin kissed the inside of her wrist. "Sounds like a great party."

"Don't be a grump." Clare whacked his arm, making him laugh and distracting him from his seduction. "It is fun. It might not be some fancy night at the opera in Boston, but it's great. Sports can be fun, you know."

"I don't like opera," he retorted. "And I'm great at sports."

"Not an opera fan?" She ran her hand down his arm and tapped his watch, which he knew didn't exactly fit with this town. "I would have thought you loved to get dressed up in a tux and be with the pretty people."

"I work. I don't have time for things like that." But he had time for Clare's hand on his wrist, that was for sure.

"Ah..." Some of Clare's excitement faded. "Yes, work."

Griffin sat up at her sudden tension. "What's wrong?"

"Nothing, I just had a tough day."

Protectiveness swirled inside him, and he leaned closer to her. "What's wrong? Tell me what's going on."

Before she could answer, a horn honked and Jackson's beater truck pulled in the driveway. He hopped out of the truck as Clare quickly pulled her hands away from Griffin. He reclaimed her hand immediately and tucked it under his arm before she could retreat.

"Griff! I'm glad I found you." Jackson grinned at Clare. "Afternoon, Clare. Looking gorgeous as always."

Griffin casually slung his arm over her shoulder and pulled her up against him, ignoring Clare's sharp look to desist. Jackson might be married, but he was a man and he'd noticed that Clare was beautiful, so yeah... "What's going on, Jackson?"

"Bruce Weller blew out his shoulder installing a dock today. We need you to fill in."

Um...yeah. That made sense. "On your construction project?"

Jackson barked with laughter. "Sometimes I forget that you're new." He pushed his ball cap back on his head, his face cheerful and happy as always. "Bruce is our pitcher, but his shoulder's sidelining him tonight. You pitched in college, right? Can you throw for us?"

Clare looked at him. "You played baseball?"

"Yeah, a bit." He shifted his arm, pulling her a little closer as he inspected Jackson with renewed interest, impressed that the man had done his research. "How do you know all this about me? Who's keeping track?"

Jackson grinned. "Trish was worried that Clare had rented a room to a serial killer, so she looked you up on the internet. There was a ton of info about you, but not a single record of charges against you, so she decided you're safe. It was her idea to track you down when we heard about Bruce. You in?"

Griffin shook his head instinctively. "I haven't thrown a pitch in almost twenty years."

"It's softball," Jackson said. "I'm sure you can manage."

"Yeah, yeah, I could manage but—" He thought of the scene Clare had painted for him. A rousing town affair. People everywhere. Women, kids, small town life. It was so not his thing. He had no idea how to be the kind of man who would fit in that scene.

"We've got no one else," Jackson said. "We're lean this year. You don't pitch, and we forfeit."

Griffin scowled at Jackson, feeling like he was losing the battle to control his evening. "You realize that's not my problem, don't you?"

Clare whacked him. "That's not nice."

"Sure is your problem." Jackson was undaunted. "You live here now."

"I rent here and I'm leaving—"

"But for now, this is your town." Jackson slammed his hand down on Griffin's shoulder. "See you at 6:30 for beer and warm up. First pitch is at seven."

"Beer before the game?" Now, that was a new one. He didn't even drink at a business dinner, let alone *before* trying to perform anything. Especially something he hadn't attempted in several decades.

Jackson winked at him. "Birch's Best sponsors us. It's our moral obligation."

Clare touched his arm. "Come on," she said. "It'll be fun. You'll totally impress Katie with your athletic prowess."

He laughed at that one. "I'm not so sure I have enough prowess left to impress a teenage girl." Damn. It had been a long time since he'd even thought about holding a ball in his hands.

She patted his stomach. "Look at that. Rock hard abs. You'll do fine."

Griffin's body tightened with sudden awareness at the feel of Clare's hand on his stomach. Rock hard abs, eh? Damn, he liked the sound of that. And he decided to ignore Jackson's snort of derision. "Well, I am a physical specimen," he admitted.

Clare's burst of laughter was a musical delight that made him feel like a king for being the cause of it.

"You'll have fun. Katie and I will cheer you on. The town will love seeing you play for them." She grabbed his hand and tugged his arm tighter around her shoulders, giving him a flirtatious look that pretty much would have brought him to his knees if he weren't the physical specimen that he was. "Anyone who pitches for Birch Crossing gets a free pass for indiscretions like murder. Public goodwill would be totally worth a couple hours of your time."

Ahh... now he got it. If he showed up, he wouldn't be such a pariah, and then, maybe, just maybe, Clare wouldn't get so much grief about him. If that made her feel better about the fact he wanted to toss her over his shoulder and cart her off to her bedroom, well, then, hell. How could he turn it down? "Okay," he said, not taking his gaze off her. "I'm in."

For her, he would do it.

CHAPTER FOURTEEN

THE HIGH SCHOOL band was playing.

Flags were waving.

Toddlers were running the bases.

A dozen grills were cooking up burgers, and three picnic tables were loaded with potato salad, fruit salad, coleslaw, baked beans and a dozen other homemade delights. A tent with a hand-printed sign proclaimed that Birch's Best had set up shop, and there were plenty of guys in red tee shirts and matching caps already camped around it, beer in one hand, baseball gloves in the other.

Griffin had to admit the atmosphere was pretty contagious, and he was feeling a little fired up to hit the ball field. It had been too damn long since he'd gripped a ball, given grief to teammates and flexed a little muscle, and there were even fans. Damned if he wasn't happy Clare had made him come.

"There's your group," Clare said, pointing at the beer tent. "Go suit up, and I'll see you later."

Griffin set the huge carton of cupcakes down on the beside the jewelry display Astrid was in the middle of arranging on a pink pashmina she'd spread on her half of the table. Clare had been a machine all afternoon, pumping out the cupcakes, and he and Katie had helped.

Turned out, his organized attorney had totally forgotten that the game was tonight, and she had failed to engage in her usual three-day pre-opening night cooking spree. Griffin had to admit that a high-stress cupcake deadline with flying icing, spinning Kitchen-Aides (not bad for a guy who didn't even know what a Kitchen-Aide was twelve hours ago), and tissue paper was one of the most entertaining afternoons he'd ever experienced.

With Clare and Katie around, it hadn't been that hard to fill the day without work. It had been a damned fine time, in fact. "You need help unpacking?"

Clare smiled and shooed him off. "Your team's waiting for you. Go play."

"All right." Griffin paused for a second, then he grabbed Clare's wrist and yanked her over to him and planted a kiss firmly on her pert little mouth.

She smacked him in the chest as she pulled away, but her eyes were dancing. "Griffin!"

"I'm a sports hero now. I need my legion of adoring fans." He winked at Astrid, who was cheerfully eavesdropping on their conversation.

Astrid had turquoise and gold ribbons woven into six tiny braids barely visible in her thick hair. Cute, but not nearly as adorable as Clare with her tossed-up pony tail and hoop earrings. Her faded jeans clung to her hips with tempting perfection, and he hadn't been able to take his eyes off the pink toenails peeking out from her braided sandals.

He raised his brows at Clare in a challenge. "Someday, maybe you won't be embarrassed for the world to know that I think you're sexy as hell."

Her cheeks turned fiery. "Go play baseball, for heaven's sake."

He didn't move, thoroughly enjoying teasing her and not feeling particularly inclined to walk away from her just yet. She was simply too damned intoxicating. "A kiss at home plate if I hit a home run?"

"No!"

"I'll kiss you," Astrid chimed in.

He didn't look away from Clare. "I want Clare."

Clare rolled her eyes, but her smile widened. "I'm beginning to figure that out."

"Griffin!" Jackson waved him over, and the rest of the guys on the team were giving him impatient looks. "Come on!"

"Right. Gotta run." Well aware that he had an audience of all the most athletic men in the town, men who might decide to make a move on Clare at some point, Griffin grabbed her around the waist and pulled her against him, kissing her again, firmly and deeply, leaving no doubt as to exactly who Clare belonged to, at least for tonight.

He was still grinning when he headed over to the boys.

"Oh, sweetheart, you're in trouble," Astrid said as Griffin walked away. "You're being hunted, big time."

"I know." Clare made a face as she began to unload the cupcakes from the box, her heart still thundering from Griffin's kiss. The man was incorrigible! How dare he attack her like that in public? But she couldn't keep from smiling to herself. It had felt kind of amazing to be claimed like that. Ed had never wanted her enough to claim her. She had to admit, it was pretty cool.

"Really?" Astrid raised her brows at Clare's grimace. "It's that disturbing to have a man like *him* after you?"

Clare finally burst out grinning, unable to contain her giddiness. "It's scaring me to death, but it's totally amazing. I've never felt like this."

Astrid smiled as she began arranging her silver charm bracelets on a blue tie-dyed cloth. Each one had a different inspirational word, thought up one night by the three friends during a wine and cupcake brainstorming fest. There were the typical ones of love, peace and dream, but a few creative ones had been thrown in. Surprisingly, "irreverence" and "be amused" had wound up to be two of Astrid's top sellers. "It's some kind of rush to be pursued by a man who makes your spine tingle," Astrid said as she slid the "snuggle" and "dance" bracelets over her own wrist. "You deserve to be pursued. You're very worthy."

"It's dangerous." Clare set a pink and gold tablecloth over her half of the table.

"Definitely."

"He'll break my heart."

Astrid set a glittery earring tree on the table. "I'm afraid it's looking that way." She straightened one of the pairs of earrings that had gotten twisted.

Clare arranged a gold tassel along the edges of her display. "And I'll never get over him if I sleep with him."

"Who could?"

Clare leaned on the table as she watched Griffin strip off his tee shirt so he could put on the team uniform. His body was hard and well-muscled, his shoulders broad. The man had a washboard stomach, and his biceps were ripped. Ed had been an eighteen-year-old actor. Muscles had not been part of his vocabulary.

But Griffin...he was all man.

Ed had wooed her with magic words and the excitement of an outsider bringing freedom to the life of a small town girl. He'd barely had to do anything to win her over. He'd been a boy with dreams and a used VW Beetle that had all his belongings in the back seat, and that had been enough for a seventeen-year-old innocent who wanted to spread her wings and fly.

Griffin, however, was power. He was strength. He was enough to break through the walls she'd so carefully constructed over the years. "He makes me laugh, Astrid."

"Oh..." Astrid put her hand over her heart, her brown eyes softening with understanding. "Really?"

"Yes. I didn't realize how much I missed laughing." Between the water fight and the baking, the afternoon with Griffin and Katie had been one of the most magical days she'd had in what felt like forever. He was such a flirt with both of them, and his humor had been so contagious. Part of the joy of the experience had been the unexpectedness of his sense of humor. She still marveled at the sight of that dimple whenever she saw it, so incongruous with the serious businessman he presented to the world.

Griffin looked over at her as he pulled the shirt over his head, and he tossed her a cheeky grin. She smiled back and gave him a small wave. "He's leaving me," she told Astrid, recalling his answer when she'd asked him whether he'd consider moving up to Maine to be with Brooke. "He's already promised he is."

Astrid sighed with understanding. "And how do you feel about that?"

She met her friend's gaze. "I don't think that's going to be enough to stop me."

Astrid gave her a long look. "You're willing to cope with the consequences if you sleep with him, knowing that he won't stay with you?"

"I know the facts, so I'm not lying to myself about what could happen between us long term. So, I guess, yes, I'm willing to accept the consequences." Oh, God. Was she really thinking about sleeping with him? Had she made her decision? Nervousness tingled down her spine, but at the same time, it felt right. So right. How could she walk away from the way he made her feel? Whether it was for a minute, or a day, or a week, didn't she deserve to enjoy it for however long she could have it? Her life had been so planned and so careful for fifteen years that the idea of releasing all the stringent constraints for a few moments was so exhilarating. What would it feel like to breathe freely again? To laugh with giddiness? To forget about rules and responsibility and obligations, and to simply live in the moment?

Astrid smiled and took her hands. "Then you must, without a doubt, let your spirit fly."

Clare's heart began to race, searching her friend's face for reassurance. "You really think so?"

Astrid nodded. "You'll survive whatever happens. You always do." She put her arm around Clare and squeezed. "And we'll be here to pick you up if it's harder than you think."

"You don't think I'm being crazy?"

"Of course you're crazy," Emma announced as she hurried up, towing a cart laden with paintings and display stands. Since it was a work day, her blonde hair was blown out and beautiful, reminding Clare of the confident, sensual woman she'd been before she'd left town. "I'm so sorry I'm late. Traffic was awful out of Portland, and I got off work late. What's Clare being crazy about?"

"The man on the mound," Astrid said, nodding at the softball field.

Emma turned to look at the game as Griffin jogged across the infield. "He's playing for the Pirates?" She dropped the handle of the cart onto the grass and set her hands on her hips as she watched him. "That's really sweet. I wouldn't have thought he's that type."

"I know." Clare looked around the ball field at all the

people still arriving, and those who had already set up blankets and beach chairs. Two towns of supporters, all cheering for the players. People were shouting Griffin's name, and he doffed his cap toward the crowd. His shoulders were relaxed as he lined up toward home plate, and he looked great in his black sweats and bright red tee shirt.

"He's like a chameleon," Emma said as she set up an easel. "He looks like he grew up here, and I bet he fits in just as well with his suit and fancy restaurants."

Clare pictured Griffin looking dashing for a night on the town, and she sighed. "I bet he looks great in a suit."

"Hard to believe that's the Slipper King." Astrid handed Clare a gold and silver peace necklace to wear. Astrid always had them well-adorned with her wares, claiming that it helped sell them if people saw them being worn. "I always thought the Slipper King should be old and fat, wearing a velour leisure suit and a toupee."

"Not a sexy, lean, muscle-bound hottie?" Emma set a painting of a loon and its baby on an easel, but Clare knew that the nature scenes weren't what really drove Emma. Somewhere in that wagon were the paintings where Emma poured her soul out, the bright colors, the angry lines, the confusion and the fear that leapt off the canvas and consumed anyone who saw them.

Clare fastened the necklace, as the Slipper King looked back over her shoulder and nodded right at her, publicly acknowledging her from his spot on center stage. "He's going to get me in such hot water with Eppie."

"So? Maybe a little hot water will be good for you." Astrid gave Emma two brooches to put on her shirt. One was engraved with the word "believe," and the other said "dream."

"Did you see who's up at bat?" Emma fastened the "believe" pin to her shirt, but handed the "dream" one to

Clare. "Didn't that guy hit four home runs off Bruce last year?"

"I think so." Clare pinned the brooch on as Griffin reared back for the first pitch. His body was so lithe and athletic, positively rippling with energy and control. It reminded her of how he'd seemed that night on the mountain. All male. So in control. So powerful.

The softball spun toward the plate, and the batter took a hard swing at it. The bat connected, and suddenly the ball exploded, throwing white shreds and remnants all over the batter, the catcher and the infield.

"Oh my God!" Clare burst out laughing. "He threw a grapefruit!"

The crowd erupted into roars of delight as Griffin pointed at Jackson, who was on second base. People leapt to their feet, cheering, as Jackson took a bow, and then pointed at Griffin, who did the same.

"That's so funny!" Astrid laughed. "I can't believe he did that! That was beautiful!"

"That's hilarious," Emma said. "We need more of that kind of thing up here." She grinned at Clare. "Okay the man has my vote. Do him, enjoy him and have a great time. Worry about the future later."

Clare grinned, her heart dancing with joy and excited nervousness. How could she fear a man who would throw a citrus fruit instead of a softball? "I agree." And she did. She really did! Terrifying, but oh, so liberating.

Griffin jogged to home plate and high-fived the batter, who was picking grapefruit off his face. They gave a manly hug with some fist pounding on each other's backs, and then Griffin waved his cap to the still-roaring crowd as he loped back to the mound. He had a shit-eating grin on his face, and held up his glove as the catcher threw another ball to him.

The batter gestured for the ball, and Griffin tossed it to

him. The batter looked at it, nodded, then threw it back, apparently satisfied that it was a real ball this time.

"Game on," the ump shouted.

Clare was still laughing as she pulled another tray of cupcakes out of the box.

"That was so cool!" Katie came racing up, wearing a Pirates cap and a hot pink tee shirt with the Pirates logo on it. "Did you see that? The grapefruit was my idea. I told him to do it. I can't believe he did it! He promised me he would, but I didn't think he would, you know? Because this is such a big game. But he did it for me! He threw a grapefruit for me."

Clare laughed at her daughter's antics, delighted by how happy she seemed. *Thank you, Griffin, for giving her that joy.* "You're a troublemaker, my dear."

"I know!" Katie skipped off, shouting at Sara, who was across the field, yelling that it was her idea.

"Well, well." Eppie walked up, sporting a Pirates visor that had been accented with two fresh violets across the bill. "A grapefruit? On the biggest game of the season?"

Clare grinned at the older lady, too happy to let Eppie bring her down. "He did it for Katie. Isn't that sweet?"

Eppie frowned at her. "Clare—"

"Oh, lighten up, Eppie." She handed the older woman a cupcake. "He's just playing softball. Give him a break."

She saw Astrid and Emma exchange surprised looks, and she smiled to herself. How had she been so scared of Eppie for so long? Right now, she just looked like a little old lady with a life so empty that she filled it by interfering in other people's lives.

"I saw him kiss you," Eppie accused.

Clare grinned. "And it was amazing."

"Clare!" Eppie looked shocked. "You aren't thinking—"

"Eppie. The man throws grapefruits. How bad can he be?"

Eppie set her hands on her hips, tossing her head so

fiercely she dislodged one of the violets, and it fluttered to the grass. "I'm just looking out for you and Katie."

"I know, and I appreciate it, but right now, I'm going to look out for myself all on my own, okay?" She picked up the flower and held it out to the older woman. "You can pick up my shattered remains after he breaks my heart, okay?"

Eppie snatched the violet from her hand. "He will, you know."

Clare looked across the field as Griffin jogged back to the bench, chatting with Jackson and a couple of the other guys. Some of her elation faded. "I know."

"And you're okay with it?" Eppie challenged.

She met Eppie's gaze. "I think I am, yes."

The older woman frowned, and some of her hostility faded. "But why?" she asked, with genuine curiosity. "I don't understand."

Griffin nodded at Clare again, keeping contact with her, and she waved back. "Because he makes me laugh."

"Ah..." Eppie followed her gaze and studied Griffin, a thoughtful gleam in her eyes. "Does he, indeed?"

"He does."

"Well, that's something, I suppose." But she didn't sound all that impressed. "I need a beer." She helped herself to two more cupcakes and then sauntered off to the beer tent, abandoning her job of haranguing Clare surprisingly quickly. It was so unlike Eppie to just cut herself off like that. What was going on in Eppie's mind *now*?

"Hot damn," Astrid said, her hands on her hips. "You actually stood up to Eppie."

Clare grinned. "I did, didn't I?"

"How do you feel?" Emma asked.

"Great, actually." Great...and a little terrified, confused and uncertain. But definitely, there was a sliver of great in there, and she would take it.

"Wow." Emma gazed out at the field. "I think I need to get myself a Griffin. Who knew a man could actually make you feel better, instead of worse?"

"Well, you can't have this one." Smiling to herself, Clare resumed unloading the cupcakes from the box. "This one is mine."

And he was.

Astrid looked at her with concern. "He's leaving, Clare. Remember that."

"I know." A ripple of fear tugged at her heart, penetrating her good mood. "I know."

AN HOUR LATER, Clare was taking a shortcut behind the ice cream truck with some bottles of water for Astrid and Emma when strong arms caught her around the waist and yanked her against the side of the truck.

She yelped as Griffin pinned her against the rainbow-colored metal panels, giving her a predatory look. Sweat was beading on his forehead, his muscles straining against the tee shirt, his whiskers rugged and untamed on his jaw. He grinned, his eyes dark with a burning desire that went straight to her belly as he braced his palms on either side of her head, trapping her. "You trying to hide from me, woman?"

"Nice home run," she said, viscerally aware of the cold metal panels against her back and the raw strength of his body as he leaned in toward her.

"You promised me a kiss." His voice was husky and low, vibrating with such heat that her belly clenched. "A kiss for the homerun. I came to claim it."

She flattened her palms against his chest to push him away, but instead her fingers dug into the hard muscle, as if she could draw him closer. "I never promised anything." Was

193

she really getting accosted behind the ice cream truck? She felt like she was sixteen again, and it was a heady, delicious sensation.

"Huh. I'm slipping then. I can't believe I forgot to get a commitment on that." His eyes flashing with wicked intent, he came at her anyway, taking her mouth in a kiss that was hot, demanding and burning with decadent promise.

All her resistance melted, and she threw her arms around his neck, kissing him back just as fiercely. He growled and locked his arms around her waist, hauling her against him as he turned up the assault, kissing her with such ferocity her whole body came alive with the need for him, for his kiss, for his touch—

A loud roar went up from the crowd, reminding Clare of where they were. What was she doing? Desperately, she pulled back, shoving at him. "Stop it." Breathless, Clare leaned her head back against the metal truck, trying to regroup. "Don't you have to get back to the game?"

He nuzzled her neck and pressed his hips even more tightly against hers. "We're at bat, and I was just up last inning. I have a minute." He growled softly and bit her shoulder. "I forgot how sports get me worked up. Sports, beer, and male bonding do wonders for a guy's libido."

She started giggling, desire leaping through her. Damn the man for being so irresistible! How could he be getting her this worked up at a family picnic? "What are you, eighteen?"

"I feel like it." He kissed her again, and her whole body trembled with longing as he tore through her defenses, stopping only when she was hopelessly tangled around him and panting for more.

He grinned, resting his forehead against hers while they both tried to catch their breath. "Tonight, Clare," he said quietly. "If your door is shut, I'm coming in anyway."

Her belly tightened with sudden desire, raw terror and giddy anticipation. "That's rather presumptuous of you."

He pulled back, looking steadily into her eyes. "If you don't want me to come in, lock the door. Otherwise, I'm coming in. Get it?"

She swallowed. Here was her chance to tell him she wasn't going to get involved. To deflect his advances before he consumed her good sense. "Griffin—"

"Dad?"

Griffin jerked away from Clare so quickly she almost fell down.

Standing ten feet away, a chocolate ice cream cone in her hand, was a girl Katie's age. She had a shocked look on her face, and her eyes were the deep, dark brown of Griffin's.

His daughter.

CHAPTER FIFTEEN

GRIFFIN COULDN'T BELIEVE how tall Brooke was. How grown-up. How beautiful. Her brown hair was long now, tossed over her shoulders. She was wearing crisp new jeans, ones bearing the logo of In Your Face's stiffest competitor. Her shirt was like Katie's, a little too snug, and she was wearing blue eye shadow. She was almost a woman, this girl. This amazing girl. *His daughter.* For a split second, his throat tightened and his chest constricted, and all he wanted to do was tear across the grass and scoop her up in his arms like he'd done so many times when she was little.

He even took a step toward her, and she stiffened, freezing him right where he was. "Brooke," he said. He had no idea what to say. He didn't want to scare her, or drive her away. Could he hug her? Tell her he missed her? He hadn't devised a plan yet. He had no strategy. Just an ache in his chest. "What are you doing here?" he finally asked, at a loss of how to approach her, how to bridge the void.

"Dan's brother plays for the Angels," Brooke said. She stared at him as if she'd never seen him before. "You threw a grapefruit."

Griffin hesitated. Was that bad? "Um... yeah..."

"But you would never throw a grapefruit. You would never even play softball." Brooke's brow was furrowed. "All you do is work. I don't understand why you're here. Playing softball." Her gaze slithered to Clare. "Kissing a woman in public."

Was that good or bad? Griffin swore under his breath. He had no idea what to say. How to respond.

"Your dad is changing," Clare said gently. "He doesn't always work anymore."

"Really?" Brooke looked at Clare. "So, he changed for you? And not for us?"

"No." Griffin stepped forward. He had to take control of the conversation. He had to take advantage of this moment, this chance to talk to her. "Listen, Brooke, I miss you. I'm up here because I want you to come home with me. Back to Boston."

Brooke gave him a look of disgusted disbelief. "And do what all day while you work? Who will do my homework with me? Who will come to my school play? Will you?"

Griffin ground his jaw. "I'll try—"

"You always *try*." Brooke's jaw jutted out in that familiar look he'd seen so many times, and suddenly she didn't look like a young woman anymore. She looked like the little girl he'd held on his knee and read stories to. Young. Breakable. Fragile. "But work always comes first with you. The softball is a lie." She looked at Clare, anger flashing in her eyes. "Don't believe it. He'll burn you."

"Brooke!" Griffin reached for her, but she sidestepped his attempt.

"Dad." Brooke took a deep breath. "I want to change my name."

Griffin frowned, trying to adjust to the change in topic. "You don't like Brooke?"

"No, I don't like Friesé." She lifted her chin. "I want to

change my last name to Burwell. I want to be Brooke Burwell."

Griffin felt like something sharp had just been plunged into his chest, and he gripped his ribs against the sudden pain. He was barely aware of Clare moving closer, but when she slipped her hand in his, he gripped it tightly, as if she could keep the world from tipping over right in front of him. "Did Mom tell you to say that?"

"It's not Mom," Brooke said. "I didn't even ask her. She doesn't even know."

"Then why—"

"Mom, Dan and the twins are all Burwells, and I'm not. I want to be like them. I want to be part of the family."

"Twins?" he echoed, his voice like some distant sound in his pounding head. "What twins?"

She hesitated. "You didn't know Mom had twins in February?"

"Shit, no." Hillary had babies?

"Well, she did, and now I have two sisters." Brooke smiled, and he saw genuine affection on her face. "I have a family now, and I want to belong. I need to change my name. I want to be a Burwell like the rest of them."

Griffin shook his head, fighting desperately against the feeling that the world was crumbling beneath his feet, struggling for a handhold to keep his head above water. "No, absolutely not. You're my daughter—"

"I don't want to be your daughter! I want to be Dan's!" Brooke stomped her foot. "You never let me be happy. If you cared about me *at all,* you would let me be happy! Go back to Boston. Leave me alone!" Then she whirled around and ran, disappearing around the front of the truck.

"Brooke!" Griffin sprinted after her, but when he rounded the bumper, he couldn't see her. Too many kids playing, people chatting, bodies moving everywhere. He searched the crowds, but he couldn't find her. "Brooke!" He bellowed her name, desperate to find her.

But she was gone.

"Griffin." Clare touched his arm as she ran up beside him. "Wait a sec."

"I have to find her. I can't let her go like that." He started to run again. He felt like his dream. Panicked. Crazed. Hopeless. The crowds were too thick, too many people. Too much noise. Somewhere out there was his daughter, and he couldn't find her. He started grabbing stranger's arms. "Where's my daughter? Where did she go?"

People looked at him, but no one pointed the way. The ocean was closing down on her, taking her away, sweeping her into its depths. "Brooke!"

"Griffin!" Clare jumped in his path and grabbed his arms. "Listen to me!"

"I can't. I have to find Brooke—"

"By playing softball and throwing that grapefruit, you showed Brooke a side of you she's never seen," Clare said, cutting off his protests. "You made progress, Griffin! You have to let her absorb it! You can't force it right now! Stop!"

You can't force it. That was like what Norm had said. He looked at Clare desolately. "I can't lose her. I might not ever find her again."

"She lives one town away," Clare said gently. "You can find her anytime."

"But I can't. I can't get in to see her." He searched the crowds, but no Brooke. No daughter. "She's gone."

"She's not gone," Clare said. "She's in that crowd, and she's watching what her dad does right now."

"So, I have to find her then—"

"No. You have to show her that she can trust you."

"She can. I swear to God, she can. I can't lose her." His throat was dry, his palms sweaty. "I can't."

"I know." Clare set her hands on his face, and the feel of her skin against his was like a shot of calmness and sanity in his crazed mind. "But she's a fifteen-year-old girl and you can't force her. Go play softball, and show her that you're different than the dad she remembers."

He gripped Clare's wrists, holding her hands to his cheeks, afraid she would let go. "You think it'll work? It has to work."

"Griff!" Jackson shouted. "Come on! We're back on the field."

"If you let down your team, she'll see that," Clare said urgently. "Softball is important in this town. She knows that. She'll be watching to see whether people can count on you."

Griffin swore under his breath and clasped his hands on top of his head, trying to think, trying frantically to strategize, to make the right move. Go after Brooke, or let her go? "I don't know."

"You both need time to process," Clare said. "You don't want to say things you'll regret, and you don't want to force her to do the same. Go play ball. Show her that you're the kind of guy who spends the evening at a family picnic instead of work. She needs to see that, Griffin. She really does."

He closed his eyes. He could feel the truth of Clare's words, penetrating his need to rip the place apart to find his daughter. "She can't change her name without my permission, can she?" He opened his eyes and looked at Clare, the attorney. "Can she?"

"No, Griffin, she can't," Clare said. "It's going to be okay. You're going to work this out. She can't disown you or change her name."

"She's still my daughter?" His voice cracked, but he couldn't help it. "You're sure?"

Clare smiled. "She's still your daughter."

"Griff!" Jackson jogged up. "Come on, man. Talk to Clare later. We've got a game!"

"Go play softball." Clare stood on her tiptoes and lightly pressed her lips to his, telling him that she accepted him exactly as he was, that he wasn't some awful bastard. "She needs to see that."

"Yeah, okay." He took a breath, trying to calm his mind. "If you see her, don't let her leave. I want to talk to her after the game."

"I'll do my best."

"Come on!"

Reluctantly, he let Jackson coerce him back to the field. But he never stopped scanning the crowd for his daughter. Was Clare right? Was she still there? He had to know.

He was already on the mound, softball in hand, preparing for the first pitch, when he finally found Brooke.

She was sitting on a red and black plaid blanket, holding a small baby in her arms. She was bent over the child, her face soft and happy as she spoke to it. Hillary was leaning over Brooke's shoulder, and she was also smiling at the baby.

His ex-wife was wearing a fleece, jeans and a pony tail, and she had a tender expression on her face. That was the woman who'd redefined cold as a household condition? The woman who'd hated him for his work schedule, but spent more money on designer clothing than he'd spent on the mortgage? He'd never seen that tender look on her face. Not ever. Not even when Brooke had been born. Who was she? Why had Burwell brought that out in her when he hadn't?

And Brooke... Griffin couldn't help but smile at the way she was wiggling the baby's nose. Brooke would be a good big sister. She really would.

On Brooke's other side was Burwell, holding another baby in his mutton arms. The behemoth had a pink burp cloth over his shoulder and was administering a bottle like he knew how to use it. Was that what it took to be a man? A husband? A father? Griffin had never held a bottle in his life or changed a diaper, and it had never even occurred to him to do it.

The five of them were huddled together, oblivious to the outside world, surrounded by baby blankets, rattles, and a picnic dinner.

Griffin felt his world sinking as he stared at the scene.

Who the hell was he kidding?

If that was what Brooke wanted, he couldn't compete with that.

"Griff." Jackson jogged over from second base. "Hey, man. What's going on?"

Griffin couldn't stop staring at the scene, and Jackson followed his gaze. "That's my daughter and my ex-wife." The words felt thick. Ex-daughter? Is that what he should say? Mother of hell.

Jackson whistled softly. "Son of a bitch. That sucks."

Griffin almost grinned at the intensity in Jackson's words. The man got it. "Well said."

Jackson clapped his hand on his shoulder. "There's only one thing to do, my man."

"What's that?" Go over and beat the hell out of Burwell?

Jackson held up the softball, then slammed it into Griffin's glove. "Kick the shit out of their softball team, of course."

Griffin laughed, some of the tension easing from his chest. "You think that'll work?"

"Crushing your opponent's hopes and dreams? Yep. It's the only way to go." Jackson slammed his hand down on Griffin's shoulder. "You good?"

Griffin gripped the stitching of the ball. "Yeah, I'm good."

And as Jackson returned to the base paths, Griffin turned his back on the perfect family and eyed the player at bat. But he couldn't pitch. He couldn't throw the ball. He couldn't think of anything but the family sitting in left field.

So, he turned and looked back at the one table he'd been drawn to all night. He had to see Clare. He had to connect with her. He had to feel her.

And there she was, with her cute pony tail, her display of amazing cupcakes and the smile she reserved just for him. And unlike his daughter or his ex-wife, Clare's attention was focused fully on him.

He jerked his chin at the Burwell clan, and he saw her gaze swivel toward them, taking in the situation. Jackson was yelling at him to pitch, the other guys were giving him grief, but he waited, unable to summon any action until he heard from Clare.

Clare knew how to be a mom. Clare knew how to love her daughter. Clare's daughter loved her. If Clare wanted him to pitch, then he would. He trusted her to know what was right.

Clare put her hand over her heart and nodded at him. *Play ball, Griffin,* she was saying. *Play ball for your daughter.*

So he did.

For Clare.

For his daughter.

For the Pirates of Birch Crossing.

~

GRIFFIN LOST.

The game.

The chance to talk to his daughter.

The night.

Brooke and the Burwells had left during the ninth inning while Griffin was on the mound. He hadn't been able to go after them, his focus had snapped, and he'd relinquished the game-winning run while his daughter drove off in an extended cab pickup.

And now it was well after midnight as Griffin pulled his truck into the driveway of Clare's house and leaned back against the seat. Beers with the guys hadn't helped his mood, and now he was back at the rambling farm house he was calling home.

The house was dark. Clare and Katie were in bed.

What was he doing playing around in Maine? Maybe Brooke was right. Maybe he should go back to Boston. But the thought tanked his mood even further.

Forget it. He wasn't going back. Not without his daughter.

He needed to focus. He needed to get his work going. He needed to get his trump card into alignment, and he needed it fast. Brooke had been wearing those fashion jeans. She was into them. He needed that company for his daughter. So he pulled his phone out of his pocket and dialed his partner.

Phillip answered on the first ring, always available no matter what time of day, just like Griffin. "Good news on Brooke?" he asked.

"No." Griffin got out of the truck and headed up the stairs. "What's the status on In Your Face? Did you get answers to my queries yet?"

"Still working on it, but I'm hearing rumors that I'm trying to track down."

"What rumors?" Griffin pulled open the screen door and walked inside. The house was quiet and still, just like his condo, and just like his house had been when he'd been married. Hillary and Brooke had always been asleep by the time he got home. Not that he'd expected Clare to wait up for him, but after today, yeah, well, he'd thought maybe Clare would be different.

But her door was firmly shut, and the light under her door

was off. He was living the same life, just in different surroundings.

"They told me that they've got other interest," Phillip said, "and that they expect an offer in the next twenty-four hours."

Griffin poked his head in the kitchen. Empty. Dark. No desserts on the counters. "Do they have a legit offer or are they just trying to drive up the price?"

"I'll know by morning. I have some leads on it. But if they do get that offer, it changes the playing field."

When Phillip told him the price, Griffin slammed the door of the kitchen shut in frustration as he headed back to the hall. "They're not worth that." Not yet. They'd be worth ten times that amount after Griffin and Phillip took them and ran the business for five years. But today? No.

"To us, yeah, but to others they might be."

"Well, maybe the others see something we don't." He had to buy that company. He had to find justification to pay that price. It was a teen jean company, and he had to get it for Brooke. "I'll go through the files again—"

"No chance," Phillip interrupted. "We're not going to offer at that price."

"We're not letting this company get away—"

"At that price, we sure are. There are a thousand businesses around," Phillip said. "There's that one for high tech kitty litter. Do you know how many tons of litter are sold each year?"

"Kitty litter? We're not buying kitty litter. I want In Your Face." Would Brooke come back to him for kitty litter? No chance. In Your Face was the only one that would suffice. "We sold Free Love to position ourselves to move on this deal. In Your Face is our focus. We're going to make it happen."

"If the price goes up, you're on your own," Phillip said. "I'm not biting."

Griffin knew that it would take a hefty investment from both of them to buy it. He couldn't swing it himself. No matter how heavily he leveraged himself. "Then preempt with an offer tonight. Lowball with a twelve hour cutoff."

"We don't have the paperwork in order. Are you losing your mind up there in the woods? You actually want us to fork over a few hundred million without ironclad paperwork?"

"Shit." Maybe he really was losing perspective. Griffin flexed his hand as he walked down the hall toward his room. Phillip was more aggressive than he was, and it was Griffin who usually had to pull him back. If Phillip was saying no, then it was a no. "See what you can do to make it happen."

"I'm on it. I'll call tomorrow. Get some sleep. You sound strung out. Later."

Griffin hung up the phone as he walked into his room. He slammed his fist into his hand as he walked to the window and hauled it open, letting the night breeze blow as he braced himself on the window frame.

He needed this company for Brooke.

In Your Face was cutting edge in the teen market, especially with girls. In five years, every female from ages twelve to forty would know the name and own the label, and anyone associated with it would be on the front lines of the fashion industry. He'd had visions of Brooke getting involved with the business. Meeting with the celebrity endorsers. Working with designers. Injecting her own vision into the company that she would help build. If she came to work with him, and got to help direct the creative side of the company, then she'd be with him, and they'd share his work together.

Together, they would create the Friesé family legacy.

That was how he was going to compete with Family

Burwell. It was all he had to offer her, but the way it was looking, it might not happen. He gripped the window sill and stared out at the dark night. What in hell's name was he going to do now?

Maybe designer jeans could compete with baby sisters and an ever-present dad, but without them? He had nothing.

He looked over at his desk, at his computer that had always been his weapon of power. It had no edge tonight. Nothing in there could change the fact that his daughter was slipping through his fingers—

There was a cupcake next to his computer.

Griffin smiled ruefully. Because a cupcake would solve his problems. Clare was naive if she thought that would make a difference. What did she know? She was a —

A mom.

Of a teenage girl who adored her.

Clare knew what it took to win over a daughter. She'd shown that tonight already at the game. *Clare was his ace.* Not In Your Face. Clare.

He pivoted on his heel and strode across the room, but just as he grabbed the doorknob, he remembered what time it was. After midnight. She'd already put the kibosh on the night by going to bed, closing her door and turning out the lights, a clear message that she wanted her space.

He should respect it. Morning was soon enough for answers.

He stood there for exactly three seconds. Screw it. Morning was too far away.

He was going to invade her bedroom and wake her up.

CHAPTER SIXTEEN

CLARE HEARD Griffin's door open.

She heard the thud of his boots on the hardwood floor as he walked down the hall.

Toward the bathroom?

He'd already walked past her door when he'd gotten home, shattering the hopes that had arisen when she'd heard his car door slam.

If he walked by again without stopping, it was for the best. For the best. For the best.

Then his footsteps stopped outside her door.

Her heart began to race, and she pulled the covers up to her chin. Why had she worn her lace camisole to bed tonight? It was far too suggestive! He would think she was some slut who would—

The knob turned and Clare jerked upright in the bed, clutching the quilt to her chest. She couldn't do this. She couldn't do this. She couldn't—

The door opened, and Griffin's large frame filled her doorway. The hall light was off, and the moon's rays didn't reach that far, so all she could see was his dark outline, a shadowed man hovering at her threshold. Nervous anticipation raced through her, and her heart hammered in her chest.

Would he kiss her right away? Would it be a silent seduction? Or would he ask if he could come in? Would he make love to her with her clothes on or off? Would he stay in her bed and hold her afterwards? Would she even know what to do? Was she supposed to touch him? Was—

"I need to talk to you about my daughter." His voice was heavy, serious and utterly devoid of any romantic intentions whatsoever. "I need your advice about her."

"Your daughter?" Clare let her breath out with a whoosh, stunned disappointment racing through her. "You're here for parenting advice?" She felt no relief at having been spared, just raw, aching dismay. Which was silly. She should be grateful that she no longer had the chance to make a choice she would regret. But she wasn't. Not at all.

God, she was a fool.

"Yeah." Griffin walked into the room, left the door open, and pulled up a chair next to the bed.

Not on the bed. He could have sat *on* the bed to get advice from a slightly panicked female who was wearing barely any clothing. But no, he'd pulled up a *chair*. And left the door *open*.

And so, the fifteen year drought continued.

With a heavy sigh, Clare flopped back in bed and rolled onto her side to face him. He was in the light from the moon now, and all her disappointment vanished, chased away by her concern for the strain on his face. What was she doing, worrying about sex when Griffin was so stressed?

She touched his arm gently. "I'm so sorry about today with Brooke." He'd looked absolutely stricken when Brooke had made her request to change her name, and Clare had wanted to hug him and, at the same time, grab Brooke and order her to get over her self-pity.

Katie would have given anything for a father who loved her, no matter how imperfect he was. And Brooke was shutting her dad out. The girl had no idea how lucky she was.

Griffin ran his hand through his hair, spiking it up and erasing the dent from his ball cap. "How do you get Katie to love you?"

Clare was almost tempted to laugh at the absurdity of the question, except that she could tell he was absolutely serious. So, she took a moment to think about his inquiry, and finally gave the only answer that she could come up with. "I love her."

He made an impatient gesture with his hands. "But what else?"

Her heart softened for his frustration. "That's it, Griffin. That's all it takes."

"No, that's not right." He stood up and paced to her window, and Clare rolled onto her other side so she could face him. "There's something else. There has to be."

She wished she had better answers for him, but she felt like she was barely hanging on with her own daughter. "I'm not the best mom, Griffin. If you asked Katie, I'm sure she would have a long list of my failings. She hates me sometimes, but she always loves me. Because I love her."

He leaned on the window frame, staring out at the trees. "I talked to Katie this afternoon, and she's so mad at you for forcing her to go to MIT, but at the game, I saw her hanging out with you all happy."

Clare felt the familiar tension at the thought of the ongoing argument with her daughter. "I wish she would just accept MIT. It will be good for her."

"She hates it, yet you insist on it, and she still loves you." Griffin faced her, his brow furrowed in concentration, as if enough analysis could give him the magical answers to parenting. "How do you do it? You weren't here today when she came home so upset, and yet she doesn't blame you for working instead of being there for her. Why?"

"Wait a second." Clare held up her hand to stop the conversation. "Katie was upset today? About what?"

Griffin waved his hand dismissively. "Jeremy doesn't like her, but that's not the point—"

Clare sat up. "Jeremy kissed her, but doesn't like her? Was she really upset?"

"Yeah, she was crying, and looking for you, but again, that's not the point—"

"She was crying?" Guilt coursed through Clare. "So she likes him? My poor girl!" She swung her feet out of bed. "I need to go talk to her. She never told me that tonight. She adores him. How can he do that to her? Why are boys like that? Why do they mess with girls? Why?"

She was almost out the door when Griffin caught her arm. "Clare."

"What?" She tried to pull herself away, but his grip was unyielding. Dammit. There were times when a strong man was just not convenient. "I need to go talk to her."

"She's okay, now." He shut the door firmly, blocking her exit. "Don't wake her up. Let her sleep."

"But—"

"We talked about it," he said as he flipped the lock on the door. "She's fine."

"Really? Are you so sure about that?" Clare eyed him, trying to figure out the best way to duck around him and make it to Katie's room before he could stop her. "Exactly how fine is fine?"

He gave her an amused look. "Well, you saw her all afternoon, during the water fight and at the game. How did she look to you?"

"Um..." Clare thought back to the mischievous grin on her daughter's face when she'd dumped the water on her, and her delighted skip as she'd raced across the field at the game. "Well, good, I guess," she acknowledged reluctantly. "Happy, even."

"See? She's fine. Now about Brooke—"

"Yeah, okay, maybe she's all right." Clare studied Griffin with new interest. "What did you say to her?" Heaven knew it wasn't easy to take Katie from tears to joy.

He shrugged impatiently, as if what he'd said was of little importance. "That she was beautiful and that Jeremy is like the rest of us males, and he's too afraid to make a move, but he's silently pining for her. I told her that whenever she looked at him, she should just remember that he thinks she's gorgeous, which is why he kissed her in the first place, but that he's too pathetic to make a move. Stuff like that."

"Oh." Clare's heart loosened. That was a good message. "And she believed you?"

"Yeah." Griffin grinned. "I think my explanation of the male stupidity had clout since I'm a male, too."

"She always argues with me when I tell her she's beautiful," Clare mused. "She says that I'm her mom so I have to say that." She smiled. "But she believed you because you don't owe her anything."

Griffin smiled, and he looked pleased. "She is beautiful."

"I know." Clare patted Griffin's cheek, her tension about Katie's well-being fading into appreciation for the fact that Griffin had been there to take care of the situation. "See? You have what it takes to be a good dad. Pulling a teenage girl out of boy-tears is not an easy task."

His smile faded. "I got lucky."

"You don't get lucky when it comes to tears. You have to be good." Her bare feet were getting cold from standing on the wood, so Clare walked over to her bed and perched on the edge of it, tucking her feet beneath her. "You did good, Griffin. And thank you." She managed a smile, though she still felt bad about not being home when Katie needed her. "It alleviates my guilt of not being here to help her."

Griffin rubbed his jaw, and she could see him contemplating. After a moment he came and sat beside her, the mattress dipping under his weight. "Here's the thing I don't get," he said. "You were at work and not here for her, and yet she wasn't mad at you for it. She didn't care that I was the one she had to talk to. How do you swing that?"

Clare hugged her arms to ward off the chill coming from her open window. The spring warmth of earlier in the day had faded, and the night was too chilly for a camisole unless she was under the covers or baking in the kitchen. "I guess it's what I said before. She knows I love her."

"That's it?" Griffin looked frustrated again. "It can't be that simple. Brooke knows how I feel about her."

Clare rubbed her arms, thinking back to the discussion by the ice cream truck. "How do you feel about her?"

"She's my daughter. I want her back."

"Do you love her?"

Griffin glared at her. "Of course I do."

She smiled at his intensity. Yes, of course this man loved his daughter. It was so obvious. "Then let her see it, and that will be enough."

"By giving a bottle to a baby? Is that what it takes to be a good guy?"

Clare laughed. "No, you goof. By actually telling her that you love her, and by showing her that you see her as her own person and appreciate who she is becoming. Show her that you love her without conditions, without limits and without judgments."

Griffin looked frustrated. "That doesn't make sense. How do I do that?"

"You'll figure it out. It will come with time." Sensing his tension, Clare scooted behind him and began to rub his shoulders. His muscles were taut, stretched to their limits across his broad back. "Here's the thing with girls. You can't mold them, and you can't force them. You have to give them space to grow and respond."

"I'm not patient." Griffin bowed his head, resting his forearms on his thighs, accepting her touch.

Clare laughed. "Really? I never would have guessed it." She found a knot by his right shoulder blade and dug in, trying to loosen it. "Your muscles are a lot tougher to loosen than Katie's."

"I would hope so," he grunted.

"Such a male comment. If you were a woman, you'd be apologizing for hurting my fingers with your beefcake back," she teased.

"Yeah?" He turned around to face her, sliding out of her grasp. "As opposed to a man who would take your sore fingers and massage them until you forgot about the pain." His eyes hooded and dark, he lifted her hand and began to rub her fingers, one by one, inch by inch.

Um...yeah. How good did that feel? "I wasn't actually sore yet," she said.

"Good." He dug his fingers into her palm, loosening the tension. "I wouldn't be much of a man if I let you get hurt taking care of me."

Clare swallowed, viscerally aware of the fact they were both on her bed now, and they weren't talking about kids anymore. "So, anyway," she said, her voice wavering slightly. "As I said at the game, now that Brooke has seen this more human side of you, she won't forget it. She'll start to wonder if there's a chance you could be the dad she wants, and she'll need to know more. You're on the right path."

Griffin said nothing for a moment, and the only sound was their breathing as he worked his fingers up her forearm.

"I envy your relationship with Katie," he finally said.

Clare smiled. "Thank you."

"I never saw the beauty in Hillary and Brooke's connection, but I feel it in yours." He was up to her biceps now, his wrist dangerously close to her breast.

"Um..." She couldn't really focus on his words anymore. Should she stop him? Had he even noticed he was encroaching on her breasts? Or was it just some absent movement while he thought about kids and—

He caught her chin suddenly, turned her face towards his. "You bring out a side in me I've never seen before."

Oh...he had that look on his face. The intense, dark look that made her toes curl up and her heart start to hammer way too fast. "That's good?"

"Yeah." He rubbed his thumb over her lower lip. "You make me think there's a chance I could be a better guy than everyone else thinks I am." He smiled. "Thank you for that gift, Clare Gray."

"You're welcome," she whispered. "You are a good man."

"I know you think so." And then he bent his head and kissed her.

Clare went utterly still at the feel of Griffin's lips on hers. The kiss was tender and gentle, not scary, not demanding. He lightly cupped the back of her head, his grip warm but loose, giving her space to get away.

But she didn't believe it. He was a man. She was a woman. They were in her bed. He would make his move at any moment. What should she do? She hadn't *really* decided yet whether or not to sleep with him. She had to know now, because he was going to make his move. Ack!

But he kept kissing her the same way. One hand still

gently sifting her hair. The other braced on the bed by her hip. He wasn't trying anything more. Just kissing.

Slowly, she began to relax. She allowed herself to notice the softness of his lips, the prickle of his whiskers against her skin, the taste of chocolate on his tongue. "You ate the cupcake," she whispered.

"Of course I did." He laid his hand on the side of her neck and nibbled on the corner of her mouth. "It's like eating heaven."

She smiled beneath his kiss. "Thank you."

"No, thank you." He kissed her again, and she kissed him back with a little more confidence.

Anticipation began to build inside her, unfurling deep in her belly, and she tentatively placed her hand on his shoulder. His muscles flexed beneath her hand, the rough cotton of his tee shirt a flimsy barrier between them. Heat rose from his skin, and she felt the power harnessed so thoroughly in his strong frame.

He deepened the kiss, coaxing her lips apart, and when she acquiesced, his grip tightened in her hair, holding her to him as he kissed her.

Slowly, he began to ease her back onto the bed, still kissing her. She gripped his shoulders, allowing him to move her, even as she trembled with nervousness and excitement. The moment her head hit the pillow, he pulled back, studying her intently.

She swallowed, her skin prickling with awareness.

Then, without asking permission or checking in with her, he sat up, grabbed his tee shirt and hauled it over his head. She could barely suppress a little squeal as she caught her first real look at his body.

His chest was lightly covered in dark hair, his muscles strong, and his belly flat. Dark nipples blended with his skin, and his sweats were low across his hips. His biceps were flexed, and she could see the strength even in his sinewy forearms.

Griffin was solid male, pure strength, absolute masculinity. Not a boy, like Ed had been. Griffin was a man.

"It's been a long time since—" She hesitated.

He smiled, the kind of possessive predatory expression that made her whole body clench. "I know."

"Am I that obvious?" Was there something she was supposed to be doing that she wasn't? She really hadn't made love that many times with Ed before he'd died. "I'm sorry—"

"No." He kicked off his shoes, then stretched out beside her, and placed his palm on her belly. "You're beautiful."

She watched his hand rise and fall as she breathed. The intimacy was incredible. That quiet touch below her belly button. Not going for the gold. Just connecting in a way that only lovers who were at peace with each other would take the time to do. "I'm nervous."

"I know." He kissed her gently, continuing the kiss until she finally began to kiss him back. "You can touch me," he whispered. "Anywhere you want."

She managed a jittery laugh. "I don't know—"

"I do." He took her hand and placed it on his chest. "Like that."

She tangled her fingers in the dark hairs. She could feel the striations of his muscles beneath her hand.

Griffin said nothing. He asked for nothing. He just waited, allowing her to touch him however she wanted.

Slowly, she moved her hand down, over his stomach. His muscles quivered beneath her touch, and she heard him suck in his breath. She smiled when she saw the hooded darkness to his eyes. "You like that?"

"You could say that."

She grew more bold, drawing circles on his belly, sliding

her hand lower and lower, until it brushed across the waist-band of his sweats.

"You're in trouble now, woman." Griffin grabbed her and tossed her beneath him. "You've stirred up the monster."

And this time, when he kissed her, it wasn't gentle. It wasn't sweet. It was hot and wet, firing up all her nerve endings and she wrapped her arms around his neck and kissed him back.

She'd never kissed anyone that way before. Not with such passion. With such relentless abandon. With such confidence. With such desire.

He shifted his position, and then tugged her camisole up over her breasts. Before she could feel exposed or vulnerable, he settled himself back on her, pressing the bare skin of his chest against hers.

The sensation of his skin sliding across hers was amazing. "That feels so good."

"Hell, yeah, it does." Griffin's voice was muffled as he kissed her neck.

Clare tipped her head back as he mixed it up. A kiss, a nip, a nuzzle, a lick. Here, and there, and then on her collar bone, and then on the swell of her breast...

"Oh, my God." She gripped his shoulders as he took her nipple into his mouth. Desire rocketed through her, and she grabbed his head. "Griffin—"

He bit lightly, and something shot through her, deep in her belly. A mini orgasm? Already? From that? No, it couldn't be—

Then he kissed her again, and she forgot about analyzing the sensations tumbling through her. All she could think of was the feel of his body against hers, the way he kissed her. His fingers in her hair. His palm cupping her breast as if it were some great treasure he had to protect.

He moved his hand to her waist. He rested his palm on

her hip, his fingers inching beneath the light fabric of her delicate shorts, the ones that Astrid had given her seven years ago, but she'd never worn. Until tonight.

Griffin's thumb circled the front of her hip bone, moving closer and closer—

And then he was kissing her again, and she couldn't keep track of his hand and kiss him at the same time. There was too much fire burning inside her, too much sensation. When he finally touched her, the orgasm that ripped through her was instant, electrifying and a thousand times more powerful than she'd ever experienced in her life.

He caught her gasp with his kiss, drawing the orgasm out as he fed it with his kisses and his touch, driving her mad until there was nothing left inside her but a quivering mass of decadent pleasure. She collapsed against the bed, her body slick with sweat, her muscles trembling. "Holy cow."

A grin of pure, male satisfaction on his face, Griffin pulled back as she tried to catch her breath. "You keep having orgasms that easily, and I'm going to think I'm the world's greatest lover."

She was so embarrassed. "I'm sorry, I—"

"No, no," he said, laughing as he kissed her forehead. "Trust me, it's all good."

She relaxed a bit at his self-satisfied tone. "You sure? Are you mad that I didn't wait for you?" Oh, God, that was an embarrassing question, but she had to know.

"Oh, sweetheart, there is nothing to worry about." He kissed her again, a little longer, a little deeper this time. "We haven't even gotten started."

Anticipation flushed through Clare. "We haven't?" Oh, wow. That was really exciting news, because that had just been incredible.

"Hell, no." Then he rolled off her, stood up and began to untie the drawstring on his sweats.

Fascinated, Clare propped herself up on her elbow to watch. Somehow, coming apart in Griffin's arms had taken away her nervousness. Now her body was jazzed, and she was totally engaged in the moment.

Griffin cocked an eyebrow at her as he tugged his sweats over his hips and let them drop.

"Silk boxers?" What would the men of Birch Crossing think of silk boxers? Then she sobered at the reminder that Griffin was not of Birch Crossing, and he never would be.

"I like how they feel against my skin." He contemplated her for a moment, as if he were debating her reaction, and then he took the boxers off as well.

Clare's breath caught at the sight of his erection, at the raw male standing before her. The outsider. The business man. The father. The man who made her laugh. The man who made her feel alive for the first time in years. He was all of the above, a magnificent combination of so many different things. She wanted him, with all his complexities.

This was her night.

This was their night.

She accepted the consequences.

So, she lifted her hand and held it out to him, in invitation.

His face was shadowed and serious. "You sure?"

"Yes."

A smile creased his cheeks, and she caught sight of the dimple before he set his hand in hers and joined her on the bed.

And this time, she had no more doubts.

CHAPTER SEVENTEEN

Intimacy with a woman had never been like this.

Never in his whole damn life.

As Griffin slid into bed beside Clare, her huge blue eyes riveted to his face, her hair tousled on the pillow, Griffin knew that this moment was a treasure that would never come again.

Moments like this came once in a lifetime.

Slowly, almost afraid to see whether the fantasy was real, Griffin leaned down and brushed his lips over hers. Her arms went around his neck, and she kissed him back. Her kiss was so tentative, exploratory, unsure, but it was laced with a sensuality that made the part of him respond that had lain dormant for years.

He ran his hand over her hip as he kissed her, marveling at the feel of her skin. It was so soft, so smooth. He could feel every curve of her body, the muscles beneath, as if she were a beautiful sculpture of angel wings and spring sunshine.

Women had just been women to him.

But this was different. This was *Clare*.

Fire shifted inside him, and he was hit with a need for

more. To connect with her. He kissed her more deeply, seducing her with his mouth as he hooked his fingers over those decadently innocent shorts and pulled them down her hips, over her thighs, past her calves—

Clare moved her feet, kicking the shorts off, and he kissed her as he touched her intimately again. And again, her body convulsed, but he moved his hand before she could go all the way. "This time," he commanded between kisses, "you must wait for me, sweetheart."

Chuckling at her groan of impatience, Griffin kissed Clare again, basking in the taste of her lips, in the growing confidence in her kisses. She ran her fingers through his hair, a sensual caress that felt so freaking incredible. Her hands slid over his shoulders and down his arms, across his hip, up his back, her touch so damned erotic he wanted to pin her to the bed and make her his right then.

It wasn't simply her touch that was so incredible. It was the way she was moving and touching him, the restless motion of her hips beneath him, the depth of her kisses as she accepted his. She wanted him. She wasn't simply tolerating his advances. She absolutely and unabashedly desired him, craved him, wanted him, and welcomed him, and that was unbelievable. Her need for him reached deep inside him to a place that had been shut down for so long, unleashing a burning passion that ripped through him.

Suddenly, nothing mattered but Clare. Her kisses, her silky skin, the way her body felt beneath his.

Raw possession surged over him, and he kissed harder, deeper, taking over the kiss, needing to claim her, to make her his. He kissed her mouth, her neck, her breasts, her stomach. Every inch of her skin needed his mark. He was consumed with his need for her, to strip away all the walls between them until there was nothing left but the burning, insatiable fire raging within him.

He sank between her thighs, moving against her, his body trembling with the need to take her, to lose himself in her body and her soul. He was desperate for more, unable to kiss her deeply enough to take away the gaping emptiness inside him that needed her so badly. Still kissing her, still moving against her, Griffin touched her and was nearly undone when he found how ready she was for him. She wanted him as much as he craved her? How was that possible? He couldn't even begin to understand how a woman as incredible as Clare, with a heart so warm and amazing could want *him* so badly.

Raw desire knifed through him, so intense it was almost painful. He couldn't wait. Couldn't hold off. He needed to be inside her, to lock her down as his, to lose himself in her—

"Astrid gave me condoms," she whispered, her breath warm against the side of his neck. "They're by the bed."

She was ready? Jesus. *She was ready for him.* He had some condoms in his room, but it hadn't been on his mind when he'd walked in here tonight. "Remind me to thank her." He found the objects in question, made quick work of the packaging and then he settled himself between Clare's hips.

He was startled to discover his heart was pounding in his chest, his breathing tight, his lungs constricted with the intensity of the moment. Then he saw Clare's wary expression, and all his frenzy vanished, replaced with a protective instinct to make sure it was right for her, to treasure the gift she was offering him.

Her eyes were wide, nearly luminescent as she watched him. Her hands were on his shoulders, almost bracing herself. Desire flushed her cheeks, but nervousness was evident in the way she watched him.

"Clare," he whispered. "I treasure you." Forcing himself not to drive deep and claim her, Griffin kissed her, lightly, gently, seductively.

Her lips parted beneath his, and he felt the moment she forgot to be nervous, when she became lost in the sensation of skin and touching and kissing and passion. The fire built inside him, licking away at his self-control and at his sanity, until all he could absorb was the woman beneath him. Her light, floral scent, the taste of her mouth, the saltiness of her skin, the softness of her hair, the power and passion in her curvy body as she moved beneath him, responding to his kiss, allowing herself to fall under the spell that was trying so hard to consume him.

"I need to be inside you." He moved his hips, testing, and Clare made a noise of desire that arched deep into his core, severing the remaining threads of his restraint.

"Yes," she whispered. She leaned her head back, and he showered kisses on her throat as he moved his hips faster now, rubbing against her, feeling her readiness for him.

Clare adjusted her legs so he could sink deeper against her. She was twisting beneath him, driven by her own desires and needs, and feeling the same intensity that was driving him. He'd never needed intimacy like this before. It had always been about sex, about physical fulfillment, but he felt like if he didn't make love to her, a part of him would forever be incomplete.

He lifted his head from her neck to look at her, and Clare immediately opened her eyes, as if she'd sensed his need to connect.

Her eyes were flooded with desire, with passion, and her face was relaxed. No fear. No hesitation. Then she smiled, and he saw the trust in her beautiful face.

Pure, untainted, *trust*...in him.

"Griffin," she whispered, "make love to me."

"*Clare.*" The sound of his name on her lips shredded the last threads of his control. Need overwhelmed him, and he shifted, plunging deep into her body.

The intensity of the connection rushed through him, and he felt like his entire world had just been made right as he felt her body accept him, as he buried himself inside the woman who had made his soul come alive.

Clare gasped and gripped his shoulders, but she didn't take her gaze from his face, and he couldn't have ripped his gaze off hers if his life depended on it. He felt like he was falling into those eyes, into the passion and humanity brimming in them.

He wanted to move, to take her, to connect them in a way only he could, but he knew she wasn't ready. He braced himself, forcing himself to still so she could adjust to him. He kissed her once, then again, and again, the kisses building a fire as quickly as before.

And then Clare wiggled her hips, and he nearly lost it right then. He gritted his jaw, holding still as she began to move beneath him, testing, experimenting, exploring.

"Yes," he whispered. "Just like that." He began to move with her, against her, coaxing her, leading her, responding to her, until he couldn't separate himself from her anymore.

He was kissing her with a fierceness and need he couldn't sate, his body thrusting, withdrawing, and again, moving with her, keeping them connected as she writhed beneath him. It was no longer about him, his need for her, and his desire to protect her. He couldn't separate them anymore, couldn't distinguish between her kisses and his, her desire and his need. All he knew was that she was his world, that nothing mattered, that the only moment that ever existed for him was right then, right there, in Clare's arms.

"God, Griffin—" she gasped, and then her body went rigid as the orgasm consumed her.

He caught her shout of pleasure with a kiss, holding her small frame as she came apart in his arms, again and again, an endless wave of pleasure that brought him to the edge and—

His orgasm hit him with violent force, ripping a gasp out of him as it surged through him. He held onto Clare, anchoring her against him as the orgasms tore them both apart, bringing them to places he had never been, and he knew he'd never get to again.

When it finally released them and Griffin collapsed on top of her, he knew that he had just been given a gift he would never, ever be worthy of.

But as Clare whispered his name and snuggled into the curve of his body, he knew that he would never, ever give it back.

FALLING asleep in Griffin's arms had been a mistake.

When Clare awoke to the feel of his body against hers, his face nuzzled against her neck, the first rays of dawn streaming over his bare back, the utter contentment that filled her was absolutely terrifying.

Clare stared up at the ceiling as she listened to him breathe. She could feel his chest expand with each breath, and his leg was thrown over hers, the heavy weight trapping her to the bed. One arm was wrapped around her upper body, tucking her against him as if he were cradling his truest love.

His whiskers were digging into her shoulder, and she was so warm and cozy against him. She never wanted to move, ever.

Her body was sore and felt thoroughly loved, and she smiled at the memory of their lovemaking. Nothing like getting back into the game in a hurry. How many orgasms had she had? It turned out, he could touch her pretty much any way he wanted, and she went over the edge.

It hadn't been like that with Ed, that was for sure.

Griffin had attributed it to the fact he was, apparently, indeed the world's greatest lover.

She had no idea what it was, or why she'd responded like that, but it had turned the night into something out of a dream. All it took was looking at his handsome face, at the passion in those dark brown eyes, and hearing the tone of his voice, and she would tumble off that cliff again.

But this morning...She wrapped her hands around his upper arm where it was across her breasts. This morning, this magnificent man was hers. This morning, for the first time in fifteen years, she wasn't waking up alone.

And it felt so incredible, so amazing, so right, that she knew she was in trouble.

Emma had been so right.

Clare wasn't an empty-sex kind of girl.

She loved her bed. She loved her independence. But after waking up with Griffin and having it feel so incredible to have him holding her, she was absolutely terrified of what it would be like when he left and she had to wake up alone again.

She rubbed her hand along his arm, feeling the softness of the hair. How could it feel so beautiful to have Griffin in her bed? Shouldn't she be trying to push him out? Shouldn't she feel a need to reclaim her space? Shouldn't she feel highly satisfied and ready to declare herself available for Mr. Right, who was supposed to follow on the heels of the rebound man?

Because that's what Griffin was, right? Sure, yeah, the rebound was a decade and a half later, but he was still the first guy she'd been with since Ed.

But she didn't feel like he was a rebound man.

She didn't feel ready to race into the sunset with another man now that Griffin had released her inner vixen.

She just felt ready to lie here, with Griffin, and never leave this spot. She'd had no idea that it would feel this amazing and right to be with him. To feel his body against hers, to have his breath mingle with hers, to have his scent tangled in her sheets.

Sighing, she wrapped her arms around him and rested her cheek against his head. For this moment, for this breath of time, he was hers and she would worry about the rest later, because it was, quite clearly, already too late to protect herself from falling under his spell—

"Mom?" Katie's footsteps padded down the hall.

Oh, no! "Just a second," she called back, trying unsuccessfully to get out from under Griffin. "Griffin! Let me up!" Clare shoved at him, but he didn't move. She tugged at his hair. "Griffin," she whispered.

He grunted and opened his eyes. A sleepy smile warmed his face. "Good morning, my darling."

Oh, God, how she wanted to melt into that smile. "Katie's outside the door."

Griffin began to nibble on her neck. "I locked it."

The doorknob rattled, and Clare tried to wiggle out from under him, but he hauled her back down.

"Mom!" Katie knocked on the door. "I want to talk to you."

Griffin rolled on top of Clare and pinned her back onto the bed, his eyes sparkling with mischief. "Tell her to give you ten minutes." He gave a low growl and kissed her.

Oh, come on! Not fair. Clare forced herself to stop kissing him and pushed at his shoulder. "I'm coming, Katie," she called out. "Hang on a sec."

The doorknob rattled again. "Why is the door locked?"

"I don't know. I didn't do it on purpose." Clare banged her fist on Griffin's back, and he chuckled and finally rolled off her. "Get in the bathroom," she whispered.

"You have your own bathroom? How'd I get the bad room that has to use the one in the hall?" Still grinning and completely erect, he strode into the bathroom and flipped the door shut behind him.

"Mom?"

Clare grabbed her shorts from the floor and pulled on her camisole. She took a quick look in the mirror as she hurried to the door, and was startled by what she looked like. Her hair was a tousled mess, her makeup was long gone, but her cheeks were flushed and her eyes were glowing.

She looked beautiful.

Stunned, she stared at herself. Never, or at least since she could remember, had she ever looked in the mirror and considered herself beautiful. She always noticed the bags under her eyes, the wrinkles by her mouth, or the new freckle on her nose. But now...

"Mom!"

"Coming!" Clare turned away and unlocked the door. Her daughter was standing in the hall, already dressed for school with a backpack over her shoulder. Her hair was curled around her shoulders, and she was wearing mascara. "Did you use a curling iron this morning?"

"Yes, you like it?" Katie fluffed her brown hair.

"Well, yes, of course. What time did you get up?"

"I couldn't sleep." Katie flounced into the room and sat down on the edge of the bed. She was wearing her new In Your Face jeans that hugged her bottom just a trifle more snugly than Clare would have preferred, but her shirt was at least modest today. "So, I was talking to Griffin yesterday, and it got me thinking."

Clare saw Griffin's underwear on the sheets behind Katie, and nearly passed out. "What did you want to talk about?" She moved into the hallway. "Let's go talk in the kitchen while I make coffee."

But Katie leaned back on the bed and braced her weight

on her hands, inches from Griffin's underwear. "So, Griffin said that he went to the MIT program, and it was cool."

"The MIT program?" This was about school? What about the boy trauma? Clare realized that she'd missed the crisis entirely. Katie had shared it with Griffin and moved on. Her daughter's first boy-crisis and she'd missed it. "Are you sure that's all that's on your mind? Anything happen yesterday that you wanted to talk about?"

"No." Katie crossed her legs, taking up permanent residence on the bed. "See, here's the thing. Griffin thought MIT was cool, so I guess that it wouldn't be that bad. I mean, if he liked it, right?"

There was a thud from the bathroom, and Katie turned. "What was that?"

"Water pipe." Clare sat down beside Katie, and patted her daughter's knee as she casually reached behind her and shoved the underwear under the covers. "So, you want to go to MIT now? That's great. You'll love it—"

"No." Katie turned her attention back to her. "See, even when I heard Griffin thought it was cool, and I still didn't want to go, I knew that it wasn't just MIT that was the problem."

"Um...what?" Where were the rest of Griffin's clothes? He'd come in fully dressed.... Clare saw that his shoes were on the floor next to her nightstand. His sweats were in a pile on the floor beside the shoes. Oh, God. No, no, that was okay. She owned sweatpants, too, right? She could say they were hers.

"I want to stay here and be in the Shakespeare festival," Katie announced. "Like Dad was."

Clare forgot about the sweats and stared at her daughter as a cold chill settled down on her. "*What?*"

Katie took a deep breath. "I want to be in the Shakespeare Festival. I'll be sixteen by July and that's old enough."

Clare stumbled to her feet. "Oh, no, Katie. You can't give up MIT for that. I mean, it's actors, it's craziness, there's no future—"

Katie lifted her chin. "Dad was an actor. Does that mean he wasn't good enough? That he had no future? That he was so weird?"

"No, no, that's not what I meant—"

Katie stood up and set her hands on her hips. "I'm tired of this whole town treating my dad like he was some freak just because he wasn't from here. And I'm tired of defending your choice to marry him. I'm going to be in the festival, and I'm going to prove that an actor can be a normal person, just like anyone else!"

Oh, Lord in heaven, this was not good. She couldn't have Katie follow the same path Clare had taken. Clare had been seventeen the summer she'd worked at the festival and met Ed, only one year older than Katie. "It's not your responsibility to defend your dad—"

"He's dead, and you won't do it, so who else is there?" Katie strode to the door, her fist bunched tightly around the strap of her backpack. "I'm going to school. We can talk later, but I'm not backing down."

"But—"

"And by the way, Mom," Katie said as she opened the door. "I'm fifteen, and I'm not an idiot. You could have told me you were sleeping with Griffin."

Clare gawked at her daughter. "We're not—"

"See? You're ashamed of him, just like you're ashamed of dad. Well, I'm tired of being ashamed. I'm going to be in that festival, and I'm telling all my friends that you're sleeping with Griffin—"

"Katie." Griffin opened the bathroom door, wearing Clare's pink robe. "I appreciate you looking out for me, but I think that's not the best way to do it."

Clare groaned and buried her face in her hands. "And there goes my chance to deny it."

"Oh, come on, Mom! His underwear is in your bed!" Katie turned to Griffin, her eyes flashing. "I'm not ashamed of you, Griffin."

"And your mom isn't either," Griffin said. "But what she does in her private life isn't the business of this town."

"Everything is the business of this town!" Katie said. "Everyone already thinks you guys are sleeping together, so at least this way we can be proud of it and not let people make us feel bad."

"No." Griffin folded his arms and leaned against the door-jamb. The robe barely came to mid-thigh, and his attempt to close the neck and hide his chest was slowly failing. "Do you want people to know Jeremy kissed you and then told you he didn't want to date you?"

Katie's cheeks flared red, and Clare glared at Griffin. "That's enough—"

"No, it's not," Griffin said. "Katie needs to understand that speaking up against the crowds is not always about spilling your secrets."

Katie glared at him. "Don't you get it? For my whole life, I've had people make this little face of disapproval whenever my dad was mentioned. The actor. The outsider. The reckless driver. And now, my mom's doing the same thing to you, not defending you. I'm tired of it!"

Clare's heart tightened for the pain she saw in her daughter's eyes. "Katie, I'm so sorry. Your dad was a good man—"

"Then why don't you ever say that when people talk about him?" Katie stomped her foot in visible frustration "Why do you just sit there with your mouth shut?"

"I don't—"

"You do! But I don't have to be like you. I don't have to be ashamed of who I am, or who my father was." She took a

232

deep breath and gave Clare a haughty look. "I'm going to be in the festival, and you can't stop me."

"If you don't like people judging your father," Griffin said quietly, "putting yourself in the festival just to stop judgment may have the opposite effect." He folded his arms over his chest. "And trust me, it won't be any better if you tell people about me and your mom, because they will judge her in ways you don't even want to imagine."

Katie's face paled, then she screamed with frustration and ran out of the room.

"Don't you dare leave this house!" Clare rushed after her, but by the time she got outside, Katie was already climbing into the cab of a truck with Sara and her older brother. "Katie!"

"I'm going to school," Katie yelled out the window. "Leave me alone!" Then the truck's engine revved, and it drove off with her daughter. They were driving toward school at least, so that was good.

Clare's first instinct was to grab her car keys and go after her, but she knew that would serve no purpose. No good words could come when they were both upset. She had to give her space.

But this was not good. Really, really, not good. She had no idea how to handle this. How to fix it. How to make it right with her daughter, because everything Katie had accused her of was true. She never defended Ed when people criticized him. Not once. There was no way she could lie about him. She wouldn't hurt Katie by revealing the truth about Ed, but God help her, there was no way she could bring herself to lie and say he was a great guy, either. But if she did nothing, was Katie going to plunge straight into the life Clare had and get knocked up by an actor just to prove that her dad was okay?

Her skin went ice-cold at the thought, and Clare stumbled back toward the house, her bare feet aching on the gravel driveway. Her daughter was gone, but her words hovered in the air, reverberating like the thick humidity of summer.

And Clare was out of answers.

It was just too hard.

CHAPTER EIGHTEEN

GRIFFIN HAD MANAGED to get his sweats back on by the time Clare came back inside. Guilt coursed through him at the haunted expression on her face. She looked furious and devastated at the same time, and she slammed the door shut when she came in. "How could you come out of the bathroom in front of Katie?"

Shit. He realized he'd totally screwed up. He really thought he'd done the right thing at the time. Once he realized Katie knew he'd been with Clare, there was no way he could have stood back and let Katie spread gossip about Clare, even if her motivation was pure, from a somewhat twisted teenage point of view. "She knew I was here, Clare. Nothing was going to be served by my hiding." Griffin found his shirt and picked it up. Yeah, too little, too late, but it still felt like the responsible thing to do to throw his clothes back on.

"She's fifteen!"

Griffin frowned, trying to understand Clare's outrage. "She'd figured it out, Clare. She wasn't buying the lies."

Clare threw up her arms in frustration. "You were *naked*!"

"I wasn't naked." He felt a little uncertain how to respond. Historically, he didn't have a great track record with diffusing the outrage of a woman, and he'd learned to stop trying. But he really wanted to figure it out with Clare. He wanted to make it okay. He wanted to work it out with her. There had never been a chance to work out conflict with Hillary, but he sensed it could be different with Clare, if he could figure out how to handle it. "I was wearing your robe. I thought it would lighten the moment."

She glared at him, still fuming, but he saw in those eyes more than anger. Loss, anguish, uncertainty, and his heart softened, realizing that her anger wasn't directed toward him, but that she was haunted by the interaction with Katie. "You were naked underneath it!"

"We're all naked under our clothes. It's the way it works." He tossed his shirt over his shoulder, searching for the right words to help her. "Listen, I'm sorry that she walked in on us. I really am." But he couldn't quite muster up too much apology. Frankly, when Katie had defended him like that, he'd felt like the king of the world. Yeah, it hadn't been Brooke, but if Katie could accept him, then maybe he had a chance with his own daughter.

"You don't get it! What if she tells people? What if they find out?" Clare collapsed back against the door. Then she slid down the door to her bottom, pulled her knees up to her chest and buried her face in them. "Oh, God, this sucks. I can't cope with everyone finding out and judging me for it."

Griffin crouched in front of her and stroked her hair, aching for her torment. "Hey, Clare," he said quietly. "Other people don't matter. You have to live your life—"

"I've tried so hard," she said as she hugged herself tighter. "I've worked so hard to make up for my mistake with Ed, and now, I've made the same error again. I've aligned myself with a man who will leave, exposed my daughter to sex, and—"

"Hey." Now he was pissed. "It wasn't sex. It was the connection between two souls and it was amazing. If they can't see that, who the hell cares what they think?"

Clare looked up then, tears brimming in her eyes. "Ed was leaving when he crashed."

"Ed?" Griffin frowned, trying to keep up with the change in topic. "Leaving town?"

"Me." There was such pain in her eyes that his heart broke for her. "He left me, Griffin. He walked out on me and Katie."

"Oh." Shit. He knew exactly what it felt like to be walked out on. It sucked beyond words. Griffin sat down beside her and leaned against the wall. He rested his forearms on his knees. "What happened?"

Clare was still hugging herself, and she looked so vulnerable he wanted to gather her in his arms and protect her. But he was smart enough to know that the last thing she wanted right now was him, not in that way.

"Katie was two months old, and I was working at Wright's part-time while Ed was working on his acting skills in our basement. I came home one day, and his duffel bags were packed. He said he was an actor and he had to follow his path, and that being in this town was stifling him."

Bastard. "There are a lot of theatres in Portland. That's not too far away."

Clare shook her head, her eyes glimmering with tears. "He said that I was killing his soul, and he wanted out. He couldn't be married to someone who had no vision beyond this town."

Griffin swore. "That's a bunch of crap. You're an incredible woman."

"I was just me, nothing glamorous or exotic. I just wanted to be a mom and a wife, and live in Birch Crossing. It wasn't enough for him."

Stupid bastard. How could anyone walk away from Clare and Katie? "Fuck him."

Clare laughed softly, but he could see the pain still etched on her features. "I tried to stop him. I cried. I begged. I told him I couldn't do it by myself. I told him that Katie needed him." She looked up at Griffin. "I even told him I'd go with him."

"And?" He didn't even need to ask. He could see from the expression on Clare's face that the stupid bastard had been completely unable to see the gift that Clare was.

"He told me he didn't want us. So, he took the car, our only car, this rusted old truck that barely ran, and he left. He crashed on his way out of town and died at the scene."

Son of a bitch. "How old were you?"

"Eighteen."

"Shit." He could only imagine the weight on Clare's shoulders on that day. "Were your parents around to help you out?"

She shook her head. "My dad had died when I was younger, and my mom was already sick at that point." She looked up, her eyes luminous. "I've never told anyone the truth about Ed. I was too ashamed to admit to everyone that they were right about him. Katie has no idea. As far as she knows, he adored her and his death was a tragic loss. How do I defend him to the town when I know they're right? He walked out on his beautiful daughter, Griffin. What kind of man does that?"

"A bastard." Griffin leaned his head back against the door, trying to imagine how Katie would respond if she knew the truth about her father, that he hadn't loved her. Maybe it would free her from his memory instead of dragging her down. "Would you consider telling Katie what he was really like?"

"No, never," Clare shook her head emphatically. "What's the point of telling her that her father didn't love her? As long as she believes her dad loved her, she can hold onto it. And maybe he did. Maybe he would have reached the Maine border and turned around. We'll never know."

Griffin looked at her. "You know."

Clare sighed. "Yes, I do. He never wanted to stay, not for a minute, and the only reason he did was because I got pregnant and Norm chased him down with a gun and told him he had to do right by me."

Griffin liked the old man already, but now? He'd buy that man a beer, or thirty, the next time he saw him. "A real shotgun wedding?"

"Yeah, well, Norm and Ophelia are the only ones who know Ed had to be threatened into marrying me. The rest of the town thinks he was a loser because he died. No one knows how bad it was." She rubbed her forehead. "I don't even know why I'm telling you this."

"Because I'm safe. I'm an outsider and I won't judge you."

She groaned and let her head flop back against the door with a thud. "Of course you can still judge me."

"But I won't." Unable to resist the need to comfort her, Griffin moved so that his shoulder was against hers. He gently unwrapped her arms from her knee and took her hand, holding it between his. "Listen to me, Clare."

She turned so she could see him, still using the door to support her head. "What?"

"You're an incredible woman. What you've managed to do with the life you were handed is extraordinary."

She watched him, but said nothing. No denial, but no acceptance either. "I should have found a way to keep him alive for my daughter," she said quietly.

"No. You can't blame yourself for any of that. The choices you made fifteen years ago were the best you could make at the time. They have no reflection on today." He rubbed her hand, not liking how cold it was. "It wasn't your fault that Ed left."

"I made a bad choice, and Katie has suffered for it."

"How? She's a happy kid."

"You heard her! The town ridicules her dad. That's not fair to her." She groaned. "And now she wants to do that festival. Do you realize what that means? She might meet a boy there like I did, and start down that path and that life. I can't let that happen, Griffin. I have to protect her from that. She needs to get a good education and have the tools to handle whatever life throws at her. I don't want her to deal with what I faced." Tears filled her eyes. "What if she got pregnant by some actor? She'll be sixteen this summer. *Sixteen.*"

Griffin pulled her onto his lap, and Clare melted into him as the tears came. He had no words to comfort her. He couldn't tell her that she was fabricating the horrors that might befall her daughter, because he knew they weren't imaginary. It was like his dream, and Katie was heading straight into the proverbial ocean, and Clare couldn't stop her.

And the worst thing of all, for her, was the truth that everyone in town who gave her grief about her choice to marry Ed had been proved correct, at least in Clare's view.

She *had* married a bastard. An outsider who had screwed up her life and then abandoned her in more than one way. Griffin kissed the top of her head as she cried in his arms, holding her and giving her comfort as best he could.

And now, after surviving through it all, here she was again. With an outsider who was going to abandon her...Son of a bitch.

Maybe his daughter was right.

Maybe he was a bastard, too.

CLARE CRIED for the loss of her childhood dream. She mourned the loss of a man she'd loved with such innocence and hope. She grieved the deprivation of a family for herself and for Katie. And she cried for the truth that she hadn't been enough to keep her husband alive.

She hadn't cried when Ed died.

She'd sat at the funeral in stunned silence, holding her tiny baby, silently resolving that she would not abandon her daughter the way Ed had. In that moment, she'd shut down her heart, she'd closed off emotions, and she'd gone into full drive to create a safe haven for her daughter.

For fifteen years, she hadn't slowed down enough to grieve. She hadn't let herself mourn the life she wasn't ever going to have. She hadn't paused to let herself feel the loneliness of an empty bed. She hadn't dared take a moment to breathe, to feel, to think.

Until now.

Until Griffin had made love to her all night and held her in his arms until dawn.

Until his own pain with his daughter and his kindness to Katie had cracked a hole in Clare's heart that she couldn't glue shut anymore.

And now... God, she wished she couldn't feel anymore. She wished she was the woman she'd been for fifteen years. Because the anguish in her heart, the pain in her soul, the sheer devastation of her spirit was beyond what she could handle.

She should push Griffin away. Run for the door. Climb a mountain and shout her strength from its peak.

But she couldn't. She simply had nothing left. The weight of fifteen years of fighting on her own was simply too much.

"Come on," Griffin said as he swept her up in his arms and stood up.

Clare clung to him, unable to stop the tears, the pain, the sobbing, and she didn't care where he took her. "Just don't leave me," she gasped through her tears.

"I won't."

Her relief at his reassurance was mind-numbing. How could she be so afraid of being alone? She had to be able to be alone, to handle it on her own. That was her life. That was what she did. She couldn't get weak. *She couldn't get weak.*

But there were no reserves to draw upon. No courage. No strength. No plucky mantra. Just pain. Grief. Loss. Hopelessness. Griffin felt like her only anchor, the one thing she could hold onto to keep from being sucked down into the abyss.

Griffin set her down on the bed, and she clung to his neck as the bed sank beneath his weight. He rolled onto his side and pulled her into his body, tucking her against him like she was a tiny child and he was a great protector.

In his arms, she felt safe. For the first time in fifteen years, she felt *safe.*

She buried her face in his chest and cried, clinging to the feel of his arms around her, of his gentle kisses on her head, of his low whispers of reassurance.

She had no idea how long she cried, but Griffin never moved. He stayed right where he was, holding her until she had no more tears, until she was too drained to cry any longer. She finally lay in exhausted silence in his arms.

"How do you feel?" His question was a whisper as he rubbed her back.

"Empty. Like there's nothing left inside me at all." She pressed her face into the curve of his neck, squeezing her eyes closed, using him to hide from her life. How could it feel so good to lean on him? How could it be such a relief to simply let herself be vulnerable and exhausted, turning to him for comfort and strength. She was the one who took care of others. She never let her guard down. She never let herself need anyone to hold her up. She couldn't afford to, and yet that was exactly what she'd done with Griffin. As terrifying as it was to fall apart, having him there to take care of her was... God...beautiful? A relief? A huge, warm breath of respite from her life?

"Good." He kissed her forehead. "It was time for all that to finally leave."

She rested her head on his shoulder and tucked herself more tightly into his embrace, wanting to crawl into the comfort he gave her. "I haven't cried like this before. Not for him."

"It's okay to cry," he said. "It's always okay to cry."

New tears filled her eyes at his acceptance of her melt-down. "I have to be strong."

"Crying doesn't mean you're not strong," he said as he combed her hair back from her face with his fingers. "It means you care."

"I don't want to care," she whispered, clenching her fists against the pain in her chest. "It hurts."

"I know it does." Griffin rested his chin on her head in an intimate gesture that softened the sharp edges digging at her heart. "I know it does."

Clare thought of his nightmare, and how his body had been trembling when she'd woken him up. He did know. He understood. "Thank you," she whispered, resting her palm on his chest, needing to feel his strength and his warmth.

"You're welcome." His voice was careful, too careful. "Clare?"

She tensed in sudden nervousness. "What?"

"I don't want to make life difficult for you." He kissed her forehead, and his arms tightened around her. "I know my presence in your life is complicating things for you with the town and your daughter, but also in here." He laid his hand over her heart. "I can't stay in Birch Crossing forever. I have a life I need to return to, and I don't want to do to you what Ed did."

She squeezed her eyes closed, as tears leaked out. She knew what he was going to say, and she didn't want to hear it.

"It might be best if I moved out of your place for the rest of my time here. I'll find a place in another town where I won't interfere with you and Katie."

The tears were hot and wet on her cheeks, and Griffin rubbed them away with his thumb.

He grasped her shoulders and gently rolled her onto her back, forcing her to look at him. His face was serious, his expression heavy, but there was tenderness in his eyes that made her want to cry even more. "You need to understand, Clare, that I think you're amazing. If my life were different, if I were different..." He sighed and brushed her cheek with the back of his hands. "I just want you to know that I don't want to move out. I want to stay here with you for whatever time we have left."

"Then stay," she blurted out.

He froze, but hope flared in his eyes. "I don't want to hurt you."

"I'm already broken inside." She touched his whiskered jaw and saw her hand was trembling.

Anger flashed in his eyes. "You're not broken—"

"I am." She placed her finger over his lips. "If you leave now, or in a week, it won't change that you've touched my heart." She swallowed and took a deep breath. "I would rather have you for a week than a day."

"Clare—"

She put his hand over her heart. "Can you feel this?"

His eyes darkened. "Your heart is beating."

"Yes, it is. And it hurts every time it beats. It didn't hurt before you."

He swore and pulled his hand away. "That's why I should leave—"

"That's why I want you to stay."

He shook his head. "That doesn't make sense. I don't understand."

"I don't either. Not really. But I know that it is what needs to happen." She put his hand back on her heart and snuggled closer to him. "My heart aches at the thought of you leaving before you have to. You're supposed to stay. You're not finished here yet."

He lightly tapped his fingers on her chest. "I have a mission?" he said thoughtfully.

"I think you do."

His gaze met hers. "To save the cupcake queen from her own demise?"

Clare managed a small smile. "Something like that, I think."

"Huh." Griffin rubbed his jaw. "How will we know when I'm done?"

"I think we'll just know."

Griffin blew out his breath. "Are you sure about this, Clare? I don't want to hurt you anymore than you've already been hurt." He studied her face. "It's important to me that you're okay."

At his words, something swelled in her heart, a warmth that started to fill the vast emptiness inside her. And she knew what his job was. His role was to make her heart beat again, until she could do it on her own. As terrible as it felt right now, it was better to have each heartbeat send pain cascading through her than to be dead inside like she had been for so long. She nodded. "Yes, I'm sure. I want you to stay until you have to return to Boston."

He searched her face, and finally he nodded. "I'll honor you every moment, I promise," he said seriously.

"I know you will." She sagged back into the pillow, too exhausted to hold herself up now that she knew he was staying. Now that she knew she could trust him to take care of her. She didn't have to do it herself anymore. Not right now. For right now, for the next day or two or three, she could lean on him.

He rubbed his thumb under her eye. "You look exhausted."

"I am." Her body felt so weak she was sure she would fall if she tried to stand. "Two hours of violent sobbing will do that to a woman, I guess."

He kissed her lightly, then snuggled her against him. "Go to sleep. I'll hold you."

Clare closed her eyes and let herself subside into the strength of his body. "You'll be here when I wake up?"

"I'll be here."

She yawned as sleep started to claim her, offering her peace in his arms. "Promise?"

He tightened his arms around her. "Promise."

GRIFFIN KNEW the moment Clare fell asleep. Her breathing deepened, and her body seemed to finally release all the tension she'd been holding. She melted into him, completely entrusting herself to him with no reservations and no resistance.

He lightly rubbed her lower back while he listened to the sound of her breathing. Her skin was so soft beneath his hand. She was so vulnerable yet admirably strong. He kissed her head, smiling at the fragrance of spring and woman drifting around them. He would forever think of her when he smelled a flower, or stood outside on a wet, spring day and breathed in the freshness of the earth.

A bird chirped, and he turned his head. Two birds were sitting on a tree branch outside the window. Little brown sparrows. One of them had a stick in its mouth, and it flew up to a crook in the tree. As he watched, they began to carry more twigs. Some of the sticks were huge, bigger than he would have thought the tiny birds could manage.

He smiled, pulling Clare closer against him. He couldn't believe how content he felt. Here it was, almost nine o'clock on a workday, and he was lounging in bed, completely at peace. He felt no urge to set Clare aside and head off to his computer. He was actually watching birds and finding them interesting. He almost laughed just thinking about it. Birds. Really.

He couldn't remember ever sitting still for this long without getting antsy. He thought back to the night he'd been waiting for Norm, and how impatient he'd been when Norm had told him to take the time to look at the stars.

He grinned. Someday, maybe he'd take Clare out in her backyard and look at the stars with her. Maybe take a bottle of nice wine from his wine closet, a soft blanket and—

His phone rang, a loud shrill in the peace of the moment. He grimaced as Clare mumbled in her sleep, and he leaned over the edge of the bed to snag the phone out of his sweatpants pocket from where they were lying on the floor after he'd tossed them, needing to feel Clare's skin against his again. He pulled it free and silenced the call from Phillip.

Scowling, Griffin set the phone on the nightstand as he repositioned himself around Clare. Screw Phillip. He didn't want to deal with that right now. He wanted to be here right now. With Clare. Giving her the comfort—

The phone rang again, and Griffin lunged for it, cutting off the ring before it could wake her up. "What?" he said as he slid out from under Clare and walked into the bathroom. "What's so important?" He made sure Clare was still sleeping, then quietly shut the door behind him.

"We're in, Griffin! We're in!" Phillip's voice was shrill with excitement, and he sounded out of breath.

"In where?" Griffin tried to keep his voice low, not wanting to wake Clare.

"In Your Face! When our lawyer told the owners that we were interested, they got really excited. Apparently, their kids wear Free Love Slippers all the time, and when they realized that we were the same crew, they wanted to meet with us."

Griffin leaned against the sink. "When?"

"Today. Can you be here by one o'clock?"

"In Boston?" Griffin looked around the pale blue bathroom with its footed tub and its antique mirror. Boston seemed so far away from where he was. It felt almost surreal, being yanked from Clare's bed into the world of fashion and high-stakes negotiation.

"Yeah, in our offices. This is big, Griff. I think if they like us, they're going to be willing to take a lower price just so it can go to us. You're our dealmaker. I need you here."

"By one o'clock?" Griffin ran his hand through his hair as he tried to focus. His mind felt sluggish, still back in the bedroom with Clare, wrung out by all the emotions he'd experienced during her tears. "That's only four hours from now."

"It's a three and a half hour drive. What's going on? You bailing on me for a bunch of pine cones?"

"No, no. Of course not." Griffin turned on the water and splashed some over his face. "I'll be there by one."

"Great. Call me when you're on your way, and we'll talk strategy." Phillip hung up without another word.

Griffin leaned his phone against his chest for a moment, trying to regroup. He'd been so immersed in Clare he'd literally forgotten about In Your Face, which he never did. The fact he'd blown off work so completely was more than a little unsettling.

And even now, with the possibility of a deal looming, he didn't want to leave her. He'd promised he'd be there when she woke up. But he had to go work the negotiation, and there was no way to be in two places at the same time.

Griffin quietly opened the bathroom door and leaned on the door frame. Clare was still asleep, and she was facing him. Her face was pale, and there were tear streaks on her cheeks. Her hands were tucked underneath her chin, and she'd curled her knees up to her belly.

She looked tiny and vulnerable in her big bed.

Griffin forced himself to look away, steeling himself against the need to crawl back into bed with her. He had to go. He had to take care of this deal. It was what he'd been angling for. In Your Face was his ticket to everything he wanted. He couldn't leave it to Phillip to win the owners over. His partner was a great businessman, but he wasn't always the most charming guy on the block, even when he was trying.

If they were going to win this deal, Griffin had to be there.

He looked at Clare again, debating whether to wake her up and tell her he was leaving. He had to. He'd made a promise to be there when she woke up, and he couldn't go back on his word. He walked over to the bed and crouched beside her so his face was level with hers. "Clare," he said softly.

She didn't move.

He touched her tousled hair. "Clare," he said again.

Still no response, except the deep breathing of a woman who was exhausted.

He'd kept her up all night, and she'd had a rough morning. She needed her sleep. Hell, maybe she'd sleep all day and he could make it back before she woke up. Griffin swore under his breath, unable to make himself deprive Clare of the peace she'd finally found.

Griffin opened her nightstand and found a pen and a scrap of paper. He paused for a moment to think, then scribbled a quick note. He propped it up carefully against her lamp, wedging it in place with a jar of lavender scented face cream to make sure it wouldn't fall to the floor before she could see it.

He rested his forehead against hers. "I'll be back tonight," he whispered. "Wait for me."

Then he kissed her lightly, grabbed his clothes and headed out the door.

CHAPTER NINETEEN

CLARE WOKE UP IN A PANIC. Her heart was racing, her mind was screaming and her hands were shaking. She bolted upright in bed, terror seizing her chest. She looked frantically around, trying to find the cause of her fear, but she was in her room. The sunlight was streaming in, making the faded bedroom look worn and tired. Everything was okay.

She flopped back in bed, pressing her hands to her chest as she tried to calm down. For years after Ed had died, she'd awoken with panic attacks, terrified that she'd forgotten to do something important, like bring her baby home from the grocery store, turn off the oven or pay a bill, but it had been a long time since she'd had one.

What had brought it on now? She tried to think of what she'd forgotten. The fight with Katie this morning. Telling Griffin about Ed— "Griffin!" She sat up again and looked around the room. The bathroom door was open, and she could see no one was in there.

He'd left? He couldn't have left. He'd promised—

She lunged to the side of the bed to check the floor. His

shoes were gone. "Oh, no." She tumbled out of bed and ran to the window. His truck wasn't in the driveway.

"Oh, God." She stumbled backward, numb with shock. He'd left? He'd really left? Despite his promise?

No, he couldn't have. He had to be there. She'd trusted him!

She turned and raced down the hall. She threw open the door to his bedroom and ran inside. "Griffin!"

He wasn't there.

His computer wasn't on the desk.

He was gone.

Her legs started to shake, and she grabbed the dresser. The room started to spin. Tears welled up. Panic constricted her lungs. Alone. She was alone. Not again. She couldn't do this again. Her dad had died. Ed had left. And Griffin. He'd promised—

She suddenly saw a pair of black socks sticking out of the top drawer. She grabbed the knobs and yanked it open.

It was filled with his clothes. Silk boxers. Socks. Tee shirts. "Oh, God." Numbly, she sank down onto the bed, staring at the dresser. He was coming back. *He was coming back.*

Relief shuddered through her, and she pressed her face to her palms as the terror faded. But she was still shaking. Her legs felt like jelly. Her throat hurt. Her chest was shuddering.

What in heaven's name was wrong with her? A total freak out that he'd left? Of course he was leaving. She knew that.

But he'd promised he'd be there when she woke up. No one had ever promised her that, and she had never trusted anyone so completely. And he'd left.

Clare lifted her head and stared at herself in the mirror over the bureau. God, how terrified she looked. Ashen. Her lips almost bloodless. Her eyes strained. All because she'd woken up alone?

"That's not good," she told the wreck of a woman in the mirror. "You need to be stronger than that."

It was a good lesson. A reminder. She couldn't become dependent on Griffin. She couldn't need him this much. She had to get back in control. Now.

Clare smoothed her hair back from her face and lifted her chin. "I'm just fine," she told the mirror.

Then she stood up, carefully closed the dresser drawer and walked down the hallway back to her room with far more dignity than her frenzied run a minute ago. So, Griffin hadn't stayed with her until she woke up. She could handle that, right? Of course right.

She strode across the room toward her bathroom, averting her gaze from the rumpled bed that had been the site of so much loving and passion and—

She noticed a scrap of pink paper propped up on her nightstand. Hope raced through her, but she forced herself not to reach for it. "It doesn't matter if he left me a note. I don't need anything from him. I'm fine."

She took three more deep breaths, and only when her breathing was no longer shaky and tremulous did she finally allow herself to pick up the note.

The paper was folded in half, and on the outside was a heart.

Her chest tightened. A heart? Really? That was so sweet—

No, she had to be strong. She didn't need a heart from anyone.

She steeled herself against the soft emotion that wanted to rise to the surface, and she opened the paper. The first thing she saw was Griffin's name at the bottom, and relief rushed through her. The note really was from him. He hadn't left her without a word.

Clare sat down on the bed, tucked her feet under her and got comfortable. Then she opened it back up.

"My sweet Clare. I got called to an emergency meeting in Boston. I'm so sorry not to be there when you wake up. I'll make it up to you tonight. Dinner at 8:30 at the Finch Grill? Last night was incredible. I'll be thinking of you all day. Have a great one. -Griffin"

Clare read it three more times before she collapsed back against the pillows, weak with relief.

He was coming back.

And he was going to be thinking about her all day.

Everything was going to be okay.

Except it wasn't.

Because her reaction when she'd thought he'd left was not a good sign. She was in over her head. Big time.

But could she walk away? She looked down at the pink paper with the dark letters scrawled across them. She should cut herself off from him. Really, she should.

But he'd left her a love note.

No one had ever left her love notes.

And dammit, she deserved them, and she was going to enjoy it for as long as she could.

The panic attacks were just going to have to go away, because she wasn't going to let terror steal this moment from her.

She deserved to be happy, and even if it was for only a moment or a day, she was going to live every second of it to the fullest.

Decision made.

Once her choice was made, a huge weight lifted off her, and she knew it was the right decision.

Even if it was just for a day or a week, she was going to let herself be happy.

~

When Griffin stepped into his plush offices in Boston's financial district, he felt like he'd lost his mind. The gleaming polished wood looked foreign, the marble floors looked ostentatious, and the huge windows gave him a view of cement buildings instead of birds building a nest.

"Griffin!" Phillip strode around the corner. His rotund frame was cleverly hidden in the expensive suit and polished shoes. His head was shiny from the fluorescent lights, and he was wearing a new pair of glasses that had a logo on it that suggested they cost probably as much as Clare's mortgage ran her each month. "What the hell are you wearing?"

Griffin looked down at his jeans, his boots and his Pirates tee shirt. Shit. He hadn't even thought about going home to change once he'd arrived in Boston. "I didn't have a suit with me." And it hadn't occurred to him to pick one up.

Phillip looked like he was about to pass out. "These designers are the cutting edge of fashion," he said. "You can't walk in there in filthy jeans and boots!"

Mud caked the treads, there was pink frosting on his jeans, and he'd sweated like hell in the shirt last night. He could only imagine what aroma it was generating. Shit. Where had his brain been? He wasn't in Maine anymore. "I have a spare suit in my office."

"Well, I'll stall them. But hurry up. And for hell's sake, shave while you're in there."

"Three minutes and I'll be ready." Griffin jogged down the hall toward his office. As he passed by the artwork and the gleaming brass fixtures, he felt his mind beginning to focus again. By the time he stepped into his office and saw his immaculate mahogany desk stretching in front of his floor-to-ceiling windows, Griffin's mind was in full gear, thinking about balance sheets, investment opportunities and the teen fashion industry.

He pulled open the door to his annex and caught a glimpse of himself in the mirror as he reached for his suit. The reflection startled him. His hair was shaggy and disheveled. He had a three-day beard, and his shirt was wrinkled and streaked with dirt from when he'd run out a triple and slid into third base. Shit. He looked like a mountain man. No wonder Phillip had panicked.

No problem. He had it under control.

A splash of cologne, new socks and a quick face wash in his sink jazzed him up. The suit slid seamlessly onto his body, and as he adjusted his tie, power surged through him. His shirt was crisp. His pants creased. His jacket fit him to perfection. Cufflinks in place. He did a quick run with his electric razor and in less than three minutes, he had become Griffin Friesé, Slipper King, once again.

Energy sizzling through him, Griffin opened his office door and strode down the hall toward the conference room. He nodded at his secretaries, and then his focus narrowed on the door at the end of the hall. He listened to the voices emanating from within, noted their intonations and their subtext, and by the time he reached the doorway, he knew exactly how he was going to play this game.

He paused outside the door to adjust his cuffs, as he always did right before he went to the mat. Power rushed through him and he smiled. This was the rush he lived for. This was who he was.

It was good to be back.

~

"HI, ASTRID!" Clare dropped into a seat beside Astrid. Wright's was packed with patrons, and the tantalizing aroma of Ophelia's delicious pizza was making Clare's stomach rumble. "I'm so glad you were able to meet me for lunch.

Emma is tied up at work and couldn't make it, but at least you came."

Astrid stared at her, a shocked look on her face.

"What?" Clare asked innocently, smiling as she thought of the night with Griffin. She was a woman now, in a way she'd never been before. There was losing your virginity to a bumbling eighteen-year old actor, and there was spending the night with a man like Griffin. She was quite certain that when it came to losing her virginity, it had happened last night. Because Griffin had awakened in her the woman that had been dormant her entire life. Who knew she had it in her?

"You slept with him," Astrid said. "Oh my God, you slept with him!"

"I did!" Clare giggled, unable to hide her giddiness. "And look at the note he left me." She waggled it in front of her friend, and Astrid grabbed it from her.

Clare leaned back in her chair and cheerfully surveyed the store as her friend read it. She waved at Norm, who gave her a nod of approval, and she smiled. The whole place looked brighter, cheerier and friendlier than it had ever been. The apples looked especially shiny, the flowers in the bins by the front door looked amazing, and the sunlight was shining through the windows like this great blossom of well-being.

"Oh wow." Astrid laid the note against her chest. "That's so sweet."

"I know." Clare smiled. "It was an amazing night."

Astrid wiggled her eyebrows as she set the note on the table. "Did you remember how to do it?"

"I did, but I was so nervous." Clare lowered her voice so Astrid had to lean forward to hear her. "I swear I thought I was going to freak out, but he was just amazing. He totally took his time until I felt comfortable and then..." She grinned.

"And then—" Astrid prompted.

"You look happy." Eppie plunked herself down in one of the empty chairs.

Clare immediately sat up, horrified that Eppie might have heard. "Um, hi, Eppie—"

"I haven't seen you with that expression on your face since before your father died," Eppie said.

"What?" Clare immediately felt defensive. "I'm always happy."

"Not like that." Eppie's sharp gaze went to the note on the table. Clare grabbed for it, but Eppie was faster. Astrid went to snatch it out of the older woman's hand, but even she capitulated to Eppie's hostile gaze.

Clare sank down into her seat as Eppie read Griffin's special words. How would she be able to read them again without hearing Eppie's disparaging comments? She needed that note. It was going to be her salvation when Griffin left, and all she had was the memory of their time together.

But after Eppie finished reading it, the older woman said nothing.

She just set the note back on the table and tipped her peacock blue bowler back on her head.

No one said anything. Clare and Astrid watched Eppie, waiting for the judgment. Finally, Eppie lifted her gaze to Clare's, and Clare was shocked by the sadness in them. "Eppie? Are you all right?"

But Eppie simply stood up, walked over and wrapped Clare up in a hug. Her mother's best friend hugged Clare the way her mom used to, so tight that Clare felt like the world could never tear them apart. Clare's throat tightened, and she hugged Eppie back. She closed her eyes, and for a moment, she could almost remember what it had felt like to be in her mother's arms.

Then Eppie pulled back, her wizened fingers gripping

Clare's upper arms so tightly it almost hurt. A tear slipped out of Eppie's eye and trickled down her cheek.

"Eppie?" Clare clenched the older woman's hand. This tough, hardened woman who had never even shown humanity was crying? "Please tell me what's wrong."

"My dear, sweet girl." Eppie trailed a gnarled finger gently down Clare's cheek. "If you could find true happiness, then your mother's spirit will finally be able to be at peace. I pray you've found it."

Clare stared at the older woman in disbelief. "You're not going to tell me that Griffin's a bad man?"

"It's too late for that," Eppie said. "All I can do is pray that he's worthy of the heart that you've given to him."

Clare's throat was so thick she almost couldn't talk. "I haven't given him my heart."

But Eppie just touched her cheek again and then turned away. As the woman who had been Clare's mentor and bane for the last decade walked away, Clare saw, for the first time, not a ramrod spine, but the hunched, weathered body of an old woman who had given her heart to Clare and her daughter. A woman who had given them love and boundaries when Clare had had nothing else to cling to.

Clare ran after her and opened the door for Eppie as the old woman reached it. "Eppie?"

The wrinkled face turned toward her, and Clare saw a deep sadness and loneliness in them that she'd never seen before. Eppie had been her mother's best friend since they were babies. "Do you still miss her? My mom?"

Eppie nodded. "I miss her every minute of every day."

Clare bit back tears. "So do I."

Eppie took Clare's hand and squeezed gently. "But her spirit lives on every day through you and Katie. She is alive through the life you breathe."

Clare hesitated, afraid to ask, afraid of the honest answer

Eppie would give her. But she had to know. "Would she be proud of me? Do you think?"

Eppie smiled, showing teeth worn of many years. "My dear sweet girl, she dances in the heavens every moment that she looks upon you, because she is so proud of everything you've done and the wonderful daughter you've raised."

She would be proud of me. Tears suddenly obscured her vision, and Clare wiped her sleeve across her eyes. She took a shuddery breath and tried to pull herself together, but she couldn't stop the tears. "Thank you," she whispered. "Thank you for telling me that."

"It's true," Eppie said.

Clare nodded. "Will you come to dinner this Sunday, Eppie? With me and Katie? And Griffin, if he's still here."

The older woman's eyes lit up. "Really?"

Clare smiled. "Really." Her mother might live on through her and Katie, but she also lived on through Eppie, and Clare had never realized it before. "Will you maybe tell us some stories about when my mom was younger?"

"It would be my greatest honor." Eppie smiled, and there was a light, a spark in her eyes that hadn't been there before. "I'll bring liver and onions. It was your mama's favorite Sunday dish."

Clare laughed through her tears. "That sounds great. Six o'clock?"

"Six o'clock. But I'm usually early, so you should be ready by three." Eppie winked and stepped out the door, a new spring in her step that made Clare smile.

She leaned against the door, watching Eppie maneuver down the stairs. "I'll be ready," she whispered. "I'll be ready." And she would be. She was finally ready to feel the pain of her mother's loss, and the joy of her life. No more empty soul for her. Not anymore.

When Eppie was in her car and had safely navigated down

the street, Clare turned to head back to her table, and she saw Norm watching her. He tapped his fist against his heart. "Good girl," he said.

"Thanks." She flashed him a smile and took a tremulous breath as she hurried back to the table. She slid into her seat, and Astrid frowned at her. "What's wrong? You've been crying."

Clare smiled at her friend. "Eppie said my mom would be proud of me."

Astrid's face softened, and she put her hand on Clare's. "You had to ask? Of course she would be. She always was."

Clare felt the tears thicken again. "I just never thought of it. I felt like I'd let her down."

"Oh, no," Astrid said. "You're a champ." She smiled. "Now, I, on the other hand, would be a vast disappointment to mine—"

"Never." Clare squeezed her friend's hand. "You're amazing. You're following your dream, and that's just the most wonderful thing ever."

"Speaking of dreams," Astrid said. "Harlan told me that Mattie and John got an offer on the Bean Pot. If you want to buy it for a cupcake store, you have to move fast."

Dread plunged in Clare's belly, eradicating the feeling of peace that had just been coming to rest inside her. "Are they going to take it?"

"He doesn't know. It's a good offer, but it's to a family moving up from New York City who wants to turn it into a place selling New York style pizza." Astrid raised her brows. "They would rather sell it to someone local, but they need the money, so they'll take it if they get nothing else."

Clare bit her lip. "I can't—"

"You can!" Astrid smacked her hands on the table "Come on, Clare! You hate your job, and you don't make much money from it anyway. Just take a risk. I did, and look where it got me."

"You don't have a daughter to support!"

Pain flashed in Astrid's eyes. "No, I don't."

Crud. "I'm sorry. I didn't mean it like that—"

"No, it's fine." Astrid waved her hand in dismissal. "But I am worried about you. I see the strain in your face while you're at work. I didn't realize how unhappy you are until I saw the difference today, when you were smiling about Griffin. That was a real smile, not the one you wear at work." She cocked her head. "Are you happy with your life, Clare? Are you really?"

Clare met her friend's worried gaze. "Truly. I don't want the store." But the words stung her throat, and she knew it wasn't the whole truth. But she had to make it the truth, because she didn't have any options right now. Maybe in ten years. But not today.

"Well, okay, then. I'll tell Harlan you're not making an offer." Astrid stood up as Ophelia called her name from the deli. "My order's ready. I'm taking it back to the office because I need to work through lunch. I have an order I need to get in the mail by two, and I'm not done with the engraving yet." She kissed Clare's cheek. "Have a good time on your date tonight."

Clare smiled, the tension leaving her body as she thought of the upcoming evening. "I will."

And she would. No matter how tough her day might be, she had Griffin to look forward to, and that gave her strength. Clare picked up the note that was still on the table, and she read the words over again. Yes, tonight would be perfect.

"How long until he leaves?" Astrid asked.

Clare looked up at Astrid's question, and a cold weight settled on her shoulders. "I don't know."

"I guess we never really know, do we? Even when promises are made." Astrid slung her purse over her shoulder. "Well, enjoy it, and don't worry about the future."

"Okay." But as she watched Astrid weave past people at the deli to get her food, Clare's thoughts disobeyed her and she began to worry about the future.

About the day when Griffin walked out of her life forever.

CHAPTER TWENTY

"CHAMPAGNE," Phillip told their tuxedo-clad waiter. "Your finest."

Griffin leaned back in his chair as the waiter laid out a fresh set of silverware for his next course. "Don't you think the champagne is a little premature? We don't have a deal yet." He was feeling a little cranky even though the meeting had gone well. Maybe it was the guilt over breaking his promise to Clare to be there when she woke up. Was she mad? He hadn't been able to get her out of his mind. He'd tried to call several times, but hadn't been able to reach her. He needed to hear her voice, to know she was all right. It was making him crazy that he couldn't get in touch with her.

Phillip barked with amusement. "Were you in the same meeting I was? They were ready to roll over and hand us the whole company for free."

Griffin tapped his index finger against his water goblet, watching the conch-shell shaped ice cubes dance off the crystal etchings on the glass. "Not quite—"

"Of course." Phillip grinned. "You were brilliant as usual. When they heard our vision for the company and you explained to them the process we went through to turn Free Love into a worldwide name, they were so excited."

Griffin had to acknowledge that truth. "They were, weren't they?" It had been a rush seeing them get so fired up about his vision. He'd liked that. Yeah, it had felt good to be in that meeting and to feed on that excitement.

"Hell, yeah. And when you said you'd keep them on as the lead designers, I thought they were going to break out into song right then."

"It was the right call." The moment Griffin had walked in the room and looked at the young artist couple who owned In Your Face, he'd known how to handle them to get them to sell at the right price. They were designers, not business people, and running their business had gotten to the point that it was draining them. They wanted the freedom to create and the money from the sale, but they didn't want to let go of their baby, so he'd offered them a deal that gave them everything they wanted.

"They'll be a great support staff when we bring in another designer, one with a brand name," Phillip said, "and then we'll ease them out."

"No." Griffin shook his head. "They need to stay as the lead designers."

Phillip frowned as the waiter began pouring the champagne. "They don't have the reputation to support our business plan. We need a big name in there—"

"Didn't you feel their passion?" Griffin thought back to the way they'd talked about their company and their designs. The two young designers had been practically vibrating with the energy of their vision. They'd reminded him of Clare while she was baking: alive, passionate and overflowing with that special talent that came only from tapping into your true self. "Their souls are wrapped up in that company, and that's what we need to drive this thing."

"Souls?" Phillip set down the champagne, giving him a strange look. "Since when is business about the soul?"

"I think maybe it always is." Griffin never thought about it before, and up until about a week ago, he would have thought it was insane. Business was about forecasts, balance sheets, good product, and smart management. But now he knew there was more involved. To get this company where they wanted to go, they had to go deeper. "We need them. They're our fire."

"I don't know what this talk is about souls, but if you feel like we need them..." Phillip studied him for minute, then shrugged. "I wouldn't be where I am today without listening to your gut. We'll keep them on." Phillip raised his glass. "To In Your Face."

Hot damn. They were really going to run this business from the soul? It was totally out of character for Griffin, but at the same time, it felt right, so completely right. Immense satisfaction rolled through Griffin and he raised his champagne. "To In Your Face."

They clinked glasses, and Griffin let the bubbly liquid slide down his throat. It was a lot smoother than Birch's Best, that was for sure. Weird, but he almost missed the feeling of his head getting blown off by Birch's.

Apparently not suffering the same issue, Phillip drained his glass and slammed it down on the linen table cloth. "Good thing my wife's getting tired of me being around, because we're going to be busy as hell once this thing closes."

Eighteen-hour days again. Griffin remembered all too well the energy it took to get a company off the ground. They'd been working hundred and twenty hour weeks for the first several years of Free Love, before it had taken off, and it had eased off to one hundred or so once things had started to roll.

"You need to take care of the Brooke situation and get

down here by early next week," Phillip said. "Brooke will be so excited about it. Have you told her yet?"

"No. Not until it's done." Shit, he hoped she was excited. If she wasn't involved, she'd never buy into his long work days. How was he going to start a business and pull off the single dad as well? "Does Pamela give you grief when you work the long hours?"

"Hell no. We have an understanding," Phillip said. "She spends the money and goes to the kids' ball games, and they make themselves available when I can be around." Phillip's eyes narrowed. "You getting grief from Hillary again?"

Griffin shrugged. "It's come up."

"Okay, here's the deal." Phillip grabbed a roll and pulled it apart. "Fuck 'em."

"Phil—"

"No, really. She wants to make you into a man you're not. You go with that, and you die." Phillip shoved a large piece of roll into his mouth. "In business, do you capitulate when someone tells you to go against your gut? Hell no. So, why give it up for your ex-wife?" Phillip gestured to the splendor surrounding them. "This is your world, Griff. If you weren't working twenty hours a day, you'd be lost. Screw Hillary. She found her dream, so go live yours and don't worry about it."

Griffin didn't even bother to look around at their luxurious surroundings. He knew what it looked like. He'd been there a thousand times, and at this point, it was just sparkles and baubles, and it didn't mean anything. Not like the smells emanating from Clare's kitchen, or the coziness of her bedroom. "But Brooke feels the same way—"

"She's been poisoned by Hillary. What fifteen-year-old needs her dad around all the time? Get her out of there, and it'll be fine. You ever have problems getting along with her before Hillary left?"

"Well, no," Griffin admitted. "She was always happy to see

me." Wasn't she? But as he thought back to it, he wasn't so sure anymore...

"See? It's all good. It's just Hillary."

Wasn't that what Norm had said? That the protests weren't Brooke's, but Hillary and Dan's? So, yeah, okay, maybe Phillip was right. Maybe it had been Hillary who'd hated his life and his work, not Brooke. "She'll be so fired-up about In Your Face," he admitted.

"You bet she will. The owners were all over having her involved. They loved the idea of their target consumer having an active role."

Yes, yes, that was true. "They were excited, weren't they?" He'd broached that subject early on, and they had thought it was brilliant. "There's room for Brooke to get involved." He'd liked the owners. He'd liked their passion and their ethics, and it would be great for Brooke to have them as role models, people who believed in working hard for the love of it.

"Hello? Teen girl on the cutting edge of fashion? She'll be the most popular kid in her class."

"True." Griffin began to warm to the idea, and his hesitation began to fade. "We could even create a line of clothing with her name on it. From one teen to another."

"Yes!" Phillip grabbed his computer out of his briefcase and started typing. "That gives us street cred. Keep the ideas coming, Griffin." He pointed at him. "Brooke is going to be our secret key. You are going to rock her world."

Griffin leaned back in his chair with his champagne glass, pleasure pulsing through him as plans began to roll through his mind about how to turn In Your Face into a father-daughter legacy. It was all coming together. He'd done it. He'd really done it. He was getting it all.

And damn, it felt good.

But hell. How was he going to tell Clare?

"KATIE, we need to talk about this summer," Clare cornered her daughter as the teenager tried to sneak up the stairs to her bedroom after school.

Clare had been in her room, trying to pick out the right outfit for her date when she'd heard the front door open. She'd hurried right out to see Katie, and had still almost missed her.

"What's there to talk about?" Katie had her hands on her hips and was sporting the same attitude as she'd left the house with ten hours ago. So much for a day at school giving her some perspective. "You want me to go to MIT. I don't want to go."

Clare tried again to explain, to help her daughter understand. "The festival will be there for years and years. MIT won't. Go to MIT this summer, and try the Shakespeare thing another time."

"Mom!" Katie made a noise of frustration. "You aren't listening to me! I don't want to go to MIT! Not ever!"

"I don't care." Clare steeled herself against the guilt of forcing her daughter. She didn't want to be the kind of autocratic mother who demanded adherence, but if she couldn't gain consensus, what other choice was there? Katie couldn't stay here and do the festival. She just couldn't. "You're going to MIT anyway."

"Dad wouldn't make me!" Katie snapped. "Dad believed in following his dreams!'

"Dad *died*," Clare snapped. For God's sake! She was so tired of Katie deifying Ed. The man had betrayed them all and left Clare to do all the hard work and all the sacrificing.

"Maybe Dad died because you wouldn't let him live his dreams," Katie retorted. "Did you ever think of that?"

Clare stared at her daughter in shock at the accusation. "Katie—"

"Think about it, Mom. Dad came to town as an actor." Katie came down several steps, getting closer as the accusation rose in her voice. "He wasn't planning to stay, was he? But he tried to give up his dream for you. And when he did that, a part of him died. Who killed my dad, huh? Was it a slippery road? Or was it you?"

Clare was too shocked to refute it. Dear God. Her daughter was right. Ed had been on that road that night because he'd had to escape from her. The storm had been raging, the tires on the car old, and she'd begged him to stay the night, to wait until morning, but he'd refused. He'd said he couldn't stay in the town with his spirit dying for one more minute, and he'd left, driving right to his death. "Oh, God."

Katie froze, her face stricken. "I'm right? I'm actually right?"

Clare slumped down on a chair. "Oh, God."

Katie leapt off the stairs and came over. "What happened that night, Mom? What haven't you told me?"

Clare looked up into her daughter's desperate eyes. And for the first time, she saw the pain etched so deeply in them. A child who had grown up with a void in her past, a father who'd never been there. Her sweet little girl was just an innocent being who'd spent a lifetime trying to piece together facts to create an image of the man who'd given her life.

Katie knelt before Clare and took her hands. "Mom," she begged. "Tell me what really happened. Tell me about my father. I need to know. You never talk about him. Not ever. You're the only one who really knew him."

Clare set her hand on her daughter's head, and she felt her heart break for her. For the need for answers. For closure. But how could she destroy Katie by telling her that the man she'd idolized and defended her whole life had actually been walking out on her? He'd left Clare, yes, but he'd also left behind a two-month-old daughter who had been the final impetus that drove him out of Birch Crossing.

"Mom?"

Clare couldn't do it. She couldn't put that burden on her daughter. Not even to defend herself. Not even to preserve her relationship with her. She couldn't destroy her daughter's spirit like that. She just couldn't. "I'm sorry, Katie. There's nothing more to tell."

"Argh!" Katie groaned in disgust and lurched to her feet. "You drive me insane! I'm going to sleep at Sara's tonight. I can't deal with you!"

"Maybe that's best." Clare had no idea what to say, or how to bridge the chasm growing between them. If only Griffin was there. Somehow, he seemed to connect with Katie in a way that she couldn't.

Suddenly, she felt the burden of being a single parent. Of not having anyone else to turn to for help or advice. She'd never felt that loss before, but seeing Griffin deal with Katie had made her realize that she wasn't perfect, that she couldn't do it all. And that was just not a good thing to realize when that new support system was going to go back to Boston all too soon. She had to find her strength again. Figure it out. Maybe Eppie could help.

But right now, she needed space from Katie before she damaged the relationship permanently. She needed time to figure out how to handle this before she caused more harm. Katie was her light, her life, and she couldn't bear the idea of causing her more pain, or of their bond cracking. "Do you need a ride?"

"No. Sara and her brother are waiting for me outside." Katie started up the stairs. "I just came home to get clothes for tomorrow."

Clare waited while her daughter retrieved her belongings,

and she walked Katie to the door. "I'm sorry, sweetheart. I do love you, you know."

Katie's jaw jutted out. "You just love the image you have of me."

"What? That's not true—"

"Yes, it is." Katie's eyes were glistening with tears, and Clare knew hers were reflecting the same. "You love the daughter who will go to MIT and make tons of money. The one you can brag about, a daughter who isn't an embarrassment like your husband was."

Clare felt like a knife had just been plunged into her heart. Did her daughter really believe that? "That's not true. I love you no matter what—"

"Are you so sure about that?" Katie challenged.

"Of course I am! How can you even doubt that? I love you!"

Katie held up her hand in dismissal. "I can't deal with this. I'll see you tomorrow. I have physics club after school, so I'll be home late. I'm sure that will be fine with you, given that it's physics and all."

"Yes, it's fine." Clare touched her daughter's arm. "I have one request."

Katie looked at her impatiently. "What?"

"Tonight, while you're away from here, take some time to think about everything. Listen to your heart, not your anger, when you think about whether I love you. Will you do that?"

To her relief, some of the anger on her daughter's face faded, and she nodded. "Okay."

"Okay." Clare held out her arms. "Hug?"

Katie sighed, but she quickly hugged her. Clare crushed her daughter to her, and she suddenly knew why her mother had always hugged her so tightly. Because sometimes, words weren't enough.

~

BY THE TIME Griffin drove up to Clare's house, his anticipation and excitement about In Your Face had morphed into tension about telling Clare.

Phillip had finalized the paperwork and sent the initial offer over to the owners, and they'd responded with excitement. Things were happening, and they were happening fast. What had felt great and right when Griffin had been in Boston had turned into tension the closer he'd gotten to Clare's house.

But when he'd rounded the corner and seen that old rambling farmhouse with its peeling paint, he realized he was glad to be home, even if he was going to have to create conflict.

He pulled into the driveway and turned off the truck. But he didn't get out. Should he tell her right away? Or later? Or—

The door opened and Clare came out onto the back step. She was wearing a pair of jeans that hugged her hips perfectly. A soft blue tank top floated over her torso like the breeze had been harnessed and turned into fabric. Her auburn hair was loose, tumbling down around her shoulders, catching the light of the bulb by the door so it appeared almost golden. She looked beautiful, feminine and radiant—

Then he noticed that her arms were folded across her chest. How many times had he caught that pose from Hillary when he'd arrived home late? Shit. He knew he was late, but he'd changed their reservation and he'd left Clare a message.

But there was no mistaking that body language. She was upset, and he hadn't even told her about the deal yet.

Then he remembered Phillip's advice, and he narrowed his eyes. She had no right to judge him. He'd busted his ass to get back here this early, and he should have gotten at least ten speeding tickets on his way. And *she* was pissed at *him*?

Well, screw that. He'd had enough of that.

He shoved the door open and stepped outside, bristling. "Clare—"

"Griffin!" She erupted into sudden movement, racing down the stairs and running at him.

He had a split second to brace himself before she flung herself into his arms and hugged him as if he'd been gone for a thousand years and a day. For a moment, he didn't know what to do, and he awkwardly fumbled in the air, not sure whether to hold her. Wasn't she mad at him?

Then he felt the warmth of her body sinking against him, the tightness of her arms around his neck and the intimacy of her face buried in his chest, and everything was all right. "It's okay, Clare." He wrapped his arms around her and held her close. "I'm home."

"I know." Her voice was muffled. "I'm so happy you're back."

Griffin kissed her hair and hugged her more tightly. There was no recrimination from Clare, no anger, no judgment. Just pure welcome. "Me, too." He caught her under the chin and lifted her head. "I need to kiss you."

She smiled and nodded.

He kissed her then, right in the driveway, in front of anyone who might drive by, and she kissed him back. And it was, he was sure, the best kiss he'd ever had. And within about two minutes, he was ready to forego dinner, toss her over his shoulder, and play the caveman role with his cupcake goddess.

But she deserved more than that. She deserved to be honored...and then tossed into bed. So, he forced himself to end the kiss. They were both breathing hard, and Clare was smiling.

"Damn, you're beautiful," Griffin mused. "A man could look at you every day for his whole life, and still want more."

Clare's smile brightened. "You have no idea how much I needed to hear that tonight."

His smile faded at the pain in her voice. "What happened?"

She shook her head. "I'll tell you at dinner. I just want to get out of the house."

"Okay." He kissed her again, then opened the door for her. "Your chariot, my dear."

She ran her hand over the dashboard as she climbed in. "I haven't been in here since that night on the mountain."

Griffin leaned on the door. "The best night of my life."

She gave him a flirty look that woke certain parts of him right up. "What about last night?"

"Hmm... good point. I'll have to think about that one. I really like rainstorms though, so I think the mud might trump."

"Mud? Hey—"

He shut the door on her protest. Laughing, he jogged around the truck to his side. Two minutes with Clare, and all the tension of the day had left. He felt like a new man again.

As he pulled open his door, he made his decision.

He would tell her about the business later.

Right now was about them.

CHAPTER TWENTY-ONE

CLARE WAS GLOWING TONIGHT, Griffin decided. There was no other way to describe her. Maybe it was the dark beams and the lake view of the quaint little restaurant perched on the northern point of the lake. Maybe it was the intimate table for two. Maybe it was the brightly colored, mismatched dishes and glasses that befitted the casual restaurant. Maybe it was the open flame grill roasting some mouth-watering steaks. Or maybe, it was just him, seeing her exactly as she really was.

He didn't know what it was, but the moment they'd arrived at the Finch Grill and been seated in the corner by the fire as he'd requested, the burden in Clare's eyes had appeared to subside. She'd been animated and happy, telling him about Eppie and her mother. The story had touched a chord in his heart he hadn't realized he had. "You never talked about your mom before."

"I know." Clare filched an olive from his plate with a mischievous expression. "It's hard to talk about her. I always felt that I was letting her down."

"How?"

"You know. Thirty-three. Unmarried. A house that's falling apart. I didn't give Katie the family my mom wanted her to have. My mom was the daughter of a minister and she was very conservative. Having her daughter married and pregnant at age eighteen was not what she'd had in mind. We had words over it, right until the day she died."

Griffin took her hand and pressed his lips to the back of it. "She was worried for you. It wasn't disappointment."

"I never understood that until today." She smiled, and the peace on her face touched him. "But after talking to Eppie, and hearing this cantankerous, judgmental old lady tell me, with total honesty, that my mom would be proud of me..." She shrugged. "All these fears I'd been holding for so long just kind of fell off me."

Griffin smiled. "Good. You deserve to be free of that burden." He leaned forward. "But you also need to know that it doesn't actually matter what your mom would think. You're an amazing woman and that doesn't change if someone disagrees with you."

She picked up her wine, the rosy tint of it sparkling with the reflection of the fire. "I know, but sometimes I think they're saying it because they're right." She took a sip. "Sometimes, I think the people in your life know you better than you know yourself."

Griffin shook his head. "No way. They only know what they want you to be. That's not the same thing—" His phone rang and he glanced down. "It's Brooke."

Clare clapped her hands in delight. "Answer it."

His heart racing, he hit 'Send' and put the phone to his ear. "Brookie?"

"It's Hillary."

"Oh." He sighed and leaned back in his chair. He was not in the mood for her grief and judgment tonight, not that he ever was, of course. "Hill, I'm at dinner—"

"Brooke told me you said no to changing her name."

Griffin drummed his fingers on the table impatiently. "Of course I'm not going to let her. She's my daughter."

"Oh, come on, Griffin! She's not your daughter anymore. I'm not sure she ever was, not in the way that really matters."

His grip tightened on the phone, trying to remember Norm's advice that Hillary wasn't necessarily reflecting Brooke's point of view, no matter what she claimed. "What's that supposed to mean?"

"You were never there for her. Not ever. And the only reason you want her now is because you want to stake your claim of ownership on her. That's not what being a father is. Let her go, Griffin, for all of our sakes."

Griffin scowled, tired of the judgment. "No chance, Hillary. Don't call me again." Then he hung up his phone and tossed it on the table. He saw Clare watching him and he grimaced. "Sorry about that." He leaned forward and took her hand, trying to get back in the frame of mind he'd been in. "Tonight is about us."

Clare cocked her head. "Can I ask you a question?"

"Of course. Anything." Griffin concentrated on the soft-ness of her hand, the gentleness of her touch, and his hostility began to fade. "You chase away my demons," he commented.

She smiled. "Good."

"Yeah." Yes, it was good.

"Why do Brooke and Hillary say you were the one who abandoned them? Did you really leave them?"

Griffin sat back as their server placed their salads before them, tension roiling through him at her question. Hell. He didn't want Hillary to overshadow the evening with Clare. "It doesn't matter. Tonight is about us."

Clare smiled a thank you at the server, then picked up her fork. "It does matter. I want to know."

Resistance darkened his mood. "What? So you can judge me?"

She gave him a placid look. "I let a potential murderer into my home. I would think that would be sufficient proof that I think you're a good guy despite all the rumors." She laid her hand on his forearm and squeezed gently. "Relax, Griffin. It's me."

He let out his breath. "Yeah, okay." This was the woman who'd given herself to him last night, the woman who'd thrown herself into his arms to welcome him home. And suddenly, he wanted her to know. He wanted *someone* to know what had happened, someone who might actually believe him. "I thought everything was fine," he said. "Life was the same as it had always been. I was working long hours, yeah, but I was making good money and Hillary was spending it happily."

Clare rubbed his arm, watching him with warmth evident on her face.

"Things got a little crazy at work. One of my directors was funneling off funds, and we had to bring in the police and sue him. It was a real hassle." He shrugged. "I was late a lot. I was stressed. It happens."

"Of course it does." She wove her fingers between his and squeezed. "So, what happened then?"

"I don't know." He toyed with his salad, revisiting that moment. "I still don't understand. It was a Thursday night, and I was supposed to go to a show at Brooke's school, and I missed it, but I called ahead, and she was like yeah, whatever. When I got home at midnight, the house was empty."

Clare raised her brows. "She'd taken all the furniture?"

"No, no, the furniture was still there. Everything was still there, except when I walked in..." He paused recalling that moment. "I stepped inside, and I knew something was wrong, that something bad had happened. I dropped my briefcase and sprinted upstairs to the bedrooms, shouting for Brooke and Hillary. They weren't there. I was panicked, terrified when I found their empty beds. I thought someone had kidnapped them. I knew they weren't just out. I could feel the difference. Their presence was gone." His heart began to pound again, just like it had that night. "I ran through the house, shouting for them, searching everywhere, but they were gone. I called the police, I called the neighbors. I couldn't even breathe."

Clare inched her chair closer, and hugged his hand to her heart.

"So, I was standing there in the kitchen, and I was leaning over the sink, trying to catch my breath while I waited for the police to arrive, and then I saw it. A note. She'd left me a note. She'd scrawled it on a piece of printer paper. Huge letters, taking up the whole page." He'd stared blankly at it for what felt like an eternity, not understanding the words, not comprehending the meaning, just numb with shock. "It said she was leaving me. That was it. Nothing else."

Clare grasped the front of his shirt and tugged lightly. "Come here."

He allowed her to pull him toward her, and was surprised when she kissed him, right there in front of dozens of patrons. And he knew, in that moment, that she wasn't going to judge him, and a lead weight fell from his shoulders. By the time she finished, his tension had eased. "How do you do that?" he asked.

She smiled. "I'm a woman. I'm naturally hard-wired to provide comfort to people in need."

"Not all women have that talent."

Her smile faded as she studied him. "During that brief time I was married to Ed," she said. "He was always working on his acting, trying to improve, trying to find local gigs. He always missed dinner, he was never around, and even if he was there, he wouldn't ever talk to me." She laid her hand on Griffin's cheek. "Not like you, Griffin. When you're with me, you are completely present in the moment. You notice me, you listen to me, and you care. You make me feel treasured."

He pressed a kiss to the back of her hand. "You deserve to feel like that."

"Thank you." She watched him closely, and he sensed she was measuring her words. "But with Ed, even while he was living with us, he wasn't connected to us. He left us long before he drove away."

Griffin narrowed his eyes. "What's your point?"

"My point is that I think it's possible that you weren't emotionally present for Hillary and Brooke the way you are for me and Katie." She held up her hand to silence his protest. "You weren't there physically, either, and the combination maybe created a feeling that you had left, even if you technically still lived there."

"I didn't leave! I was working my ass off for them!" He pulled his hand free of hers. "You're like them, judging me—"

"No, no, no." She tried to take his hand again, but he didn't let her. "I'm just trying to help you get your daughter back. Don't you get it? You can't just demand her back or say you love her. You have to actually feel her in your heart, the way you do with me and Katie! You did abandon them, but you don't have to be like that anymore." She set her hand on his shoulder. "You *are* the man you want to be, but you won't get your daughter back until you let her into your heart. It's not about the money, Griffin. It's about the connection."

Griffin glared at her. "You're interfering where you aren't welcome."

Clare scowled back at him, and she took her hand off his shoulder. "So? What's your point?"

"My point? My point is that I want you to back off. I'm done being judged."

Clare glared at him. "Did it ever occur to you that I might be pushing at you not because I'm judging you, but because I'm tired of you judging yourself? Because I see this amazing man whose heart is breaking because he doesn't understand how wonderful he is? For God's sake, Griffin, not everyone who yells at you is your enemy. Some of them shout at you out of love!"

"That's crap! You don't yell at people you love."

"Oh! You drive me mad!" She shoved her chair back and threw her napkin on the table. "Forget it. I can't deal with you on top of Katie. Doesn't anyone understand love around here? I'm trying! Doesn't anyone get that?" Tears filled her eyes, and she whirled away and raced for the door.

Oh, *shit*. The hurt on her face told him the truth: that she did believe in him and she did think he was worthy of his daughter. Shit. He'd totally overreacted and hurt her. "Clare!" Griffin leapt up and gave chase, catching up just as she stepped out onto the sidewalk. He caught her hand. "Clare—"

She spun toward him and yanked her hand free. "Leave me alone!" Her fists were clenched, and her eyes were flashing fire, but the anguish in her voice and the tears streaming down her cheeks eviscerated him.

"I'm so sorry," he said. "I'm so sorry, Clare."

"You're a jerk! I was just trying to help."

"I know, I know. I'm an ass." He held up his hands in surrender. "A complete jerk."

She sniffled. "That's my point. You're not an ass. You just act like one sometimes."

He smiled. "I know. I understand that now." He held out his arms. "Come here."

She folded her arms over her chest. "I'm still mad at you."

"And you should be." He took her wrist and tugged her so she fell into him. He immediately wrapped her up in his arms and hugged her. Really, really hugged her. Not the reluctant, impatient hug he used to give Hillary, but the kind of embrace where their bodies meshed, and his soul wrapped around hers to protect her and keep her safe. "I'm so sorry, Clare. I really am."

She sighed, and then she softened her body, melting into his. When she finally wrapped her arms around his waist, he knew he hadn't blown it. Clare had forgiven him, and it felt amazing.

For a long moment, they just stood there, holding each other, and it was a perfect moment. Griffin had no urge to end it, no desire to get to work, no calling to move on, and no drive to be productive. He was content to simply hold her.

"Do you think they took away our salads?" Clare finally asked.

"I doubt it. I haven't paid and my phone is still on the table." He pulled back so he could look at her. Tears streaked her cheeks, and she looked exhausted. "What happened with Katie today?"

She shook her head. "Never mind. I'm too tired."

He kissed her lightly. "That's what I'm here for. Sometimes it doesn't go away until you talk about it." He took her hand. "Come on. We'll give it a three minute limit, and then there's no more heavy discussion tonight, okay? We'll just discuss how beautiful you are, how great your cupcakes are—" He frowned at the flash of pain on Clare's face "What did I say? Something about the cupcakes?"

"Nothing." She sighed and leaned her head against his shoulder as they walked, in an intimate gesture that made him want to sweep her up in his arms and cradle her.

"There's no chance I'm going to believe you that there's nothing wrong." He held open the door for her. "I won't give up until you tell me."

"Maybe you really are a pain in the ass." She wrinkled her nose at him.

He laughed. "Probably, but I have it on good authority that I'm still a great guy even when I'm being an ass." He guided her across the dining room, to where the waiter was standing over their table wringing his hands. Griffin jerked his chin at him, and the waiter nodded with visible relief and vanished back into the kitchen.

Griffin pulled out Clare's chair and helped her sit. Then he took his seat, moved it closer to hers, and then took her hand again. "Now, tell me. Cupcakes first."

"It's nothing." Clare picked up her fork and fiddled with her salad. "It's just that Astrid told me at lunch today that there is an offer on that place she thinks I should buy for a cupcake store."

Griffin studied her. "You want to buy it?"

"No." She finally looked at him. "No, I wasn't going to buy it. But I felt a little sad. Like I don't want it, but I don't want anyone else to have it either."

"Clare, maybe you should think about it—"

"No." She shook her fork gently at him. "I don't want to talk about any of this stuff anymore tonight. My life is always about dealing with one problem after another. Tonight, I want to simply be with you." She gave him a small smile. "You take away the chaos and bring peace into my heart. I need that tonight. Can we do that?"

He cupped the back of her head and drew her close to him. "Yes, we can." He kissed her again. Her lips were soft and welcoming, and he felt the turmoil within him cede to a feeling of peace and rightfulness. "I want it, too."

"Okay, then." She smiled.

He set her wine glass into her hand and picked up his own. "To the most beautiful woman in the world, who makes my life better simply by being in it." He tapped his glass against hers. "To Clare."

To the woman he was going to have to leave tomorrow.

~

"I CAN'T BELIEVE you blindfolded me," Clare laughed as she heard Griffin open the door of the truck. After dinner, he'd announced he had a surprise for her, blindfolded her with a tee shirt he'd apparently brought along for that purpose, and put her in his truck. "You're crazy."

"It wouldn't be a surprise if you knew where we were, would it?" He took her hand. "Step down, carefully. I've got you if you fall."

"I'm not going to fall," she teased, though she was happy to let him guide her. "I didn't have that much wine at dinner."

"You didn't? Damn. I was hoping to get you drunk so I could take advantage of you later on."

Feeling a little giddy, Clare giggled as Griffin wrapped his arm around her waist, keeping her solidly against him. "I'm not that kind of girl. There will be no hanky panky tonight." She certainly hoped that was a complete lie. To spend another night in Griffin's arms would be a beautiful gift she would treasure forever.

"Yeah, well, we'll stop at Norm's and get some of Birch's Best and then we'll see how long you can resist me. Come on." He swept her up into his arms. "Allow me."

Clare locked her arms around his neck. "Where are we?" She didn't hear any water, so he must not have brought them to the lake. What romantic spot had Griffin found to cap off their evening?

"You'll see." He climbed a few stairs. "I have to set you down for a second. Don't go anywhere."

"Really? I thought I might go for a run." She set her hand on his back to ground herself, her heart dancing. After their fight in the restaurant, the night had turned magical. It was as if their fight had unleashed a spark between them, and the connection had been wonderful. Griffin had wooed her like a prince, with magical words and champagne, and she'd felt like she was in a fairy tale. And then when he'd blindfolded her in the parking lot and told her he had a surprise, well, she'd really kind of melted.

It had been a very, very long time since anyone had given her a surprise.

Griffin muttered something to himself, and then she heard the sound of a key sliding into a lock. A building? Where in the world were they? It was almost midnight already. "Did you rent a motel room for us?"

"Why would I want to sleep anywhere but at your house?"

She smiled at the honesty in his voice. "It's not the Ritz."

"And thank God for that." A door creaked, and then she felt Griffin's hands on her waist as he picked her up again. "Okay, sweetheart. Here we go."

Light glared, and she knew he'd turned on some lights. He set her down carefully, and kept his hands on her hips. "I want you to promise me something," he said.

"What?" Her heart began to race. She couldn't imagine what he was about to unveil.

"I want you to see with your heart, and not with your mind."

Clare frowned. "See what?"

"What I'm about to show you. I don't want you to think about it. Just feel it, okay?"

Now she was confused. "Um, okay—"

"Good." He sounded excited. "Here you go." He dropped the blindfold, and Clare squinted at the sudden brightness.

It took her eyes a moment to adjust, and then she was able to see. She was in a small, empty café with round wooden tables and matching chairs. A beautiful pine counter with a glass display case on the right. A huge blackboard on the wall by the ceiling, listing every kind of coffee beverage known to human kind. Disappointment killed her excitement. "You brought me to the Bean Pot? But I told you that I'm not going to buy it—"

"No." Griffin pressed his finger to her lips. "I told you. No thinking. Just feeling. Agreed?"

She sighed but nodded. Anything to get this over with and get home.

"Okay." Griffin freed her lips and then put his arm around her shoulders and turned her toward the seating area. "I want you, just for a minute, to envision it in a different way." He gestured to the dark wood tables and plain chairs. "Those are pale pink with white legs. The chairs match." He turned her toward the counter. "The chalk board is covered with beautiful writing in blue and pink and yellow and white. Names like Brooke's Sweetie. And Honeymoon Surprise. And Fairy Wings."

She started to smile. "Fairy Wings?"

"And here—" He jogged over to the display case. "This is covered with bright, clear glass, and the shelves are brass so shiny it sparkles like gold." He spread his hands over the area, as if he were casting a magic spell across it. "Inside are dozens of cupcakes. Pink ones. Chocolate decadence. Mint delicacies. Even some made with Birch's Beer. Those are called Man Cakes."

She broke out in a laugh. "Man Cakes? Really?"

"Of course, really. The construction guys love 'em. They're loaded with beer, extra sugar and fat, and they're made from chips and pizza dough."

She set her hands on her hips, grinning at Griffin's silliness. "Griffin—"

"And look up! Do you see it?"

Cobwebs, old wood beams and a few fluorescent lights. "The spiders?"

"No, no, no." He came up behind her and set his hands on her shoulders, rubbing gently. "That pink and white ceiling fan, shaped like a cupcake. And the paintings on the ceiling. Have you ever seen such bright colors or so many different cupcakes? Emma did a great job on the mural, didn't she? Who knew she could paint with such whimsy?"

And suddenly, Clare could see it. The place came to life with Griffin's vision, and excitement rushed through her. She could see the sparkly gold paint decorating the lemon cupcake with sprinkles. Little children's faces delighting in their desserts. The pink and white striped panels of the ceiling fan. "It's so alive," she whispered.

"And here? Do you see them?" He was standing behind one of the chairs, his hands resting on the back. "This family from Virginia? The mom and dad and three kids? See how happy they are?" He did a sweeping gesture of the table. "They're staying in Portland for a week, but they heard about Clare's Cupcakes, and they had to come see. They drove for almost two hours, and look how happy they are. They bought an extra box to take home and even ordered some to be mailed to the mom's sister in Idaho as a surprise."

Clare set her hands on her hips, laughing with delight as Griffin stopped at each table, regaling her with his stories about the imaginary patrons dining there. His magic was infectious and she could hear the music coming from the jukebox in the corner, she could smell her own creations baking, and the happy energy of the place swirled around them.

Griffin came back and caught her upper arms, his expression intense. "Can you see it, Clare? Can you feel the magic?"

"I can." She really could. "All this from cupcakes?"

"All this from *your* cupcakes." He put his arm around her

shoulder and turned her to face the room. "This is your dream, Clare, and you can make it come true. Right here. Right now. It's time."

At his words, her excitement faded, replaced by a sensation of emptiness. She ducked out from his arm and walked toward the door. "It's not time."

"How can you say that?" He blocked her path to the door. "I saw your face when you were picturing it. I know you saw the magic. I know you felt it." He tapped his fingers on the left side of her chest. "Your heart beats for it. I know it does. Can you really deny it?"

"I don't—" Her denial died under the urgency of Griffin's expression. His dark eyes were full of fire and passion, and she knew she couldn't lie anymore. Not to him. Not to herself. "It is my dream," she finally said quietly. "I would love to do this."

He smiled, a gentle, supportive smile. "Then do it."

"I can't."

"Why not?"

"I have a daughter to support. I have to provide a home for her and pay for her college and whatever else she needs." When Griffin started to shake his head, she grabbed his arms. "It's my job as her mother! I have to provide a safe world for her. I can't give her a family or a father or siblings or grandparents, so I have to do what I can."

"You've given her a family. You're all she needs."

"But if I take out a loan to buy this place, and it fails, I have nothing. Her college funds will be gone, and—"

"She'll get scholarships."

"No!" She pulled away, her eyes burning. "I'm still paying off my student loans. It's a burden I don't want her to deal with. I want her to graduate from college free and clear, ready to follow her dreams."

"Really?" He folded his arms over his chest, looking smug. "That's what you want? For her to follow her dreams?"

"Yes, of course—"

"How is she supposed to learn how to follow her own dreams if her only role model is a mother who won't follow hers?"

"That's not fair! I don't have the choice—"

"Of course you have a choice," he said. "Do you really think you're doing Katie favors by slaving away at a job you hate? Don't you think the better message is to teach her to follow her dreams? She idolizes her father for following his, doesn't she? Don't you think she'd rather see you happy and fulfilled, than unhappy and financially solvent?"

Clare thought of Katie's desire to be in the festival, and she folded her arms. "There are limits to dreams. She might want to be an actress, but now is not the time to find out. She needs to be responsible and diligent and get her education right now."

"You don't want her to follow her dreams?" Griffin challenged. "You just said you did."

"When she's older! She's too young to know what her dreams are right now." Clare glanced over at the counter again, and could almost see her cupcakes arranged on the display. "Dreams should be planned carefully and embarked upon at the right time."

"What if you wait too long?" He challenged. "What if you let this go, and you spend the next thirty years going to that office every day to draft another will for a client? Sitting there at night, unable to make time to bake because you're manipulating legalese to make sure that the favorite son will get the farm and the unloved daughter will wind up with the skunk cabbage? You want that?"

Clare ground her jaw. "It's not that bad—"

"Of course it is! You hate it, Clare."

"I don't hate it! I'm proud of what I've accomplished! I've worked hard to get where I am." Anger rushed through her. "I created a stable home for my daughter, and I'm not going to risk it for a stupid dream about cupcakes!"

Griffin said nothing. He just looked at her.

Clare's fury faded into silence, and she sank down into one of the chairs.

Griffin sat next to her and took her hand. "You can always go back to being an attorney. But you'll never know if you don't try."

Clare felt so defeated. Her heart ached for the dream she was facing. "I can't do it right now."

"Why?"

"Because I'm getting sued."

Griffin laughed softly. "Seems to be even more of a reason to get out."

"I can't afford to." She finally looked at him and confessed the weight that she'd been too embarrassed to share with anyone. "A will I wrote was successfully contested in court, and the heirs who lost out are suing me for malpractice. They want me to compensate them for the value of what they lost."

Griffin frowned. "They'll never win—"

"It doesn't matter. I have to pay an attorney and go to court, or I have to settle." She looked at him. "It's already depleting my savings. I can't afford to sink a down payment into a new building and then invest everything I have in startup costs. I need to bear down and re-stabilize and then maybe try again in ten years or so."

"Ten years." Griffin leaned back in his seat. "That's a long time."

"I know."

He rubbed his jaw. "I could lend you the money."

Clare smiled at his offer. "No, but thank you."

"Why not?" He sat up. "I'll be part owner. It won't be a

favor. It'll be a business investment. I'll just be the silent investor. You can send me repayment and profit sharing once a month."

She looked at him. "How in God's name could I possibly write your name on checks once a month and ever be able to recover from losing you from my life?"

He looked startled. "Clare—"

"No." She slid her hand beneath his. "This time with you is a treasure, and it will break my heart when you leave. There's no way on earth I will ever be able to move on if we own a business together." She paused, and hope flared in her eyes. "Unless you would move here to run it? Is that what you meant?"

For a moment, Griffin wanted to say yes. He really did. But like Clare's dream, it wasn't reality. It wasn't who he was. Owning a cupcake store wasn't how he was going to win his daughter back. He wasn't the man Clare wanted and needed in her life. "No," he said quietly. "I can't do that. I belong in Boston."

"Do you? Are you so sure?"

"Clare." He took her hand. "If I tried to stay here, I would be like Ed. My focus would be in Boston, and eventually I would leave. I won't do that to you. You deserve more."

She pressed her lips together and nodded. "I know. I know all that." She smiled. "But a girl can have dreams."

"Yes, she can." He took her hand and kissed it. "Let's go home, Clare. I want to be with you tonight."

She squeezed his hand. "Yes, I need that."

"Me, too."

CHAPTER TWENTY-TWO

GRIFFIN CARRIED Clare across the threshold of her bedroom.

It wasn't much. She deserved so much more, but it was all he had to give.

When he set her down on the bed, and he saw those pools of blue staring up at him, he knew that he had to make this moment last forever. He had to sink into her and imprint the moment in his mind so it would always be with him. It was almost desperation, the need to memorize her. To record every curve of her body. Every lilt of her words. To wrap her memory up so securely that he could feel like he was with her every minute of every day.

Because he knew what tomorrow was bringing, even if he hadn't shared it with her yet.

Griffin?" She touched his face. "What's wrong?"

He held her hand to his cheek. "I wish I was a different man."

She shook her head. "No, no. If you were, I wouldn't love you."

His chest constricted. "You love me?"

She nodded. "I didn't realize it until I blurted it out at the restaurant."

She loved him. For a moment, Griffin was too overwhelmed to respond, just consumed by a wash of emotions so intense, so powerful, so deep he felt like his chest was going to explode. *She loved him.*

His body trembling, Griffin eased down beside her, needing the comfort of her body against his. Her words had shaken him, rattled him deeply, and he needed her touch to ground him. "Yeah, I noticed that, but I figured it was just because you were mad." Oh, he'd heard those words. And he'd wished, so deeply, so intensely, that they were true. Because if a woman like Clare loved him, then that had to mean there was something redeemable in him.

"That's what I thought." She raised her arms and let him tug her shirt over her head. "That's what I hoped, at least."

He began to kiss her bare shoulder. "You hoped you didn't love me?" Of course she would hope that. Clare was a smart woman.

"Yes." She wrapped her arm around him, holding him close while he kissed his way up her neck.

"Because?" He eased her down, and stretched on top of her, relishing the feel of her body beneath his.

"Because I do have some sense of self-preservation." She hooked her arms around his neck. "But the truth is, that I think I fell in love with you the minute I saw you drive your ridiculously big and shiny truck up the side of the cliff for me."

He grinned, and he sorta felt like jumping off the bed and doing push-ups, he was so fired up by her confession. "My truck is not ridiculous."

"It is." She raised her brows. "But that's not the point."

"I know, I'm teasing." He grinned. "I'm a man. It makes

me uncomfortable to talk about emotions and doing so renders me incapable of coherent speech. So, I make jokes."

"You're such a liar." She punched his shoulder lightly. "You talk about deep things all the time."

He paused to consider her comment while he nibbled on her collar bone, and after a moment, he realized that she was right...when it came to her, that was. "Damn, woman. You've turned me into a softie."

She smiled. "You're welcome."

He cupped her face, needing to get serious. "Clare Gray, you're an amazing woman, and I'm the luckiest guy in the whole damn world to have your love." He kissed her mouth, once, then again. "You honor me," he whispered between kisses. "You amaze me." He kissed her again. "And you make me so happy to be in this place, right now, with you."

He was too overwhelmed with words he didn't know how to articulate. So, he told her in the only way he could. Through his kisses. Through his touch. Through his tenderness.

～

GRIFFIN'S KISSES were different tonight. They were deeper, more passionate, more intentional.

Last time had been a seduction, an introduction to passion, an ascension to the heavens and back.

Tonight, his touch was more tender. The way his hand caressed her shoulder. His light grip on her elbow as he kissed his way down her belly. The sensual slide of his hand across her hip. There was an ownership in his touch. A possession.

Clare closed her eyes and rested her hand on his head as he lightly bit her belly, and then her hip. "You're mine," he said as he nipped her again.

Excitement rippled through her at his deep growl, and she realized she wanted Griffin to stand up and claim her. She wanted to be his, at least for tonight.

He crawled back up her body and kissed her again. Hard. Deep. Relentless.

Her body pulsed in response, and she kissed him back. She needed to taste him. She needed to feel him. She needed all of him. Restlessly, she tugged at his jeans. He caught her hand and pinned her to the bed. "I'm in control tonight," he said.

She smiled in anticipation at the idea of him taking over. "Okay."

He nodded, then kissed her again. He nibbled and kissed his way back down her body and then he was sliding her jeans over her hips. So slowly and deliberately that chills raced down her spine. His palms were warm and seductive as they eased her pants over her legs, and he palmed the back of her calf as he slipped them off.

His dark eyes focused on hers, he kissed her toes, one at a time, as if each one was a present from the angels. His lips drifted to the arch of her foot. A kiss on each side of her ankle. The back of her knee. It was as if he were staking his claim on every inch of her body, memorizing every curve as his hands slid over her thigh and he set her foot on his shoulder.

The other foot now. Toes. Arch. Ankle.

She began to tremble, her nerves singing in anticipation as he kissed the inside of her knee. And then her inner thigh. And then—

"Oh, God." She came off the bed as his mouth closed down on her. He flanked her with his palms, holding her still as he continued to kiss her. Not giving her a moment to breathe or to recover or to—

The orgasm exploded through her and she shouted his name, clutching his shoulders. It hadn't even finished rolling through her when Griffin had ditched his jeans, grabbed a condom and sank himself inside her.

She gasped as he took her again to that peak, moving inside her as he kissed her, awakening in her a restless, insatiable need for him. White hot desire cascaded through her, and this time, she didn't feel nervous. It felt amazing and beautiful, a passionate and natural extension of the beautiful connection between them. She let him stoke the fires, losing herself in the feel of his body moving inside her, claiming her, making her his forever and ever. She knew he was leaving his mark on her, not just her body but her soul as well, but it didn't scare her. It was simply too poignant to fear. Tonight, this night, was their magic, and she breathed his very essence into her heart and let him fill her with his kisses and his lovemaking.

"Clare," he whispered her name, his voice so full of emotions that tears filled her eyes. "I will never forget this moment."

Then he kissed her again, and the intensity of his kiss shattered her. The orgasm crashed over her. He kissed her screams away as he continued to move in a most delicious motion, driving her to that edge relentlessly, with a ruthless desperation, almost as if he was afraid that he would lose her if he stopped, if he let them take a breath.

"Yes, Clare," he whispered. "Let me take you. Let me make you mine."

And then he kissed her so deeply, she knew she was lost to him.

Forever.

And the night had only just begun.

~

AT EIGHT O'CLOCK the next morning, the last thing Clare wanted to do was leave Griffin behind and go to Portland for one last attempt at settling the lawsuit before going to trial, and Griffin really wasn't making it any easier for her.

"You're sure you have to go?" Completely ignoring the fact he was wrinkling her suit, Griffin locked Clare in his arms, trying to stop her from walking out the door. "Take the morning off. Stay with me."

"I wish I could." She leaned into the strength of his body, yearning to be back in that bed with him. They hadn't slept until dawn, filling the night with lovemaking, stories of their childhood, and whispered secrets. Neither one of them had wanted to waste a moment on sleep, and she couldn't stop the terrifying feeling of time passing too quickly.

Her alarm had gone off less than an hour after they'd fallen asleep, and Griffin had kept her in bed for another half hour before finally capitulating to her laughing demands for him to release her. Their joint shower had been quick and non-sexual, but it had the intimacy of a daily ritual, of learning how to share the same space. The way he'd washed her back and combed the conditioner through her hair. The bumping of elbows and knees in a tiny area barely big enough for one. The laughter around a dropped bar of soap, and even a clump of her hair in the drain.

It had been very hard for her to leave that shower.

And even harder to put on her business suit and prepare to leave his arms for a day in Portland.

"Why don't I come with you?" he suggested. "I'm a great negotiator. We could have lunch on the pier and—"

"No." She rested her cheek against his chest. "I have to do this myself."

"Why? Why stand alone when you don't have to?"

She closed her eyes and inhaled the musky scent that was

so Griffin. "Because I can't forget how to manage my life on my own."

He said nothing, but his arms tightened around her.

His phone rang, and he stiffened but he didn't answer it.

"You should get it." She pulled away. "Maybe it's Brooke. I have to go anyway."

He tugged her against him and fished his phone out of his pocket. She saw it was a man named Phillip Schnur. Griffin swore and shoved the phone back in his pocket. "My business partner. We're working on something."

Clare stiffened at the sudden tension in his body, the evasion in his gaze. "What?"

He finally met her gaze. "Nothing yet. I'll fill you in tonight."

She hesitated, knowing he wasn't telling the truth, but not sure she could handle pressing him on it. She was already too tense about today. "You'll be here when I get back?"

"Yes, of course." But he was distracted, and she could tell he was already thinking about whatever Phillip wanted to discuss with him.

She clasped his chin and forced him to look at her. "Last time you promised, you weren't here." She held up her hand over his protest. "I just need to know what to expect. If you won't be here, tell me."

He caught her hand and kissed her palm. "I'll be here tonight," he said fiercely. "I swear it."

"Okay." She accepted his truth, but when he grabbed her and kissed her again, the kiss was off. It was tense.

It wasn't right.

Not anymore.

Something was about to go terribly, terribly wrong.

GRIFFIN LEANED against the door frame, watching Clare drive away.

She paused at the end of the driveway and waved. She looked so small and vulnerable in her well-worn Subaru with one hundred and fifty thousand miles on the odometer. Protectiveness welled inside him and he jumped down off the porch. "Take my truck," he called out, beckoning for her to come back, wanting her in his safe, new vehicle.

But she just waved back and then pulled out of the driveway, and all he could do was watch the taillights disappear around the corner.

He knew she'd sensed his tension. Her face had been pinched and vulnerable when she'd said good-bye, and he knew it was his fault. He should have told her the deal was close. She deserved to know.

He grabbed his phone and called her, but it went right into voicemail. "Come on, Clare," he muttered. "Turn on your phone." He tried again, but no response. She was going to drive all the way into the city without him being able to check up on her? No way. Unacceptable.

Screw it. He was going after her.

He grabbed his keys from the front hall table and sprinted out the door. He yanked open the door to his truck, jumped in and revved the engine. He shifted into reverse—

His phone rang.

He answered it instantly. "Clare? I'm so glad you called, I—"

"We got the deal," Phillip crowed. "We got the deal!"

Griffin froze. "We did?"

"Yes! But we have to close quickly. Turns out, they're expecting a baby and they want to buy a house, and they need the cash. Tomorrow morning, my man. Tomorrow morning!"

Griffin sank back in his seat, staring blankly out the windshield. "Tomorrow?"

"Nine in the morning, partner. At nine-fifteen, the proverbial keys are ours and we get to work. Hot damn! This is fantastic! They didn't even counteroffer! You impressed the hell out of them. They loved you, man." Phillip whooped again. "Let's go get drunk. It's our last day of freedom, Griff."

His last day of freedom.

Griffin let his head fall back against the seat. "I don't know if I can wrap things up here by then. Can we move it out a couple of days?"

"No, we can't, and why the hell would we want to? This is it. It's what we've been building for. I'm going to go get drunk. Congrats, man! I'll have the papers sent to you this afternoon for proofing, and then we'll be good to go in the morning." Phillip let out another roar. "Go get your daughter and come on home, big guy. Life has just begun. Hot damn!" He hung up the phone without another word.

Griffin dropped the phone on the passenger seat.

This was it. They'd done it. They'd reached the pinnacle. By the time they finished with In Your Face, he'd have more money than God, and more fame, too. And most importantly, he would have a way to connect with Brooke.

It was everything he wanted.

Everything.

He looked at the red farmhouse in front of him, and knew it wasn't entirely true.

If only he wasn't who he was. If only Clare didn't have her past. If only there was a way to bridge the gap. But he wouldn't ask that of her. He wouldn't put her through what she'd gone through again.

He wouldn't make her love a man who wouldn't be there for her.

He had to let her go.

And it would be tonight.

He would wait for her to come home, and then he would leave.

Forever.

~

GRIFFIN DIDN'T bother with the front steps or the doorbell when he drove up to his daughter's house an hour later.

He just parked his truck in the driveway of the small colonial in River Junction, and he strode around to the rear of the house. As he'd suspected, given the trusting nature of people in Maine, the back door was unlocked, just like at Clare's house.

He didn't knock.

He didn't announce his presence.

He just walked into the house that he wasn't welcome in.

Right into that faded, undersized kitchen, which was hosting the family of five for breakfast.

Their shock was so vivid he almost laughed.

Dan was the first to react, and he rose to his feet with impressive speed for a lumbering beast of a man. "Get out of my kitchen."

Griffin ignored him, he ignored Hillary and he blew off the twins. He just strode across the kitchen to his daughter, who was staring at him as if he'd gone insane.

He grabbed Burwell's abandoned chair and pulled it up next to Brooke. He took his daughter's hand, and was pleased that she was still too startled to pull away. "Here's the deal, Brookie."

"Get out of here," Burwell said, his hand coming down hard on Griffin's shoulder. "Leave her alone."

Griffin gave a hard look to both Hillary and Dan. "My divorce agreement gives me rights to my daughter, and I'll sue both of you for violation of it if you try to keep me away from her." He let his fury show in his face. "I'll strip you of every asset you have, and I'll keep you in court until you don't have a cent left, or the rights to even breathe around her if you don't back off right now."

Hillary's mouth opened in stunned surprise.

Burwell scoffed. "You don't scare me—"

"No." Hillary touched her husband's arm. "He's not bluffing. Let him talk to her."

Damn right he wasn't bluffing. He was tired of playing games, and he was taking control now.

He didn't bother to see how long it took for Hillary to knock some sense into her husband. He just turned back to his daughter, who now looked pissed. "Don't threaten them," she said hotly.

"Do you know the company In Your Face?"

Brooke blinked. "Of course I do." She pointed to her pants, and Griffin saw the familiar logo on her right hip."

"I'm buying it tomorrow."

Brooke's eyes widened. "What? Seriously?"

"Yeah." Griffin leaned forward and squeezed his daughter's hand. "The designers plan to create a new line called Brooke's Closet, designed by you, with their help."

Brooke stared at him. "You're kidding?"

He grinned. "They and I think that having a fifteen year old on board gives legitimacy to the brand." He laughed. "Heck knows, I'm not legit when it comes to teen fashion."

"Wait a sec." Brooke's face was flushed with excitement. "I'm going to design a line of clothing for In Your Face? With my name on it?"

"And you'll do some commercials, so that the kids can see that there's someone on the inside who knows what they need."

"Oh my God!" Brooke screamed and threw her arms around him. "That's so awesome! Wow!" She whirled around and raced over to Hillary. "Did you hear that? In Your Face! My friends will go crazy!"

Griffin leaned back in his chair, grinning as he watched his daughter's excitement. Relief cascaded through him. He'd done it. He'd really done it.

"Griffin?"

He looked over at Hillary, not bothering to keep the smug look off his face. "Yeah?"

"Where is this company located?"

"Boston."

"Boston." Hillary cocked her head. "And are you moving it up here?"

"No, of course not. It would be impossible. Too many moving parts."

Brooke stopped dancing and turned to look at him. "I would have to move to Boston?"

Griffin's exhilaration faded, replaced with a rising sense of unease. "I've kept your room exactly as it was," he reassured her. "We'll get you a new computer with design capability, so you can start to work on designs and—"

"And what will your hours be?" Hillary asked. "Will you be home at three when she gets out of school?"

Griffin shifted. "I'll try when I can. Brookie can come to the office after school and work with the designers—"

"You want a fifteen-year-old girl to go to your office every day and work?" Hillary asked.

Brooke was standing very quietly beside her mother, saying nothing.

"It's not work," Griffin said. "It's In Your Face. It's living a dream, for both of us."

"Whose dream?" Hillary put her arm around Brooke's shoulders. "Brooke loves her family, Griffin. She can't replace that with an office or a commercial. Your dream is not hers."

Panic began to hammer in Griffin's chest as he turned to Brooke. "I'm buying it for you," he said.

"I don't want to move back to Boston," Brooke said in a small voice.

"Oh, come on, Brookie." Desperation ripped through him and he dropped to his knees in front of her. "Don't do this to me. I'm doing everything I can for you. I don't know what else to do. You're my daughter. I miss you. I need you to come home."

Brooke looked away and folded her arms over her chest.

"Brooke!" He felt like his soul was breaking, like everything that mattered to him was slipping out of his reach. "For God's sake, tell me what to do. Tell me how to get you back. I'm sorry for whatever I did. I am. But when you walked out on me, I thought my soul was going to die right there."

Brooke bit her lip, and tears shone in her eyes. Son of a bitch. She was going to say yes, wasn't she? Joy leapt in his chest and—

She turned and walked toward the hallway.

"Wait!" He lunged after her and caught her arm. "I love you, Brookie. Don't you understand? *I love you.*"

Brooke looked sharply at him as Hillary sucked in her breath.

"Brooke." He felt like the word was going to break him in half. "I love you. I can't lose you like this. *Tell me what to do.*"

Tears were streaming down Brooke's cheeks, and her hands were shaking. "You want to know what to do?"

"Yes, God, *yes.*"

"Let me change my name to Burwell."

Griffin felt like a knife had just cleaved his heart in half. "But why?"

"Because this is my family! Everyone is here at breakfast

and dinner. They come to my games. They know my friends' parents. They love me just for being me!"

"But I love you—"

"No. You don't," Brooke said fiercely. "You don't even understand what love is! Just let me change my name and leave me alone!" Then she ran out of the room, sprinted up the stairs, and he heard her door slam.

Griffin bowed his head and closed his eyes, fighting against pain so deep he felt he would never breathe again.

Hillary touched his shoulder gently. "I'm sorry, Griffin."

He summoned his breath and turned to face her. He saw the genuine sorrow in her eyes, and realized it hadn't been her words coming out of Brooke's mouth. Brooke had been speaking with her own heart. "You didn't try to get her to hate me, did you?"

Hillary shook her head. "I wanted you to be her father, Griffin. The pain of not having you in her life has been great. I wanted her to have it all."

He nodded. "Whose idea was it to change her last name?"

Hillary met his gaze, and her face was softer than he'd ever seen. "Hers, Griffin. We had nothing to do with it."

He nodded. "Okay."

Hillary frowned. "Okay, what?"

"She can change her name." His voice started to crack, and he took a breath. "I'll give her the family she wants." His throat got tighter, and he knew he had to leave. "Send the paperwork to my office. I'll give my consent."

Then he turned and walked out, past Burwell, that big ass mountain man with a beard, a baby in each arm, and a pair of jeans off the rack. But he had something that Griffin didn't have.

He had Brooke's heart.

Son of a bitch.

By the time Griffin reached his truck, he was crying.

He could barely see to maneuver out into the road, and he pulled into the first dirt road he found. And there, in his ridiculous truck, he finally grieved for the family he had lost.

And there, in that ridiculous truck, he experienced pain beyond what he'd ever felt in his life.

And there, in that ridiculous truck, he made his choice.

CHAPTER TWENTY-THREE

THE FAINT SHREDS of hope that Clare had been clinging to were finally gone. Totally and completely destroyed.

As she drove around the corner onto her street, she glanced down at the tan envelope on the seat beside her. The one that contained the settlement agreement she had signed two hours ago. The risk of a prolonged lawsuit was over, but she'd had to agree to more than she could afford to stop the nightmare.

No new roof.

No MIT this summer.

And no cupcake store.

There was nothing left of the fifteen years she'd given to her work, to her life, to her daughter's future. After all that, she was left with no savings, nothing to fall back on, no safety net. Nothing for her daughter. She'd failed them both.

She'd failed.

Clare pulled into the driveway and parked beside Griffin's truck. It was dark out, and the lights in the house were off. No one welcoming her home. Just an empty house.

Tears suddenly burst free and she hit the steering wheel

with her fist. It wasn't fair! After working so hard to build a life for herself and Katie, paying off loans, working at a job that she really didn't like, she'd lost it all. In one minute, a group of undeserving heirs had stripped her of everything she'd accomplished.

What else was she supposed to do to get it right? How many times was she supposed to pick herself back up and pretend she could soldier on? She didn't want to live this life anymore. She stared at the dark house. How could she go back in there? Sleep alone after Griffin had shown her what it felt like to have someone she loved hold her all night? Go back to her office after her imagination had envisioned that cupcake store? Harden her heart after Griffin had opened it?

She didn't want to go back, and yet, here she was, not just returning to the life she'd had, but to an even worse one. No money. No nest egg. No options. "Dammit!"

The door to Griffin's truck opened, and she realized he'd been sitting inside his cab the whole time. Relief flooded her at the sight of him. She needed him now, more than anything. She pushed open her door and raced around her car. "Griffin —" She threw her arms around him and buried herself in his bulk. "Hold me," she whispered. "Just hold me."

But he didn't.

He stood there stiffly, his body rigid, his hands by his sides.

Clare slowly pulled back. "Griffin?"

"I'm going back to Boston tonight." His face was hard as he gestured at his truck, and she saw his suitcases on the back seat. "I'm leaving."

Her stomach dropped, and her hands started to shake. "So soon? But why—"

"I sign the papers on my new company tomorrow at nine," he said, his voice still so harsh and unyielding. He was nothing like the man she knew. There was nothing soft and warm about him. Just emotionless and stoic. Cold, even. "Back to work at nine-fifteen."

"But what about Brooke?" This couldn't be happening. Not now. Not in this way. Why was he so angry? What had happened to him while she'd been in Portland? She knew it must have been terrible, to make him so cold and furious. "Did something happen with your daughter?"

He said nothing.

Oh, it had. No wonder he was so upset! "Don't give up on her. She loves you—"

"She's staying here. She doesn't want to come." He raised his chin, shutting down the slight tremor in his voice. "I'm letting her go."

"No." She grabbed his arms. "She's fifteen! She doesn't know what she wants. You're the grown up. Don't let her—"

"Stop it!" He knocked her hands away. "Give it up, Clare! I'm not some doting father. I never will be. I work. I make money. That's what I do, and I'm a stupid fool for thinking that fits with a daughter or family."

"But you love her!" *And me? What about me? Don't you love me?* But she couldn't ask those questions. Not now. Not to the man in front of her, who was acting like the cold, emotionless man Hillary had accused him of being.

"Let it go, Clare," he growled. "Stop trying to make me into something I'm not." He glared at her. "You tried to convince me that I was something else, and I'm not. So back off, and let me go be who I am."

"You're not cold," she said urgently. "You have a good heart. It doesn't need to be like this—"

"No," he interrupted. "Don't try to make me into something that I'm not just because you don't want to be alone anymore."

She gaped at him. "What? I'm not doing that—"

"You tried to make Ed into something he wasn't, and you

tried to convince me of the same. Well, give it up. Pick a man who is actually what you want, and stop trying to change the others."

Anger fueled inside her. "You're a bastard!"

"I know." He looked at her coolly. "And it's time we both realized it." He got back in his truck. "I'm going to Boston."

"Just like that?"

"Just like that." He hesitated, and for a second, she saw a flash of vulnerability in his face.

That was all it took for her to realize that his anger and coldness was just a facade for the tremendous pain he was feeling. "Griffin," she said softly as she set her hand on his arm. "Don't run away from this. Please stay. Let's talk about this."

"No." He took her hand and pressed a kiss to her palm, holding it for so long she thought she was going to start to cry. "I can't pretend anymore, Clare. I can't pretend to fit where I don't." He met her gaze, so much torment in his dark eyes. Gone was the cold shield, and there was nothing hiding the raw anguish tearing him apart. "It's too damn hard."

"I know it is," she said. "It hurts. But it's worth it."

He laid his hand on her cheek. "I can't do it, Clare. I can't do it anymore." Then he leaned forward and kissed her, and it was a kiss of farewell.

Of a final good-bye. "Griffin—"

He shook his head. "No more, Clare. Let it be, so we can at least hold onto the beautiful memories." He gently pushed her back out of the way, shutting her out of his life.

She couldn't believe it was happening.

But it was.

She wanted to scream and berate him for leaving her, like she'd done to Ed. But protests hadn't kept Ed home, and it wouldn't keep Griffin from leaving. His departure had always been part of the deal, but she'd had no idea how badly it would hurt.

She wouldn't kill another man's spirit.

She wouldn't lower herself to begging for whatever crumbs he would give her.

Not this time. Not again. Even if she kept Griffin for another hour, or another day, the end would be the same. Another Ed. And she couldn't survive that again.

So, even while her heart was breaking, Clare didn't fight for him. She simply wrapped her arms around herself as he shut the door. The bang of the door shutting made her jump, and he shifted into reverse without even looking at her again.

His truck reached the end of the driveway. "Please come back," she whispered, knowing it had to be his choice, his decision, his own heart's calling. "Please don't give up."

But the tires spun on the dirt, and then the truck peeled down the street, until the dark vehicle disappeared into the night, and all she could see were the taillights.

And then even those disappeared.

As GRIFFIN DROVE AWAY from Clare's house, all he wanted to do was turn the truck around, haul ass back up the gravel driveway, and claim his woman.

But for what purpose? For nothing. He'd played all those cards, and it was a dead hand.

So, instead, he forced his attention toward the life that he actually fit, and he dialed up his business partner. Phillip would give him the fire he was looking for.

"I'm on my way," he said the moment Phillip picked up. "I'll be down by midnight. Let's meet at the Cafe Florence for a drink." Like a full bottle of Grey Goose, straight up. Because right now, all he wanted to do was erase the memories beating at him and find a way to look at his new company without wanting to blow the damn thing to hell and beyond.

"You got it." Phillip sounded so psyched that Griffin felt like his partner was talking at him from another planet. "It'll be good to be back, won't it?

Griffin fisted the steering wheel. "Yeah," he lied, unable to muster the matching excitement. Once he was back at work though, the rush would return. He was sure of it. It was what he lived for. After Hillary and Brooke had left him, his work had taken away the pain. Work had filled the void, and it would do so again. The office was his oasis, and he'd been a damned fool to try to play in someone else's fountain. "I'll see you soon."

"Drive fast," Phillip ordered. "Let's get going."

Drive fast. Griffin snorted as he disconnected. Clare would have commanded him to drive safely—

Clare.

Her name bit deep.

Driving out of her place had been the hardest thing he'd ever done. So much more gut wrenching than he'd anticipated. After his hellish day in River Junction, all he'd wanted to do was pull Clare onto his lap and tell her about Brooke. He'd wanted to hold her in his arms and listen to her arguments about why he was a better dad than he thought. He wanted to feel her body against his as she talked him down from his bottomed-out state of mind.

Except the moment for delusions was over.

It was time to let go of certain dreams and focus on the ones that mattered. In Your Face. That was what he was good at. That was his calling. That was where he fit.

Not in this town.

Not as a lover and a partner.

Not as a father.

Son of a bitch. He felt like shit. He tightened his grip on

the gear shift and hit the gas. He needed to get away from this town. Go back to where he was from. Reclaim the life where he excelled. Connect with the people who thought his business genius was a veritable blessing from the gods.

He tried to picture how it had felt to walk into that conference room to seal the In Your Face deal. The excitement of working on a project until four in the morning, taking a nap on his couch and then being back at work an hour later.

It would take only a day, maybe two of being back in the office, and he'd be in his groove again. He wouldn't remember this town. The thought of Clare's blue eyes wouldn't make his chest hurt. He wouldn't lie in bed at night and remember what it was like to make love to her. He would stop replaying that moment last night in the restaurant when she'd shouted her love for him loud enough for the whole damn place to hear.

Shit. He shook his head, trying to get the thoughts out of his mind as he sped around the corner onto Main Street. Emergency vehicles were crowding the front of Wright's store. What the hell was going on?

There was an ambulance, a fire truck and two police cars, probably the entire fleet of emergency vehicles in the service area. Adrenaline spiking, Griffin peered intently through the windshield, checking out the store, but he didn't see any smoke coming from it. The place wasn't burning down, so that was something, right? So, it was okay.

People were crowding around the front of the store. People he recognized. Eppie and her friend Judith. Some of the guys from the softball team. Jackson and Trish. Ophelia. People he knew. He slowed the truck so he could get out and check on everyone, and then he realized what he was doing. This wasn't his deal. This wasn't his world. He was leaving, and sitting around here wasn't his deal.

He didn't belong here.

He never had.

He never would.

It was time to let it go and return to where he belonged. To the place that accepted him for who he was. The life that made him happy.

He gunned the engine and drove on.

He made it as far as the fork that would take him to the highway before he turned around, unable to leave until he knew that the people he'd come to care about were all right.

A few minutes later, Griffin parked his truck in front of Clare's office and got out. He strode across the street to where Jackson was standing, his face reflecting the blue and red from the emergency vehicles flashing lights. Two minutes. That's all he would give it, and then he was gone for good. "Jackson," he barked. "What's going on?"

Jackson looked at him, and Griffin tensed at the anguish on his teammate's face. "It's Norm."

"Norm?" Griffin took a sharp look at the building as a stretcher was wheeled out the front door of the store. "Norm!" He raced toward the stretcher, and then stopped hard when he saw that the sheet was over the old man's face.

He was dead?

Holy shit.

Norm was dead.

Griffin stood numbly while he watched Ophelia run over and take Norm's hand. She was sobbing openly, her whole body shaking with grief. Eppie clasped her shoulders, and Trish supported her waist, keeping Ophelia from falling as she stumbled down the front steps beside the stretcher that was taking away the man she'd loved for fifty-three years.

Griffin realized everyone around him was crying. Some of the women were sobbing, and the men were silent, but there were tears on their cheeks. Men, women, even some kids.

As the paramedics walked Norm's body down the stairs, Jackson took off his ball cap and laid it over his heart. Everyone else did the same. Those without hats used their palms, and the town went quiet.

Then one old man, a guy that looked as wizened and wrinkled as Norm, began to sing. At first Griffin couldn't make out the tune, but then the man beside him joined in, and then others, and he realized they were singing the national anthem. Hailing Norm with the song of their whole damn country.

The paramedics stopped wheeling Norm toward the ambulance, and they put their hands over their hearts and joined in. And standing there, beside the man she loved, was Ophelia, holding his hand while the town showed their respect and their love for the man who had held them together for so long.

Griffin thought of the stars that Norm had taught him to see, and he slowly placed his own palm over his heart, and he began to sing, joining in with the town that had become his own. Emotions welled deep, and he felt tears burn in his own eyes as he paid tribute to Norm.

When the song ended, the night was silent. Not a sound. Not a movement. Just townspeople honoring a legend, a man who had been the cornerstone of their community.

Ophelia raised her chin, and, with tears still streaming down her cheeks, she spoke, her voice strong and determined. "Norman is smiling right now, because his greatest joy was to provide a place to bring the community together. To have everyone here, in this moment, is everything he would ever have wished for. He loved you all." Then her voice broke, and Eppie and Trish wrapped their arms around her and helped her into the ambulance.

Trish told Jackson to have someone bring Ophelia's truck to the hospital for her, and one of the men from the

Pirates loped into the store, apparently to retrieve the car keys.

But for everyone else, silence reigned while the paramedics loaded the ambulance. And then lights flashing, it slowly drove away, followed by the police cars and the fire truck. The crowd dissipated quickly, and within moments, there was a procession of cars following the ambulance. The last car in line was an old, blue pickup truck that pulled around from the back of the store, with Wright & Son painted in faded letters across the side.

In less than five minutes, the town was empty as its inhabitants escorted their leader on his journey.

The store was locked up, and Griffin was alone on the porch of the building that had always been bustling with activity since the day he'd arrived. Now? Abandoned.

The sign on the door said to ring the doorbell if it was after hours, and someone would be down to help. How many times had Norm come downstairs in the middle of the night to help someone who needed diapers, or baby formula, or even beer? Griffin suspected that Norm would have deemed all requests sufficient to rouse him from his sleep and his wife's arms.

And now he was gone.

Griffin sat down in the chair that Norm had used the night they'd had their talk. The one Norm would never use again. He leaned back and looked up at the sky. The stars were bright tonight, just like that evening he'd been out here with Norm.

How could Norm be gone? He was the town. He was Wright's. Would the store stay open? And what would Ophelia do? Would she even be able to live there anymore? Or run the store? Or would she lose everything on top of her husband?

Griffin's chest tightened and he leaned forward, pressing

his forehead to his hands as his body began to shake. Ophelia's courage and strength had been astonishing. Her life, her soul mate, her reason for being had been stripped away from her, and her heart had been breaking, and yet somehow, she'd had the capacity to share Norm's love with the town he'd loved so much.

Norm had been Ophelia's life, and she'd loved him so much, yet she hadn't broken under the agony of losing him. Shouldn't her love for him have brought her to her knees? How had she used her love to survive that moment? But she hadn't simply survived. In that moment, he'd seen her glow with something powerful. With an inner spirit that had carried her through. Was that love? Was that—

"Dad?"

Griffin looked up to see his daughter getting out of the passenger door of Hillary's Mercedes. "Brooke?" His voice was raspy and thick, and he couldn't clear it.

She walked to the bottom of the steps. She was wearing jeans and a tee shirt, a pair of old flip-flops, and her hair was shoved in a crooked ponytail. It was the most disheveled he'd ever seen her, and the most beautiful, because her spirit wasn't hidden behind makeup, fancy hair and designer labels. His daughter. So precious. So alive.

Brooke peered at him. "Are you crying?"

He was too drained to lie. "Yeah, I am."

"Why?"

"Because a good man died tonight."

"Oh." Brooke hesitated.

Griffin patted the seat beside him. "Come sit, Brookie."

She hurried up the stairs and perched on the swing that Griffin had used the night he'd been talking to Norm.

For a moment, neither of them spoke.

Finally, Brooke said. "I've never seen you cry."

"I don't much." It was difficult to talk, his throat was so heavy and thick.

Again, conversation faded until the only sound was the squeak of the swing as Brooke pushed off, back and forth, back and forth. How many times had Ophelia sat in that seat while Norm had occupied Griffin's? Hundreds? Thousands?

And now, it was over. How did love like that end? It was too soon for them. They had so much more they were supposed to live.

Hillary got out of the car and leaned on the roof to watch them. But she said nothing. She was just waiting. For what? Why were they in Birch Crossing? Not that he could muster up the energy to figure it out. Not right now. After all the energy he'd spent trying to win his daughter over, he had nothing left.

"Dad?"

"Yeah." He rested his forearms on his thighs and clasped his hands, staring at the gray paint on the porch. How vividly he recalled Norm walking across those boards, accompanying his wife to the door. He could still see their wrinkled hands entwined, the way they'd parted, with a promise of love and intimacy and foreverness. It had been a moment of beauty. And it would never happen again. He pressed the heels of his hands to his eyes again and his shoulders began to shake. "That's not the way it should be."

He felt a soft touch on his shoulder. "It'll be okay, Dad."

He couldn't look up. He couldn't talk. He couldn't respond.

His daughter's arms went around him, and she leaned her head on his shoulder.

"Oh, God, Brookie." He grabbed her and pulled her onto his lap. He held her as he trembled, as his beautiful child hugged him for the first time in far too long. "I missed you."

"I missed you too," she whispered. "I love you, Daddy."

"I love you, too, Brookie." He hugged her, so tightly, so fiercely, and he knew he could never let go, not ever.

It felt like an eternity before his body stopped shaking, before his throat loosened enough that he could speak, and Brooke held him the whole time, never letting him go.

He swallowed finally and lifted his head. To his surprise, tears gleamed on his daughter's cheeks. "Brookie," he said softly, brushing his thumb over her face. "Why are you crying?"

She sniffled. "I don't know."

He managed a smile, and kissed her forehead. "You're so beautiful," he said. "You're growing into the most incredible young woman. I'm so proud of you. I'm sorry I'm such a bad dad. I'm sorry I can't get it right, but you need to know that I love you every minute of every day, and I will always do anything you need me to do." He held her face. "I love you, Brookie. I just wanted you to know that."

She smiled through her tears. "I know you do."

"You do?" At her nod, the most intense relief rushed through him. "Oh, God, you really do, don't you?" His daughter believed him. She knew his love. She did. He grabbed her and hugged her again, pressing his face in her hair like she used to beg him to do when she was little.

Brooke laughed and pushed him away. "You're messing up my hair."

He grinned and tousled her hair even more, feeling like a tremendous weight had fallen from him. "Sorry, pigeon. You know I'd never mess it up on purpose."

"Stop!" She swatted his hand away, but her eyes were sparkling. "I'm not five! You can't call me pigeon anymore."

"You'll always be my pigeon," he said. His little girl, no matter who she called Dad or whose last name she carried. He suddenly understood that truth. Just as Norm's spirit would always remain, kept alive by the people of Birch

Crossing and by Ophelia even though he was gone, his daughter would always be a part of his heart, regardless of whether her last name was Friesé or Burwell. She would always, always be his daughter, and the love would always be there.

And by God, that felt damn good.

"Dad," his daughter groaned. "I'm not your pigeon."

"Okay." He laughed softly. "You're right. I'll try to remember. But you might have to remind me."

She studied him, her face suddenly solemn. "But will you listen to me?"

He nodded, his amusement vanishing. "Yes, I will." He turned toward her, giving her his full attention. "I swear I'll listen to you from now on, Brooke. I promise it."

She smiled and took a breath. "Then I'll come to Boston with you."

Griffin felt like something had knocked the wind out of him, and he looked sharply at Hillary. And that's when he saw the tears on her cheeks. He returned his gaze to his daughter, barely able to fathom her words. "That's why you're here? You came after me?"

Brooke nodded. "When Mom told me you said I could change my name, I freaked." She hit his shoulder. "I never thought you would say yes. You weren't supposed to actually let me go!"

He was so shocked by her words that he couldn't speak. *She didn't really want him to let her go.* "Oh, God, Brooke." He hugged her again, so fiercely, fighting the surge of emotion that threatened to bring back his unmanly tears again. "You broke my heart today," he told her thickly. "I thought that's what you wanted."

Big, huge tears trickled down her cheeks as she buried herself against him. "I just wanted my dad," she whispered.

"Well, you've got him." He looked again at Hillary, who

was standing there, patiently waiting for Brooke to leave her. Hillary was giving her daughter the freedom to make her own choice, even if that meant losing her forever.

"My stuff is in the car," Brooke said. "I'm ready to go tonight."

"Tonight?" Griffin saw then that Brooke was holding her pink stuffed poodle. The one she'd had since she was a baby. He touched it. "Do you still sleep with Ponzo?"

She hugged him to her chest. "Of course. Ponzo would get very upset if I didn't."

And in that moment, as his daughter peered at him over the head of a very ragged poodle, Griffin realized how young she was. How fragile. How delicate. She wasn't a commodity to be pulled back and forth. She was a tiny, vulnerable person with a heart that had shut him out because she'd been afraid of losing him.

He saw Hillary had her head down, and her hand was covering her eyes and the tears he knew were on her cheeks. Tears like the ones Ophelia and the others had shed tonight, tears of loss for the one they loved.

No. It wasn't supposed to be like this. No more loss.

He took his daughter's hands. "Brooke," he said. "Do you love mom? And the twins?"

She nodded. "Of course."

"And Dan? Tell me the truth. I won't be mad."

She looked down. "Yes," she whispered.

Yes. She loved them all. But she also loved him. How could he cause her the kind of pain he'd felt and seen tonight with Norm's death? How could he make her choose between those she loved? He couldn't.

Brooke pulled back. "Well, let's go, then." Her voice was impatient, but tears were glistening in her eyes, and her mouth was pulled into a tight line. He knew that expression. It was the one he'd seen so many times, moments before his

322

little girl exploded into tears and sobs. She was being so brave, but he knew her pain.

"Dad? Let's go."

Griffin didn't move. "I can't."

She frowned. "You can't what?"

"I can't take you away from your home."

Hillary's head came up, disbelieving hope etched on her face.

Brooke's face crumpled. "You don't want me."

"No!" He grabbed her arms. "Never think that. I just can't take you away from them, either. It's not right for us to be apart, but it's not right to take you away either."

"But—"

"Brooke," he said. "I'll find a way for you to have both."

And there, in that moment, he finally saw his daughter's face come alive with the joy and love he'd always wished for her. "I don't have to leave them? Or you? I don't have to choose?"

"No." He brushed her hair back from her face. "Never."

"Really?"

"Really." He realized his hand was shaking. "I'll never ask that of you again, I promise."

She grabbed his wrist, her delicate fingers tight on his arm. "And you'll still come by? A lot? You promise?"

"I swear it."

Brooke shook her head, confusion and doubt wrinkling her forehead. "But your work—"

He laid a finger over her lips, silencing her. "I'll make it happen. I promise."

She searched his face, those dark brown eyes so intent as she sought to understand if she could trust him. He met her gaze. He didn't look away. He allowed her to see his love.

And then she smiled, a great big smile that broke like the dawn over her face. "Thank you!" She threw her arms around him and hugged him, and he held her tightly. "I love you, Daddy."

"I love you, too, pigeon." And by God, he did.

She pulled back and stuck her tongue out at him. "Dad! You called me pigeon!"

He laughed. "Go back home with Mom. I have to go to Boston tonight."

Excitement danced in her eyes. "Can I still be involved with In Your Face?"

He smiled. "Of course. We'll figure out a way." He winked at her. "Maybe we'll have you skip school on Fridays so you can come down and hang with me."

"Oh, yeah! That would be awesome! No school on Fridays!" She hugged him and then raced down the stairs. "Mom! Mom! Guess what! I don't have to go to school on Fridays anymore!"

"Is that so?" But Hillary's voice was light and happy as she hugged her.

Griffin smiled as he watched his daughter jumping up and down with excitement. It was the way it should be. Somehow, someway, he'd finally gotten the dad thing at least a little bit right, and it felt damn good.

Hillary bundled Brooke into the car, and shut the door. Then she looked up at Griffin. "Thank you," she said.

He nodded, then leaned back in the chair as he watched them go. But this time, as his daughter drove away, he didn't feel sad or empty. He knew he was going to make it right. It wasn't going to be easy, but if Clare could balance work and being a mom, then he could do it, too.

Clare.

The thought sobered him up pretty damn quickly. He glanced in the direction of her farmhouse. Was there a way to make that work, too? A way to—

No.

Just as he couldn't ask his daughter to leave her family, he couldn't ask Clare to love a man who lived in Boston, who belonged in Boston. It was time for him to let her go. It was time for him to leave.

But he didn't get up.

He just leaned back in his chair, looked up at the stars, and asked Norm for advice.

CHAPTER TWENTY-FOUR

CLARE WAS STILL SITTING in the driveway when Sara's mom dropped Katie off at the house a while after Griffin had left. Her phone had rung several times, but she hadn't bothered to move to answer it. She had nothing left to say to anyone, no reserves left to cope.

So, she stayed where she was and let the night swallow her up.

Katie paused when she saw Clare camped out on the gravel. "Why are you sitting in the driveway?"

"Because it's too much effort to go inside."

"What's wrong?" Katie's brow furrowed with dismay. "Aren't you cold?"

Clare was vaguely aware that she was shivering. She didn't know what it was from. Shock. Fear. Cold. Hunger. Dread. She felt so empty inside. "I've messed everything up."

Katie dropped her backpack beside her. It landed with a thunk on the gravel, so heavy with books that Clare knew Katie must have come straight from the library. "What happened?"

Clare sighed and hugged her knees to her chest. "I'm so sorry, Katie. I'm so sorry I let you down."

"What are you talking about?" Katie kneeled in front of her. "You're scaring me, Mom."

"I can't send you to MIT this summer."

She was expecting Katie to cheer, but her daughter just looked worried. "Why not? What happened?"

She didn't want to burden her daughter with this. She wanted Katie to go through life thinking everything was okay. But she just couldn't hide it anymore. "I can't afford it."

Katie frowned. "What do you mean? We have plenty of money."

"We don't." Clare rested her chin on her knees, staring blankly at the empty spot where Griffin's truck used to be. "I made a mistake on a will, and it was successfully contested in court. I got sued by the heirs."

"You never make mistakes," Katie protested. "They're wrong."

Clare shook her head, finally admitting the truth that had been weighing on her. "Actually, I did make a mistake. I did screw up. And I had to pay them quite a lot of money to settle the lawsuit." She managed a smile. "So, at least we don't have to go to court, but there will be no MIT this summer."

"Oh." Katie crossed her legs, propped her elbow on one knee and rested her chin on her palm. "If money was that tight, why would you send me to MIT in the first place?"

"Because I wanted a different future for you than what I had." And how well that plan was turning out.

Her daughter picked up a stick and drew a heart in the dirt. "Is your life really so bad, Mom?"

Clare laughed softly. "I have a job I hate, I don't have enough money to give my daughter the life she deserves. I wasn't enough to keep your dad around, and I never gave you the family you wanted."

Katie stopped drawing. "What do you mean, you couldn't keep Dad around?"

Clare winced. "Sorry. I didn't mean to say that." What was she doing, burdening her daughter with this? She patted Katie's knee. "Never mind, I'm just feeling a little melancholy because Griffin went back to Boston. Everything's fine, and you don't have to go to MIT this summer. See? Life is good."

Katie set the stick down. "Don't lie to me anymore, Mom. Tell me the truth. I'm almost sixteen. I can handle it! Tell me!" Katie looked at her intently. "What did you mean about Dad? Did he leave you? Did he leave us? Is that what you meant?"

Clare was too surprised by the specificity of the questions to remember to deny it. "How did you know?"

Katie shrugged. "It was the only reason I could think of for how you talked about him." She retrieved the stick and drew her dad's name in the dirt. "What happened? Will you tell me?"

Clare watched Ed's name scrawled in her driveway, a shadow that would never leave. "You really want to know?"

"Yes." Katie drew a heart around Ed's name.

"Okay." Clare averted her eyes from her daughter's design, and she finally released the truth she'd been holding onto for fifteen years. She told Katie about the forced wedding, the lonely nights, and Ed's words the night he'd left. She told her daughter everything about the man she'd idolized, and Katie listened to every word. Never interrupting. Never questioning. Never defending him. Just listening.

And then Clare finished. There was nothing left to say.

And to her surprise, Katie leaned over and hugged her. "Thank you for telling me that."

Clare hugged her back, confused. "Aren't you mad?"

Katie shook her head. "Do you have any idea what it's like not to know the truth? I had to know." She took a deep breath, raised her arms over her head and flopped back onto the driveway. "It feels so good to know. I feel so much better."

"Really?" Clare took a deep breath, and the air felt fresher and clearer than it had in years. "You're sure?"

"Yes."

Clare realized that she did too. She stretched out beside Katie and stared at the brilliant stars. "I'm so sorry I held back for so long. I thought it was better for you to believe he was a good man."

"I'm not a baby." Katie pointed her stick at the night sky, sketching words Clare couldn't decipher. "I can handle the truth. It feels better, actually. I hate it when I know you're hiding things from me."

"I'm so sorry. I won't do it again." She laughed softly. "There's nothing left to hide. That was my only skeleton." She felt so good, so liberated not to be weighed down anymore.

"What about your job? Do you really hate it?"

"Oh, now, all my secrets are out," Clare teased. "No, I don't hate it. I just don't like being sued."

"You're lying again, aren't you?" Katie propped herself up on her elbow to look down at her. "Why? Why won't you be honest with me?"

Clare sat up. "Because I'm trying to protect you! It's my job as your mom to make the world safe for you. What was I going to do? Tell you that my job is sucking the life out of me, and that I never should have incurred all this debt to go to law school, and that I want to chuck it all and go open a cupcake store, even if it means risking your college money and our house and everything else? How would that make you feel, huh? It would scare you and—"

"That would be awesome!"

Clare stared at her daughter. "What?"

"A cupcake store? How cool would that be? Could I work there, too?"

"I'm not going to do it. I was just saying—"

"Why not?" Katie jumped to her feet. "That would rock. That would be so much cooler to have a mom who was a cupcake goddess than a lawyer."

"I can't do it! I don't have the money—"

"So? We don't need this huge house. And I'll get a scholarship. Who cares?"

"I care!" Clare stood up. "I'm not going to let you suffer because I can't make money—"

Katie rolled her eyes. "So, you'll make me suffer by watching you be so unhappy at work? While I lie in bed at night, listening to you mutter to yourself while you type away at the computer all night just so you can find time to bake another batch of cupcakes? Seriously, Mom, that totally sucks."

"But—"

"I hate seeing you unhappy," Katie said. "Why do you think I joined the physics club? I hate it, but I did it so you would be happy. If your work made you happy, then maybe I wouldn't have to." She groaned. "God, that would be *awesome*. No more physics club!" She spun around like a ballerina. "Do it, Mom! Just do it! Ditch the lawyer thing. Come on!"

Emptiness filled Clare as she watched her daughter's exuberance. "It's too late, anyway. Someone already made an offer on the place I would have bought."

"So?" Katie set her hands on her hips. "Then find another place."

"I don't have the money—"

"So borrow it!"

"I can't! I have a mortgage on the house, student loans, a car loan and a huge debt I have to pay off. No one is going to lend me the amount of money I would need to buy the store and start the business." Clare spread her palms. "There are no choices, Katie. I can't do it."

"Hello? It's so obvious." Katie gave her an impatient look that only a teenager could do justice to. "Griffin has the money. Ask him."

At his name, the empty feeling dug even deeper. She would never forget how cold he was when he left. His rejection of her. "Griffin and I are over. You and I are on our own now."

"What?" Katie looked devastated. "You drove him away? Like Dad?"

"No." Clare fisted her hands in self-defense. "Don't even start with me on that—"

"Well, it's true! Griffin loves you!"

"No, he doesn't—"

"Of course he does. Anyone who saw the way he looked at you would agree. How could you let him go?"

"I didn't let him! He left!"

"Because you let him." Katie stomped her foot. "You just want to be miserable, don't you? That's the real reason you won't open a cupcake store or fight for Griffin. You think being some sort of martyr makes you more admirable. Well it doesn't!"

"I'm not a martyr! I'm trying to be responsible!"

"Well, you suck at it! How could you let him go? Griffin was the best thing that ever happened to us, and you're not fighting for it. For any of it! Did you even try to keep Dad? Did you even *try*?"

Clare opened her mouth to defend herself, to say she had fought for Ed, but the words didn't come out. They were a lie. A big fat lie. "I didn't know how," she finally said. All she'd done was sit there by the window, watching for his car every evening. Or lie beside him in bed, wishing he would touch her. She'd waited, she'd yearned, she'd dreamed, but she'd never done anything to try to win Ed's affections. Nothing other than wait until it was too late.

"I would have fought, and if you really wanted to be a good mom, like you claim, then you would have fought, too!" Katie spun around and stormed into the house, leaving Clare behind in the driveway.

Clare clasped her hands on top of her head as Katie stomped up the stairs to the second floor, her feet echoing in the night.

Her daughter was right. She hadn't fought. Not for Ed. Not for Griffin. Not for any of it. She'd lived her life in fear of doing it wrong, so she'd done nothing. Nothing that she really wanted to do.

But that realization was useless. What could she do now? Griffin was gone. The store had been sold. And she didn't have the money. It was over, just like Griffin's chances with Brooke. Her hands fisted at the thought of him. How dare he take her to the Bean Pot and tell her to dream, when it wasn't possible? He was such a bastard—

Oh, who was she kidding? He wasn't a bastard. He'd offered to buy the store for her and make her dreams possible. If she'd taken the deal—

"No." Even if Katie was right, and even if Griffin loved her, she deserved more than that from him. His love wasn't enough, not when he would always be looking past her in the direction of Boston. She didn't want a man who rolled into town every month or so to check on the business and spend the night in her bed. She'd accepted less than she deserved with Ed, and she wouldn't do it again.

Katie was right. Griffin was right. She did deserve to be happy. Really happy. Not pseudo-happy.

So, what would make her happy? What did she really want?

She knew the answer even before the words formed in her

mind. She wanted to be loved. She wanted a man who was there every night for her. She wanted a man who wanted to be a part of her life every day, who treasured everything about her, including the fact that her life was in this town.

And that wasn't Griffin. Even if he, by some miracle, decided to stay, he would never be present. Boston would always be calling to him, just like it had been with Ed.

If he lived in Boston and popped in for an occasional visit, her soul would die from the loss of the dream, from being in love with a man who could give her only part of his heart and his time. If he stayed and gave up his world, it would be his turn for his light to fade, and then hers would as well. There was no way for it to work. Her future, her love, her vision, her need for completeness...

It couldn't be filled by Griffin.

Her heart ached as she made that realization, and the last shred of hope shattered. Emptiness filled her and she allowed herself to grieve. To release her dream for him. To release her willingness to accept what little she could get from him, even if it wasn't enough.

She finally began to allow herself to believe that she really did deserve to be truly happy, to have it all. Griffin might have awakened her heart, but now it was time to let him go. It was time to keep her heart open, and to bring in a man who would be in her life the way she wanted.

And so, in that driveway, under the stars and the moon, she let go of Griffin, she released the old Clare, the one who accepted a life of emotional emptiness, who did her best to make everyone else happy instead of herself. She took owner-ship of the passion and the fire that Griffin had stirred up those moments in his arms and that night in the Bean Pot, and she made a promise to herself to channel that into the life she wanted.

"Okay, Clare," she said to the night. "If you want that

store, how are you going to get it?" She remembered Griffin talking about his business, how he always managed to get the deals he wanted because he figured out what people really desired more than the money, and he gave it to them. So how did that apply here?

She clasped her arms behind her head and began to pace, just as she did when she was trying to figure out a tricky solution to a client's issues.

What did the owners of the Bean Pot want? A local owner, right? To unload themselves of real estate.

What did she want? A chance. A store.

They had a store. She was a local owner. So, what about the money? What if she could convince them to be a partner? Like Griffin had offered?

Her heart began to race. Yes, yes, that would make sense! Maybe they would do it. Mattie and John loved her. They might just agree—

She ran over to her car and grabbed her phone. There were several missed calls from people in the town, but not Griffin. Of course not Griffin. Steeling herself against the disappointment, she called Astrid, who she knew was in the next town for the evening with Emma visiting a local art exhibit.

Astrid answered on the first ring. "Hi, Clare Bear. What's up? Are you going to meet up with us after all?"

"No, I need Harlan's phone number. I want to talk to him about the Bean Pot."

Astrid paused, then said quietly. "The offer was accepted today. It's not available."

Clare gripped the phone. "It can't be over!"

"It is. I'm so sorry, Clare. I really am—"

"No, no." Clare hung up, staring numbly at her phone. How could it be over, just when she'd made the decision to start her life?

It was over because it was supposed to be over.

It was too risky. Even if Mattie and John agreed to lease the store to her and to go in as partners, it was still risky financially. This was the universe's way of telling her to go back into the house, fire up her computer and be responsible.

Clare began to edge toward her car instead of heading into her house, thinking of one possible solution that might get her that store. Yes, she knew she shouldn't do it. For Katie, she had to be responsible.

But she thought of her daughter's outburst, and knew that it wasn't true.

For Katie, she had to follow her heart.

No, for herself. She had to do it for herself.

She was no longer willing to live with the emptiness.

She deserved more, and she was going to take it.

Maybe there was no way to make it work with Griffin. Maybe she had to let him go. But dammit, she wasn't going to lose out on everything. Not this time.

This time, she was fighting for it.

As she got in the car and turned on the ignition, she realized that it felt really, really good to fight for something. Not just for *something*.

To fight for herself.

GRIFFIN STILL HADN'T MOVED from Norm's chair several hours later when a battered pickup truck pulled in and parked behind the building. Someone wanting frozen peas for a midnight snack?

As he sat there, he heard the shuffle of tired feet, and he looked up to see Ophelia round the corner, holding Norm's cap in her hand.

He immediately stood up. "Ophelia, I'm so sorry—"

"Can it, young man." She waved him off. "Sit yourself back down for a minute."

Griffin sank back into the chair while Norm's widow shuffled across the porch and eased herself down into the swing. She leaned back with a soft groan of relief, and began to swing gently. "We used to sit here, you know," she said. "As long as it was over fifty degrees, we sat out here after the store closed. Norm liked to watch people drive by. He wanted to know who was going where."

Griffin smiled. "He knew everything about this town, didn't he?"

"He sure did." Ophelia looked tired, and her face looked far more wrinkled than before. She was still wearing her nightgown, and a ratty pink robe covered in roses. "He was the pulse of this town, just like his father before him."

"He was a good man."

"He was." Ophelia opened her purse, and dug out a key. She held it out to him. "Go inside and get us a couple beers, will you? Get a couple from the cooler in the back room. Those are the coldest."

"Sure thing." Griffin took the key and hustled over to the front of the store. The key barely fit the rusted lock, and he couldn't get it to turn. "Is there a trick to this?"

"Yep." Ophelia continued to swing, watching him struggle, but never offering to help him or tell him the trick.

He finally got the key to turn, and he opened the door. "Got it." He was actually a little proud of himself for getting the door open. He had a feeling Ophelia had watched many people struggle unsuccessfully with it, amused by their failings.

The store was eerily silent as he walked inside. Shadows fell across the shelves from the parking lot light outside, casting darkness where there were usually people and noise and activity.

Norm's stool was behind the register where it had been every time Griffin had walked in. But now, it was empty. The red seat was bare, worn from years of use. Griffin could almost see the older man there, giving him a knowing smile.

The place was stocked, the shelves full, indicating a healthy business. Stock was expensive, and most small stores like this one had a lot of empty space. But not Norm's store. Griffin suspected Norm knew exactly what his town needed, and he always had exactly that on his shelves. Nothing less. Nothing more. He probably even matched the sizes of the diapers to the ages of the babies in the town.

Griffin pushed open the swinging door to the back room. The place was packed with crates and boxes, all on top of each other, with no markings or labels. It looked like utter chaos that hadn't been inventoried in a hundred years, which it probably hadn't been. The store was likely run in a manner that defied every business school class Griffin had taken, and every business decision he'd made. And yet, it worked perfectly.

It almost made Griffin wish he had the balls to run a business by the seat of his pants as well.

On the far wall was an old-fashioned freezer, the kind that might store a deer that was going to feed the family for the winter. Griffin lifted the lid, and inside was an assortment of beer. All of it Birch's Best, of course.

He grabbed two, and then picked up a third. On his way back out, he set one on Norm's stool. "Safe journey, my friend." He raised his beer in salute, then headed back outside.

Ophelia was still sitting on the swing, her frame diminutive and fragile. But she smiled when Griffin handed her the beer. "Thanks."

"Any time." Griffin resumed his seat and took a drink. It

wasn't as bitter as last time. He wouldn't call it smooth, but it worked. "What happened tonight?"

Ophelia took a long drink. "He said it was his time." She was staring off into the distance, a faraway look on her face, as if she could see her husband smiling down at her from the heavens. And maybe she could. "He took my hand, and he said, 'Ophelia, you're not done here, but I am. I found my son, and it's time to go.'" She rubbed her palm thoughtfully. "He said he would always be holding my hand. If I needed him, to just close my eyes, and he would be there."

Griffin's throat thickened. "I believe him. I could feel him on his chair in there."

Ophelia nodded. "He'll always be on that stool."

Griffin cleared his throat. "Do you need money to keep the store running? It would be my honor to help you out."

"Oh, no," Ophelia said, laughing softly as she looked at him. "I'm not going to run it. I only do the deli."

He frowned. "Who's going to run the store?"

"His son." Ophelia nodded at the sign over the front of the store. "Wright & Son. It has to be a son."

Griffin had never heard anyone talk about Norm and Ophelia having children, and he sure as hell hadn't seen any son running around helping out. "Does he live around here?"

She smiled. "Not yet, but he will."

"When's he coming?" Griffin leaned forward. "If you need help until he gets here, I can maybe arrange something to help keep things going."

Ophelia's smile faded. "You don't understand, do you?"

"Understand what?"

"You're the one he found. You're the one who's going to run it." She gestured at the store. "You're the son."

Griffin stared at her, completely confused. "What are you talking about?"

"You." Ophelia leaned back against the swing and gazed

out into the night again. "We talked about it the day you arrived. Norm knew that you were the one, but he said you weren't ready. Tonight, he said you were."

A chill rippled down Griffin's arms. "You're trying to tell me that Norm died tonight so that I could take over the store?"

"Yes, of course."

Yes, of course. The old man had died for *him?* Sweat began to trickle down Griffin's back, despite the cool breeze. "Ophelia, I'm sorry, but I can't do that. I'm buying a business in Boston, and I'm headed back down there tonight. I don't belong here. This isn't my town, and I sure as hell can't run this store."

She looked at him, and he felt the intensity of those silver eyes bearing down on him. "Norman was never wrong about anybody."

"Well, that may be true, but—"

"Feel the night," she said, returning her gaze to the invisible scene only she could see. "Can you feel how fresh that air is in your lungs?"

Griffin was too tense to breathe any damn air. "Listen, Ophelia, I'll be happy to give you money—"

"There's an envelope under the register with your name on it," she said. "Go get it."

Griffin stared at her, a sense of foreboding growing in his chest. "Ophelia—"

"Get it."

"Yes, ma'am." He lurched to his feet and went inside. He stood at the counter for a minute, feeling weird about going into Norm's space. He looked at the beer sitting on the stool. "What the hell were you thinking? How the hell could you tell Ophelia I would run the store?"

The stool, of course, did not reply, and Griffin finally walked around the corner. He stepped around Norm's perch and crouched so he could see under the register. In the far back was a large manila envelope.

Griffin withdrew it, and on the outside was his name, scrawled in shaky lettering. He leaned against the counter and opened it. Inside was a thick contract. He pulled it out, and saw it was a purchase and sale agreement for the sale of Wright & Son to Griffin Friesé. It was dated two days ago, and already executed by both Norm and Ophelia. "Son of a bitch."

Then he saw the price, and he started laughing. It was too high by at least one zero. "Fleecing me from heaven, eh, old boy?"

He flipped the pages, and a piece of paper fell out. He picked it up and saw it was a handwritten note. Chills ran down his spine for the second time that evening when he realized it was from Norm.

Griffin, don't underestimate yourself. Norman P. Wright
Shit.

"Just so you know," Ophelia said from the doorway. "There's a clause in there that says I run the deli, and that I live upstairs. Non-negotiable."

"I'd never kick you out."

"Good." She smiled. "Then get to bed, young man. The store opens at seven, and you should be here by six."

"I'm not going to buy Wright's—"

"Why not?" She marched into the store. "What's wrong with you? Marry Clare. Adopt Katie. See your daughter all the time. Run a business. Play softball. What in God's name is wrong with that?"

He stared at her, and he couldn't think of a damn thing.

Ophelia smiled. "See? It's all good." She picked up a pen. "Sign it. We'll all pretend that it was executed before he died. Then we avoid all that hoopla about wills and estates and everything."

He didn't take the pen. "My daughter is counting on In Your Face."

Ophelia grabbed a New York Times, rolled it up and then smacked him in the side of the head. "She's counting on her dad. She doesn't need a damn business!"

Griffin looked around the store. He pictured all the people coming in and out. He imagined himself sitting in Norm's seat, looking over the crowd. For a moment, rightness swelled inside him, a sense of belonging, of finally coming home.

Then he thought of Clare, of Brooke, of Boston, and he shook his head. Clare had trusted Ed to be what he wasn't, and if Griffin tried to stay, it would have the same result. He wouldn't be able to commit, not the way they all deserved. He wouldn't make a promise he couldn't keep, not to Clare, not to Brooke, not to Ophelia, and not to the entire town of Birch Crossing. "No." He set the contract on the counter. "I can't. I'm sorry."

Ophelia dropped the newspaper on the counter. "Keep the key so you can come back and sign it later. Remember, the door opens at seven. Be here early."

"I'm not—"

Norm's widow clasped his shoulder and reached up on her wobbly tiptoes to kiss his cheeks. "Welcome, my boy. We've been waiting for you." Then she turned and disappeared through a door at the back of the store. He listened to her feet slowly work their way up the steps, pausing every so often, and then he heard no more as Ophelia entered the home that she'd shared with Norm for fifty-three years.

He wanted the kind of peace she and Norm had shared. He did. But to try to step into Norm's shoes, to pretend he could be that man who took care of an entire town on every level...he'd be an imposter. It would be a lie, and everyone,

341

including himself, would find out soon enough. He would fail, and everyone would suffer for it.

He would stick with what he did best. The place he was meant to be.

"I'm sorry, Norm," he said to the stool. "But I can't make your vision into reality. Forgive me."

He reached into his pocket and pulled out a checkbook. Then he wrote a check for the full amount of the purchase and sale, left it on the counter, and walked out without signing the contract.

He couldn't offer himself, but Ophelia could have his money.

It would have to be enough. For all of them.

CHAPTER TWENTY-FIVE

It took only forty-five minutes for Clare to drive to the southern tip of Black Bear Lake to the cabin that belonged to Harlan Shea. The building was dark, the lake was still, the pine trees thick, giving Harlan's cabin a feeling of isolation and loneliness that was in stark contrast to the effervescent energy of his sister.

Keeping her headlights trained on the house so she could see her way across the rocks that seemed to discourage rather than welcome visitors, Clare hurried across the bumpy terrain and banged on the door. "Harlan! Wake up! It's Clare Gray!"

The door opened so quickly she lost her balance and almost tumbled into the half-naked brother of her best friend. Harlan was wearing only a pair of cut-off shorts, and his dark hair was tousled from sleep. She was surprised to see how muscled he was, but she instantly decided that he fell short of Griffin. *Griffin.* Sudden tears burned in her eyes, and she fisted her hands to will the emotion away.

Harlan's eyes were alert. "What's wrong?" he asked, taking her arm and drawing her inside. "What happened?" He looked out the door, as if to make sure there was no one chasing her.

Clare pulled her arm free of his protective gesture. "Can you call Mattie and John right now?"

"Now?" Harlan turned back toward her, a look of confusion on his face. "It's almost midnight."

"I know. That's why we have to talk to them now. It's about the Bean Pot."

He sighed. "They already accepted the offer—"

"Did they sign the paperwork?"

He rubbed his eyes. "No, I FedExed it to them today."

"So, call them now! Please." She grabbed his arm. "They can change their mind, right?"

"They won't—"

"Harlan!"

The man that looked so much like her best friend finally ground his jaw. "I swear I'm going to shoot my sister for having too many friends."

"Oh, yay! You're the best!" Clare hugged him, and then quickly pulled away from the sensation of his naked chest against her. Dammit. What was wrong with her? Harlan was a handsome, fit, attractive single guy, and now that she was open to men again, she should be appreciating him. But it just made her cringe to touch him.

All she wanted was Griffin.

And that was just great, wasn't it?

"Hang on, let me get their number." Harlan disappeared into the darkness, and a faint desk lamp turned on over his desk at the far end of the one room building.

Clare stood in the tiny, darkened cabin while Harlan rustled around. The cottage was quiet and neat, but, like the homes of most single men she knew, it was stark and bare.

Was this like the home Griffin was returning to? Some high-priced version of loneliness, only without the beautiful lake and trees? Griffin deserved more than that. He was walking away from people by going back to his job. He was leaving his daughter, her, Katie and this whole town, so he could marry his work and live in his office.

He was so much more than that. Why couldn't he see it?

"Okay," Harlan said, walking back with his phone. "If they shoot me, you're going to have to foot the bill for the funeral."

Anticipation rushed through her. "Okay."

He dialed the phone. "What's your offer?"

Oh...she wasn't sure Harlan would buy into the joint venture proposal, and she didn't want him screening her. "Is it okay if I present it to them myself?"

Harlan shook his head. "They don't like talking directly. It puts too much pressure on them."

Oh, come on! This was no time for rules! "Ask them if they'll talk to me," she urged. "They love me. You know they will."

Harlan raised his brows at her, but before he could argue, someone answered. "Hey, Mattie, it's Harlan Shea. Did I wake you?" He relaxed and gave Clare a thumbs up. "Yes, I forgot about your Friday night poker games. Listen, do you remember Clare Gray?" He paused. "Well, she wanted to speak with you about the Bean Pot. She's right here. Can I put her on?" He listened to Mattie's response, and Clare shoved her hands in her pockets while she waited.

Come on, Mattie.

Harlan finally handed the phone over. "Your game."

As she reached for the phone, Clare was suddenly nervous. For the first time in her life, she'd taken ownership of what she wanted, and it was actually kind of terrifying to finally be facing the opportunity to get it...or not. It was so much easier not to want anything.

Harlan gestured for her to talk, and she took a breath to

steady herself, then she put the phone to her ear. "Mattie? Hi, it's Clare Gray."

The crackly voice of the woman who'd been part of her summer experience for so many years was so familiar. "Clare, my darling, how are you? And how's that sweet girl of yours?"

Clare relaxed at the friendly greeting. "We're both great. Doing really well."

"Excellent. Are you married yet?"

Clare laughed, even as a vise clamped around her heart. "No, I'm not, but maybe I'll start working on it."

"Well, that's a beginning at least. Now, what can I do for you? The poker game is starting again soon, and I need to be back at the table."

Clare glanced at Harlan, then turned her back on him so she was facing the lake. "It's about the Bean Pot."

"Oh, sweetie," Mattie said. "We've already accepted an offer. Didn't Harlan tell you?"

"Yes, but you didn't sign the papers. You could tell them you decided not to sell."

"We won't lie, Clare," Mattie said stiffly.

"It wouldn't be a lie," Clare interrupted. "What if you kept the store, and I opened a cupcake cafe instead of the Bean Pot? I could pay rent, or we could share profits, or some of both. Astrid's going to help me with an internet business, so it could really take off. Then you would still be a part of the community and I could do the rest. Please?"

Mattie sighed. "Clare, we live in Florida almost all year now. We don't need to own a store in Birch Crossing anymore—"

"But you lived here for thirty years! This is where your kids grew up, and—"

"Clare," she said gently. "Even if we were willing to partner with you, we already gave our word to the buyer from New York to sell it. We can't go back on our promise."

Clare gripped the phone. "Please, Mattie, this is my dream. I don't have the money to buy the store outright, but I know I will in a year or two. I have enough to invest in what I need to run the store, just not buy it as well. I know it will take off and—"

"Heaven knows your cupcakes are the best we've ever had," Mattie said. "John was just commenting the other day that the one thing Florida doesn't have is Clare Gray's cupcakes. But we can't do it, Clare. We don't want the store anymore, and we already committed."

Clare heard the finality in Mattie's voice, and she knew that it was over. The dream was done. Her shoulders sagged and she bit her lip. "I understand," she said quietly.

"Isn't there somewhere else you could do it?"

Clare shook her head. "It's not that big of a town, Mattie. You know that." And what other owner did she know well enough to ask them to run the business together? Mattie and John were dear, and she had really thought they would be up for it.

"I'm sorry, honey," Mattie said. "But keep your chin up. Another opportunity may surprise you."

"Yes, yes, of course it will. Thanks for talking. Enjoy your game." Clare hung up the phone and handed it back to Harlan. "Thanks."

He gave her a sympathetic look. "I'm sorry, Clare."

"Yes, me too."

"I'll keep an ear out for other opportunities."

She managed a smile. "Okay, thanks."

He gave her a steady look. "You want to stay for a beer? Stars are out tonight, and I have a heater on the deck."

She laughed softly, almost amused at how strongly she did not want to be snuggled down with another man, even if it was a man as good looking as Harlan. She didn't know him that well, and Astrid had made vague reference to some baggage he had with women, but he'd always been thoughtful and nice to her. But the only man she wanted right now was Griffin. "Thanks, but I just want to go home."

Not to Griffin, because he wasn't there. Just to her home.

Griffin had opened her heart to dreams she didn't know she had. And the moment she'd accepted them, allowed herself to love him and acknowledge the dream of a cupcake cafe, she'd lost it all. It was great to finally acknowledge her dreams, but the timing of it all wasn't so outstanding.

Harlan nodded. "Some other time, maybe."

"Maybe." She bid him goodnight and scurried out his door. As she made her way across the rocky soil, her heart aching with disappointment, she knew she wouldn't go back to the life she'd lived, to the woman she had been.

As much as everything hurt right now, it was better than the veritable coma she'd been in for the last fifteen years. So, yes, she wouldn't go back to who she'd been...though she might have to go crawl into bed and cry for a day or two before trying to figure out her next steps.

Sometimes broken dreams and broken hearts couldn't heal instantly, and for the first time in her life, she didn't want them to. If she didn't feel pain, it would mean she wasn't living, and she was ready to start living again, no matter how much it hurt and no matter how terrifying it was.

But what now? She had no idea.

GRIFFIN WAS five miles down the highway when his cell phone rang. He glanced down and saw it was a Maine area code. Clare's office? He grabbed the phone. "Clare?"

"No, it's Jackson. I need ice cream."

Okay, yeah, that was a little random. "Then go get some."

He moved into the left lane to pass a car from Maine. Yeah, he was on his way back to his life.

"Hah, funny," Jackson said, not sounding amused. "How long 'til you'll be here?"

What in hell's name was Jackson talking about? "Be where?"

"At Wright's." Jackson lowered his voice. "Dammit, Griffin, I'm dealing with a pregnant woman's cravings. Get your ass over here before she loses it entirely."

Griffin was completely confused. "Why do I need to come to Wright's?"

"Because the sign on the door says that after-hours customers are no longer supposed to ring the bell for service," Jackson said impatiently. "It says to call you."

Griffin realized he still had the key in his front pocket. That woman had probably bespelled him to forget to give it back. "Well, ring the damn doorbell. Ophelia's upstairs."

"In fifty-three years, Ophelia has never once handled an after-hours request," Jackson said. "And she's not going to start now. If you don't get your ass back here and get me some ice cream, I'm going to come after you and shoot up your pretty truck until it's so full of holes that even Ralph won't accept it as a trade-in."

Griffin almost laughed. "You covet my truck. You'd never hurt it."

"I'm a desperate man, Griff, and desperate men will do anything for their women. Get back here before I start loading up." Then he hung up.

Griffin gripped his phone as he sped down the highway. Jackson wasn't his problem. The store wasn't his responsibility. They would deal without him.

His mission was two hundred miles south.

His mission was blue jeans, not ice cream.

His clients were millions of teenage girls world-wide, not a pregnant woman and her doting husband.

It was not his deal.

It was not his deal.

It was not his—

He suddenly hauled right across three lanes, cut off an eighteen-wheeler, and bounced over a grassy mound to get to the exit he'd almost missed.

He was going back for ice cream.

JACKSON WAS STANDING on the top step, his arms across his chest and his ball cap pulled low over his head when Griffin drove up. Jackson's old beater was idling in the parking lot, the headlights too dim, but the rust was hardly visible in the darkness.

Griffin shoved open the door to his truck and vaulted up the stairs. "I was on my way to Boston—"

"Thanks, man." Jackson grabbed him in a full-on bear hug, and hammered his back with his fist. "I was afraid to go home without it."

Griffin grinned. "Yeah, well, you're letting her manipulate you too much." He shoved the key in the lock and managed to get it open with much less effort than last time. Yeah, quick learner.

"Hell, man," Jackson said as he followed him into the darkened store. "There's nothing better than letting the woman I love manipulate me."

Griffin shot a surprised look at Jackson as the ball player pulled open the freezer door. "Seriously?"

"Oh, yeah." Jackson helped himself to six different kinds of ice cream. "I don't know what she's going to want when I get there, so one of each, don't you think?"

Griffin laughed. "You forgot rocky road and vanilla frozen yogurt."

"Can you get those?" Jackson was already heading toward the front of the store.

Griffin grabbed the last two, added a box of popsicles to his stash and then strode after Jackson.

By the time he reached the truck, Jackson was already behind the wheel. He slapped Griffin on the shoulder. "Thanks, man. Put it on my tab. You're the best."

Griffin nodded. "Any time." The words were out of his mouth before he realized it, and then he frowned at the slip.

"Double date, Friday night, eight o'clock," Jackson said. "Come to our place. Trish makes a mean ravioli and she wants to show off the baby's room to Clare."

Griffin shook his head. "I'm moving back to Boston tonight. I won't be here."

"What?" Jackson stared at him. "Why?"

"Because that's where I live."

"Screw that. When I came here, I lived in New York City. Men like us don't go back, Griff." Jackson winked. "Once we find our women, they lock us down and life finally gets meaningful."

"She's not my woman—"

"Not until you get her," Jackson agreed. "So go do it." He shifted into reverse. "And if you need a job, come work with me. We could always use another hand."

Griffin stepped back from the truck. "You bought the business?"

"Hell, no," Jackson said. "If I bought that business, I'd never be home and the stress would knock me on my ass." He winked. "Trish loves me exactly as I am, and why would I ever mess with that?" He saluted as he backed up. "See you on Friday, Griff. Bring beer."

Then he sped off in a squeal of tires, spraying up gravel on Griffin's jeans.

Griffin looked up at the windows of the apartment above, and he saw Ophelia peering down at him. Keeping track of the town, keeping up the tradition she and Norm had begun.

He held up the key, and set it down in the driveway. But when he looked up again, she was already gone from the window.

Dammit. She'd never find the key.

He jogged up the steps to leave it under the mat, but just as he bent down, another car pulled up into the parking lot. He recognized the shape of it instantly, and his heart leapt to life. "Clare!" He raced down the stairs to the Subaru, then stopped when a woman he didn't recognize stepped out.

The disappointment was so intense his chest actually hurt, and he looked past her, as if he might see Clare in the passenger seat. But it was empty, and he saw the seats were beige instead of black. Not Clare's car. Not Clare.

He was hit with a sudden sense of absolute wrongness, that Clare was supposed to be there with him. At that store. At that moment. That she belonged with him, by his side, on these steps.

The woman hurried past him. She was frazzled and looked exhausted. She was wearing what looked like pajamas and bedroom slippers. Griffin watched as she ran up the stairs. She started to press the bell, then stared at the note. "Oh, come on!"

She tried the door, but it was locked. When she turned around, tears were streaming down her face as she ran back down the stairs.

Griffin almost let her go. He really did. But he couldn't stop himself from reaching out as she rushed by. He caught her arm. "Do you need something?"

"Yes." She turned toward him. "I just discovered that my

dog ate my last canister of baby formula, and I have to get more. Do you have a phone? I don't have mine and I have to call that number. Why don't they have a phone next to the sign? Who brings a phone with them at this hour? I mean, what am I supposed to do?" She wiped her forearm across her eyes. "I'm so tired. I can't take it anymore—" Tears started again, and Griffin put his arm around her.

"I have the key, come on." He helped her up the stairs and unlocked the door for her.

She knew exactly where the formula was, and she was back in a second. "I don't have my purse. Can you tell Norm to put it on our charge? It's Harry Burns."

He nodded, and committed the name to memory. "Good luck. Try to get some sleep."

"This will help. Thank you so much. I thought I was going to fall apart out there before you arrived. I owe you." Her words were so heartfelt, Griffin felt himself stand a little taller.

"It's no problem."

She waved at him and hurried down the stairs.

Griffin stood in the door and watched her get into the car that was so much like Clare's. She waved at him, the same as how Clare had waved at him so many times.

And as her car pulled away, Griffin was hit with the most extreme sense of loneliness he'd ever felt. And he knew there was one more stop he had to make before going back to Boston.

CHAPTER TWENTY-SIX

By the time Clare reached the end of Harlan's dirt road, she'd stopped crying.

By the time she reached the edge of Main Street, she'd made a decision.

By the time she was driving past Wright's, she was dialing her home phone number.

Katie finally answered the fifth time she called. "What?" she mumbled sleepily.

"I'm quitting my job as a lawyer," Clare announced.

"Good."

Clare frowned at her daughter's sleepy acquiescence. Maybe she didn't really understand what Clare was saying. "I don't have a way to start a business yet."

"Okay." Katie yawned.

Um, hello? This was a big deal! Her daughter should be freaking out on her by now. "We're probably going to have to live in our car and eat pine cones for dinner," she said, enunciating very clearly, in case Katie was too asleep to grasp the tragic situation Clare was thrusting upon her.

"Yeah, sure, fine," Katie mumbled.

Fine? That was fine? Well, then... "And your father was an ass who didn't deserve us."

Katie laughed then. "Mom, I love you."

Clare realized then that her daughter actually did understand. Katie got it, and she was really, truly okay with it. Clare's tension faded, and she smiled. Granted it was a somewhat forced smile loaded with terror and uncertainty, but it was also illuminated with relief and hope. Katie wasn't judging her, or trying to make her choose a path she didn't want, and that was a precious feeling. "I love you, too, sweetheart. I'll be home soon. I just wanted to tell you."

"Want me to get the champagne out?"

Clare laughed, and suddenly she knew it was all going to be okay. She and Katie would find their way together. "You're fifteen, and we don't have champagne."

"How about milk and cupcakes, then?"

Clare grinned. "That sounds great. I think tonight is a night to celebrate, and cupcakes are definitely the appropriate choice." She paused, then added, "Thank you for your support, Katie. I would never have made this choice without your encouragement. You and Griffin gave me the courage to make this leap."

Katie was quiet for a second. "I wish Griffin was here."

"I do, too." Clare let herself feel the pain and the sadness, she faced it and she let it fill her. "But we deserve more than what he can give us. We deserve a man who will give us everything. We deserve it all."

"But what if he could do it?"

What if... No. She knew he couldn't. His soul was elsewhere, and she would accept nothing less than his full commitment to her and Katie. "We deserve it all," she said fiercely. "And we're going to get it. Okay?"

"You're cool, Mom," Katie said, approval evident in her voice.

Clare smiled. "I think that's the first time you've ever called me cool."

"Well, it's the first time you've ever been cool." Katie sounded more awake, and Clare could hear her feet on the stairs. "I'll go get our feast ready. See you in a few minutes?"

"Yes." Clare hung up the phone as she turned onto her road. She'd said brave, strong words to her daughter, but how was she really going to get it? Any of it? Because—

There was a big, black truck in her driveway.

Clare slammed on the brakes, her heart pounding as she stared at it. Why was he back?

As she watched, the driver's door opened and Griffin stepped out. He slammed his door shut and faced her. Waiting.

He was difficult to see in the dark. The shadowed outline of a man with broad shoulders, lean hips and thick hair. Just like the night she'd met him. And just like the night she'd met him, something turned deep in her belly at the sight of him.

"I can't do this," she whispered. He was too much. He was too compelling. He was her other half. What if he was there to offer her some part-time deal? Come see her on weekends? The occasional trip to Boston for her? Or just one more night of loving before he walked out on her forever?

She would do it. She knew she would. She couldn't say no to him.

Her foot trembled on her brake with the need to go see him. To take whatever he was offering. To take it, to pretend it was okay, and to shut down the part of her that wanted it all. To betray the woman inside her that wanted a husband, a family, a man who thought she and her daughter were the most important things on this earth.

She couldn't pretend anymore that she was okay with leftovers.

"I deserve it all," she whispered.

So she eased her foot off the brake, turned her steering wheel back toward the road, and drove away from the man she loved more than she'd ever thought she could love again.

~

GRIFFIN COULDN'T BELIEVE it when Clare drove off, leaving him behind.

Hadn't she noticed he was waiting for her?

But a hardening in his gut told him she had. He was sure of it. She'd paused so long at the end of the driveway, he knew she'd seen him and then made the choice to reject him.

She'd walked away from him just like Hillary had.

Clare was the only one who had believed in him. She saw his value where no one else did. She was his last grasp of humanity. If there was anything redeemable in him, she would have seen it.

But she'd driven away. She'd finally accepted all supporting evidence and given up on him.

Son of a bitch.

That bit like hell, and he didn't like it. Not one bit. Probably because he knew she was right. As long as Clare had deemed him worthy, he'd held out hope, a thin, fragile, unraveling thread of hope that had been tied together by Norm and Jackson and the woman with the hungry infant.

But now that he knew Clare didn't believe in him anymore?

Shit.

If she didn't believe in him, who would?

"Griffin?" The back door opened and Katie came out on the back step. "Griffin!" She screeched with delight and raced down the steps toward him.

"Katie!" Her joyous welcome made him feel like a king, and he caught her as she threw herself at him. "It's so good to see you," he said. "I missed you." He'd been gone only for a few hours, but it felt like an eternity now that he was back. "I think you've grown since I last saw you."

"I missed you, too." She beamed up at him, and he saw the genuine happiness on her face.

Shit. She really had missed him? "Does your mom miss me?" The question snuck out before he could stop it, but once it was out, he wanted the answer. He wanted a yes.

But he didn't get one.

"She's mad at you." Katie's excitement faded, and those blue eyes narrowed in accusation. "You left. Why would you leave us?"

"I didn't—" He cut off his customary denial, the one he'd perfected whenever anyone had asked why he'd abandoned his wife and daughter. He understood now that he had left them, in some ways, but this time... driving away from Clare and Katie? That was really and truly leaving, and he would no longer deny responsibility. "Because I'm a jerk."

Katie laughed. "No, you're not. You just pretend you are." And he saw, in those blue eyes that were so much like Clare's, an acceptance of who he was. "Mom knows that," she added cagily, "even if she's pissed at you."

His fist tightened around his car keys. "Really?"

Katie nodded. "Yeah."

Griffin looked down the road to where Clare had driven. The street was empty. She wasn't coming back. But according to Katie... Was there really a possibility that Clare hadn't completely given up on him? He thought back to Clare's driving off. She'd waited a long time before turning away. Second thoughts?

Dammit. He wanted a chance.

But she'd made her choice when she'd driven off. He had to respect it—

Or did he?

Screw that. Clare didn't have the right to dismiss him. No one did. He didn't give a shit what anyone thought about him or his ability to make it happen outside the office. Not anymore. "I have to go." He set Katie back from him.

Katie's face crumpled. "You're not coming back, are you?"

He met her gaze. "I don't know," he answered honestly. "But I'm going to go find out." He got in the truck. "I'm going after your mom."

"Oh...you'll need good luck, then." Stepping back from the truck. Katie crossed her fingers and held them up. "She's feeling pretty hostile toward you."

"Yeah, but she loves me, too." Or she used to. If she still did... would it even be enough?

He decided to cross his own fingers, and he held up his hand, mimicking Katie's pose.

She grinned, and then he shifted into reverse. Gravel sprayed up as he peeled out of Clare's driveway, and he took off after the only woman that mattered.

~

CLARE WAS CRYING SO HARD she could barely see the road, when bright headlights came barreling up behind her. The headlights blinded her, reflecting in the mirror, and she pulled over and slowed down. "Stupid driver," she shouted as it sped past her.

Then the offender careened in front of her, spraying up dirt as it cut her off.

"Hey!" She slammed on her brakes, and her car slid across the dirt toward the car. She screamed and held up her arms, bracing for impact, but her car stopped inches from the side of the vehicle. "Oh my God." She closed her eyes and leaned back, her whole body shaking. "It's okay, it's okay, it's okay—"

Her passenger door was ripped open, and she screamed as a dark body loomed beside her.

"What do you think you're doing, taking off on me?"

The deep voice was unmistakable. "Griffin?"

His familiar visage was in her car, and he was glaring at her.

"You jerk!" She punched his chest, fury rising fast inside her. "You could have gotten us killed!"

"I would never have endangered you." He caught her fist. "I gave you space to stop."

"Leave me alone!" It felt too good to have his hand on her. "Get away from me!" She tried to hit him again, desperate to make him leave.

But he just reached over her, unsnapped her seat belt and pulled her out of the car, completely ignoring her protestations. "Calm down," he said. "I need to talk to you."

"I don't want to hear it." She was out of the car now, and she could barely breathe under the impact of his presence. She'd been prepared to never see him again, to never be in his presence, to never feel the hugeness of his spirit and strength engulfing her.

She had not been remotely prepared to face all that again and still walk away. He looked beautiful and powerful and her heart cried for his embrace. "I really don't want to hear it," she repeated. "Please, just leave me alone."

Like the stubborn, arrogant man he was, he completely ignored her request. "I have a business decision I need to discuss with you."

A business decision? Seriously. She shook her head. "I can't—"

"You can." He took her hands then, ever so gently, and she almost started to cry again. "It will just take a minute."

"Griffin," she begged. "Please, let me go. I can't do this. I really can't. Just let me go."

He was silent for a moment, and at first she thought he was going to agree. As much as she had meant her words, the terror that seized her at the thought of him leaving nearly made her legs buckle. Griffin must have sensed it, because he swept her up in his arms and set her gently on the hood of her car.

The brief moment in his arms was too agonizingly short, and too agonizingly long, as it stirred up memories and longings and desires so powerful her body trembled.

Griffin braced his hands on either side of her hips and leaned into her space, boxing her in, overwhelming her with his presence.

She fisted her hands against the urge to touch him. To stroke her hands over his face one last time. To feel his mouth against hers one last time. To take whatever he could give, and deny her need for more. She deserved more, and she couldn't live with less.

"What do you need from me?" he asked.

She stared at him, totally confused by the question. "What?"

"What if I was like Jackson? What if I had a regular job and made a few hundred bucks a week? What if I couldn't buy you things? What if my truck was rusted? What if it was just me?"

"That's not you. You aren't regular." She pushed at his arms. "This is ridiculous. Let me go."

He didn't budge, but his eyes narrowed. "You said you loved me. Who did you love?"

She shook her head. "Oh, no, I'm not going there again—"

"Clare. I need to know. Tell me. Do you love the guy who has vast reserves in his bank account and an expensive truck? Or is there something else?"

She heard the urgency in his voice, the desperate plea, and

she forced herself to look at him. His eyes were dark, and there was strain about his mouth. He didn't look like the confident businessman and she'd gotten to know. He was a man carrying the weight of a thousand lifetimes, a fierce warrior who was about to crack under the strain.

"Oh, Griffin." She set her hands on his face, unable to stop herself. His skin was warm, his whiskers prickly, and she recognized every curve on his jaw. "How many times do I need to tell you?" She put one hand on his chest, over his heart. "This is what I fell in love with. Your heart. That's it. Nothing else. Just this."

Griffin bowed his head, and his shoulders shook with emotion.

Clare kissed the top of his head, and then laid her cheek against his hair. It felt so right to be with him again. To hold him.

He wrapped his arms around her waist and held her, resting his face against her chest, almost like a small lost boy. Only he was a strong, powerful man, with a life and a future so enormous that he would never be able to stop long enough to fit her in.

She kissed his head again. "Griffin, I need to go home. Katie's waiting for me."

He lifted his head but didn't loosen his grip on her. "I'm the one who's been waiting for you, Clare. I need you."

"Oh, no." She pushed him back. "No."

Confusion flickered across his handsome face. "But you just said you loved me."

"I do, I do." She slipped under his arm and moved away from him, needing space. "But it was a lie."

His face hardened. "It was a lie that you loved me?"

"No! I would never lie about that, I swear!" Clare protested.

"Then what's the lie?"

"That I was okay with what we had." At his puzzled expression, she tried to explain. "I said I would take you for a few days, that whatever you could give me was enough, and I could let you go. But I can't do that." She hugged herself, the words breaking her in half. "I can't open my heart to you and know that your soul is calling you elsewhere. I can't take another day or another night with you, and know you're leaving or that your attention is two hundred miles south," she said softly. "I want the fairytale, and I can't accept anything less."

Griffin leaned against the hood of her car, his arms folded across his chest. "What's your fairytale, Clare? What do you wish for in your Prince Charming?"

"What do I wish for?" She looked up at the stars, at the way they lit up the sky. "That's what I wish for." She gestured to the expanse of twinkling darkness. "A love so huge and so powerful, that it sweeps across everything. It's always there. It's fuller than a heart can hold, so it spills out into the world and fills everything around it with more love. It's there when I fall asleep. It's there when I wake up." She met Griffin's gaze. "It's there every time I breathe in, every time I breathe out, and with every beat of my heart."

"That's it?"

She stared at him in disbelief. "That's a lot, Griffin. That's everything."

A slow, tremendous smile filled his lovely face, and he held out his hand. "Come."

She shoved her hands into her front pockets.

He laughed softly and dropped his hand. "Here's the thing, Clare. I don't know how to be a dad. I don't know how to be a husband. I've pretty much failed at both. I don't know when to hug or when to get ice cream in the middle of the night, or any of that."

Something began to stir inside her. Was it hope? No, no,

not hope. Please not hope. She folded her arms over her chest and lifted her chin. "So, what's your point?"

"My point, Clare, is that there's one thing I can do. I didn't know I could, but you showed me that I can."

"And what's that?"

He met her gaze. "Love."

Tears filled her eyes. "No, don't, Griffin. I can't—"

He began walking toward her. "But you have to promise to believe in me. Because when you look at me like I'm this amazing man, I seem to do what's right. I know when to hold you, or when to tell you to toughen up. As long as you love me like that—"

"Stop it!" She scrambled backward as he reached for her. "I can't handle a man who wants to be somewhere else—"

"I don't want to be anywhere else."

She backed into the side of his ridiculous truck, and there was nowhere else to go as he approached her. "Griffin—"

"I want to be right here." He stopped in front of her. "I want to be with you. And Katie. And Brooke."

"But—"

"I don't want to go back to Boston," he said. "I don't want to go back to my condo." He took her hand and went down on his knee.

She stared at him. "Don't—"

"Clare Gray," he said. "I was dead when I came up here, and you opened my heart. A man would be a damned fool to walk away, and I am one of the smartest damn people I know."

"Please don't make promises you can't keep," she whispered. "Please. I can't let myself love you and then have you leave in six months. I can't do that."

"You don't have to." He tugged her hand, and she eased down to her knees in front of him. He held up his finger to tell her to wait, then he pulled his phone out of his pocket.

He put it on speaker phone and then dialed. She saw from the display that he was calling his business partner.

"What—"

He pressed his finger to her lips as Phillip's voice slurred out into the night. "Griff? You down here already? I've got your seat all ready and a bottle of champagne waiting for you—"

"I'm out," Griffin said.

"Out of what?"

"In Your Face."

Clare sucked in her breath, certain she'd heard wrong. "What?"

"What?" Phillip said, all amusement gone. "What the hell are you talking about? We're signing papers in eight hours—"

"I'm staying in Birch Crossing. I'm going to marry Clare, I'm buying the local general store, and I'm going to learn how to be a dad to two teenage daughters." He looked at Clare. "And maybe have a son, too."

Phillip swore. "But—"

Griffin hung up and tossed the phone over his shoulder. He grinned. "So, yeah, don't say you won't marry me, because I've thrown away all my other options."

She was too stunned to react. "I don't understand. That's your dream."

"No." He took her hands. "You're my dream. What you bring into my life, that's my dream. I just didn't know how to get there, and you showed me the way. Marry me, Clare Gray. Marry me right now, so that neither of us has to go another moment without each other ever again."

She shook her head. "I can't."

He didn't seem to believe her, as he simply raised his eyebrows, and gathered her into his arms. "And why is that?"

"Because you never said you loved me. I can't marry a man who doesn't love me."

He smiled and stroked her hair back from her face. "My dear, sweet, Clare, I love you more than my heart can hold. I love you more than all the stars in the sky, and I love you for the beauty of your soul, the lightness of your spirit, and for the way my entire being comes alive when you focus those beautiful blue eyes on me and tell me that you love me."

And then he kissed her, the most beautiful, most magical, the most wonderful kiss that had ever been, and she knew that the young girl who had given up magical fantasies at age eighteen, had finally had her dreams come true.

"Yes," she whispered. "I will marry you."

CHAPTER TWENTY-SEVEN

NORM'S HAT was exactly where it belonged.

Griffin grinned as he caught sight of one of the town's old timers setting a cold bottle of Birch's Best on Norm's stool beside his old, worn hat. In the month since Norm's passing, there had been a cold beer on that stool every minute of the day that Wright's was open.

As it should be.

Griffin shut the door to the storage room with his foot and walked into the main section of the store, holding the box he'd gone in there to retrieve.

Sam White, one of Norm's buddies, slammed his hand down on Griffin's shoulder. "Griff! Didya hear the news?"

Griffin grinned. "I sure did. Three baby loons from the pair by your place. It's been, what, eighteen years, since a nesting pair on this lake has had three chicks?"

"Nineteen years, Griff! Nineteen! It's a sign that new life is coming to the region, I'm telling you. You gotta come see them. It's a damned record." Sam leaned forward, his Pirates baseball cap askew on his head. "All the local artists are hanging out in my woods painting them. You should see this old gal." He waggled his bushy eyebrows, giving Griffin a lecherous look. "She may be close to seventy, but she's got a spring in her step enough to make an old man sit up and take notice." He raised his brows, vulnerability flashing in his weathered face. "You think I oughta go for it?"

Griffin grinned. "How many times has she come by to paint?"

"Been there every day for a week. She's done at least ten paintings so far."

Griffin raised his brows. "Sam. How many paintings of the same damn birds does she have to do before you figure it out?"

The older man's eyes widened, and then he got a big shit-eating grin on his wrinkled face. "You think?"

"I do." Griffin jerked his head toward the deli. "Ophelia!"

His deli manager waved a spatula at him, a hot pink scarf from Astrid tied in her hair. It was a new look for her, but Astrid had insisted that Ophelia could pull it off, and she'd been right. It seemed to give Ophelia even more attitude than she used to have, and he was damned glad to see the exuberance shining in her eyes. The woman's inner strength was awe-inspiring, and the whole town had rallied around her. The gal hadn't spent an evening alone in her apartment in the last month, and she was getting a killer reputation around the bridge table. "Your omelet's coming, Griffin, and you're getting ham this time. You're too damn skinny!"

Griffin didn't bother to argue. It was an argument he knew he'd never win. "Sam needs to go woo a girl. Can you put together a picnic basket for him?"

Ophelia whistled loudly. "That old coot is too ornery to fit a woman in his life, but if it gets him out of our hair, then it's worth a try." She gestured at him. "Get over here, Sam, and tell me about her so I can set you up right."

Sam slugged Griffin on the shoulder, straightened the

collar of his tee shirt, and then hauled ass across the crowded store toward the deli.

Griffin grinned, then headed back toward the register. He set the carton on the counter in front of Heather Burns, the woman he'd gotten formula for that night a month ago when Norm had died. "Joey is in size three diapers now, right?"

Heather smiled at him, her face so much less stressed than it had been that night. "I was just going to ask you to order size threes!"

Griffin winked as he rang up her order. "Harry told me that the size twos were getting tight, so I figured you'd need them soon. It was easy to toss them into my order last week."

"You're the best." She blew him a kiss as she hurried out of the store, her arms full.

The line of customers taken care of for the moment, Griffin did what had become such habit over the last month and checked out the table in the corner. The familiar sight filled him with such a sense of rightness.

Clare and Astrid were huddled up with her computer, working on her website. Sitting at the same table were Brooke and Katie, and he could see their colored drawings of new ideas for cupcakes.

As he watched them, Clare looked up. The moment her eyes met his, the chaos and bustle of the room melted away, until it was just them, just her, a connection that would hold him forever. She smiled at him, and lightly laid her hand over her heart. Griffin's throat tightened, and he gave her a single nod, just for her, for no one else. Tonight was date night at the Finch Grill, and he couldn't wait to lose himself in her without the chaos of the town around them.

Brooke looked at Clare, then turned around to see what she was looking at. When she saw Griffin watching them, her face brightened and she waved at him. "Come see, Dad! You should see our displays! They look awesome."

Griffin grinned. "Yeah, sure." He started to head over there, and then the front door flew open and Jackson strode in, wearing his customary jeans and boots.

He waved a cardboard tube at Griffin. "Here are the latest plans for the addition you want me to build onto Wright's. We need to move the cupcake display more to the left to make room for the tables, and I adjusted the ceiling height to allow more space for Emma's paintings and the ceiling fans."

Anticipation coiled through Griffin. He took the plans out of the tube and spread them over the counter. He nodded with satisfaction as he saw what Jackson had done. The amount of knowledge Jackson had acquired during his years of construction was impressive, and his talent with designs was even better than Griffin had suspected after his first visit to Jackson's house. The nursery Jackson had designed and built had been incredible, and Griffin had known immediately that it was Jackson who needed to design Clare's store. "Damn, you're good man."

Jackson grinned. "I know. How about that, huh?"

Griffin studied the drawings. "When we finish with the cupcake shop, I want you to design and build an addition to the farmhouse next. We need a master suite, and Brooke needs her own room, even though she and Katie are enjoying their sleepovers when Brooke stays over."

Jackson nodded. "I'll check with my boss and see when we can fit it in."

Griffin shook his head. "No. You need to build it. Your vision is what I want, not his."

Interest flashed in Jackson's eyes. "I thought having me build the addition to Wright's myself was a one-time-thing."

Griffin shrugged his shoulders, not wanting to push the soon-to-be-dad too far. Not yet. But he knew Jackson's talents wouldn't remain a secret once people saw what he was doing with the store's addition. "One more project. That's all. You game?"

Jackson shrugged. "Yeah, I guess I can fit it in. Got a few more months before the baby arrives and I could use the extra cash" He thudded his hand on Griffin's shoulder. "Thanks for the extra work. I appreciate it."

"It's not charity. You're the best, and I want the best." Griffin rolled up the plans to take them to Clare. "Do you have time to go over these now?"

"Nope." Jackson winked. "Trish is waiting in the truck for me. We're going shopping for paint colors for the nursery. I want blue, she wants green." His grin widened. "It's gonna be a battle. Wish me luck."

Griffin smiled. "It's just paint, Jackson. Let her win."

Jackson inclined his head as he strode toward the door. "I always let her win, my friend. Seeing her smile is all I need." Then he saluted Griffin and jogged out the door.

"My boy, we've got a problem." A gnarled hand closed down on Griffin's arm as Eppie moved in front of him to block his path. She was wearing a hat decorated with fresh sunflowers that were far too big for the white brim, taking up the entire damn hat so it looked like she had the whole garden stuck on her head.

Griffin straightened the hat that had begun to slide off-center. "What's up, Eppie?"

Eppie shook her head, her mouth pursed in dismay. "It's Astrid."

Griffin glanced over at the table again. Astrid was in deep conversation with Clare, wearing a pair of earrings that dangled almost down to her shoulders. A polka-dotted scarf barely taming her curls, and her turquoise tank top was bright and audacious, just as he would expect of her. "What's wrong with Astrid?"

Eppie sighed. "She hasn't created a new design in almost

three months, Griffin. That woman is a veritable font of creativity, and the well has dried up."

Griffin frowned. "How do you know?"

Eppie rolled her eyes. "I keep track of these things, young man. Someone has to." She hooked her arm through his elbow, declaring him her escort. "Now, let's go over there and find out what's wrong with her."

"I'm sure she's fine."

Eppie looked at him, and in those old eyes, he saw genuine concern. "No, she's not."

Griffin's amusement faded, and he realized the old lady had sensed something he hadn't noticed. Over the last month, he'd come to really appreciate Astrid's spunk and her loyal friendship to Clare. She might come across as flamboyant and artsy, but her heart was full of warmth and love, making it clear why she and Clare were best friends. But he was well aware that Astrid never spoke of her past, and he'd sensed a layer of pain beneath her cheerful exterior. If Eppie said they needed to worry about Astrid, then he would believe her. "Okay, then, let's do it."

She beamed at him and patted his arm. "It's great to have a man around again, Griffin. Welcome to Birch Crossing. We've been waiting for you."

Griffin grinned at her as he picked up Jackson's plans to bring them to Clare. "Thanks." Then they headed toward the table and the three most important women in his life.

As he approached, Clare lifted her head to watch him, a slow smile growing on her face as he neared. Intense satisfaction pulsed though him, and he smiled back, unable to take his gaze off the face of the woman who had brought him to life, the woman he loved to the very depths of her soul.

Eppie released him to grab a chair and park herself next to Astrid to start the interrogation, and Griffin walked over to Clare, needing to connect with her before he could do anything else.

Clare's smile widened, her eyes dancing with anticipation as he grabbed the back of her chair and leaned over her. "Hi, Griffin," she said cheerfully.

"Hello, my love." He bent his head and kissed her lightly, and a sense of absolute rightness settled over him when she leaned into him and kissed him back.

Right there.

In the middle of the store.

In front of everyone.

Claiming him every bit as much as he was claiming her.

A moment that would never, ever lose its beauty, no matter how many times it happened.

"I love you, Clare," he whispered against her lips. "Always and forever."

She smiled, her eyes full of such love. "Always and forever," she whispered back. "I love you, too."

He grinned at her, the moment sheer perfection. "Clare—"

"Dad!" He felt a tug at his shirt.

Laughter danced in Clare's eyes, and they shared an amused smile before he turned toward his daughter. "What's up, Brookie?"

"Look at our cupcake designs." She held up a sketch of a cupcake with a theatre mask on it. "It's for the Shakespeare festival. What do you think?"

Griffin pulled up a chair and sat down between Clare and Brooke as he handed the plans to Clare. He rested his arm over the back of her seat, brushing his fingers over her neck as he leaned toward his daughter. "I like it. How'd you come up with the idea for the design?"

"It was Katie's idea, actually. See, it started like this—"

Brooke took out a black and white sketch, and then she and Katie began explaining what they'd done.

As the two teens tried to talk over each other, he glanced over at Astrid and Eppie. Eppie had her hand on Astrid's arm and she was talking urgently in a low voice. Astrid looked up at Clare, and Griffin was shocked by the raw pain in her eyes. It wasn't simply despair at being tormented by Eppie. It was something deeper, a pain and loneliness so stark it would strip her bare and destroy her.

He recognized it, because he'd been there. He'd lived with it for so long, until Clare had saved him. How could Astrid have been able to hide such pain so well? And how much deeper did it go?

"I have to go work," Astrid said cheerfully as she stood up. "Lots of big orders to fill by tonight." She leaned forward to hug Clare, and he saw her hold on a little tighter than usual, as if she was using Clare for strength before she waved good-bye to the rest of them and sauntered off with a swagger he no longer believed.

Shit. Eppie was right. Astrid was in trouble. He looked over at Clare and raised his brows. "She's not okay, is she?"

Clare looked at him with troubled eyes. "I don't know," she admitted. "She's so private."

Son of a bitch. Protectiveness surged through him as he watched Astrid leave, a need to help her, to make it right for her, to—

Clare set her hand on his arm. "Griffin?"

He turned his gaze toward her, his heart softening when he saw the love in her expression. "What is it?"

She squeezed his arm softly. "Thank you."

He raised his brows. "For what?"

"For caring about the people who matter to me. For caring about this town." She smiled at him, that special smile of love that still made his chest tighten.

"Of course I care." He looked at the two teens girls at his table, at Eppie critiquing their designs, at Ophelia on her way over with his omelet, and at the woman he loved.

Yeah, he was home.

~

Want more Birch Crossing? Can Astrid find happiness? Check out Accidentally Mine, *when a one-night stand results in Astrid's accidental pregnancy, finally giving a single-dad widower his chance at true love...and Astrid a chance for the family she's never had.*

"Heartwarming doesn't even begin to describe this romance! Wow!"
-Vickie R. (Amazon Review)

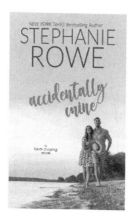

"I absolutely loved this story from beginning to end." ~Christina (Amazon Review)

When a one-night stand with a sassy, spunky woman results in an accidental pregnancy, a single-dad widower finally gets his chance at true love.

〜

Jason Sarantos sank down beside his sleeping son and dropped his head to his hands, digging his fingers into his temples. "Think, Jason," he said aloud, his voice echoing through the crumbling café that he'd bought sight unseen and moved three hundred miles to run, so his son would have a chance at a normal life. But this place was nothing like what he'd thought. *Nothing.* What the hell had he done? "There has to be a way to make this right."

"Of course there is," a woman said, her melodic voice drifting across the dust-filled café. "A fresh coat of lilac paint on the walls and maybe a blue-green turquoise on the ceiling, don't you think?"

Jason jerked his head up at the intrusion, and then froze when he saw who had spoken. It wasn't the old lady with cookies that he'd imagined when he'd decided to move to this rural New England town. He'd been off by several decades and a whole lot of femininity.

She was leaning against the doorway to his shop, her brown eyes sparkling with merriment he hadn't felt in years. Her dark brown hair tumbled around her shoulders with a reckless abandon that spoke of a spirit that would never be tamed. Some of the curls had been woven into a yellow and green braided scarf that seemed to disappear into her thick hair. From each earlobe dangled several pairs of earrings, gold wire twisted into designs so intriguing he wanted to stride right over to her and see what they were.

She was wearing a pair of faded jeans that showed womanly curves that he hadn't thought about in way too long. The delicate straps of her pale yellow tank top rested across her collarbones, revealing a smooth expanse of skin that shot right to his core.

But it was her smile that he couldn't look away from. It was so full of life and vitality, that it made him want to grab her and yank her into his store so she could inject the dying place with her energy.

Her eyebrows arched up, and there was no mistaking the glint of interest in her eyes. "So, should I take your lack of response as a statement that you disagree with the lilac paint suggestion but you're too polite to tell me that? Or maybe you're just overwhelmed by my mind-numbing beauty and stunned into disbelieving silence?"

Shit. He was staring? Jason swore and quickly stood up, brushing the dust from the store off his jeans. "My name's Jason Sarantos. I bought the place."

Her smile widened, lighting up her eyes even more, like this great gust of relief breaking through the gloom trying to consume him. "Jason, everyone in this entire town knows your name, that you bought the store, and that it was twelve minutes after three when you drove your Mercedes SUV past Wright's General Store when you arrived in town, not to mention the fact you were drinking a coffee as you went by." She set her hands on her hips and tilted her head, giving him a teasing grin. "Everyone was pretty offended you didn't stop in to buy your coffee at Wright's and introduce yourself."

Jason blinked, suddenly thrust back into the past, into his childhood, into the small town in Minnesota he'd grown up in, where his mother had found out about his first kiss before he'd even lifted his lips from those of Samantha Huckaby. That was why he'd been drawn to Birch Crossing: because it reminded him of everything he liked about his home and his childhood, yet it had the appealing bonus of being two thousand miles away from the sixteen cousins, five aunts and uncles, and four sisters that had driven him east to find his own path. "Shit. Sorry. I wasn't thinking."

She laughed, a beautiful, melodic sound that went right to his gut. God, when was the last time he'd seen anyone effuse such life? He was riveted by her, by the irreverence of her smile, by the fire in her eyes. This was a woman who was so damn alive that nothing could bring her down. He wanted that. He needed that. God, he needed that.

"Don't worry about it. The town will have you trained in no time, trust me." She raised her eyebrows. "I don't suppose you're dialed into the gossip chain enough to know my name?" She wrinkled her nose, and he thought he saw a flash of vulnerability in her eyes. "I tend to be fodder for talk in this town. I'm not always a fit."

Yeah, he could imagine. She seemed to carry the kind of spunk that might knock an old New England town on its ass. Jason grinned, and he was almost surprised to realize he still knew how to smile. It felt like a long time since he'd smiled, and actually meant it. "Yeah, sorry, I figure I need at least twenty-four hours to recognize everyone in town by sight."

"I'll be back to quiz you in twenty-four hours." She inclined her head and held out her hand. "Astrid Monroe. My brother Harlan is the one who sold you the shop. He's out of town, so he asked me to stop by and see if you needed anything."

Instinctively, Jason reached out to shake her hand. "Nice to meet you. Thanks for the offer." Yeah, he knew what he needed. He needed a damned angel to sweep into his life and fix everything that he'd screwed up, to make this okay for his son. He needed—

Then as he felt the warmth of her palm against his, the light touch of her fingers on the back of his hand, his gut knew what he needed.

He needed *her*.

Like it? Get it now!

A QUICK FAVOR

Did you enjoy Clare and Griffin's story?

People are often hesitant to try new books or new authors. A few reviews can encourage them to make that leap and give it a try. If you enjoyed Unexpectedly Mine *and think others will as well, please consider taking a moment and writing one or two sentences on the eTailer and/or Goodreads to help this story find the readers who would enjoy it. Even the short reviews really make an impact!*

Thank you a million times for reading my books! I love writing for you and sharing the journeys of these beautiful characters with you. I hope you find inspiration from their stories in your own life!

Love,
Stephanie

STAY IN THE KNOW!

I write my books from the soul, and live that way as well. I've received so much help over the years from amazing people to help me live my best life, and I am always looking to pay it forward, including to my readers.

One of the ways I love to do this is through my mailing list, where I often send out life tips I've picked up, post readers surveys, give away Advance Review Copies, and provide insider scoop on my books, my writing, and life in general. And, of course, I always make sure my readers on my list know when the next book is coming out!

If this sounds interesting to you, I would love to have you join us! You can always unsubscribe at any time! I'll never spam you or share your data. I just want to provide value!

Sign up at www.stephanierowe.com/join-newsletter/ to keep in touch!

Much love,

STAY IN THE KNOW!

Stephanie

BOOKS BY STEPHANIE ROWE

Do you know why I love to write?

Because I love to reach deep inside the soul, both mine and yours, and awaken the spirit that gives us life. I want to write books that make you feel, that touch your heart, and inspire you to whatever dreams you hold in your heart.

"This book has the capacity to touch 90% of the women's lives. I went through all the fears and anguish of the characters with them and came out the other side feeling the hope and love. I would even say I experienced some healing of my own." -cyinca (Amazon Review)

All my stories take the reader on that same emotional journey, whether it's in a small Maine town, rugged cowboy country, or the magical world of immortal warriors. Some of my books are funnier, some are darker, but they all give the deep sense of emotional fulfillment.

"I adore this family! ...[Wyoming Rebels] is definitely one of

my favorite series and since paranormal is my usual interest, that's saying something." -Laura B (Amazon Review)

Take a look below. See what might strike your fancy. Give one of them a try. You might fall in love with a genre you don't expect!

≈

CONTEMPORARY ROMANCE

WYOMING REBELS SERIES
(CONTEMPORARY WESTERN ROMANCE)
A Real Cowboy Never Says No
A Real Cowboy Knows How to Kiss
A Real Cowboy Rides a Motorcycle
A Real Cowboy Never Walks Away
A Real Cowboy Loves Forever
A Real Cowboy for Christmas
A Real Cowboy Always Trusts His Heart (Sept 2019!)

A ROGUE COWBOY SERIES
(CONTEMPORARY WESTERN ROMANCE)
A Rogue Cowboy for Her, featuring Brody Hart
(Coming Soon!)

LINKED TO A ROGUE COWBOY SERIES
(CONTEMPORARY WESTERN ROMANCE)
Her Rebel Cowboy

BIRCH CROSSING SERIES
(SMALL-TOWN CONTEMPORARY ROMANCE)
Unexpectedly Mine
Accidentally Mine

(FUNNY PARANORMAL ROMANCE)
Not Quite a Devil
The Devil You Know (Coming Soon!)

ROMANTIC SUSPENSE

ALASKA HEAT SERIES
(ROMANTIC SUSPENSE)
Ice
Chill
Ghost

YOUNG ADULT

MAPLEVILLE HIGH SERIES
(FUNNY CONTEMPORARY ROMANCE)
The Truth About Thongs
How to Date a Bad Boy
Pedicures Don't Like Dirt
Geeks Can Be Hot
The Fake Boyfriend Experiment
Ice Cream, Jealousy & Other Dating Tips

BOXED SETS

Order of the Blade (Books 1-3)
Protectors of the Heart (A Six-Book First-in-Series Collection)
*Real Cowboys Get Their Girls (A Wyoming Rebels Boxed Set,
with bonus novella!)*

For a complete list of Stephanie's books, click here.

ABOUT THE AUTHOR

New York Times and *USA Today* bestselling author Stephanie Rowe is the author of more than forty-five novels, and a 2018 winner and five-time nominee for the RITA® award, the highest award in romance fiction. As an award-winning author, Stephanie has been touching readers' hearts and keeping them spellbound for more than a decade with her contemporary romances, romantic suspense, paranormal romances, and YA contemporary romances.

For the latest info on Stephanie and her books, connect with her on the web at:

www.stephanierowe.com
stephanie@stephanierowe.com

ACKNOWLEDGMENTS

Special thanks to my core team of amazing people, without whom I would never have been able to create this book. Each of you is so important, and your contribution was exactly what I needed. I'm so grateful to all of you! Your emails of support, or yelling at me because I hadn't sent you more of the book yet, or just your advice on covers, back cover copy and all things needed to whip this book into shape—every last one of them made a difference to me. I appreciate each one of you so much!

Special thanks to, Jeanne Hunter, Sharon Stogner, Jan Leyh, Summer Steelman, Teresa Gabelman, D. Alexx Miller, Holly Collins, Janet Juengling-Snell, and Jenn Shanks Pray. There are so many people I want to thank, but the people who simply must be called out are Denise Fluhr, Alencia Bates, Rebecca Johnson, Karen Roma, Nicole Telhiard, Denise Whelan, Tamara Hoffa, and Ashley Cuesta. Thank you also to the following for all their amazing help: Judi Pflughoeft, Deb Julienne, Julie Simpson, Mary Lynn Ostrum, Shell Bryce, Jodi Moore, Jacqueline Wilson, and Amanda

Tamayo. You guys are the best! Mom, you're the best. It means so much that you believe in me. I love you. Special thanks also to my amazing daughter, who I love more than words could ever express. You are my world, sweet girl, in all ways.

*For the town of Lovell, Maine, whose charm and character inspired
me to share the wonder of Maine with others.*

Made in the USA
San Bernardino, CA
08 August 2020

76709019R00244